I0671847

JOYCE OF THE NORTH WOODS

HARRIET T. COMSTOCK

1st WORLD
LIBRARY
Literary Society

Joyce of the North Woods

Harriet T. Comstock

© 1st World Library, 2007
PO Box 2211
Fairfield, IA 52556
www.1stworldlibrary.com
First Edition

LCCN: 2007901805

Softcover ISBN: 978-1-4218-4272-1
Hardcover ISBN: 978-1-4218-4174-8
eBook ISBN: 978-1-4218-4370-4

Purchase *"Joyce of the North Woods"*
as a traditional bound book at:
www.1stWorldLibrary.com/purchase.asp?ISBN=978-1-4218-4272-1

1st World Library is a literary, educational organization
dedicated to:

- Creating a free internet library of downloadable ebooks

- Hosting writing competitions and offering book
publishing scholarships.

Interested in more 1st World Library books?
contact: literacy@1stworldlibrary.com
Check us out at: www.1stworldlibrary.com

1ˢᵗ World Library Literary Society

Giving Back to the World

"If you want to work on the core problem, it's early school literacy."

- James Barksdale, former CEO of Netscape

"No skill is more crucial to the future of a child, or to a democratic and prosperous society, than literacy."

- Los Angeles Times

Literacy... means far more than learning how to read and write... The aim is to transmit... knowledge and promote social participation."

- UNESCO

"Literacy is not a luxury, it is a right and a responsibility. If our world is to meet the challenges of the twenty-first century we must harness the energy and creativity of all our citizens."

- President Bill Clinton

"Parents should be encouraged to read to their children, and teachers should be equipped with all available techniques for teaching literacy, so the varying needs and capacities of individual kids can be taken into account."

- Hugh Mackay

TO

EVELINA HEMINWAY SMITH

"SISTER--FRIEND"

Accept the dedication of this book of mine as a very slight recognition of your encouragement in my work; your faith in me.

To you I first read the story; from you I received my first approval; I believe its chances will be brighter in the book-world if your name and good-will go with it.

HARRIET T. COMSTOCK

Flatbush—Brooklyn, N. Y. February, 1910

PREFATORY NOTE

"Love is the golden bead in the bottom of the crucible." And the crucible was St. Ange.

* * * * *

Fifty years before this story began, St. Ange was a lumber camp; the first gash in that part of the great Solitude to the north, which lay across Beacon Hill, three miles from Hillcrest.

When the splendid lumber had been felled within a prescribed limit, Industry took another leap, left St. Ange scarred and blighted, with a fringe of forest north and south, and struck camps farther back and nearer Canada.

Then Nature began to heal the stricken heart of the Solitude. A second growth of lovely tree and bush sprang to the call, and the only reminders of the camp were the absences of the men during the logging season, and the roaring and rushing of the river through Long Meadow every spring, with its burden of logs from the distant camps.

In the beginning St. Ange had had her aspirations. A futile highway had been constructed, for no other purpose apparently, than to connect the north and south forests. A little church had been built—there had never been any regular service held in it—and a small school-house which promptly degenerated into the Black Cat Tavern, General Store, and Post Office. A few modest houses met the highway face to face;

a few more turned their backs upon it and were content with an outlook across Long Meadow and toward Beacon Hill, beyond which lay the village of Hillcrest which grew in importance as St. Ange degenerated. There were scattered houses among the clumps of maple and pine growths, and there was a forlorn railroad station before which a rickety, single track branch ended. Sometime during the day a train came in, and after an uncertain period it departed; it was the only link with the outer world that St. Ange had except what came by way of Hillcrest.

Toward Hillcrest, as the years went on, there grew in St. Ange a feeling of envy and distrust. Its prosperity and decency were a reflection, its very emphatic regard for law and order a menace and burden. St. Angeans sent their aspiring youths to the Hillcrest school—it was never an alarming constituency—it was cheaper to do that than to support a school of their own. There were emergencies when the Hillcrest doctor and minister were in demand, so it behooved St. Ange to keep up a partial show of friendliness, but bitterly did it resent the interference of Hillcrest justice during that season immediately following the enforced sobriety and isolation of the lumber camp.

Were men not to have some compensation for the hardships of the backwoods?

And just at that point in the argument Beacon Hill received its name and significance. From its top a watcher could view the road leading to Hillcrest, and by a well-directed signal give warning to any chance wrongdoer on the St. Ange side. Many a culprit had thus been aided in his plans of escape before Justice, striding over the western hill, bore down upon the town.

Beautiful, unappreciated St. Ange! The trees grew, and the scar was healed. The soft, pine-laden breezes touched with heavenly fragrance the dull-faced women, the pathetic children, and the unambitious men. Everything was run down and apparently doomed, until one day the endless chain which encompasses the world, in its turning dropped the Golden Bead of Love into St. Ange! Down deep it sank to the bottom of the crucible. Jude Lauzoon was blinded by it and stung to life; Joyce Birkdale through its power came into the heritage of her soul. Jock Filmer by its magic force was shorn of his poor shield and left naked and unprotected for Fate's crudest darts. John Gaston, working out his salvation in his shack hidden among the pines, was burnt by the divining rays that penetrated to his secret place and spared him not. And then, when things were at their tensest, Ralph Drew came and tuned the discordant notes into sweet harmony. St. Ange became in time a home for many whom despair had marked for its own; a Sanctuary for devoted service.

CHAPTER I

The man lying flat on the rock which crusted Beacon Hill raised his head with a snake-like motion, and then let it fall back again upon his folded arms. His body had not moved; it seemed part of the stone and moss.

The midsummer afternoon was sunny and hot, and the fussy little river rambling through the Long Meadow was talking in its sleep.

Lazily it wound around young maples, and ferny groups—it would crush them by and by, poor trusting things—then it would stumble against a rock or pile of loose stones, wake up and repeat the strain it had learned at its mother's breast, far up in the North Woods.

"I'm here! here! here! I'll be ready by and by, by, by, by." Then on again, a little faster perhaps, but still dreamily. Children's laughter sounded far below; a slouching man or woman making for the Black Cat bent on business or pleasure, passed now and then; all else was still and seemingly asleep.

Again Jude raised his head and gave that quick glance around.

Jude was awake at last. Little Billy Falstar had roused him two days before and set the world in a jangle. The child's impish words had struck the scales from Jude's eyes, and the blinding light made him shrink and suffer.

"Him and her," the boy had whispered, hugging his bruised and dirty knees as he squatted by Jude's door; "him and her is sparking some." Then he laughed the freakish laugh of mischief.

Jude was polishing the gun which John Gaston had given him a year before, and had trained him to use until he was second only to Gaston himself for marksmanship. "Him and her— who?" he asked, raising his dull eyes to Billy's tormenting face.

"Joyce and Mr. Gaston. Him and her is beaux, I reckon. She goes to his shack; I listened outside the winder once—he reads to her and tells her things. They walks in the Long Medder, too, and once I saw him kiss her."

Again the teasing laugh that set every nerve tingling.

Then it was that Jude awoke, and his hot French blood, mingled with his canny Scotch inheritance, rose in his veins and struck madly against brain and heart.

He stared at Billy as if the boy had given him a physical blow—then he looked beyond him at the woods, the sky, the highway and the dejected houses—nothing was familiar! They all seemed alive and alert. Unseen happenings were going on— he must understand.

"You saw—him—kiss—her?" The gun fell limply across the man's knees.

"Yep," Billy whipped his dramatic sense into action. He arose and strode before Jude with Gaston's own manner. "This way. His arms out, and him a-laughing like, and Joyce she kinder run inter his arms and he held her, like this—." The close embrace of the childish gesture seemed to strangle Jude, and he gave a muffled cry. This acted like a round of applause upon Billy.

"Yep, and he kept on hugging and kissing her like this—" Billy

Harriet T. Comstock

went into an ecstasy of portrayal. Suddenly, however, he reeled into sanity, for Jude had struck him across the cheek with the back of a hand trembling with new-born emotion.

"Take that, you impish brat," he had said, "and more like it if you stand there another minute with your lying capers."

"They ain't lies," wailed Billy, edging away and nursing his smarting face; "he did! he did! It was in his shack—I saw 'em!"

"Get out," yelled Jude, glowering darkly; "and you tell that to any one else and," he came nearer to the shrinking child, "I swear I'll choke yer till yer can't speak." So changed was Jude that Billy trembled before him.

"I won't," he whispered, "I swear I won't, Jude; don't—don't hit me again; I won't tell."

He was gone, but the old Jude was gone also. The new man finished the gun cleaning, his breath coming hard and fast meanwhile, and then, taking the gun with him, he went into the deep woods on the northern edge of the village.

All the rest of the day he watched Gaston's shack from a distance; as the darkness drew on he crept closer.

Joyce did not come near the place, and Gaston himself only returned when the night was well advanced.

Jude watched him light his lamp, and prepare his supper. Watched him, later, go into the inner room, and then he crept close to the broad window to see what Gaston was doing in there where no foot but Gaston's own, so it was said, ever entered. As he had raised his eyes to the level of the casement, Gaston's calm gaze met his with a laugh in it.

"Hello, Jude," the voice was unshaken; "playing Indian Brave? Got your gun, too? What you after, big game or—what?" Jude rose to his feet. He was trembling violently. Gaston watched him closely. "Come in?" he asked presently.

"No. I was only passing—thought I would look in. I'm going now."

"Hold on there, Jude, what's up?" Gaston leaned from the window. "Are you alone?"

"Yes. There ain't anything the matter."

"All right." Gaston looked puzzled. "Good night." He watched Jude until he was lost in the shadows, then he drew the heavy wooden shutters close, bolted the door and placed his pistol near at hand.

All the next day Jude haunted the vicinity of Joyce Birkdale's home, but he kept hidden, for Joyce was safe within doors and a drizzly rain was falling. Night again found him on guard; and now he lay on Beacon Hill in the hot sun, napping by snatches (for he was woefully tired) and scanning the Long Meadow, with his feverish eyes, in between times.

In his dreams the scene Billy Falstar had so luridly described was enacted again and again, until he felt as if he, Jude, had been the onlooker.

The people whom he had taken for granted in the past now assumed new meaning and importance. Gaston had slipped in among them three years before, and after the first few months of observation he had aroused no interest. He had minded his business, paid his way, taken his turn in camp at greenhorn jobs, accounted for his presence on the ground of seeking health, and that was all. Life went on as usual, sluggishly and dully—but on.

Jude had, before Billy's illumination, been thinking that after the next logging season he would annex Joyce Birkdale to his few belongings—the cabin, his dog and gun. The idea had not roused him much, but it had been a pleasurable conclusion to arrive at; and now? Every nerve was aching and the boy's heart was thumping heavily. Again he dropped his head, and he cursed everything his thought touched upon—even the girl he meant, in some way, still to have.

One, two, three hours passed. Jude's hilltop was touched by the sun, but in the meadow the purpling shadows were gathering slowly.

Suddenly Jude sprang up—something was happening down there below. Something in him had warned him.

From the southern edge of the meadow a tall man was swinging along with easy strides. He carried his broad-brimmed hat in his right hand and waved it as if in greeting. From the opposite direction a girl was approaching. She wore a blue-checked gown, and her pale hair seemed to shine in the dimming light. She wore no hat, and she walked with the quick freedom of a child who longed to reach something precious.

Midway of the meadow the girl and man met. He stretched out his arms, and they closed about the slim form.

Then he bent his head over the fair one on his breast—but he did not kiss it! Jude was burning and palpitating. He strained his hearing, forgetting time and space. They were talking, and he would never know what they said.

Presently the girl slipped from the enfolding arms, and, clinging to the man's hands, looked up into his face. Some-times she bowed her head, and once she passed her hand across her eyes as if to wipe away tears. Then the man drew her close again. He raised the face that was crushed against his shoulder; he kissed the brow, the eyes, the chin—and then the lips.

Something blinded Jude. Something thick and hot like blood, and when he could see again, the two had parted. The man stood with bared head watching the slim, drooping figure as it retraced its steps with never a backward turn. When it was gone he replaced his hat and took his way—this time, toward the Black Cat.

Jude stood alone on his hilltop and watched the lights spring to life in cottage and tavern. The stars twinkled above him in the calm evening gloaming. The little river trilled a vesper hymn as it felt its way along the dark rocky path—and then tears came to Jude's relief, impotent, boyish, weak tears, such tears as he had not shed since his father and mother lay dead, and in childish fright and sorrow he had not known what to do next. But now, as then, he pulled himself together and set his teeth grimly.

He did the wisest thing he could have done. He went down the hill and strode toward the Birkdale house.

But he did not walk alone. Almost forgotten memories rose sharply and kept him company as he pushed on to meet his Fate.

Womankind in St. Ange was monotonous. There was a shading of individuality in the girls and newly-wed women, but it faded soon into the dull drab that seemed the only possible wearing-colour of the place. Occasionally, though, the sameness had been relieved by a vivid touch, but only for a short hour. The Fate who snips the threads, had invariably clipped such colouring from the St. Ange design, and tossed it aside as useless.

Jude remembered Marsena Riddall. What a woman she had been! What a menace to man's rights and woman's position.

She had demanded, and got her husband's wages as he returned from camp. She met him at the edge of the North Wood, and held him up, morally and physically. That she kept a clean and respectable house; that her children were well fed, clothed and cared for, had not counted to her credit one jot among the powers that be. Her husband was not safe on the man's side of the Black Cat screen. At ten o'clock, did Riddall brave his chances to that hour, Marsena would march boldly into the arena and claim her quarry. If a man rose to expostulate, Marsena was equal to him with tongue and wit. Masculine superiority trembled during Marsena's reign, which lasted five years; then Fate downed her.

Riddall was called away from his jailer by the command that even Marsena could not defy, and she and her children faced life in a village where a man was an absolute necessity unless there was money to take his place. Jude grimly smiled as he recalled how the men and boys gave Marsena and her brood a jeering send-off as the rattling train bore them away soon after Riddall had been laid behind the disused church.

So while Marsena was still in Jude's memory, he came upon the deserted and decaying cottage where once Lola Laval had sung her pretty French-Canadian song.

It was odd how Lola came always with that song accompaniment. Try as he might, even now, in this disordered moment, Jude heard the rippling little lark song rise and fall in the fragrant darkness.

Jude, while but a boy, liked to draw water for Lola and run her errands when young Pierre, the husband, was in camp. When the logging season was over, Lola's cottage vied with the Black Cat in popularity. Pierre was a noted card player, but, oh! Lola's song sounded above the slap of pasteboard and the click of glasses. How pretty she was—and how the women hated her! The men were eager to serve her. She had no need to command; her desires seemed granted before she voiced them—poor, pretty Lola!

Alouette, alouette, alouette, alouette.
Oh, alouette, chantez alouette,
Alouette, je te plumerai.
Alouette, chantez alouette,
Alouette, je te plumerai.

Je te plumerai le bec,
Je te plumerai le bec
A le bec,
A le bec,
Alouette,
Alouette.

Lola had not lasted long; only nineteen she was when Pierre in his jealousy struck the light from her eyes by a cruel blow, and the song fled from her lips; then taking warning from a well-directed signal from Beacon Hill, he had sought the Southern Solitude just before Justice, in the form of the Hillcrest constable, came stalking into St. Ange.

But the song was not dead. Again and again a man or woman would revive it and so it had become a part of the place. To Jude, now, it was painfully evident as he again plunged forward; it followed him sweetly, mockingly as it used to when Lola sent it after him to keep him from being afraid as he left her for his lonely home; he, a neglected little boy.

And now here was Joyce! With a stinging consciousness Jude realized this new personality that heretofore he had not suspected. Even as jealous anger spurred him on, a vague something he knew awaited him, calmed him and made him cautious.

While he longed to grip and command the situation, he was aware of a power in Joyce—a power he had unconsciously, perhaps, sensed before—that bade him stand afar until she beckoned him.

As he neared her little house, before even he saw the lights, he heard a song. It was that song! It met the rhythm in his own heated fancy—he and Joyce seemed to be singing it together:

Alouette,
Alouette.

The light was streaming through open window and door. Inside Joyce was preparing the evening meal, stepping lightly between table and stove as she sang. Jude dared not enter unannounced, and his pride held him silent.

What was he afraid of? Was he not he, and Joyce but a girl? Still he kept his distance.

"Joyce!" The song within ceased, and the singer stepped to the open doorway.

"That you, father?" No answer came. "Father?"

Then Jude came into the light.

"You, Jude? Come in; father's late. I never wait for him and I am as hungry as a wolf."

Joyce had been one of the few girls who had gone to the Hillcrest school as long as paternal authority permitted, and she showed her training.

"I ain't come for no friendly call," muttered Jude, slouching in and dropping on to a wooden chair beside the table.

Joyce turned and looked at him, and the glow from the hanging lamp fell upon her.

She was tall and slim, almost to leanness, but there were no awkward angles and she was as graceful as a fawn.

Her skin was pale, clear and smooth, her eyes wide apart and so dark as to be colourless, but of a wondrous softness. Her hair was of that shade of gold that suggests silver, and in its curves, where the sun had not bleached it, it was full of tints and tones.

"What have you come for?" she asked, as a child might have asked it, wonderingly and interestedly.

"I want to ask you something, and I want the truth."

"Oh!" Joyce sat opposite, and let her clasped hands fall upon the table laid out for the evening meal with the brown bowl of early asters set in the centre. She forgot her hunger, and the steaming pot on the stove bubbled unheeded.

"What you want to know, Jude? You look mighty upset."

Jude saw with his new, keen vision that she was startled and was sparring for time. "It's about," he leaned forward, "it's about you and—and him. I saw you in the Long Medder. I saw him hold your hands and—and kiss you." The words smarted the dry, hot lips. "I—I want to know what it means."

Jude was trembling visibly as he finished, but Joyce's silence, her apparent discomfort, gave him a kind of assurance that upheld him in his position.

The girl across the table had been awakened several weeks ago in Gaston's little shack among the pines. Since then she had been living vividly and fervently. The question with her, now, was how best to voice herself—the self that Jude in no wise knew. Womanlike, she did not want to plunge into what might prove an abyss. She wanted to take her own way, but with a half-unconscious coquetry she desired to drag her captives whither she went.

In the old stupid life before her womanhood was roused, Jude had held no mean part in her girlish dreams. He was the best of the St. Ange boyhood and Joyce had an instinctive relish for the best wherever she saw it. Whatever the future held she was not inclined to thrust Jude from it. In success or failure she would rather have him with her than against her. Not that she feared him—she had boundless belief in herself—but, hearts to the woman, scalps to the savage, are trophies not to be despised.

"I—I want to know what it means." Again Jude spoke, and

Harriet T. Comstock

this time a tone of command rang through the words.

The corners of Joyce's mouth twitched—she had a wonderfully expressive mouth. Suddenly she raised her eyes. They did not hold the expression Jude might have expected from her disturbed silence. His growing courage took a step back, but his passion rushed forward proportionately.

The witch-light danced in the steady glance she turned upon him; she threw her head back and her slim throat showed white and smooth in the lamp's glow.

"Suppose he did hold my hand and—and kiss me, Jude Lauzoon, you'd like to do the same yourself, now wouldn't you?"

She was ignorantly testing her weak, woman's weapon on the man's metal.

Jude felt the mist rising in his eyes that once before that day had hid this girl and Gaston from his sight. Like a mad mockery, too, Lola's lark song sounded above the rush of blood that made him giddy. He got to his feet and staggered around the table. He held to it, not so much to steady himself as to guide him, but as he neared the girl the blindness passed, and the tormenting song stopped—he stood in an awful silence, and a white, hot light.

"Yes, by God, I do want to, and if yer that kind I'll take—my share and chance along with the rest of 'em."

It was his own voice, loud and brutal, that smote the better part of him that stood afar and alone; a something quite different from the beast who spoke, and which felt a mad interest in wondering how she would take the words.

"You go and sit down over there!"

No clash of steel or dash of icy water could have had the effect those quiet words had, combined with the immovable calm out of which they came.

The instinct of frightened womanhood was alive. If she could not down the beast in the man by unflinching show of courage—she was lost.

They eyed each other for an instant—then Jude backed away and dropped into the chair across the table.

Still, like animal and tamer they measured each other from the safer distance. Presently the girl spoke, laying all the blame upon him for the fright and suffering.

"What right have you, Jude Lauzoon, to come here insulting me?"

"What right had you," he blurted out, "to make me think you was that—that sort?"

"I didn't make you think it—you thought it because you—wanted to think it—it was in you."

The beast was quelled now, and a stifled sob rose to the boyish throat.

"I—I didn't want to think it—God knows I didn't, Joyce, it was that that drove me mad."

"Can a man only think bad when he sees what he doesn't understand?"

Revulsion of feeling was making Joyce desperate. While her new power brought her a delirious joy, it also, she was beginning to understand, brought a terror she had never conceived before. She wished the house were nearer the other human habitations.

"If you're that kind, Jude, you had better take yourself to the

Harriet T. Comstock

Black Cat; you'll find plenty of your liking down there."

Jude was visibly cowering now.

"Why did he kiss you?" he pleaded.

"Suppose I gave him the right?"

"Then what am I to think? Have you given him the right? Does he want the right? I mean the right first—and last?" Jude was gaining ground, but neither he nor the girl to whom he spoke realized it yet. Joyce drew back.

"What is that to you?" she murmured hanging her head. For the moment she was safe—but she felt cornered.

Jude again bent toward her over his hands clenched close.

"It means everything," he panted, "and you know it. I've always liked you best of anything on earth—ever since I went to school, to please you, over to Hillcrest; ever since I tried to keep from the Black Cat, because you asked me to. I've gone following after you kinder heedless-like till—till he gave me a blow twixt the eyes, with his hand-holding and kissing. It drove me crazy. I never thought of any one else with you— least of all John Gaston and you. He didn't seem your kind—I don't know why, but he didn't. Howsomever, if it's all right— God knows I ain't in it—that's all."

A hoot of an owl outside made Joyce start nervously. She was unstrung and superstitious—the fun of the game died in her, and she felt weak and nauseated. She spoke as if she wanted to finish the matter and have done with it forever.

"Well, I didn't give him the right. He didn't want it. I guess it was all foolish—everything is foolish. When he found out how I liked books, and how I wanted to know about things, he just naturally was kind and he let me go to his shack to read. Sometimes he was there, sometimes he wasn't. He just thought about me as if I was a little girl—Maggie Falstar used to go sometimes—he told her fairy stories—it was all the same to him, until—" the wonderful colour that very pale people often have rose suddenly to Joyce's face, and the eyes became dreamy—"one day a week ago."

"Well," Jude urged her on—he was sensing the situation from the man's standpoint.

"It was nothing. I had been reading a book there by myself. It was the kind of story that makes you feel like you was the woman it tells about. Then Mr. Gaston came in, and stood looking at me from the doorway; he seemed like the man in the book too. We looked at each other, and—and I was frightened and I guess he was—for I was grown up all of a sudden. Jude"—the girl was appealing to the familiar in him, the comradeship that would stand with her and for her—"he took me in his arms and—and—kissed me. Then he begged my pardon—and he pushed me away; then he led me to the door and said he—he didn't understand, but I—I mustn't come again to the shack alone, but to meet him in the Long Meadow to-day."

"Curse 'im," muttered Jude; "curse 'im." But the move was a wrong one. Joyce rose to her own defence and Gaston's.

"If you feel that way," she cried, "you can take yourself off."

"I—I don't feel that way," Jude returned illogically and meekly; "go on."

"He's a good man, Jude Lauzoon; better than any one here in St. Ange; and he isn't our kind—not mine, yours, or any one else's around here. He just made me feel ashamed of myself out in the Meadow to-day. I felt as if I had been bold and—and all wrong, but he wouldn't let me feel that way. He acted like I was a little girl to him again—only different; and—I'm going to tell you something." The pink flush dyed even the white throat now. "He said he wished I would get married—it

Harriet T. Comstock

was for the best. That's the way he wanted me for himself!" Joyce laughed with a bitterness that changed suddenly as she recalled the subtle power she had felt over Gaston even while he was forcing her out of his life.

"He asked me about Jock Filmer."

"Jock Filmer?" Jude's jaw dropped. Was all St. Ange hurtling around Joyce? "Jock Filmer—why—why—" Words failed him and he laughed noisily.

"Oh, I don't know," Joyce tossed her head. "You seem to think nobody would want me—I guess—they would—if I wanted them!" The girl was worn out; racked by the emotions that were reflected from the new attitude of others toward her.

And now Jude came around the table again. This time he walked steadily, and he was quite himself. The best self he had ever yet been.

"I want you Joyce—God knows I do."

"He said you did."

"Who?"

"He—Mr. Gaston."

"He—said that? Then why in thunder did—he kiss you?"

That rock Jude dashed against at every turn.

"He didn't until—until I told him—I liked you."

Poor Joyce! She was never to tell any one that that admission had been wrung from her in order to make Gaston think he himself had not been deeply in her thoughts. It had been a difficult fencing match that afternoon.

"You told him that?" A light came into Jude's handsome, heavy face, which quickly vanished as the torturing jealousy, feeding upon a new hope, rose, defiantly. "You told him you cared—and then he kissed you, damn him! Maybe he thinks he'll get you to take me, and then he'll go on with hand-holding and kissing all the safer."

"Take that back," cried Joyce harshly. "Take that back, Jude Lauzoon." Yet as she resented the implied insult, the primitive woman in her admired Jude as it had never admired him before.

"I didn't mean it against you, Joyce, I swear it. Can't you see how I love yer and I don't want yer hurt? No one ain't going to hurt yer!" He had clutched her to him roughly but tenderly. "Maybe he wouldn't want ter, maybe I don't understand—but he can't, anyway!"

She was sobbing hysterically against his breast.

"You're mine, lass; you're just a little one; you don't know things. You're no older than you was when you toted over to Hillcrest and—and never felt afraid."

Jude tried to kiss the tear-stained face, but she pressed it closer against him. He had to be content with the satin softness of her thick hair.

Suddenly she sprang from him. A sickish odour was filling the room.

"Everything's burned," she gasped; "everything!" She drew the pot from the stove and ruefully carried it outside. "Nothing left, Jude;" she laughed nervously. "Nothing but crusts and leavings."

"You go to bed," commanded Jude authoritatively; "that's what you need more than anything!"

Harriet T. Comstock

"Yes, yes, that's what I need—sleep. I'm almost dead, I'm so tired."

Jude looked at her hungrily. The sudden happy ending of his torture gave him an unreal, unsafe feeling.

He wanted to touch her again in the new, thrilling way, but she was forbidding even in her sweet yielding.

"You go to bed," he said vaguely; "I'll go down to the Black Cat, and see that your father gets home all right."

Joyce stepped backward to the chamber door beyond.

"Thank you," she murmured; "I certainly am dead tired."

CHAPTER II

There was only a path leading from the highway to John Gaston's shack. A path wide enough for a single traveller, and the dark pointed pines guarded it on either side until within ten feet of the house. The house itself sat cosily in the clearing. It was a log house built by amateur hands, but roughly artistic without, and mannishly comfortable within.

The broad door opened into the long living room, where a deep fireplace (happily the chimney had drawn well from the first, or the builder would have been sore perplexed) gave a look of hospitality to the otherwise severe furnishings. The fireplace and mantel-shelf were Gaston's pride and delight. Upon them he had worked his fanciful designs, and the result was most satisfactory. There was a low, broad couch near the hearth piled with pine cushions covered with odds and ends of material that had come into a man's possession from limited sources. A table, home-made, and some Hillcrest chairs completed the furnishings, except for the china and cooking utensils that ornamented shelves and hooks around the room.

An inner door opened into Gaston's bedchamber and sanctum. No one but himself ever entered there.

There was a broad desk below the one wide window of that room and a revolving chair before it. A boxed-in affair, filled with fragrant pine boughs, answered for a bed. This was covered with white sheets and a pair of fine, handsome, red blankets. An iron-bound chest stood by the bed with a padlock strong enough to guard a king's treasure, and around the walls of the room there were rows of books, interrupted here and there to admit a picture of value and beauty out of all proportion to the other possessions.

Over the window hung a large-faced clock that kept faultless time, and announced the fact hourly in a mellow, but convincing, voice. Just below the window and over the desk, was a pipe-rack with pipes to fit every mood and fancy of a lonely man. There were the short stumpy ones, with the small bowls for the brief whiff when one did not choose to keep company with himself for long, but was willing to be sociable for a moment. There were the comfortable, self-caring pipes that obligingly kept lighted between long puffs while the master was looking over old papers, or considering future plans. Then there were the long-stemmed, deep-bellied friends for hours when Memory would have her way and wanted the misty, fragrant setting for her pictures that so comforted or tormented the man who wooed them.

By the rude desk Gaston was sitting on the evening that Jude and Joyce were clinging to each other in the house under the maples. His hands were plunged deep in the pockets of his corduroy trousers, his long legs extended, and his head thrown back; he was smoking one of his memory-filled pipes, and his eyes were fixed upon the rafters of the room.

He was a good-looking fellow in the neighbourhood of thirty-five; browned by an out-of-door life, but marked by a delicacy of feature and expression.

The strength that was in Gaston's face might puzzle a keen reader of character as to whether it were native, or the result of years of well-fought battles. Once the will was off guard, a certain softness of the eyes, and a twitching of the mouth muscles came into play; but the will was rarely off guard during Gaston's waking hours.

An open book lay upon the desk, and the student lamp cast a

full light upon the words that had caught the reader's thoughts after the events of the day and their outcome.

"In the life of every man there occurs at least one epoch when the spirit seems to abandon the body, and elevating itself above mortal affairs just so far as to get a comprehensive and general view, makes this an estimate of its humanity, as accurate as it is possible, under the circumstances, to that particular spirit. The soul here separates itself from its own idiosyncrasy, or individuality, and considers its own being, not as appertaining solely to itself, but as a portion of the universal Ego. All important good resolutions of character are brought about at these crises of life; and thus it is our sense of self which debases and keeps us debased."

Poe and Gaston were great friends. The living man knew that had he known Poe in the body he would have feared and detested him, but there was no doubt he had left trails of glory in his wake, for the comfort of struggling humanity, if only one could lose sight of the man, in the spiritual effulgence of his genius.

Gaston, in his detached life, practised many arts upon his individuality and character. He had time and to spare to "abandon the body," and he was growing more and more confident, that in these self-imposed crises he was gaining not only strength, but a keen and absorbing interest in others. If the sense of self debased, then this detachment was his great salvation.

The rings of smoke curled upward, lost shape and formed a haze of blueness. The heat became intense, and the noises of the summer night magnified. The windows and doors were set wide, Gaston's wood-trained senses were alert even in this abstraction.

"What next?" That was the question. He had just come through a conflict with flying colours. He was flushed with victory, but the after details annoyed him. With the waning

Harriet T. Comstock

enthusiasm of achievement, from his point of vantage of abandonment, he was trying to see beyond this confident hour—see into the plain common days when a sense of self would control him, tempt him, lure, and perhaps, betray him. What then?

The realization of Joyce Birkdale's womanhood a time back had shaken him almost as much as it had the girl herself.

It had all been so peaceful, so elemental and satisfying before: that companionship with the little lonely, aspiring, neglected child. She was so responsive and joyous; so eager to learn, so childishly interested in the fairy tales of another sort of existence that he kept from decay by repeating to her. And then that sudden, upleaping flame in the purple-black eyes. The fierce rush of hot, live blood to the pale face. The grip of those small work-stained hands as they sought dumbly to stay the trembling until he had taken them into his firm control.

Well, confronted by the blinding flash, he had acted the man. That was good. He had not acted thoughtlessly, either. He had sent the quivering little thing away quietly, and with no sense of bitterness, until he had threshed the matter out. And then in the Long Meadow, he had set the girlish feet upon the trail he had blazed out for them during the nights of temptation and days of lonely self-abnegation.

It was a hard, stumbling way he had fixed upon. His heart yearned over the girl even as he urged her on. But Joyce was demanding her woman's rights. Demanding them none the less insistently, because she was unconscious of their nature. He knew, and he must go before her; but there was small choice of way.

When he had held her in his arms out there in the open, he had bidden her farewell with much the same feeling that one has who kisses the unconscious lips of a child, and leaves him to the doubtful issue of a necessary surgical operation.

But the victory over self was his, and Joyce was on Life's table. There was a sort of feverish comfort now in contemplating what might have been. Many a man—and he knew this only too well—would have put up a strong plea for the opposite course.

What was he resigning her to at the best? There was no conceit in the thought that, had he beckoned, Joyce would have leaped into the circle of his love and protection. Not in any low or self-seeking sense would the girl have responded—of that, too, he was aware; but as a lovely blossom caressed by favouring sun and light, forgetting the slime and darkness of its origin, she might have burst into a bloom of beauty.

Yes, beauty! Gaston fiercely thought. Instead—there was honour! His honour and hers, and the benediction of Society—if Society ever penetrated to the North Solitude.

Joyce would forget her soul vision, she would marry Jock Filmer—no; it was Jude Lauzoon who, for some unknown, girlish reason, she had preferred when she had been cast out from the circle of his, Gaston's protection.

Yes, she would marry Jude—and Jock might have made her laugh occasionally—Jude, never! She would live in cramped quarters, and have a family of children to drag her from her individual superiority to their everlasting demands upon her. Perhaps Jude would treat her, eventually, as other St. Ange husbands treated their wives. At that thought Gaston's throat contracted, but a memory of the girl's strange, uplifted dignity gave him heart to hope.

Again the reverse of the picture was turned toward him. He saw her flitting about his home—who was there to hold her back, or care that she had sought dishonour instead of honour?

He might have trained and guided that keen mind, and cultivated the delicate, innate taste. Yes; he might have created a rare personality, and brightened his own life at the same time—and the years and years would have stretched on, and nothing would have interrupted the pure passage of their lives until death had taken one or both. Gaston sat upright, and flung the pipe away. Suppose he should choose to—go back? Well, in that case it would have gone hard with Joyce. The soul he had awakened and glorified would have to be flung back into the hell from which its ignorance shielded it.

That was it. In giving the girl the best—yes, the best, in one sense—he must forego his own soul's good; forego the hope that he might some day choose to go back—and in that hope, lay Joyce's damnation.

Through dishonour—as men might have classified it—he might have lifted Joyce up, but to save her soul alive from the hope he reserved for himself—his open door—he must drive her back to squalor and even worse.

He had chosen for her and for himself. He had his hope; Joyce was to have her honour; and now, what next?

His renunciation had strengthened him. His good resolutions steadied him; in the regained empire of his self-respect he contemplated the loneliness of exile, self-imposed, but none the less dreary. He was so human in his inclinations, so pitifully dependent upon his environment; and since he had stepped from the train three years ago, these rough people had taken him at his face value; desired nor cared for nothing but what he chose to give. Desolate St. Ange was dear to him.

No, he would remain. There was really no reason why he should abdicate the little that was his own. All should be as it was, except for Joyce, and even she, now that he was sure of himself and had the rudder in hand, even she might claim his friendship and sympathy in her new life.

He started. His quick ear detected the slow step outside.

"Hello, Jude," he called without getting up. "Step in; I'll fetch a light."

"How did you know 'twas me?" Jude asked from the outer darkness. The salutation made him feel anew the awe of constant supervision.

"I thought you'd drop in," Gaston carried the lamp into the living room and set it upon the table.

Jude shambled in, drew a chair up to the table and sat down. Gaston took his place opposite and kept his eyes upon his caller. Jude grew restless under the calm inspection. He had come with a goodly stock of self-assertion and sudden-gained dignity, but they withered under the inquiring gaze.

"You've come from Joyce Birkdale's? I congratulate you, Jude."

So he knew that too! Jude felt a superstitious aversion to this man he had but recently begun to have any feeling toward whatever outside the ordinary give and take of village life.

Over the ground he had come laboriously to discuss, Gaston strode with unerring instinct. There were no words ready for this friendly advance, so Jude halted. He had meant to approach the announcement of his engagement to Joyce by telling Gaston what he had seen from the hilltop that afternoon and what he had gained since, and then he had intended, in man-fashion, to warn Gaston off his preserves. Instead, he sat twirling his cap and foolishly staring.

"Smoke?" Gaston felt his guest's discomfort and tried to ease the strain. He pushed the tobacco-jar forward; no St. Ange man ever travelled without his own pipe.

"Given it up," muttered Jude, "and cards likewise, and—and drink; I'm going to get married right away."

This was rather startling. Gaston had expected some faltering on Joyce's part, some dallying with the past. The smoke of his

Harriet T. Comstock

burning bridges was still in Gaston's consciousness. He had lighted the fuse, to be sure, but had not expected the demoralization to be so prompt.

For a minute his gaze faltered, then he said cordially:

"Good! And you won't drink to it—or smoke over it? Well, then, shake, old man."

For the life of him Jude could not decline. So their hands met over the bare table.

An awkward pause followed. Gaston took refuge in smoke. He drew the inevitable pipe from his pocket, filled and lighted it, and during the time of grace, got himself in hand.

"Jude," he said between puffs, "I want to see her married."

Jude's anger rose. The words and the tone brought back his suspicions and jealousies.

"I want that girl to have a chance at life." Gaston looked over Jude's head, and drew hard upon his pipe. "She's never really waked up. Just got the call, you know. Before this, she's been dreaming, and God alone knows where she got her dream material. Like the rest of us, until she finds out, she's going to expect her dream to come true. In heaven's name, Lauzoon, help her to make it true."

The import of all this touched Jude not at all, but the meddling of this outsider did mightily stir him to depths he had never fathomed before. Suddenly a kind of courage came to him, partly worthy, but wholly unreasonable.

"I ain't no wooden-head, as some thinks I am," he blurted out, while his dull eyes flashed; "and, by gosh, I want that darn well understood between you and me, Mr. Gaston! I don't want any interference in my affairs; but as to what you're drivin' at, perhaps, I'll say this. I'm going to let Joyce have her head—in reason."

"You better," Gaston laughed unpleasantly. He rather liked Jude the better for his uprising; but he had no intention of showing a flag of truce now.

"Why?" asked Lauzoon; the laugh irritated him.

"Oh, it's plain common sense to be with her, instead of against her, when she gets fully awake. Her kind goes well enough in harness if the other one pulls a fair share—if he doesn't—why, the chances are—she'd break the traces and—clip it alone."

"Alone, hey?" It was Jude's turn to laugh now. "You ain't got the lay of the country yet, Mr. Gaston, not so far as the women is concerned. How in thunder is a woman to go alone, I'd like to know, in St. Ange? Once she's married, she's married, and she knows it. Go alone? I'd like to know where she'd go to?"

A breeze was now stirring outside. Gaston felt it and he shivered slightly.

"Jude," he continued after a moment, "they sometimes go to the devil, you know. Even St. Ange's ideals do not prevent that, judging from things I've heard."

"Not her kind," Jude muttered. He was harking back to Lola Laval. How the girl rose and haunted him to-night! "Not her kind, Mr. Gaston."

"No, you're right, Jude—not her kind as she is now. That's just the point. It's poor work, though, to draw on your bank account without noting how your balance stands. If you do, you'll get a surprise some day. Joyce wants the best she can get out of life. She's had a vision, poor little girl, and she's making for that vision, believing it a reality. We all do that, old man, and it's up to you to give her as much of what she wants as you can. She's been building a place for her soul"—Gaston was

Harriet T. Comstock

thinking aloud. Jude had vanished from his horizon—"and she's going up to take possession some day. God, how that woman is going to love—something!"

And just then Jude shifted into view again upon the line of Gaston's perceptions. He had risen to his feet and was glaring at his companion. There was an ugly look on his face, and his hands trembled with the effort he made to restrain himself.

"Say, Mr. Gaston," he blurted out, "all that talk is damned moonshine, and I ain't such a fool but what I know it. Such gaff ain't nourishing. Now as to Joyce, I'm going to do the square thing by her. Her book-learning is all right if she keeps it to herself, and don't let it get mixed up with her duties 'long of me. And right here, Mr. Gaston," Jude choked miserably, "I guess her and me don't want no coaching from you. No harm intended, understand, but just a clean showing."

Indignation and a realization of his own insignificance, had hurled Jude along up to this point, but he was suddenly landed high and dry by the calm, amused look in Gaston's eyes.

"Too bad you don't smoke, Jude," Gaston said quietly, refilling his pipe. "But sit down, and loosen your collar. The room is infernally close. I've been thinking some of leaving St. Ange—"

"When are you going?" Jude broke in with an eagerness that intensified the smile on Gaston's face, and bade the devil in him awake. The same devil that in boyhood days had made him such an irritant to the bullies of his class.

"Oh, I'm not going," he replied, puffing luxuriously upon his pipe; "I've changed my mind. All I wanted was new scenes and occupations. I've decided to stay on awhile. But I've been thinking, Jude, you don't want to take Joyce into your shack. Let's build her another up on the sunny slope beyond the Long Meadow on the Hillcrest side. I'm gaining strength each year; I like to keep myself busy and the work would be a godsend to me. What do you say? I can lend you a little money, too, if you need it."

Need it? Unconsciously Gaston had touched the spring that unlocked the evilest part of Jude's nature. Jealousy, love, hate, were blotted out by this unlooked-for suggestion. His dark face flushed and his dull eyes gleamed. Money! Money! To handle it, spend it and enjoy it without great bodily effort in earning it. This had ever been a consuming passion with Jude. A passion that had remained smouldering because no favouring chance had ever fanned it. Lazy and hot-blooded, Jude, in a prosperous community, might have developed criminal tendencies young; in St. Ange there had been nothing to tempt him—until now.

"Thank you," he said, and Gaston saw the change in him. "I—I may be glad of a small loan—just at the start, you know, and before I get my pay from the camp boss. It's almighty kind of you, Mr. Gaston, to think of this here building and all. Me and Joyce will take it grateful, I can tell you."

"Going?" Gaston asked, for Jude had risen and was awkwardly shifting from foot to foot. "Well, so long! Good luck—and a speedy marriage."

Then the door closed upon the transformed Jude.

"Now, what in thunder," mused Gaston in the hot, smoky room, "has got into that fellow, I wonder!" Could they know of his money? The amount, and manner of getting it? Was he, in offering Jude this assistance, letting the leak in upon his own safety?

A cloud gathered on Gaston's face. A sensation of coming evil possessed him. He felt as if, in an unguarded moment, he had given an enemy a power over him.

The memory of the look in Jude's face when the money cast a gleam over his hate, repelled him. Gaston was as fully alive to the possibilities now as Jude was—perhaps more so; but there stood the pale, innocent girl between them. He recalled her hurt, quivering face when he had urged her into Jude's keeping. It had seemed her only salvation—hers and his! But it began to look now like a hideous damnation.

"Poor little devil," he murmured taking the lamp and going back into his bedroom.

The window of this room he closed carefully, and set the lamp upon the rude desk. He drew the pistol from the drawer, and laid it conveniently at hand, then he turned to the chest with the mighty lock and, having unfastened it, drew forth a small package and went back to the chair before the desk.

The package contained a photograph and some letters. The letters were tied together, and these the man placed beside the pistol. The photograph he took from its various wrappings of tissue paper and braced it against the lamp.

The big clock hanging over the window frame struck one. The heat in the little room became stifling, and the lamp flickered in its duty—for the oil was running low.

With arms folded before him Gaston gazed upon the pictured face. It broke upon the senses like a revelation of womanhood. At the first glance it seemed as if just that type had never been conceived before. The artist had grasped that conception evidently, for with no shading or background, with only a filmy scarf outlining the form from the colourless paper, the compelling features started vividly upon the vision, as the individuality of the girl did upon the imagination. An irritation followed the first impression. Was this child, or woman? What was she to become, or what had she become already? Was she a soul reaching out for realization, or a well-developed personality, having gained, with all its other attainments, a power of self-concealment from the inquisitive eye?

The brow, low and broad, bespoke gracious womanhood and a

possible radiant maternity, rather than intellectuality. The masses of hair were braided and wound coronet-style about the small uplifted head. The eyes, deep, dark, and mystical gave no clue to the inner woman; but the mouth, while it was tender in its curves, had a rigidity of purpose in its expression that fixed the attention. A pretty, rounded chin, a slender, slightly tilted nose, an exquisite throat set off by the cloud of lace—such was the face that Gaston beheld, and presently it wrung a groan from him.

"Ruth, Ruth, Ruth," he muttered, and then his mind took to the memory-haunted highway that led back, back of the lonely years of St. Ange; past a certain black horror that had stood, and would always stand, as a thing that should not have existed; but which had been, and would always remain, an object that cast a shadow before it and behind it.

"Did you do this thing?"

"I did."

Question and answer made up the vital happening in Gaston's life. Everything before led up to them, and all that had occurred since was the outcome.

They had admitted—or so he once thought—of no shading nor explanation. The questioner was not the type to deal unsteadily with a problem, and Gaston had been too simple and direct to note fine points or shadings. Perhaps neither of them had understood. Life had been so fair until the terrible thing had loomed up. It had come like a cataclysm—how could they, young and inexperienced as they had been, deal with the situation justly?

Suppose *now* she stood before him, wonder-eyes raised, seeking his soul's truth; hands resting in his until he should speak. Would he speak again those two crude, fatal words? Would she drop her hands letting his soul sink, by so doing, into the blackness which had engulfed it?

That was the torturing problem that Gaston was working out up in the lonely St. Ange woods; but he seemed no nearer the answer than when he had come to the place, by mistake, a few years back, and decided to stay there simply because it was as desirable as any other forsaken spot, while he was debarred from the Paradise of life.

The lamp flickered fretfully, and the spasmodic flare showed the rigid face torn with the emotions that were racking the soul laid bare before its God and its own consciousness.

What had the dreary, desolated years done for him? He was a fool. Why had he not taken what was possible, since the ideal was dashed from him?

This girl, way off there behind the hideous shadow, had been wiser. She had replaced his memory by living love; why should not he take the poor substitute that the Solitude offered, and warm the barren places of his heart and life with the faint glow?

It was a bad hour for Temptation to assail John Gaston.

The armour of self-wrought strength was off. Suffering was flaying the naked despair and yearning; and just then Temptation knocked softly and pitifully at the door of the outer room!

Gaston had done more while he had hidden in the woods than he was aware of. He had developed something akin to second sight. Loneliness and empty hours had strengthened this as blindness intensifies other senses to abnormal keenness. Gradually he had grown to believe that a man's life, complete and prearranged, lies stretched before, and occasionally some, when the circumstances are propitious and the soul has a certain detachment that ignores the bodily claims, can leap over the *now* and here, and catch a glimpse of the future and what it holds. This vague sense had come to Gaston more than once during the past year or two—the seeing and hearing of that which had held no part in what was, at the moment, occurring, but which he noted later had become a fact in his life.

That feeble knock dragged the man's consciousness away from the pictured face; away from his wavering indecision; away from the darkening room with its foul smell of oil: he knew who stood outside in the moonlighted, fragrant summer night, and he wondered if he were going to open that barred door to her. He waited for a glimpse of what was in store for them both.

But his spiritual sight was blinded by a firm, deadening blankness! Whatever was to be the outcome must be of his own choosing.

Again she knocked, that poor little temptress in the dark. What had Fate decreed that he was to do? Gaston knew as well as if Joyce had told him, *why* she had come. Her soul had revolted from her concession to Jude. In the bewitched hours of darkness, the primitive, savage instinct had driven the girl to the only one who could change her future. Worn, weary, defiant, she had come to him; not questioning further than her despair and his power.

Well, why not? Who would be the worse, and who the better—if he drew her within and closed the door upon—St. Ange?

Another tap—this time upon the wooden shutter of the bedchamber!

Gaston shivered and trembled. He was not outside; he was stifling in the dark room. The light had gone entirely, and he was struggling to free himself from an intangible enemy or friend; a thing that had, unknown to himself, evolved during those isolated years among the pines, and was restraining his lower nature now.

He battled to get to that little, insistent girl. He heard her sob, a childish sob, half desire, half fear. The veins stood out on his forehead and his hands gripped the edge of his desk as he got upon his feet.

The sob outside was echoed by a stifled groan from within— then all was still.

Slow retreating steps presently sounded without. She, that sad, broken, little temptress, was going to meet the fore-ordained future that lay before. There was nothing else left for her to do. All her reserves were taken.

Then Gaston, when all was beyond his power of recall or desire, opened the window.

Softly, sweetly, the fresh morning air entered. It was a young and good morning. A morning cool and faintly tinted, a morning to soothe a hurt heart, not to stimulate it too harshly.

Gaston's lined face smoothed under the caress. His armour arose as if unseen hands guided it, and placed it again upon him. Once more he was the strong, quiet man that St. Ange had taken upon faith, and accepted without question.

As he looked at the scene, his self-respect giving him courage to meet the day, Jude Lauzoon's soft-stepping figure materialized upon the edge of the pine woods.

The humour of the situation for a moment gripped Gaston's senses. Had all St. Ange stayed awake and been on guard while the night passed? But the smile faded. How long had Jude been there? Long enough to *know all*, or just long enough to know half?

What should he do? If Jude knew but half, no explanation could possibly avail. If he knew all; if he had been on guard before Joyce came—been camping out with no definite purpose, since his late talk in the shack—why, then it was simply a matter to be settled between Lauzoon and Joyce. God help her! He, Gaston, could serve best by retiring. This he did physically.

He put away his treasures and locked them fast; then, flinging himself upon the pine-bough bed, dressed as he was, he soon fell into a troubled sleep.

Harriet T. Comstock

CHAPTER III

Jared Birkdale, with a contemplative eye, looked at his daughter through the haze of his tobacco smoke as if seeing her for the first time. In a way this was so. He was not one to take heed of time or happenings. When he was not obliged to work, he was enjoying himself in his own way, and so long as nothing jarred him, life slipped by comfortably enough.

When he worked he was away, as all St. Ange men were, in the camps. Occupation, outside of Leon Tate's profession, was the same for all the men after first boyhood was past. When the logging season was over Jared, more temperate, perhaps more cruel for that reason, settled down. When he was not occupying the chair of honour at the Black Cat—given him by common consent because of his superior mental endowments—he was lounging at home and idly appreciating the plain comfort for which Joyce was responsible; a comfort Jared neither understood nor questioned.

But little Billy Falstar, the day before, with the fiendish depravity of a mischief-making child, had set the match to a fuse of gunpowder all ready for it down at the Black Cat.

Resenting the treatment Jude had given him when he had voiced his observations about Gaston and Joyce, he had gone to the tavern to nurse his wounded feelings where company and safety abounded. His fear of Jude had departed.

Several men, Birkdale among them, were sitting about when

Billy, sniffing and rubbing his knuckles in his eyes to such an extent that of necessity notice must be taken, drew their attention.

"What's up, Billy?" asked Jock Filmer good-naturedly; "shingle struck a thin place in your breeches? Go around and buy a peppermint stick. Here's a cent. Peppermint ought to be as good for a pain in your hindquarters as it is for one in your first cabin. Let up, kid, and get cheerful!"

Billy accepted the coin, but turned a calculating eye on the others. If his news had had power to rouse Jude, how would it act now? Billy, freckled and sharp-eyed, was a born tragedian.

"'Tain't Ma," he said. "No more was it Pa; it was that Jude what beat me most to a jelly."

This was startling enough to awaken a new interest. Jude was too lazy on general principles to reduce any one to jelly unless the provocation had been great.

"What divilment was you up to?" Filmer asked with a leer.

"I didn't do nothing! 'Pon my soul, I didn't. I swear!"

This Billy did, fervently and fluently. The children of St. Ange swore with a guileless eloquence quite outside the sphere of wickedness. The matter was in them. It must, of course, come out. So Billy swore now with only an occasional hitch where his indignation muddled pronunciation.

"Billy's got a fine flow of language," Birkdale put in amusedly. "For a youngster, I don't think I ever heard it equalled." Birkdale was about to urge Billy to renewed effort, when something the boy was wedging in among his evil words caught his attention.

"I was just a-telling him—" more lurid expressions—"'bout Joyce and Mr. Gaston. It didn't seem like nothing; just them two being beaux like all girls and fellers, but Jude he did me dirt, he did!" Billy stopped rubbing his eyes.

He was interested, himself, in the effect his words now had. For a moment he feared all the men were going to rise up against him as Jude had done. A silence fell upon the group. Filmer gave one keen glance at the imp on the doorstep, and then refilled his pipe and leaned back in his wooden chair.

Tom Smith, the ticket agent of the Station, looked as if some one had dashed water in his face, so startled was he; and Jared Birkdale simply stared open-mouthed at the spy in their midst. Then Tate, the proprietor, with the tact for which he was noted, went to the bar and began filling glasses.

St. Ange had received a shock; but St. Ange took its shocks in a peculiar way. It reserved its opinion until it had drunk on them.

Soon after the revelation Birkdale went home without a word having been spoken by any one on the subject so suddenly thrust upon their notice.

Jared had gone home to assure himself that Joyce had actually grown up to the extent of making Billy Falstar's remarks possible.

The afternoon's contemplation had caused him some astonishment.

Joyce *was* grown up! Then he had slept on the knowledge, and dreamed of other days—a life apart, and beyond St. Ange.

St. Ange was a young place; it had no antiquity; almost all who lived there had had a setting in some other time and environment.

Jared recalled, in his thoughts that night, the beginnings of things in his life. Joyce's mother, and the babies who had come and gone like little ghosts, each one taking more of the wife's and mother's beauty and power.

Then that flight to the St. Ange lumber camp—it was really that, nothing less—the attending discomfort and paralyzing reality of what lay before!

Joyce was born the year after the settlement in the rough forest home, and then poor Mrs. Birkdale gave up the struggle.

She told Isa Tate that had the baby been a boy she would not have felt the way she did, but to face the life of another woman in her own life was more than she could bear.

Isa had tried to hold her to her responsibility: Isa had more than her own share of trouble—but Jane Birkdale had slipped away in the middle of the severest winter St. Ange had known for many a year and Isa had been obliged to have "an eye" to the baby Joyce. The small girl responded in health and joyousness, and Jared, when he was himself, had had the grace to be grateful.

As the years slipped by the fire of Jared's own little private hell aroused him to a consciousness that he deserved anything but a happy future.

He hoped, in due season, that he would forget the wrongs he had done his wife, but they gathered strength with time. His sins walked with him through the sober lumber season; their memory drove him to the Black Cat; but his keener wit evolved a desire to "make good," as he termed it, in his relations with his daughter.

He would so conduct himself with her that she, at least, should have nothing against him; and when age, sickness or accident befell him, he might turn to her and find refuge. Jared had always had some kind of sanctuary to flee to when overtaken by the results of his own evil nature.

Harriet T. Comstock

And now, by the impish words of Falstar's Billy, he was brought face to face with a possibility that staggered and unnerved him.

Joyce and Jude, or Joyce and Jock Filmer, had been possibilities in Jared's distant future. But Joyce, already a woman, and that silent man Gaston who had come from a Past that he rigidly reserved for his own contemplation—Gaston, who lived among them as a traveller who might depart with the day into a Future Birkdale instinctively knew would hold no possible connection with St. Ange—Joyce and Gaston! Here was a situation indeed.

Astonishment, anger, a dull fear and a determination to grip something out of it all for himself, swayed Jared as he sat tilted back, eyeing his daughter after the night's travail.

He had come from his troubled thought imbued with a forced strength and singleness of purpose that made themselves felt by the quiet girl at the window.

Joyce had brought no strength from her disturbed night. She was ill-fitted for the encounter.

"By Jove," Jared suddenly ejaculated, "it's just struck me all of a heap, Joyce, that you're more than ordinary handsome."

The girl raised her eyes with a dull show of surprise, then went on with her sewing.

"With the learning I've given you over and above the other girls of the place, you *ought* to do pretty good for yourself—and me—and no mistake. You always was a real grateful child, and you ain't one ever to forget the fifth commandment, Joyce—the only one with a promise."

"The only one needing it," Joyce returned, with a bitterness for which she was sorry the moment after. But when Jared turned to quoting Scripture the girl grew rebellious. It was always distasteful to her to see, or hear, her father parade his superior knowledge. For some reason she always felt more ashamed of him then than at any other time.

"You've got a nasty bit of a temper, Joyce." Jared's eye gleamed. "I hope you ain't going to take the first chance you get to shirk your duty to me."

"I guess not, father, but I hate to be dragged to my duty; and I have a headache."

"What give you that, Joyce?"

"I don't know." Again the fair head bent above the coarse sewing in the trembling hands.

She had seen the light in the chinks of Gaston's shutter. She had felt his nearness, but rigid aloofness. The memory of these things had tortured her and left their trace in worn-out nerves and hurt pride. She felt that she hated Gaston and in revolt her thought now clung to Jude. She forgot her father.

"Joyce!"

"Oh, yes, father." How the insistent invasion of paternal intimacy jarred.

"I've been thinking lately how you and me might do better than stick here in St. Ange."

A sudden illumination flashed into the pale face. Was there a possibility of escape that did not include Jude?

"Where could we go, father?" Joyce was all attention.

"Oh! there are several places. I wasn't always here by a long shot. I've always meant to tell you some day, Joyce. It has sometimes struck me as singular that you never asked."

"I never cared. I was here—and the rest didn't matter—or it never did, until now."

"Well I was a handsome young buck once, my girl." Jared glanced at the mirror hanging over Joyce's head, and smirked. "I ain't a bad looking feller now. A little trimming of the beard, fashionable clothes, refined surroundings and you'd have a father that any girl might be proud of!"

Joyce noted now, as she had more than once before, since Hillcrest training had given her a certain power of discrimination, her father's style of speaking.

"What happened, father, before you came here?" she asked quickly. Her directness, and the slight she paid to his personal reflections, ruffled Jared's complacency. He was not ready to confess more than was absolutely necessary.

"Just one of them misunderstandings," he replied, slipping into St. Ange's carelessness of speech, "that happens now and again to any young man with a fine taste and slim purse. A matter of business! I always calculated to go back and make it straight, after the first flash had passed and I had money enough. I never give up or got discouraged. It was your mother losing grip sort of set me back; and then your raising and expenses here, kinder held me down. But the spirit in me has soared nevertheless."

"Sometimes it seems to me," Joyce's eyes grew dreamy, "that every one in St. Ange has something to keep still about. Every one seems to be here because he has to, not because he wants to. People seem to drift in here like logs after a spring freshet—and they get jammed."

Jared laughed. The idea caught his fancy.

"You've hit it, Joyce!" he said, "You've hit it all right. Jammed, by damn! that's it; but to carry the simile further, when the jam is loosened up, there's going to be some logs as gets away."

"*Where* could we go, father, and how?"

The pleading intensity of the girl encouraged Jared. He refilled his pipe, imagined himself in the mirror trimmed up and fashionably attired, and then drove his axe to the heart of the matter.

"When all's said and done, girl," he began, "I've been a pretty good dad to you. Given you years of schooling and stood by you when I might have skipped and led my own life. Many a man with his wife dead, and a kid on his hands, *has* done it. I've worked for you, and given you the best home in St. Ange; and now if you let me play the cards that you've got in your hands, we'll get out of this and live in clover to the end o' time."

"I don't know what you mean," Joyce gasped.

This was no idle talk. She was fascinated and frightened. It seemed as if her father had his fingers on the rope that was strangling the life out of her.

"You've got the winning cards, my girl, if I don't miss my guess. It's all in the playing now. I've had one eye on you all along, Joyce. I've seen, like any kind father might, that there ain't a young feller between here and Hillcrest but would be glad to have you. But like a rap on the *shut* eye it has just been sprung on me that Myst. has had his mind on you as well!"

Joyce's eyes dilated and the colour rose through her soft paleness, but she did not speak.

"It's always the way. Them most concerned gits wind of scandal last. Even the brats have caught on before me. But once your father has both eyes open, folks better watch out."

"Who do you mean by Myst.?" asked Joyce, and her strained voice sounded unnatural.

Harriet T. Comstock

"Gaston, to be sure! I've got a wit of my own, Joyce. Myst.—short for Mystery. That's what Gaston is. No one knows a damned thing about him."

"Well, that's to his credit, anyway." Joyce flung up a defence now. She must fight, but she must keep herself out of sight.

Jared glared angrily. He did not like the tone.

"Oh! I ain't the one to object to you keeping your mouth shut," he returned. "Jammed logs"—the phrase stuck in his mind—"jammed logs don't creak any; but when it comes to joining forces, like two jams together for instance, there's got to be, in the nature of things, some demonstration. What I'm aiming at is this. Has this here Myst. meant business or has he not? I'm a man of the world—so is Gaston—he ain't never hoodwinked me. I had my reasons for coming here, and likewise, so has he. That's my business and his, by thunder! but when *he* meddles in my affairs he's got to show his hand. Now is it, or ain't it, business 'twixt you and him?"

"What kind of business?" Joyce's voice was low and even. She was approaching her father cautiously and fearfully.

"Honourable—or otherwise?"

A silence followed. Something was born, and something died in the sunlighted room while that silence lasted.

The child's dependence upon its father fell, torn and quivering, before the new-risen self-protection of the pitiful girlhood.

For the first time, consciously, Joyce experienced the soul-loneliness for which there is no aid. Her deep eyes pleaded for help and mercy where there was no help, and alas! no mercy. Birkdale had his answer now, though no word had been uttered by those quivering lips.

"You can't be expected to act for yourself in these matters."
Jared put his pipe on the table and brought his chair to the
floor. "You ain't the first girl as has been game for such as
Myst., but he's made a damned mistake if he thought two
couldn't play at his game here in St. Ange. We'll make something out of him no matter which way you put it."

"Make something—out—of—what?" Joyce bent forward and
real horror filled her eyes. Was even the security of Jude to be
wrenched from her?

"Out of Myst. He's got money, It comes in letters—checks.
Tate has ways of finding out. Myst. has a fat account over to
Hillcrest. He thought we took him on trust. We knowed what
we wanted to know."

"And so, and so," panted Joyce, "what next?"

"Well, by the living God, if he wants to marry you, let him
come out and say so, and I won't hold back my presence nor
my blessing."

It was quite plain now. Gaston was the target at which Jared
aimed. In some way she must shield him and shield him so
effectually that no harm could reach him. There was no escape
for her. Every path was closed through which she had hoped to
go free and happy.

"I ain't going, though," Jared was whining in his semi-religious
tone, "to have my reputation smirched. Either he marries you,
or he pays well, and we'll get out. See?"

"Oh, yes, I see!" Joyce shivered in the hot room; "I see what
you think, but *why* do you suppose I'd marry Mr. Gaston if he
did want me? Sometimes girls don't—marry—men even when
they are asked. Books are full of such things." A heavy sob
came after the pitiful words.

"Oh! that's your dodge, eh?" Jared laughed comfortably from

Harriet T. Comstock

the secure position he had gained for himself from this misery. "Trying to shield him, eh? It won't do, Joyce. Your daddy's too much a man of the world for that. Now here it is in a nutshell: The boys at the tavern are back of me. How do I know? You leave that to me. Now I calculate that Gaston don't want any of the dust of his past stirred up by us. If he's been playing with you, it's for *you* to say whether you'd rather have him forced to marry you, or have him pan out money enough to hush the matter up. I'm willing to sacrifice something for you, Joyce. I'm willing to go so far as to say I don't want the dust of *my* past raised—I'm actually willing to sacrifice—anything."

"Even me!" The words were a moan of fear and misery.

"Sure!" Jared did not catch the point. "This is an opportunity that don't come often. Retribution for Myst., by thunder, and clear gain for me and you! Out beyond the high trees, girl, there's better diggings for us. God! how I've smothered, these long years. The end justifies the means—you will say so, too, when you see what lies down to the south."

Jared laughed wildly as if the ambition of all the desolated years had been achieved. Joyce, compelled by his delirious words and excitement, almost felt a responsive sympathy; but her words, slow and hard, brought her and Jared down to the bleakness of St. Ange again.

"You are wrong, terribly wrong. Mr. Gaston never wanted to marry me, and I can take care of myself—I always have—taken care of myself! Why—why, I'm engaged to Jude Lauzoon. I'm going to marry him right away. We can't even wait for him to build a new shack. If a minister doesn't happen this way, we're going over to Hillcrest. Oh, what a joke we've played on you!"

Jared stared idiotically, and Joyce's laugh rang wildly out.

"Mr. Gaston and me! What an idea! Why, he's helping us"—the inspiration to say this came from a blind belief in Gaston's quick adaptability—"he's helping me and Jude—to what we want."

"The devil he is!" It was all that Jared could clutch from the rout. "I—I believe it's a thundering lie," he added as an afterthought, and as a cover to his retreat.

"It's no lie." Joyce had regained her calmness. She was panting, but she had reached safety and she knew it. An unlovely, unhallowed safety, but such as it was it was her salvation and Gaston's.

When she had stolen to him the night before it was her last ignorant impulse to gain her own ends. From now on she must be on guard, or her world would come clattering about her heart and soul. It took Jared some minutes to digest the information that had been flung at him so unexpectedly, and then anger and baffled hope swayed him. Joyce married to Jude would make *his*, Jared's, future no securer than it now was. Indeed it might complicate matters, for Jared had no belief in Jude rising above the dead level of St. Ange standards.

"You're a durn fool!" he ejaculated at last, while the new impression of his daughter's beauty stirred him painfully. "You are a durn fool to fling yourself away on Jude when you might have done most anything with yourself—if you was managed right."

Then in an evil moment Joyce laughed. Her lips parted in an odd little way they had showing the small white teeth and forming the dimples in cheeks and chin. So great was the girl's relief; so appalled was she at what might have been, that the conflict of emotions made her almost hysterical.

"Daddy," she said, between ripples of laughter, "you thought you had me then, didn't you? But being your daughter, you know, I had wit enough to take care of myself."

Jared listened to this outburst in sheer amazement. Unable to

Harriet T. Comstock

understand, in the least, what was passing over the girl before him, he weighed her by his own low standard, and drew the worst possible conclusion as Jude had done before him.

He looked steadily at Joyce, and he saw the colour and fire come to cheek and eye. The ringing laughter struck through his brutality and hurt something in him that was akin to paternal love; but so long had that protecting tenderness been ignored by Jared, that now when it was called upon to act, it did so in a savage rage.

"By heaven!" he thundered, "I catch your drift, you young divil. And if that Myst. ain't a slick one! Going to use Jude is he, to pull his chestnuts out of the fire?"

Then Jared strode forward with arm upraised as if to strike and, by so doing, again command the situation. In like manner had he downed and controlled Joyce's mother. But he paused before the pale undaunted girl. Her laugh died suddenly, to be sure, so suddenly that the gleaming teeth and pretty dimples outlived the mirth long enough to give a stricken, death-like expression to the face, but the change brought no fear; it brought something worse.

Joyce's moral sense was an unknown quantity in her present development. Her father's true meaning affected her not at all; what she felt was—a loathing disgust, and a conviction that if she was to hold even Jude for herself against her father's anger and purpose, she must flee to other shelter.

She drew herself up and cast a look upon Jared that he never forgot to his dying day. It was an added faggot to that hell of his.

"Isa Tate," the even voice broke upon him, "Isa Tate said you killed my mother. But I'm not afraid of you, and I'm going to live my life. You can't kill me! I know when and where to go."

With that she gathered up the work that had fallen to the

floor, and almost ran into the little bedchamber beyond the kitchen, closing the door after her.

Jared sat dumbly staring at the wooden barrier. He longed to call her, but his tongue pricked with excitement.

He dared not go to her—so he waited. He heard her moving about inside the room. A half-hour passed, then an hour. Noon came and went. The fire was out, and dinner, apparently, was as distant as it had been two hours before.

Jared fell asleep in his hard chair, his dishevelled head lying on his arms folded on the bare table. When he awoke it was three o'clock and Joyce stood before him.

She was very white, and the drawn look was still in evidence. She wore a blue-and-white checked gown; short and scant it was, but daintily fresh and sweet. She had her poor little best hat on—a hat with a bunch of roses on the side—and she carried a large basket in her hand.

Jared stared at her as if she were part of a nightmarish dream.

"Where are you going?" he asked hoarsely, a new fear gripping him.

"It doesn't matter to you, father. I'm just—going."

Jared experienced a shock as he realized how far this girl had already gone from him.

"Good-bye," she faltered; "good-bye, father."

She turned from him and walked to the door. Then a latent power for good roused Jared.

"Joyce," he called after her; "there's twenty dollars left—take it all, girl."

"No."

"Then for God's sake take half!" He was pleading, pleading with a woman for the first time in his selfish, depraved life.

Joyce turned and looked at him, and the tears filled her eyes.

"No," she repeated, "I—I couldn't take it. I don't want it; but I'm going to Isa Tate, father."

How frightfully still and lonely she had left the little house. Jared looked at the old furniture and found it strange and unnatural. The summer day grew dim as he waited there among the ruins of all that he thought had been his own. No dinner; no probable supper—Jared thought upon the physical discomfort, too, but he was sober enough, and shocked enough to give heed to the graver side of the situation.

What he suffered as the afternoon faded and the ticking of the clock thudded on his senses, no one could ever know.

We may leave retribution for sin out of our scheme of things-as-they-should-be for others. Each sin takes care of itself, and burns and blisters as it strikes in. Men may suffer without giving outward sign. Justice is never cheated, and we may trust her workings alone. Jared suffered. Suffered until nerves and body could bear no more, and then he went down to the Black Cat to face the situation Joyce had created and deal with it in his own fashion.

CHAPTER IV

When Joyce went with bowed head from the only semblance of a home that had ever been hers, she carried with her, in the rough basket, all that she could rightfully call her own in personal effects. The load was not heavy and she scarcely noticed it as she walked rapidly through the maple thicket which divided her father's garden-place and the Long Meadow.

She felt like an exile, indeed. A friendless creature who had no real hold upon any one.

She thought of Gaston—but he no longer suggested safety to her. She thought of Lauzoon, and a wave of fear and repulsion swept over her. She knew she was driven to him. She knew she must accept whatever fate he offered, but with the remnant of her intuitive belief in her personal charm and beauty, she paused at the edge of the wood, to plan some sort of attitude that would secure Jude's admiration as well as his protection. She must not call upon him in a moment of weakness and defeat. That would be putting a weapon in his hand that no St. Ange man could be trusted to wield mercifully.

She must hide all traces of outraged feeling; she must find a vantage point from which Jude might take her. He must come to her; she must not go to him. Thus she pondered. For one wild instant she turned her face toward Hillcrest. There were those over the hill who might give her work—what work? What could she do? But granting that she obtained work, how

Harriet T. Comstock

long could she retain a position, with her father and Jude in pursuit? No; she was a product of St. Ange and had all the faltering distrust of other environments common to the shrinking childhood of the poor village.

Down beside the last tree of the thicket the girl crouched with her shabby basket beside her.

The elemental woman in her saw, as clearly as any cultivated sister might have seen, that if she hoped for success in her married life, she must not throw herself upon Jude crushed and downed. A brave front must be the breastwork behind which she was to fight.

When she had told her father she was going to Isa Tate, she had spoken wildly; but the inevitable closed upon her. Every one went to Leon Tate in trouble. Leon, like the old gods, first made mad whom he wished to destroy; for the trust that all St. Ange put in Leon's bland generosity was nothing short of madness. When any difficulty arose, private or public, it was carried to the Black Cat for adjustment and final settlement. By putting every individual under deep obligation to him, Leon controlled money, loyalty and obedience. Every man in St. Ange was in his debt, and every woman had accepted, in some form or other, his wife's services. The difference between Isa and her husband was, however, vital. Tate was a friend to man in order that he might draw his victims into his net. Isa had a woman's soul hidden under her rough exterior and, while she played the part assigned her by her diplomatic lord, she found comfort for her own lonely nature in giving comfort.

Joyce, in going to Isa for protection, would in no wise interfere with her father's welcome at the tavern. Leon would arrange that, and bring about a brilliant climax for himself; at least he always had done so in emergencies.

Crouching under the tree, as the sun went down behind Beacon Hill, Joyce saw the future unfold itself. There was nothing to do but go to Isa. Then Leon would, by his subtlety, make it seem that she had come there to get ready for her marriage to Jude. He'd even arrange, perhaps, the marriage, and so clutch Jude and her closer to his power. He'd smooth the way for her father, too, and hush tongues and smile—oh, how he would smile on them all!—and no one would ever know.

The sun went down and the stars came out. Still the girl sat there; but presently a healthy appetite was the call that roused her. She had not eaten since noon of the day before. She was weak and suffering. She thought with a kind of comfort that perhaps it was hunger alone that was now causing her mental and physical agony. After she had eaten, all would be well with her. She could control Jude and her own fate. She would never let any one think—Gaston above all—that she was not mistress of her own shabby little life.

She got up dizzily, and was shocked to find how heavy the basket was; still, with a constant shifting from hand to hand, she could manage it.

Lola's giddy little lark song sprang to memory out of the ashes of her hurt and pain, and rose and rippled in the fragrant darkness as she entered the Long Meadow.

Beacon Hill stood gloomily to the west, and above it gleamed a particularly bright star. Across Long Meadow the lights in the houses flickered from open windows, and the Black Cat's glare seemed to control her motions. It drew her on and on. It was to play a part in her future as it did in the futures of all—sooner or later.

Wearily she mounted the steps of the tavern and went to the side door that opened into whatever there was of privacy in Leon's establishment. Isa was washing the supper dishes. She was a tall, gaunt woman with a kindly glance that Nature had, for a safeguard, hidden under heavy black brows.

"You, Joyce?" she said, going on with her task. "I thought maybe it was some one else."

"Isa," the girl stepped cautiously forward, "I want to tell you something."

The gathering hilarity in the tavern made this moment secure. Isa put down her dish and faced the girl.

"What?" she asked bluntly.

Quickly, breathlessly the truth, with all its hideous colouring, truth bald, and yet with a saving clause for Gaston, was whispered in Isa's ear.

When the parting with Jared was confided, the woman put her arms about the girl.

"Now you hush, Joyce, I've heard enough. This is a man's world, God help us! Us women, when we can, must cling together. Me and Tate pull in harness because we find it pays—we'll help you out—Tate in *his* way, me in mine, but, Lord a-mighty, don't I hope there'll be a heaven just for women, some day!

"Sit down, you poor, little haggled thing, I don't believe you've eat a morsel. You look fagged out. They ain't worth it, Joyce, men ain't. Father, husband—not one of them. But since we've got to use them, we must make out some kind of game. Here!"

She set food before the wan girl, and the readjustment of life, in her masterful hands, seemed already begun.

It was comparatively easy, later on, to go into particulars with Isa. With the roar and clatter growing hourly more deafening in the tavern, Isa and Joyce, sitting on the back porch under the calm stars, spoke freely to each other.

Isa, like a dutiful wife, had, while Joyce satisfied her hunger, confided as much of the girl's trouble to Leon as she thought advisable. Leon had recognized the opportunity as one by which to capture what was left of Jared's independence, and rose to the emergency.

"Leave it to me," he said. "Everything will be blooming tomorrow like—like a—garden—er—Eden."

So now Isa had only Joyce's sore little heart to deal with.

"Come, girl," she began at last; "tears never yet unsnarled a knot. Be you, or be you not, going to marry Jude?"

"Yes—I am." There must be no doubt upon that score and Joyce sat up stiffly and faced her helper.

"Well, then, look at the thing sensible. In a place like St. Ange, where there ain't women to spare, you either got to be a decent married woman or you ain't. Long as I've lived in St. Ange, and that's been more'n twenty years, I ain't never yet seen a comfortable, respectable, satisfied, old maid—they ain't permitted here, and you know it. In season, of course, you'd marry—that's to be looked for. It chances to be Jude—and after you get over the strangeness, he'll do as well as any other. They are all powerfully alike when they have their senses. The sameness lies in their having their faculties. The only man as was ever different in St. Ange was Timothy Drake. He got smashed on the head by a falling tree up to Camp 3, and his wits was crushed out of him. But do you know, what was left of Tim was as gentle and decent and perticerlar as you'd want to find in any human. He never drank again, never cussed nor stormed, and I've laid it by as an item, that the badness and sameness of men lies in their wits—if you want a companionable, safe man, you've got to turn to sich as are bereft of their senses—and most women is that foolhardy they prefer wits and diviltry, to senselessness and decency."

Joyce smiled feebly at this philosophy.

Harriet T. Comstock

"You are the one to decide," Isa went on. "Now see here, girl, I ain't lived fifty years for nothing. I ain't been in and out of my neighbour's houses, in times when all the closets are open, without learning a heap about things. Men is men and there's no getting around that. So long as you can, you better let them think they amounts to something even when you own to yourself they don't. Private opinions ain't going to bring on trouble; it's only when they ain't private. Now granting that man is what we know he is—it's plain common sense to get as much out of him as you can. Make the place you live in the best thing he's got; and just so long as you can, keep yourself a little bit out of his reach—tantalize him. There ain't nothing so diverting to a man as to claw after a woman, when he's got the belief in himself that when he *wants* to clutch her, he can.

"I know the kind of naked feeling you've got when you sense your power with men first; but that wears off when you get your bearings and find out that it's only a shuffle in the game, anyway. Land of love! if man and woman was *all*, then when they came face to face with life they would get smashed; but housework tempers the matter powerfully; and man's work out among other men; and then when children come and you have to contrive and pinch, why you just plod along and don't ever get flustered. It's just the first dash of cold water in the face, child; after that all lives is pretty much the same."

Joyce had grown quieter as Isa's words droned on. It was, for all her commotion, a very humdrum thing that had happened to her.

As it was she, Joyce, was going to be very respectable. She'd manage, and Jude would always find her worth his while to be decent for. She would wrench what she could from him and St. Ange and be a commonplace married woman.

Now that all the fuss and fury were over, it seemed quite a silly exhibition she had made of herself. She almost wished that she had stayed at home.

"The little loft room is yours, Joyce, for as long as you want it," Isa was saying, through the sobering silence. "I ain't going to side with Jared Birkdale when a woman's sense of right has been roused. Jared's wits are the keenest and the cruelest round here, and the poison in his tongue is the deadliest; I guess *I* know. Are you coming in, child? The bed's made, but you best carry a pitcher of fresh water up with you."

"I'll be there in a minute, Isa, and the cracked pitcher's by the well, isn't it?"

"Yes," Isa replied; "and I'll leave a lighted candle for you, the ile is pretty low in the lamp. Good night, child, and don't fuss. I never saw fussing hurt any one but the fusser."

Joyce rose stiffly and stood by the open door. She stretched her limbs and winced at the pain in them. Then she clasped her aching hands above her head and permitted her tired spirit one long, heavy sigh.

She stood for some time in that relieved state. The chill of the deepening night soothed her, and the late new moon looked down through the pines at her—then she turned sharply. Some one was near!

Her startled glance fell upon Jude Lauzoon. He was crouching upon the step of the porch.

"I thought you was sleeping, standing up," he whispered hoarsely. "I didn't want to scare you none."

"Why are you here?" Joyce's heart fluttered. Had he heard all?

"Why are you?" Jude turned the tables.

"Where else should I be—to—to—" she looked at him appealingly, "to get ready to be married?"

Jude was master of the situation in a way Joyce did not know.

He could afford to be condescendingly gracious. He, of all who had taken part in this poor little drama, now held the centre of the stage, and the knowledge gave him a certain manliness highly becoming.

"Stay here until we get married—is that it?"

Joyce nodded.

Jude felt a pity for her that would have been contempt had not her beauty and charm mastered him. He was going to clutch her once and for all, but he was willing to let her see that he only meant, since he must have her, to clutch close enough to bind her to him. He was not going to strangle her: he meant only to stifle her. Jude was cool now, and alert.

"I've got something to say to you, Joyce, and it better be said and done with. I slept on it last night and most of to-day. I went to your father's this evening to have it out, but you wasn't there. I met Jock Filmer in the Long Medder and he told me where you was, and why. Your father had aired his affair in the tavern."

Joyce clasped her cold fingers nervously. There was nothing for her to do but wait Jude's pleasure. Leon had not been able to overpower Jared's personality evidently.

"I saw you go to Mr. Gaston's shack night before last! I'd been there before you, and I was lying off in the pine grove when you came a-visiting."

The widening eyes of the listener were the only sign that this information was startling.

"Do you know," Jude gave a chuckle, "up to that minute when I saw you a-knocking, and him taking no heed, I had thought 'twas him as had been shining up to you. I was actually hard agin him, and once went so far as to go up there with my gun!" Joyce shivered. "Yes, by gosh! with my gun. Just suppose I'd killed him, and him not to blame either?

"Now there be some men, Joyce, that wouldn't have you after knowing what I know, but I ain't one as goes off the handle without looking on both sides. Since I know *he's* all right, I can manage you proper enough—and I own up to wanting you, and I'm willing to let bygones *be* bygones, only—and you might as well know this—once I've had my eyes open, I ain't going to shut them again. I'll always be within call if you should forget yourself, and take to attracting Mr. Gaston's attention. He's my *friend* now, by gosh! He's going to stand by me. He's the real stuff and shows up to me in the finest colours, never once hinting that your seeking him had made you cheap. He's a bigger feller than I ever thought, and I ain't going to have no foolishness. You understand?"

"Yes; oh, yes; I understand!" Again the shivering seized Joyce.

"I should think to have a man turn a deaf ear to you like that, would end any nonsense without more fuss."

"It—it will." The low voice shook.

"But you see, protecting a young girl agin herself is one thing. He might feel different if a married woman wanted to turn fool. Now, Joyce, I ain't ever going to say anything more about this, 'less it's necessary. I know you're pretty and maybe a bit more flighty along of that, but being married and having your own work, may tone you down. If you'll stick by me, I'll stick by you; and in time Mr. Gaston can be a friend to both of us and no harm done. You understand, don't you? I ain't hard, I'm only letting light in on the whole thing."

"I—I understand, Jude."

"And now, as to marrying. Mr. Gaston is going to lend me money, and I'm going to put up an addition to my shack, and get some fixings over to Hillcrest. If you want, we'll get married over there and rough it together before the buildin's done."

"I—I'd rather wait, Jude if you're willing. I want to get some—some things." Joyce's teeth were chattering. "But if a minister should happen in St. Ange in the meanwhile, I'd—I'd marry you." This seemed a reasonable request—"I don't like the minister over at Hillcrest, he's so fearful in his sermons, he makes me afraid."

"Well," Jude rose, "when the house gets along, we'll see. Things are tight and trim now. Good night! Go to bed—and forget it."

He put his hands on her shoulders and bent and kissed the cold, upturned face. Then he laughed: for he had got what he wanted, and she was very sweet and pretty.

"Go to bed now—trot on!"

Joyce staggered indoors and hurriedly bolted the door behind her. She took the spluttering candle and mounted the steep stairs. Once alone in the small stifling room, she gasped, and put her hands to her throat as if to remove a pressure that was there.

Presently she blew out the light, set the shutters wide to the pale moonlight, and undressed herself quietly and methodically.

Already she seemed used to her lot. It was very ordinary, tame and familiar.

She had received the first dash of cold water in the face, and had accepted the new situation.

There was no longer even the excitement of trying to dangle a little above Jude. He had her close in his grip. She must accept whatever he doled out to her—and that was the fate of all respectable married women in St. Ange.

CHAPTER V

The late September afternoon held almost summer heat as it flooded St. Ange. The breeze gave a promise of crispness as it passed fitfully through the pines; but on the whole a calmness and silence pervaded space which gave the impression of a summer Sunday when a passing minister had been prevailed upon to "stop over."

However, it was not a summer Sunday, as St. Ange well enough knew, for every able-bodied man in the place had that day signed a contract with the Boss of Camp 7 for the lumber season; and the St. Angeans never signed contracts on Sunday.

The calmness was accounted for by the fact that Joyce Birkdale was to be married. The circumstances leading up to this event had been sufficiently interesting to demand sobriety. St. Ange did not believe in putting on airs, but it had its own ideas of decorum; things had sort of dovetailed lately, and, according to Leon Tate, "it was up to them to spread eagle and plant their banner for knowing a good thing from a rotten egg."

Leon was above consistent figures of speech. He had power of his own that controlled even language.

After Jared Birkdale had defied Leon in his own stronghold, and, instead of agreeing with Tate that Joyce had come to Isa as to a mother, had insisted upon bare, unglorified fact, he had betaken himself into oblivion. Tate was confronted with the predicament of having a helpless girl on his hands to do

Harriet T. Comstock

for—unless another man was forthcoming.

Jude rose to the occasion. He confided to Jock Filmer his desire for immediate marriage, and good-natured Jock, his system permeated by gossip, consented to send down to the Junction—since Joyce objected to the hell-fire minister at Hillcrest—and bring a harmless wayfarer of the cloth, who Murphy, the engineer of the daily branch train, had said, was summering there.

"He's a lean, blighted cuss," Murphy had explained; "what God intended for an engineer, but Nature stepped in and flambasted his constitootion, and so he took to preaching— that not demanding no bodily strength.

"He comes pottering round the engine, using the excuse of saving my soul, and I don't let on that I see through him. I give him pints about the machinery; and if I tell him he can ride in the cab with me anywhere, he'd marry a girl, or bury a tramp, if he had to go to hell to do it."

So Jock detailed Murphy to decoy the side-tracked gentleman at the Junction up to St. Ange.

The stranger was expected on the afternoon train, and Tate had the guest room of the Black Cat in readiness.

Jock had lazed about the Station since noon. The wedding preparations bored him, and the train's delay angered him.

"See here!" he exploded to Tom Smith, the agent, "ain't it stretching a point too far when that gol-durned train gives herself four hours' lee-way?"

Tom spat with dignity, and remarked casually:

"Long as she ain't likely to meet any train going down, seems to me there ain't any use to git warmer than is necessary."

"If she keeps on," drawled Jock, "she'll have a head-on collision with herself some day. Is that the dying shriek of the blasted hussy?"

Tom stopped the imminent expectoration.

"It be," he announced, and went out on the track to welcome the guest.

"She do look," he contemplatively remarked, "like she had an all-fired jag on."

The train came in sight, swaying unsteadily on its rickety tracks. Puffing, panting and hissing, it reached the platform and stopped jerkily.

Murphy sprang from the engine; the conductor strode with dignity worthy a Pullman official, to the one passenger coach behind the baggage car, and assisted a very young and very sickly man to alight.

Tom Smith, with energy concentrated on this single activity of the twenty-four hours, began hurling mail-bag and boxes about with the abandon that marks the man whom Nature has fitted to his legitimate calling.

Filmer eyed the passenger with disapproving interest; Murphy, after looking at some part of the machinery, lolled up to Jock.

"Is that it?" Filmer nodded toward the stranger, who sat exhaustedly upon a cracker-box, destined for the Black Cat, with his suit-case at his feet.

"It ain't, then," Murphy returned. "It got on the Branch 'stead of the Mountain Special, by mistake. It's a lunger bound for the lakes, and some one gave him a twist as to the track an' we caught 'im. But shure, the rale thing, the parson, when I was after tellin' 'im of the job what was at this end of the game, he up and balked—divil take 'im!—an' said he wasn't goin' to tie for time and eternity, two unknown quantities. What do ye think of that?"

Jock thought hotly of it, and expressed his thought so fervidly that the boy on the cracker-box gave attention.

"Say," Murphy continued, "give it straight, Filmer; does it be after meanin' life or death for Birkdale's girl? What's the almighty hurry, anyway?"

He leered unpleasantly. Jock squared himself, and faced the engineer.

"Come off with that guff!" he drawled. "What hurry there be is *my* hurry, you blamed idiot! And my reasons are my own, confound you! I've set my mind on having that affair come off to-morrow, gol durn it, and I'm going to have a parson if I have to dangle down to the Junction on that old machine of yours, myself."

A few added words of luridly picturesque intent gave force and colour to this declaration.

The stranger on the cracker-box rose weakly and drew near.

"Excuse me," he began, in a voice of peculiar sweetness and earnestness, "I wonder if I can be of any service? I am a minister!"

Filmer reeled before this announcement, took the stranger in from head to foot, then remarked in an awed tone:

"The hell you are!"

"I am. My name's Drew, Ralph Drew."

Murphy beat a rapid retreat. The scene was too much for him. Filmer, in doubt as to whether this was a joke or not, stood his ground.

The young fellow laughed good-naturedly.

"I know what you think," he said, and coughed sharply; "I got my credentials all right. I nearly finished myself in getting them, but they're all right. Graduated last June, went under soon after, got on my feet two weeks ago, and am making for Green Lake. I got side-tracked at the Junction through my own stupidity, and landed here. Perhaps you can direct me to a quiet place for the night, and I'll be glad to help you out in any way along my line, if I can."

This lengthy explanation was interrupted by short, hacking coughs, and Filmer's eyes never dropped from the eager boyish face through it all.

Presently he leaned down and took the dress-suit case from the other's hand.

"Drop that," he drawled, "and you follow me. There's the Black Cat Tavern, but I guess that ain't your kind. Do you think you can make my shack? It's a half-mile, and pretty uppish grade."

The boy began to thank Filmer.

"Hold on!" Jock commanded. "Keep your wind for the climb, and stop gassing."

The two started on, and the climb was a silent one. Filmer appreciatively strode ahead, speechless. Drew, panting, accepted the situation gratefully, and made the most of his position and his leader's silence.

Filmer's shack was a lonely place, standing on a little pine-clad knoll facing the west. It had four small rooms, a broad piazza, and a thrifty garden at the rear.

The room assigned to Drew had a cot-bed and rough, home-made toilet accommodations that suggested comfort and a sense of refinement. When Filmer made him welcome to it, he said quietly: "Now kid, you make yourself trim and dandy. Come out on the piazza when you get good and ready, and we'll have supper out there later." It was evident that Jock's sympathies had been touched.

Once alone, Drew sank upon the low bed, and permitted the waves of weakness and weariness to engulf him.

The young face grew pinched and blue, a faintness rose and conquered him. The eyes closed, and the breath almost stopped. But it was only momentary, and with returning consciousness came renewed hope and sudden strength.

From the broad open window the boy could see the western hills, already gay with glistening autumn colour, shining under the glowing sunset sky. The tall pointed pines, standing here and there in clumps, rose sharply dark in the early gloaming of the valley.

"It's my chance," thought the boy, his eyes widening with enjoyment of the beauty; "and, by Jove, I believe I've caught on!"

He got to his feet. The giddiness was gone. He flung off his dust-stained garments, as if they held all of his past weakness and misery. He plunged his head into the clear, cold water in the big basin on the pine table; when he emerged, colour had mounted to his pale face, and depression was a thing of the past.

"Hang it!" he exclaimed, rubbing his face and head with the rough towel that he took from the back of a chair; "this is good enough for me. No Green Lake in mine! I'll send for my trunk"—he had begun to whistle in the pauses of his thought—"and put up my fight right here. Filmer's good stuff; and there's a job ready-made for me, I bet! This is where I was sent, and no mistake. What's that?"

It was the odours of supper, and Drew stood still, inhaled the fragrance and grinned broadly.

"Gee whiz!" he cried; "I'm as hungry as a ditch digger." He dashed over to his suit-case, opened it and pulled out the contents. A pair of flannel trousers, a heavy flannel shirt and thick shoes were selected, and soon Drew, radiant and revived, went forth from the disorder he had created, eager for the meal that he heard Filmer placing on the piazza table.

Drew was to eat many of Filmer's meals in the future; he was to learn that Jock was a master-hand at cooking, but he was never again to know just the positive joy that he felt during that first meal; for he brought to it an appetite made keen by the hope of recovered health—the health he had squandered so foolishly, poor fellow, while he was making for his goal at college.

At last he tilted his chair back and laughed.

"I haven't eaten like that," he said, "nor with such enjoyment, since I went tramping up in the Maine woods when I was a youngster."

Filmer was removing the empty dishes. There was a sense of delicacy about his host that was compelling Drew's notice. He watched him passing from kitchen to piazza, and he saw that he was big, strong and handsome, but with a certain weakness, of chin, and a shyness of expression that came and went, marring the general impression.

Filmer's shyness was increasing. Never before in his life had he been brought into close personal contact with "the cloth" as he termed it, and even this "swaddling garment" was having a slow-growing hold upon him.

Presently Jock came timidly out, after his last visit to the kitchen, with pipes and a tobacco-box.

Harriet T. Comstock

"I'm not certain," he began, "how your kind takes to tobacco, but if I don't get my evening smoke, I get a bad spell of temper—so, if you don't object—I'll light up."

"If you'll wait a moment," Drew returned, "I'll join you. I always smoke my own pipe—I've got sort of chummy with it—but I'll share your tobacco."

Filmer grinned, and the cloud passed from his face.

"I calculated," he said, "that your kind classed tobacco with cussing and jags. Light up, kid."

They were soon lost in the fragrant smoke, the bliss of satisfied appetite, and a peaceful scene. The sun went down, and left the hills and valley in an afterglow of glory. The beauty was so touching that even Filmer succumbed, shook the ashes from his pipe and delayed refilling. Presently he looked at Drew's face. It had paled from emotion, and shone white in the shadow of the porch.

"You look peaked." Filmer's words brought the boy back to earth. "Been through a long siege, maybe?"

"Oh, overstudy and weak lungs!" Drew spoke cheerfully. "Bad combination, you know, and I didn't pull in as soon as I should have. I crammed for exams. Made them, and then collapsed. I'm all right now, though. All the struggle's over. I've only to reap the reward. There was a big doctor down in New York who told me that the air up here was my one chance. I'm going to take it. A few months here, and a life anywhere else I may choose, he said.

"What do you say to letting me have your room and company—you needn't give any more of the latter than you want to, you know—for a spell? You'll find me easy to get on with, I fancy, no one has ever complained of me in that way. I don't care what Green Lake is like, I like *this* better. I like this, way down to the ground. I've gone daffy over the whole thing." He drew in a long, happy breath. "What do you say?"

"I'd like to ask, if it ain't too inquisitive," Jock inquired, ignoring the boy's eagerness, while he put forth his own claims, "why in thunder a chap like you took to the preaching business? Somehow you look like a feller that might want to enjoy life."

Drew laughed heartily.

"Why, I mean to enjoy life," he replied, "and I chose this profession because I like it. I believe in it. You see, I was born to be a fighter. If I'd had a big, lusty body like yours, I might have been—anything. As it is, I had to choose something where I could fight with other weapons than bone, muscle and bodily endurance. I'm going into the fight of helping men and women in the best way I can, don't you see? I suppose I must sound cheeky and brazen to talk this way, but I'm full of the joy of it all, and I've made the goal, you see, and for all the breakdown I've come out ahead. It's enough to stir one, don't you think?

"The night I graduated, I don't mind telling this to you, I went down on my knees when all the excitement was over and the lights were out, and I said, 'I am here. I've got money; the good God need not have me on his mind along that line; he can send me where he chooses, to do his work; I'm ready.'"

"It was like consecrating myself, you know. Well, when the sickness came, I thought perhaps he didn't want me or my money either; but I came out of the Valley and here I am now, and I tell you—it seems good."

Filmer folded his arms across his chest, and looked steadily ahead of him.

"Do you know," he said at length—"and I hope you'll excuse me—I think you're the most comical cuss that ever happened."

Drew met this frank opinion with the boyish laugh that was having the effect of clearing up all the dull places in Filmer's character. He had never heard that laugh equalled but once, and he rarely went back to that memory—the path was too hard and lonely.

The reserves were down between the two. Without reason or cause, perhaps, they had fallen into a confident liking.

"Have you done much marrying and burying yet?" The question startled Drew, then he recalled the conversation on the Station platform.

"Well, no," he said, "practical demonstration comes after graduation generally. I've substituted for ministers—preached a Sunday, now and then, you know; but of course, I *can* perform the marriage ceremony, or read the burial service."

"You look pretty young," Jock spoke slowly; he was noting the strange dignity of his guest. Any reference to his profession brought with it this calm assurance that held levity in check; "but it's this way. There's a wedding fixed for to-morrer. I've set my heart on it coming off, and there ain't a durned parson to be had, that the girl favours. Now under these circumstances, you can't afford to look a gift horse in the mouth so to speak, and no offence intended. I can give you a tip or two before you trot in, and as for you, why you know, there ain't nothing equal to being thrown neck and crop into a job.

"The first time I went logging I got one leg broke and my head smashed, but I haven't ever regretted it. That accident, and the incidental scare, did more for me than any two successful seasons could have done. Now, your plunging right into a marrying may prove providential. Sermons and infant christenings will seem like child's play after. What do you say?"

Drew was laughing and the tears stood in his eyes.

"I'll—I'll do my level best," he managed to say through his

spasms of mirth. "This seems like a horrible approach to anything so serious, but it is the way you put it, you know, and—and the air, and the supper. The laugh comes easy, you see."

"Oh! enjoy yourself." Filmer waved his pipe aloft. "I'm glad you *can* take life this way, with the handicap of your trade, I don't quite see, by thunder, how your future parish is going to account for you, but so far as I'm concerned you can laugh till you bust."

Filmer was delighted. Not in years had he been so taken out of himself.

"Now this here town," he explained, "likes to have its buryings and weddings set off with a sermon with the principal actor as text. They like to get their money's worth. See? This girl, what I want spliced, is a devilish—" he paused—"you don't mind *moderately* strong language, do you?" he asked. "We all get flowery up here. What is lacking in events, talk makes up. I'll hold back when I can—in reason."

"Don't mind me!" Drew was trying to control his mirth.

Filmer nodded appreciatively.

"Well, as I was remarking—and I've got to be open with you—this here girl will be safer married, and so will some other folks. I ain't much of a reader of character, but I sense things like all creation, and I *feel* that getting the girl in harness as soon as possible is the only plain common-sense method. She's mettlesome, you know, the kind that kicks over the traces, and slams any one happening to be handy. She ain't never done it yet—but she's capable of it."

"Is—is the girl a relation or—?"

Jock flushed.

Harriet T. Comstock

"Neither. Nor the man. The feller—Jude Lauzoon is his name—I don't care a durn for, but he's all gone over this girl, and if any one can steer him straight she can, and when she gets the reins in her hands, I believe she's going to keep her head, in order to steer straight.

"The girl's name is Joyce Birkdale. Mother dead; raised sort of promiscuous on the instalment plan. Father an old buck who only keeps sober because he want's to see what's going on. He lit out and made himself scarce a time back, and this here Joyce took refuge after a hell of—excuse me! after a row with the old man—up to the Black Cat. Leon Tate acts the father-part to any one in a fix—it helps his trade—keeps folks in his debt, you know, but he ain't going to hamper hisself past a certain point, and if this here Jude Lauzoon should get a beckon from old man Birkdale he'd skip as quick as thunder—that's what is troubling Tate, and, by gosh! it's troubling me, but for another reason what needn't enter into this here conversation.

"If it was trusting you with a funeral or a christening," Filmer felt his way gingerly, "I wouldn't care a durn. You can't hurt the dead and the kid might outgrow it; but when it comes to tying folks together tight, it's a blamed lot like trusting something brittle in a baby's hand. It mustn't be broke, you see, or there'll be h—I mean trouble, to pay."

"See here!" Drew sat up straight, "I'm not much younger than you, if the truth were known. So let us cut extreme youth out of the question."

"Maybe you are about my age, kid," Jock gazed indulgently upon him, "and don't let your necktie choke you; but you're pretty raw material, and I'm seasoned. That's the difference. It ain't anything against you. It's the way you've been handled. Burying is looked upon by young *and* old, solemn-like; but I didn't know how you looked upon—marrying."

"It's the solemnest thing in life." Drew spoke clearly and

impressively. "I think death is a light matter in comparison. I've always thought that—since, well—for several years."

"Now you're talking!" Jock leaned over and gave Drew a friendly slap on the shoulder. "Now you're getting on the right course, and I want to give you this tip. Lay it on thick with Jude. Tell him he'll be everlasting blasted in kingdom-come if he don't act clean and hold on. Specially slap it on about holding on. Jude's intentions are good enough. He's powerful promising at the start, but he's the d—, the gol-durndest quitter anywhere around.

"Every new boss bets on Jude when the season begins, but every man of them would like to kick him out of camp before the spring sets in. All the hell-fire threats that that religion factory of yours drilled in you, you plank on Jude to-morrow, when you make him and Joyce man and wife. How fervent was that factory of yours? There is a difference in temperatures among them, I've heard."

"Oh! mine was mild," Drew was again helplessly convulsed, "so mild that I'm afraid you'd call it frigid. But that doesn't matter. Future damnation is a poor threat when every man among us knows that a present hell is a much worse affair. It's the awakening of a soul to *that* fact, that is going to save the world of men and women."

A full moon was sailing high in the heavens now, and Drew's animated face showed clear in the pale gleam. Jock hitched his chair nearer.

"Do you mean to insinuate," he asked, "that you've been wasting your time and health studying a line of preaching that hasn't got a red-hot hell in the background for sinners?"

"I mean just that." Drew threw back his head proudly.

"What in thunder do you do with them, then?"

"We try—by God's help *I'm* going to try—to take fear from them. Make them *want* to be decent. Make them *want* to use the powers they have in themselves. Make them want to work *with* God, not alone *for* God."

Jock's face was a puzzle. Admiration, pity, bewilderment, and a desire to laugh, waged war. Finally he drawled:

"Well, I'll be eternally durned, if I ain't sorry that a bright chap like you has wasted his youth, and pretty nearly drowned the vital spark, in arriving at such a cold-storage conclusion as this here one you've been airing. Why any one with half an eye can see that if hell-fire can't stir sinners, a slow call to duty ain't going to get a hustle on them. I swear if it wasn't so late, I'd get Gaston over here to listen to your views. Gaston is open to all kinds of tommy-rot that has a new mark on it. I'll be jiggered if I don't believe Gaston will want to pay you a salary to keep you here just for a diversion. But take my advice, and keep to old-fashioned lines, to-morrer 'specially, when you come to the marrying. Lord! Lord! But Jude would be having a picnic if he grasped that rose-coloured streamer of yours."

Drew made no reply. He was thinking, and his thoughts led where he knew Jock could not follow.

Presently a thin, blue-veined hand stole out in the darkness and found Filmer's.

"I—I—didn't know such men as you—such a place as this—existed," said the low, eager voice. "It's like having died and awakened in a new atmosphere, where even the people are different. It's—it's quite an inspiration."

Jock kept the hand, delicate as a woman's, in his strong, rough palm.

"You're somewhat of an eye-opener yourself," he said. "I've always held that mixing is learning on both sides. As long as you've got strength and inclination to stretch out, you'll always find something stretching out to you.

"And now as to that proposition of yours a time back, about bunking here for a time. I'm agreed, with this understanding: I've got a devil of a disposition, but it ain't ever going to be no better and them as don't like it can find new quarters. I came here over ten years ago to indulge my disposition, and I'm going to indulge it. When I don't want folks, I take to the forest, or, if the weather is bad, I shut and lock my door. If, after knowing this, you care to take that room I gave you this afternoon, it's yours for as long as you want it. I like you. I'm sudden in my likes, but I don't like your hell-less doctrine. I advise you not to turn that loose in St. Ange. We're none too good now, but if a soothing syrup was poured out, them as valued their lives would have to navigate to the Solitudes."

"I don't believe it!" cried Drew. "As God hears me, I believe it is just the place to try it."

"Oh! Get to bed." Jock stood up and laughed good-naturedly. "Go to bed and get up steam for to-morrer. When you see the whole collection you'll warm up your ideas. You're a terrible plucky kid to trust your own soul on a trifling little raft like this religion of yours. You better not overload it with more souls, though; the risk's too tremendous.

"Go sleep on your fairy story, boy. I don't see for the life of me how your health could have broken studying such a mild mixture as that. You must have been real run down at the start. But never mind, don't lay the laugh up against me, kid, I ain't enjoyed myself so much in ten years as I have to-night."

The two parted the best of friends. Drew fell quickly into a deep, undisturbed sleep, but Filmer tossed about till morning. The grim Past gripped him; he pulled the flask, that stood ever ready, nearer; but the cowardice of the act swayed him, and he flung the bottle to the floor.

Then he swore, and tried to sleep again, but the Spectre

jeered him.

"The powers they have in themselves." The words struck again and again on Filmer's aching brain.

What powers? Oh! he had had powers. He might have been— what? He might have been where? If—if—

The sunrise of Joyce's wedding day was just breaking when Filmer's Spectre gave up the struggle and sleep came. The only trophy of the victory was the discarded flask, which lay untouched where the hand of the master—for that time at least—had flung it.

CHAPTER VI

The word had passed along, and all St. Ange knew that Jock Filmer had a raw specimen of a parson up at his shack, in safe keeping for the Sunday events. For Joyce's wedding-day fell upon a Sunday.

"He's fattening him up," said Tom Smith, "and the Lord knows he needs it! Such a spindling youngster I *never* saw—a parson!" The contempt was too deep for Smith's expression, so he gave up. "And to think," added the train conductor, stretching his long legs in Tate's tavern, "there he was on my car, and I never sensed his ideas. Talk about entertaining angels unaware, it ain't in it! He even cussed mild when I told him his ticket was punched for Green Lake, and he was headed for St. Ange. I never would have took him for anything but a plain milksop till he let forth his opinions."

"I don't call it a proper attitude," broke in Tate, mixing a glass of vile dilution for Murphy's consumption. "I don't call it a *proper* attitude for a parson to appear so much like other folks that you can't tell 'im. It's suspicious, says I. How do we know as he *is* a parson?"

This suggestion caused the company a moment's pause.

"He better be!" muttered Peter Falstar. "He'd better be what he claims to be, even if it *is* a parson. We don't stand for any tricks from strangers."

Harriet T. Comstock

This lifted the spirits somewhat. Looked at *that* way, they had the matter in their own hands.

"I wonder"—Tate's face assumed its cheerful placidity—"if his marrying of Jude and Joyce would hold in any court o' law?"

At this the listeners laughed.

"Who ever heard of a marriage in St. Ange getting to a court o' law?" asked Tom Smith.

"But Jared ain't never had a daughter married before." Tate nodded his head sagely. "Jared's a deep one, and, taken off his guard, shows he knows more about law and order than any one man I ever let my eyes fall on."

"He must be all-fired off his guard," jeered Falstar, "when he talks order of any kind. Where is he, anyway?"

"Exactly." Tate held his own glass high and firm. "*Where* is he? Here is his daughter's wedding day—Where is he? I tell *you* if that marriage ain't hard and fast, it's *my* opinion Birkdale will trifle with it to suit his own ends. Jude's taking chances when he annexes Jared to his responsibilities, and don't you forget it! If that marriage ain't hide-bound, or if Jude don't provide for Birkdale, it's going to be broke if Jared has to raise all damnation to do it. He's got his eye to a knothole somewhere, you bet your life on that."

By superhuman sacrifice St. Ange had kept itself sober the Saturday night preceding the wedding but it did not sleep much. The male population discussed the day's doings and the women searched their meagre belongings for appropriate trappings for the next day's festivities.

Their resources were limited, and the day being Sunday, added to the difficulty.

"You can't," said draggled Peggy Falstar, "put on real gay

toggings in a church and on a Sunday."

Isa Tate, as leading lady in the place, solved the problem.

"We've got our mourning," she said to Peggy and the others gathered in Peggy's dirty kitchen. "We always have that on hand. Now we can leave off the long veils and put some false flowers on our bonnets—real spruce ones. They will lighten up the black. Them as has black gloves can wear them, but by carrying a clean handkercher real conspicuous, the gloom will be brightened some."

"I ain't had a pair of gloves in seventeen years," moaned Peggy.

"Well, you can sort of wind yer handkercher around your hands," comforted Isa.

"My feelings may be overcome," said Peggy; "they generally is in public, and then I'll have to use my handkercher and show my hands."

"You'll have to control yourself." Isa looked grim. "And, land o' love, a wedding ain't no place for wailing. Tate and me has given Joyce a real smart white dress, and she's trimmed her old hat all up with little frost flowers. She's a dabster at fixin' things. She's going to look real stylish. You know her mother was that way, though it was sorter knocked out of her, but the last thing she said to me was, 'Isa, I want you to put my grandmother's specs on me when I'm gone. Specs is dreadful stylish, and I've always looked forward to my eyes giving out so I could wear them. My eyes,' says she, 'has lasted better than me, but I want to be buried in my specs'; and so she was!"

The women all wiped their eyes.

"She was a powerful impressive corpse," whimpered Peggy, "but them specs gave me a terrible turn when I saw them first. The second look sorter took away the shock. I do hope," Peggy sighed, "I do hope them specs was long-distance ones. The good Lord knows Mrs. Birkdale had favourable reasons for seeing as far off as possible!"

"They was," Isa nodded. "I tried 'em, and things was all blurred to me."

And then the women parted gloomily, to meet again at Joyce's wedding.

It was such a day as only the mountains know. A hushed, golden day with a mysterious softness of outline on the distant hills.

The little crumbling church was open to the beauty of the morning, and John Gaston had decked it within with every flowering thing he could gather from wood and meadow.

Jock came early and stood in one of the narrow doors of the church, opening upon the highway. His hands were plunged in his pockets, and a look of concentration was on his handsome face.

He was going to "set," so he thought, his baby parson on to Jude. There was excitement in the idea. While he stood there Gaston came and took his stand at the other narrow door. The architect of the St. Ange church had had ideas of propriety in regard to established rules.

"Looks—some! don't it?" Jock asked.

"Yes," Gaston replied; "I was bound to have it look as wedding-like as possible."

"You did the decorating?" Jock asked, and a curious frown settled between his eyes. "I thought it was the women."

"They're thinking of themselves. Is your parson on to the game, Filmer?"

"He's all right. Gone off to commune with Nater. There he is now."

Drew had entered the rear door, and went at once to the small bare pulpit.

"Umph!" whispered Gaston. "Looks like a picture of John the Baptist."

"He don't act like it." Jock was in arms at once against any suspected criticism. "He's got more sand than many a blasted heavyweight. You ought to hear his gab—it's the newest thing in soul-saving. Sort o' homeopathic doctrine. Tastes good, but bitter as pisen under the coating. Real stuff inside, and all that. Get's working after it's taken, and the sweet taste lasts in your mouth while your innards are acting like—"

The people were gathering. They passed by Jock and Gaston without recognition. Social functions in St. Ange ignored all familiar intimacies.

Jude and Joyce came through the rear door, and sat in the front pew.

The girl moved with the absorption of a sleepwalker beside Jude whose shufflings bespoke nervous tension. Every now and then he glanced sheepishly at Joyce. Even to his senses, accustomed as they were to the girl's beauty, there was a slight shock of surprise.

The little round hat was gracefully wound with frost flowers until it looked like a wreath upon the pale gold of the glorious hair. The face was white and luminous, and the eyes looked as if they were expecting a vision to appear.

The white dress, home-made and cheap, had the unfailing touch that innate taste always gives, and it fell in soft lines about the slim, girlish figure. The little work-worn hands were folded loosely. They were resting a moment before taking up

Harriet T. Comstock

the labour of the new, untried life.

Drew glanced down as the two came in, and when he saw Joyce he started, and leaned forward.

He tried to take his eyes from that pale, exquisite face, but could not. It moved him powerfully not only by its beauty, but by its expression of entranced expectation.

Could the crude fellow at her side inspire such emotion? It was puzzling and baffling, but it roused Drew's sympathy, and held him captive. The rough faces of the men, the pitiable, worn faces of the women, the sprinkling of freckled, childish faces were blotted out for him. Like a star in blank space shone that one sweet, waiting face with its wreath of fairy-like flowers.

*　　*　　*　　*　　*

She was waiting for something she expected him to give. Drew became obsessed with this thought. Not the consecration of marriage—No! but something she—the soul of her—wanted.

Out among the pines in the early morning Drew had made a few notes, these he clutched in his feverish right hand. When the hour fixed upon arrived, he arose and stood beside the rickety pulpit stand. He made a short prayer; he knew it was feeble and rambling.

"Scared to death," thought Gaston, and he heard Filmer breathe heavily. Then Drew lifted his notes to the desk; tried to fix his eyes and attention upon them, failed and gazed helplessly at that one face in the appalling vacancy. Presently the bits of paper fell from his nerveless hand and fluttered to the floor.

Back in his college days he had had his dream of the vital word he would say to his people—*his* people—on that first day when he was to come to his own. Strangely enough he felt that his time had arrived. Called only by God, to a people who would never think of desiring him, he must say his word though only that pale, wonderful face thrilled to his meaning. If only he could make *her* understand, he would take it as a sign from on high that his mission was not to be an unworthy one.

Drew always had the power, even in his weakest moments, to utilize his panic to more intense concentration. It was the faculty that had made his college president point to him on more than one occasion as a success. Now, with the anchor of his notes fluttering in the September breeze, he put out to sea.

"We brought nothing into this world, and it's certain we can carry nothing out."

"He's mistaking this for a funeral," thought Gaston, and he struggled to conquer his inclination to laugh.

But what was happening? The boy up aloft was refuting the statement. His voice had a power wholly out of proportion to the frail body. He was getting hold of the people, too, Peggy Falstar was crying openly, and slow, hard-brought tears were dimming many eyes.

They were being told, those plain, dull people, and by a mere boy, too, that they had brought something into the world. A heritage of strength and weakness; of good and evil, bequeathed to them by those who had gone on. From these fragments their souls must weave what is to be taken with them when Death comes. The effort, the struggle, the success or failure, will be the part that they leave behind for them who remain, or who are to come later. In words strangely adapted to his listeners, that frail boy, with glorified face, was beseeching them, as they valued their future hope, as they desired to make better the ones who must live later, to gain a victory over their heritage of weakness and sin by the God-given elements of strength and goodness, and to blaze the trail for themselves, and to leave it so free behind them that weak, stumbling feet might easier find the way.

He was speaking to fathers and mothers for the sakes of their children. He was urging the two about to marry to see to it that they prepare by their own consecration, the *path on before.*

A silence filled the little church. The boy, pale and exhausted, was asking Jude and Joyce to come forward.

Gaston saw them go, side by side, Jude shambling as usual, Joyce stepping as if hastening to receive something long-desired.

It was the briefest of services. Simple, unadorned, but dignified and solemn.

Amen!

It was over. Jude and Joyce were married! The people were stirring; were moving about. The sodden, familiar life was awaiting every one of them. No; something had happened in St. Ange. Gaston knew it. Filmer knew it. Peggy Falstar had hold of her little Billy's hand, and Peter followed with his little daughter Maggie drawn close to him.

Leon Tate was red in the face, and Isa looked stern and thoughtful. Yes; something had happened in St. Ange. It would never be the same.

Drew went outside the church and joined Filmer. He had seen the uplifted expression on Joyce's face. He had had his answer from on high; and he was strangely moved.

He stood beside Filmer, motionless and flushed. Jock contemplated him from his greater height as if he were a new and startling enigma.

"Say, kid," he drawled presently, striving to hide the excitement that was causing the perspiration to stand on his forehead; "what got into you?"

"I reckon it was something getting out of me," Drew replied with the short cough.

"I don't know as them few words you spoke are capable of holding Jude and Joyce eternally. What you think?"

"If they cannot, no others could." Again the quick, harsh cough.

"But that sermon!" Jock shrugged his shoulders nervously; "that's what's shook the foundations of this here town. Leaving out the fact of you being *you*, standing up there handling folks's feelings as you did, I want to know if you stand by them ideas you passed out?"

"With all my mind!"

"Not elocuting and acting?"

"Surely not."

"Why, see here, kid, if what you said is true—which, by thunder it ain't!—don't you see that doctrine, 'bout coming with an outfit, adding to it, and taking away what you want, and leaving what you must; blazing trails, clearing away underbrush and what not; why, don't you see that's worse, by a confounded lot, than the old-fashioned hell?"

"Much, much more solemn." Drew leaned against a tree. His new strength was exhausted. Jock was too absorbed to notice the weakness and pallor.

"Why," he went on excitedly, "when you know you're going to frizzle at the end—just you, yourself, you can see the justice of it, and respect what sent you there, but to eternally be thinking of others, and messing up their lives—why that's durn rot."

"Filmer," the tone was low and faltering; "we're all one with God, no matter how you put it. All working together; all

Harriet T. Comstock

bound on the same journey. Think back; was there never one you loved who suffered with you and for you? Have you ever considered how much of that one's life you were hampering, when you dragged him—or her—down?"

Filmer's face twitched.

"Now, see here," he blurted out, and his eyes flashed, "the folks round here ain't going to stand for this rot, and I don't blame 'em. When they think it over, they'll get drunker than ever, and they'll even up with you later. You've got to learn more than you've learned already. Feelings are private property and outsiders better keep off. Come home to dinner. You look like a pricked bladder. This here gassing 'bout things what ain't worthwhile don't pay. Here, lean on me. It's all gol-durned nonsense using yourself up so."

He took Drew firmly by the arm, and led him away.

Drew was too weak to continue, even had he desired to do so, the conversation Filmer had forced upon him, but when they were smoking in the late afternoon Jock returned to the subject.

"I was just wondering," he said, through the haze; "ain't there never no let up to that new-fangled idea of yours?"

"None. That's the beauty of it."

"Beauty? Huh! Well, we'll drop it. Feel like toddling down to Gaston's?" Drew rose at once.

They passed down the pine-covered path slowly, and as they neared Gaston's shack, Filmer paused.

"Wherever you be," he began slowly, "as occasion permits, you're going to air them sentiments?"

"I'm going to live them. I may never have a chance to preach them. I'm a bit discouraged about the weakness that followed my first attempt."

"Oh, thunderation! You're going to pick up flesh and strength fast enough—it's that slush you've got on board that's getting my grouch. I'd rather you had a natural death, kid. I've taken a liking to you; and you don't know St. Ange."

CHAPTER VII

Joyce stopped her wild little song, and stood still to listen. Then she stepped to the window, drew aside the white muslin curtain, and looked out upon the white, white world.

She had thought she heard a step on the crisp snow, but probably it was the crackling of the protesting trees, for the weight of ice was almost more than they could bear.

The lights in the scattered houses shone red and steady in the still glitter. A full moon dimmed the stars, but a keen glance showed that every one was in its place and performing its duty in the glorious plan.

A white, holy night! Only such a night as comes to high, dry places where the cold is so subtle that its power is disguised; where the green-black pines stand motionless in the hard whiteness, and where the silence is only broken by mysterious cracklings and groanings, when Nature stirs in the heart of the seeming Death, while she weaves the robe of Spring.

Joyce was beginning to feel the wonders of her little world; she was timidly feeling out the meaning of things. Sometimes the sensation hurt and frightened her; often it soothed and thrilled her to deep ecstasy.

Presently she left the window, and turned to the warmth and glow inside.

Jude's old cottage had been transformed, and Joyce was developing into one of those women who are inherent home-makers. Such women can accomplish more with the bare necessities of life than others with the world's wealth at their command. It is like personal magnetism, difficult to understand, impossible to explain.

Comfort, grace, colour and that sweet disorder which is the truest order. Chairs at the right angles, tables convenient, but never in the way. A roaring wood fire on a dustless hearth; pictures hung neither too high nor too low, and no sense of emptiness nor crowding. A room that neither compelled attention, nor irritated the nerves—a place to rest in, love in, and go out from, with a longing to return.

On the south side of the room, Jude, with Gaston's financial and personal assistance, had added a bay window.

That innovation had quite stirred St. Ange. Ralph Drew had designed it and, through the summer, while the building was in process, the inhabitants had watched and expressed their opinions freely and enjoyably.

"Up to Joyce's," Billy Falstar, that indefatigable gatherer and scatterer of news, announced, "they are smashing a hole in the off side of the house."

An hour later, a good-sized audience was occupying the open space on the south side of the garden.

"Why don't you have it run *in*, instead of out?" Peter Falstar suggested. "It's just tempting Providence to let out more surface to catch the winter blasts."

"And it's wasteful as thunder," added Tom Smith. "Just so much more heating of out-door space enclosed in that there semi-circle."

"There ain't nothing to see from that side, anyway," Leon Tate remarked, as if possibly the others had not considered that. "If you want a more extended, and rounded outlook, you'd better smash the north side out. From that hole you could see the village, and what not."

"And the Black Cat," Jock Filmer drawled.

"It's no kind of an outlook at all that don't include the Kitty, eh, Tate?"

Tate scowled. He held a grudge against Filmer. It was he who had discovered, sheltered, and abetted the young minister who had so interfered with trade a time back. Tate held his peace, but he had never forgotten.

The laugh that followed Jock's interruption nettled the tavern-keeper.

But the pretty window had been finished before Drew and the autumn went. It was Joyce's sanctuary and pride. In it stood the work-basket, a gift from the mystical sister of Drew, who lived off somewhere beyond the Southern Solitude, a girl about whom Drew never tired of talking, and about whom events seemed to cluster as bees round a hive.

In that nook, too, hung the three wonderful pictures—Gaston's wedding gift.

There were spaces between the sides and centre of the window, and in the middle place hung a modern Madonna and Child. This Joyce could comprehend. Gaston knew the older, rarer ones would be beyond her.

That pictured Mother and Child were moulding Joyce's character. Gaston had wondered how they might affect her.

To the left of the Madonna was an ocean view. A stretch of sandy shore, an in-rolling, white-crested wave—with a limitless beyond.

To the wood-environed mind of the girl this picture was simply a breath-taking fairy fancy.

It existed, such a thing as that. Gaston had sworn it, but it was incomprehensible. However, it led the new-born imagination to expand and wander, and when Joyce was at peace, and the sun shone, she went to that picture for excitement and worship.

To the right of the Madonna hung a photograph. Gaston had taken it himself long ago. A foreground of rugged, cruel rock; black where age had stamped it; white where snow traced the deep wrinkles of time. But out of this rough light and shade, rose a glorious peak, sun-touched and cloud-loved. A triumphant soul reaching up to heaven out of all the time-racked rock.

The dwarfish peaks, that had surrounded Joyce's outlook all her life, made one understand the girl's love for this picture. As this was great, compared to the small things she knew, so life held possibilities that her life hinted—she might struggle with that ideal in mind.

The ocean scene was her fancy's fairy space; the towering peak, her philosophy.

But Joyce knew nothing of all this, consciously. Marriage, as Isa had foretold, brought its many cares and new interests. The strangeness and importance dwindled. No one considered the matter different from any other joining of St. Ange forces into a common life—the girl herself grew to take it for granted and sometimes wondered why she *imagined* her lot different.

She piled on more wood now, and laughed at the roar and glow. Then she drew up the arm-chair that Jude liked; he would be cold and tired when he returned. With a little laugh she pulled her own chair, a low, deep rocker, from the bay window, out into the fire's warmth, opposite Jude's spacious chair. Between them she placed a hassock—it was nearer her

Harriet T. Comstock

rocker than Jude's chair.

This she evidently noticed after a moment's contemplation, for the smile faded, and with strict impartiality she moved the stool to a position exactly between the two chairs, and directly in front of the fire's full light and heat.

"There!" she said, as if satisfied with her own sense of justice and propriety. "That ought to suit everybody."

The smile returned, and the little neglected song was taken up where the imagined footsteps had interrupted it.

The room was rosy and warm; even the window that was to tempt Providence was cosily heated, and the box of plants that fringed its outer edge stood in no danger of the frost's touch.

A plate of deep-red apples on the table sent forth a homely fragrance, and they were almost as beautiful as a vase of roses would have been.

Presently there was no mistake—steps were approaching. The crusted snow gave way under the heavy tread, the steps of the little porch creaked under the weight of strong bodies. It was Gaston's voice that came first to Joyce.

"It's too late, Jude. Past nine."

"Come in! Come in!" Jude was stamping noisily. "It ain't never too late, when I say come. Maybe Joyce can tempt you with a mixture she's a dabster at. After the walk you need it, and so do I."

The outer door was pushed back, the waiting cold rushed in with the two men, but the home glow killed it as the kitchen door swayed inward, and Jude and Gaston stepped toward Joyce.

She stood with her back to the fire, a pale straight figure

against the red light.

"Hello! Joyce." Jude was energetically pulling off his short, thick jacket. "Get busy at that 'mix' of yours. Put plenty of the real thing in and don't be sparing with the tasties. Off with your coat and hat, Mister Gaston. Make yourself comfortable. To folks as is already up, what's an hour or two?"

Gaston had taken Joyce's hands in welcome.

"It's too bad," he said, "to set you to work after your stint's over. The room looks as if you'd bewitched it. I tell you, Jude, there never was a man yet who could juggle with a house and put the soul in it."

Joyce flushed happily, and took Gaston's hat from him, as he pulled off his coat.

"I'll have everything ready in a jiffy," she said briskly. "Sit down, and tell me about it, while I mix the brew."

Jude sank, without giving Gaston a choice, into his own chair. Gaston took Joyce's—he knew her fancy for the stool when he and Jude were both present.

"Well," said Jude, stretching his legs out toward the blaze, and putting his heavy, snow-covered boots so near the fire that an odour of scorching leather filled the room; "we got some men over to Hillcrest, and we've bargained for lumber and other materials; we're going to begin at once, clearing, and soon as the cold lets up, we'll start building."

"Just think!" Joyce stirred the concoction in the jug jubilantly. "Just think of Mr. Drew coming here and bringing folks with him. Isn't it wonderful?"

She was all aglow with interest, excitement and pleasure. Gaston looked at her musingly.

"I used to think," she went on, coming forward with the jug and setting it on a low table near the hearth, "that nothing could ever happen here in St. Ange. Nothing that hadn't already happened over and again. Isa has always said the place would get a jog some day. She always seemed to sense that," the girl smiled; "and she was right. Didn't you have to put money down for men and things, Jude?"

"Sure!" Jude spoke from the depths of his mug.

"Did Mr. Drew send money?"

"Send nothing." Jude laughed foggily from the depths. "That's how I got the deal so prompt, I told him I'd undertake the job without any settlement till he got here to boss the doings."

"But where did you get the money, Jude?"

"It's partnership, Joyce," Gaston broke in. He set down his own emptied mug, and drew a little farther from the fire's revealing light. "Lauzoon, Filmer and Gaston, Contractors and Builders.' How does it sound?"

"But the money?" There was a little line of care, now, between the girl's deep eyes.

"Oh, that's all right! When Drew planks down the dollars, Mr. Gaston will get them back." Jude wiped his heavy lips on the back of his hand.

"But—it must have taken—a good deal?"

"Come, Joyce," Jude scowled, "you creep back to your corner. When women get to tangling up money with their own doings, it's the devil. You keep to your business, girl, and leave deeper matters alone."

Gaston frowned. Something lay back of that care-traced line

on Joyce's forehead. Something lay back of her questioning—what was it? And Jude's assumption of the male superiority over his young wife disturbed Gaston. He had not noticed it so sharply before.

Presently Joyce took the low stool, and clasped her knees in her enfolding arms. The two men had filled their pipes, and now, through the dim haze, looked at the fair, dreamy face between them. Then Jude laid his pipe aside—and snored. The clock ticked softly. The logs fell apart in a red glow. In drawing away from the flying sparks, Joyce placed her stool nearer Gaston, and the pretty bent head came within easy distance of the hand lying inert on the chair arm.

"Jude gets awfully sleepy in the heat," Joyce whispered; "you don't mind?"

"No, why should I? But I ought to be going. You are tired, too?"

"No." The sudden upward glance was all a-quiver with alertness. "I don't ever seem tired now. Keeping one's own house—is great! and it seems like everything is waking up every minute. Sometimes I hate to go to sleep for fear I'll miss something."

And now Gaston's hand touched the heavy curves of pale, gold hair.

"You have made a *home*," he said; "I wonder if you know what a great achievement that is? I wonder if Jude knows?"

Joyce winced.

"Oh! if he's a bit cross with me," she whispered softly, "don't you mind. He thinks that's the way, you know. *I* understand."

"I suppose you do," Gaston smoothed the silken hair, "but make *him* understand, Joyce. It takes understanding on both

Harriet T. Comstock

sides, you know."

"And, Mr. Gaston"—the girl changed the subject as adroitly as a more worldly wise woman might have done—"you helped me make this home. I ain't *ever* going to let you forget that. These pictures," her loving glance took them all in, "and the books coming and going just fast enough to keep me nimble. It seems like you'd opened a gate and let some of the big world in."

"There's plenty of it on the other side of the two Solitudes, Joyce." Gaston's hand fell gently along the warm throat and rested on the bent shoulder.

Jude gave another gurgling snore. The two did not change their positions, but there was silence for an instant.

"That mountain-top, all jagged and high—my! how it just makes me want to climb; climb through my work all day long; climb to getting somewhere out beyond. And that great empty picture with the awful white wave coming from nowhere—it just makes me hold my breath. Sometimes it seems as if it was going to swallow up everything and—me. It don't ever do that, does it, Mr. Gaston?"

"It has done damage of that kind in its time; but generally it obeys orders and stops at the safety line." Gaston smiled into the wondering eyes.

"I like the—picture—I like it terribly," breathed the girl, "but I'd *hate* the real thing. I am sure it makes a terrific noise." Gaston nodded, and old memories seemed beating in upon him. "It would wear me out by its own—"

"Restlessness." Gaston's thought ran along with the cruder one. "Its restlessness is at times—unbearable, unless—one is very young and happy."

"But I am young—and happy." Joyce spoke lingeringly and

her eyes grew fixed upon the heart of the coals. "Still I would hate it—and be afraid of it. It's beautiful—but it's awful. I don't like awful things. I like to look up at that brave old mountain, and know—it will always be the same no matter what happens down below."

Suddenly Gaston felt old, very old, beside this girl near him with her intuitive soul-stretches and her hampered life.

"So the mountain is your favourite picture, Joyce?"

A grandfatherly tone crept into his voice, and the caressing hand touched the round, pale outline of cheek and chin with the assurance of age and superiority—but the girl tingled under it.

"No," she said, almost breathlessly, "I like *that* best of all." And she pointed a trembling finger toward the Madonna and Child.

Gaston was conscious of a palpitating meaning in the words and gesture.

"Why?" he asked softly.

"Because," the fair head was lowered, not in timidity, but in deep thought, "because I want it—my baby—to look like that one. I look and look at the picture, and I dream about it at night. I know every little dimple and the soft curls—and all. I pray and pray, and if God answers—then—" a gentle ferocity rang through the hurried words—"I'm going to *keep* it so. It's going to be different from any other little child in St. Ange. And it all fits in, now that Mr. Drew is coming back. It's just wonderful! It was Mr. Drew that set me thinking about leaving something better for them as come after. He said terrible strange things—but you can't forget them, can you? I've been—well, sort of weeding out my life ever since he was here—and there can't be so much—for my baby to do—if I clear out my own faults. Can there?"

The girl's absolute ignoring of any reason for withholding this confidence from him at first staggered Gaston, and then steadied him.

Never before had Joyce so appealed to him, but the sacredness of the position she had thrust upon him for a moment appalled him. He looked intently at the girlish, innocent face. What he saw was a blind woman, groping through the child, seeking a reality that evaded it.

Never greatly impressed with his own importance, Gaston became cruelly aware, now, that in a marked way he still was the one being in the girl's world to whom she looked for guidance. The knowledge made him withdrawn for an instant.

Drew had appealed to her spirit—but he was elected Father Confessor, Judge and General Arbiter of her daily life. For a moment Gaston's sense of the ridiculous was stirred. Suppose they—those—people who inhabited the Past, and peopled the possible Future—suppose they should know of this? The eyes twinkled dangerously, but the girl in the glow of the red fire was terribly in earnest.

"You are perfectly happy, Joyce?" It was an inane question, but like some inane questions it touched a vital spark.

"Why, if I get on the top of the things that might make me unhappy if they conquered me; and if I shut my ears and eyes—why, then, I guess I'm perfectly happy. I won't *let* myself feel sad any more, and I make believe a lot—about Jude. You have to when you've been married long; and I guess he has to about me. So you see, living that way it comes out all right. And then when you have beautiful things, like this house, and the books and pictures, and some one ready to help—like you—why *those* things I just hold up in the light all the time. Isn't *that* being happy?"

"What a philosopher!" Gaston bent forward and again pressed the slim shoulder. The piteousness of this young wife getting her happiness, all unknowingly, by self-imposed blindness of the inner soul, clutched at his heart.

"Hold hard to that, Joyce," he said. "Hold fast to that. Let all the light in that you can upon your blessings, and as to other things, why, don't acknowledge them! You're on the right track, though how you've struck it so early in the game, beats me."

"Well," Joyce was all aglow, "Mr. Drew helped. He was so funny and jolly. Just a big boy, but he had the queerest ideas about things. When I think of him, sick and weak like he was, and yet living out all his brave thoughts just as if he was a giant—why, sometimes I go off and cry by myself."

Jude from his shadow and aloofness was staring dumbly at the pair opposite while the low-spoken words sank into his drowsiness. Jude was primitive. Actions were *things* to him; things that admitted of no shades of meaning. What the two were saying in no way modified the situation. Gaston's hand was caressing his wife—his woman, Jude would have expressed it—and the bald fact was enough.

A hot anger rose in him—an anger calculated to urge a personal assault then and there, upon the two who dared, in his own house, set his rights—his alone—aside.

The sleepy eyes widened and closed; the teeth showed through the rough beard—and then, like a smarting blow, came the memory of all that Gaston meant to him. Money! Gaston's money. There had been loans, trifling, but many, and now Gaston stood ready to advance money for this new building project. Money enough to make Jude master of the situation. But with this thought came others that crushed and bruised him.

He had been wrong. It was not his wife's folly alone that stood between him and her. Gaston *had* been using him. He was lending him money—hush money! And while he had gone his stupid way, thinking he held the whip hand over Joyce, the two had had their laugh at him. Money has done much for good and evil in this world, but it saved Gaston that night from a desperate attack.

A low cunning crept into Jude's thoughts. Very well, two or three could play at the same game.

More money! More! More! and who knew? Why he might make a choice in the future—a choice for himself.

He settled back and snored long and deep. Then he stretched and yawned and gave ample notice of his advance, in order that the conspirators might cover their tracks.

When he opened his eyes, Gaston was leaning forward with clasped hands stretched out toward the fading glow, and Joyce, crouched upon her stool with huddled knees, gave no sign that confusion held part in her thoughts.

"Say," Jude had already adopted the guise of the man with a purpose, "you don't suppose, do you, that that young parson is coming up here with any idea of saving souls?"

"Only his own, I fancy." Gaston replied, without turning. "He wants to keep his soul and body together. Seeking his lost health, you know."

"What makes him fancy he lost it up here?"

"He doesn't. He lost it down there among books, bad air, and foolish living. His physicians tell him his only chance for life is up in this region. Some day more of the big doctors will shut down on drugs and give Nature a try."

"Umph!" Jude shook himself. "Put a log on," he commanded Joyce. Then: "He preached a durned mess of nonsense the last time he was visiting us," he continued. "I didn't have any inclination to take his guff myself, but I don't half like the idee, now that I've slept on it, of his coming in here as a disturbing element, so to speak. Living and minding your business, is one thing; interfering with other folks' business is another. Filmer, he told me a time back that he ain't had a comfortable spree since that young feller was here. He sort of upset Jock's stomach with his gab. The women, too, was considerable taken with him—he's the sort that makes fool women take notice. It ain't pleasant to think of that sissy-boy actually setting up housekeeping here, and reflecting upon old established ways, with any tommy-rot about clearing trails and such foolishness."

Joyce smiled. So that thought rankled in more lives than her own?

"Going to retire from the contractorship, Jude?" Gaston got up and crossed the room for his coat and hat.

"Not much!" Jude rose also. "Only beginning right is half the battle, and I say for one, and Tate he was saying the same this morning, that we'd better stamp out any upraisings in the start, now that it's likely to be a staying on, 'stead of a visit. When I select a teacher," Jude was following his guest to the outer door, "I ain't going to take up with no white-livered infant. See you to-morrow, Mr. Gaston?"

"Oh, certainly. Good night, Jude. Good night, Joyce." Gaston looked back at the little figure by the fire, and he saw that the upturned eyes were fixed on the Madonna and Child.

"Why don't you speak, Joyce? Mr. Gaston is saying good night." Jude's words reached where Gaston's had failed. The girl rose stiffly.

"Good night," she said slowly, and a great weariness was in her face.

When Jude returned she still stood in the middle of the room, her hands hanging limply by her side.

Something had gone out from her life with Gaston's going. But she was still thrilled and her soul was sensitive to impressions.

"What's up?"

Jude came close to her and stared boldly into the large, tired eyes.

"Nothing, Jude."

"You ain't so spry as when—there's company."

"It's late—you've had a nap. I'm dead tired."

"That's it," Jude laughed coarsely. "I've slept and kept out of mischief—you've been too durned entertaining—you're feeling the strain. See here, Joyce, maybe you better not be so—amusing in the future. Maybe you better leave Gaston to me—business is business and I guess we can do without petticoats in this camp."

He was losing control of himself.

"Jude," Joyce came close and tried to put her hands on her husband's shoulders. "Jude, I want you to pay Mr. Gaston back as soon as you can. It's been on my mind for quite a spell. We must owe him a lot. How much, Jude?"

"None of your—durned business."

"And Jude—don't borrow any more. I know Mr. Drew would advance anything for the building. His family is terribly rich. Mr. Gaston knows about them. I'd rather owe Mr. Drew than Mr. Gaston. Please, Jude!"

For a moment the sweet, quivering face put forth its appeal to the lower nature of the man. The girl was young enough, and new enough to sway Jude after a fashion, but the charm died almost at birth.

"See here." Jude slipped from the clinging hands, and glared angrily. "You ain't ever properly learned your place. You better let go any fool idee that you can budge me with your wiles. I don't have to buy your favours—they're mine. What I do, I do, and you take what I choose to let you have. See? If you get more than what is rightfully yours, don't get sot up with the notion I don't know what I'm permitting. I guess I've got to let you see what you're up against a little plainer. I had a kind of dim idee that your schooling and book-learning made you a bit keener than most about the real facts of the case, but you're all alike. Don't you question me in the future, girl, and you go your way—the way I *let* you go—and be thankful, but don't you forget you and me is *man* and *wife*, and that means just one durned thing in St. Ange and only one."

Joyce staggered back as if the man before her had dealt her a blow.

What had happened? Then she remembered that Jude was always irritable when he had been roused from sleep, or when he was hungry.

The blindness was mercifully clouding her soul now; but its duration was brief. It only gave her time to stand upright.

"Did you think I was asleep to-night?" Jude almost hissed the words.

The suddenness of the question had all the evil power of reducing the girl to an appearance of guilt.

"You were asleep," she whispered back.

Jude laughed cruelly.

"With my eyes opened," he snarled—"It pays to *seem* asleep, when you want to catch on to some kind of doings. Your old man, Joyce, ain't half the fool you'd like him to be. I wasn't napping when Billy Falster blabbed his warning. I wasn't napping when I saw that hand-holding and kissing from the top of Beacon Hill. I wasn't snoozing that night when you went crawling to Gaston's shack just after you'd given your word to me, and"—Jude had worked himself into a quivering rage—"I wasn't sleeping when you and him sat *there* to-night, blast ye!"

The convincing knowledge broke upon Joyce with full force. She would never be able to ignore the fact again. Try as she might, dream as she could, she was but a St. Ange woman, and he a St. Ange man.

There was only one way. She must deal with the rudest of materials.

"Jude," she said slowly, "you pay Mr. Gaston back all that you owe him—I'll stint here in the house—and I'll promise never to speak to him again. Could anything be fairer than that?"

She was in deadly earnest; but Jude laughed in her face.

A fear grew in the girl's heart at the sound. Not even an appeal to his selfishness could move him. She had lost the poor little power she once possessed. He did not care! And when that happened with a man like Jude—well, there was reason for fear.

"I'm the boss, girl, and you better hold to that knowledge. Keep your books, your pictures and what not as long as I say you can, and let that do you for what *I* am getting out of it. See?"

"Yes—I see!" And so she did, poor girl; and it was a long barren stretch on ahead that she saw. A stretch with hideous possibilities, unless luck were with her.

"Don't you let on." Jude was striding toward the bedchamber

beyond. "I guess you're smart enough to hold your tongue, though. Pile on a log or two, before you turn in; and you better draw the shutters to the north window—it's getting splitting cold."

Joyce turned to obey the commands. Not slavishly; after all it was but part of her woman-task. Jude feeling it necessary to tell her was the lash. It was cruelly superfluous—that was all.

She laid two heavy logs on the red embers, and stooped to brush the ashes from the hearth. Then she went to the north window and raised the sash. Before she drew the shutters she stood and looked out into the brilliant night.

Black and white. Sharp, clean and magically glittering it all looked; and the keen cold cleared the fear and fever from her head and heart.

Yes, off there in the distance Gaston was entering the pine thicket through which his private path ran. He must have walked slowly—or had all this new knowledge come so rapidly?

Gaston stood still at the entrance to the woods. Was he looking back?

Then something occurred. Once or twice before Joyce had been conscious of this. Something seemed to go out from her and follow Gaston. She, or that strange something, escaped the fear and smothering closeness of the little house. It was free and happy out there with Gaston in the night. He was strong—stronger than anybody in St. Ange. Nothing could really happen while *he* was near. She saw his smile; felt his compelling touch—no, not even Jude would dare hurt her, or go too far.

Gaston passed into the dim thicket. Joyce, too seemed to be going on quite happily and lightly, when—

"I say, Joyce, shut that winder, can't you?"

A silence. As Joyce had followed a certain call the night she had promised to marry Jude, and had gone to Gaston's house, so now she was going on—and on—and—

"Joyce!" At last the real clutched the unreal. The girl, for the first time, was conscious of the biting cold. She shivered and seemed to travel back to that rough call over frozen distances. With stiff fingers she drew the heavy wooden shutters together and lowered the sash. Then feeling her way with outstretched hands, like a bewildered child, she made her way to the inner chamber and Jude.

CHAPTER VIII

The following June Joyce's little boy was born. It was a most inconvenient time for him to make his appearance.

The late spring had delayed the logging season. The winter had been a long-continued, cold one; the men at the different camps had fretted under the postponed ending of their jobs, and severe discipline had been necessary in more than one camp. Hillcrest's ideas of decency had been deeply outraged; its courts of justice had been kept busy by men, who, unable to resist temptation after restraint had at last been removed, carried lawlessness to an unprecedented excess.

The river, too, with the depravity of inanimate things, had taken that occasion to leap all bounds and run wild where never before it had ventured. Not being content in carrying its legitimate burden of logs to the lower towns, it bore away, one black night, more than half of the lumber that Jude had piled near the clearing for Ralph Drew's new house.

This occurrence sent Jude into one of the fits of sullen frenzy which were becoming more and more common to him. He had been obliged to track the stolen lumber many miles to the south, seize it there, and make arrangements for bringing it back. This absence from the scene of his life battle, turned Jude into a veritable fiend for the time being. He had enough self-confidence to believe he could hold things in his own hands, when his hands and eyes were on the spot, but with absence and distance—bah!

Harriet T. Comstock

Many a horse and man suffered that spring from Jude's evil temper.

Whether Gaston was aware of conditions or not, who could tell? He took a keen delight in the manual labour of working on Drew's house. He and Filmer, with or without Jude, hammered, sawed and made rough designs that filled their days with honest toil and brought healthy sleep to their tired bodies.

And just when the early wild flowers were timidly showing themselves, after the winter's long reign, little Malcolm Lauzoon opened his eyes upon the scene.

How could he know that the festivities at the Black Cat were interrupted by Jude's necessary absences, and Isa Tate's voluntary visits to Joyce's home?

Leon Tate, good-naturedly reaping a belated prosperity, had insisted that his wife serve Joyce how and as she might.

Jude was becoming a man to be considered. He evidently had a future, and the tavern's attractions had never held a sure power over Jude. Here was Leon's opportunity for putting Jude under obligations.

Tate thought fit to place himself and his wife on a social equality with the Lauzoons. So Isa was in command when small Malcolm arrived.

It was an early June morning, after a night of black horror, when Joyce became aware of the singing of birds out of doors, and a strange, new song in her heart.

The latter sensation almost stifled her. She tried to raise her head and look about the room, but the effort made her faint. She waited a moment, then slowly turned her head on the pillow and opened her eyes. There by the low, open window sat Isa Tate, swaying back and forth in the old-fashioned rocker, with something on her lap.

Again the strange faintness overpowered Joyce, and the big tears rolled down her face. It had not, then, been all a hideous nightmare? Something sweet and real had remained after the terror and agony had taken flight?

"Isa!" So low and trembling was the call that Isa, drowsing luxuriously as she rocked to and fro, took no heed.

It was many a day since she, detached from the demands of home cares, could make herself so comfortable.

"Isa!"—and then Isa heard.

"What is it?" she turned a steady glance toward the bed. She did not intend that Joyce should be exacting. Women were apt to be unless the nurse was rigid. "Do you want anything?"

"Oh! Isa is that—my baby?" There was such a thrill in the voice that Isa was at once convinced that Joyce was delirious.

She was going to have her hands full. A mere baby, to Isa, was no cause for that tone, and the glorified look.

"I guess there ain't any one else going to put in a claim for him," she replied with a vague sense of humorously calming the patient.

"Him!" Joyce's tears again overflowed. "Did you say 'him' Isa?"

"There, there! do be still now, Joyce, and take a nap. You won't have any too much time for lazing. You better make the most of it."

"It's a boy. Oh! It seems too, too heavenly. *My* little boy! Isa, is—is—he beautiful?"

And now no doubts remained in Isa's mind. She must pacify

this very trying case.

"'Bout as beautiful as they make 'em," she said slowly, and tried to remember what was given to patients when they became unmanageable.

"Does—does he look—like—" the words came pantingly—"like the picture in the other room?"

Isa was sitting opposite the door leading into the living room, and her eyes fell, as Joyce spoke, upon the Madonna and Child.

Then, in spite of her anxiety and weariness, Isa laughed. The entire train of events since her arrival the day before had appealed to her latent sense of humour.

"Oh! exactly," she answered and rolling the baby in a blanket she strode over to the bed, and placed him hastily beside Joyce.

"There," she said soothingly; "now lay still or you'll hurt the little beauty. I'm going to fix something comforting to drink."

She was gone. In the mystery of the still room and the early morning, Joyce was alone with her little son!

As she felt, so all motherhood, as God designed it, should feel. Before the acceptance of the wonderful gift, motherhood stood entranced. Fear and awe hold even love in abeyance. Into poor, loving, human hands a soul—an eternal soul—was entrusted. No wonder even mother-love held back before it consecrated itself to the sacred and everlasting responsibility.

Joyce only dumbly felt this. All that she was conscious of was a fear that her joy, when she looked upon the blessed little face, would kill her, and so end what had but begun.

A new and marvellous strength came to her. She raised herself upon her elbow and reverently drew the corner of the blanket from the tiny head.

Suddenly the birds ceased singing. The June morning was enveloped in a black pall. The ominous stillness that precedes an outburst of the elements held breath in check.

Joyce was perfectly conscious. In the hideous blackness she saw her baby's face clear and distinct, and with firm fingers she tore the wrappings from the small body—she must see all, all.

Misshapen and grim in its old, sinister expression of feature, the baby lay exposed. The face was grotesque in its weazened fixity; the little legs were twisted, and the thin body lay crooked among its blankets. The big eyes stared into the horrified ones above them as if pleading for mercy. The sight turned Joyce ill.

"In spite of all," the stare seemed to challenge, "can you accept me?"

In that moment when the bitter cup was pressed to mother-hood's lips, Joyce received the holiest sacrament that God ever bestows. In divine strength she accepted her child. This little, blighted creature would have no one but her to look to—to find life through. All that it was to receive, until it went out of life, must come first through her. Should she fail it?

With fumbling and untrained hands she drew it to her, and pressed it against her breast. With the touch of the small body at her heart, the dawn crept back into the room, and from afar the birds sang.

With all her striving, poor Joyce had not eliminated from the baby's life the inheritance of others' sins. He had come, bearing a heavy load of disease and deformity. All that was left for her to do now, was to lift the cross as she might from this stunted and saddened life, and walk beside him to the farther side.

Harriet T. Comstock

The poor, little wrinkled mouth was nestling against the mother-breast. Instinct was alive in the child. Joyce laughed. At first tremblingly, then shrilly. Suddenly she began to sing a lullaby, and the tune was interrupted by laughs and moans.

Higher and higher the fever rose. Isa Tate, beside herself with fright, screamed for help, and for days Jude Lauzoon's house was the meeting place of Life and Death; then Life triumphed, and people breathed relievedly.

"A homely young-un often makes handsome old bones," comforted Isa. Now that Joyce was creeping back from the dangers that had beset her, Isa felt a glow of pride and interest. She was an honourable diploma to Isa's skill as nurse. In the future, Mrs. Tate was to feel a new importance. She was assuming the airs of a woman who has learned the market value of her services. Tate was to reap the effect of this later.

"Oh! It doesn't matter much with boys," Joyce answered, indifferently. "A girl would have been different."

"That's a sensible way to look at it," Isa agreed. "I often think that a man with good looks has just that much temptation to be a bigger fool than what he otherwise would be. It's one agin 'em whichever way you take it. They don't *need* looks. They gets what they wants, anyway, and if they are side-tracked by their countenances, it's ten to one they will get distracted in their aims, and make more trouble than usual.

"Now that I hark back, the only men as I can remember that amounted to enough to make you willing to overlook their cussedness, was men as had a handicap in looks.

"There was Pierre Laval's brother Damon. He was born with twelve toes, twelve fingers—two extry thumbs they was—and four front teeth.

"He certainly was the most audacious ugly young-un I ever set eyes on. I wasn't much more than a girl, to be sure, when I saw him first, but I went into yelling hysterics, and took to my bed. Pierre was handsome—and, you know how he ended? Damon, he gritted his teeth—and in his case he could do that early—and made up his mind to make good for his deficiencies—if you can say that 'bout one as had more rather than less than Nature generally bestows. Land! the learning that child was capable of absorbing! Hillcrest School just sunk into him like he was a sponge. When he got all he could over there, he just walked off as natural as could be, without a cent to his name—and they do say, so I've heard, that down the state they set an awful store by his knowledge of stars and moons and such-like. And Mick Falstar, cousin to Pete—"

"Never mind, Isa." Joyce looked wan and nerveless. These tales only accentuated the agony she felt whenever she was forced to concentrate her thoughts upon actualities.

When she was left to herself, she was beginning to regain the power of ignoring facts and living among ideals. She was growing more and more able to see a little spiritual baby at her breast—a beautiful child. And with that vision growing clearer she felt her own spirit gaining strength for flights into a future where this little son of hers, borne aloft by her determined will and purpose, should hold his own among men. Surely, she thought, God would not cripple mind, body and soul. God would be content with testing her love by the twisted body. The mind and soul would be—glorious!

Day by day, the young mother, creeping back into the warm, summer life, watched for intelligence to awaken in the grim little face; the first flying signal of the overpowering intellect that was to make recompense for all that had been withheld.

The misshapen body was always swathed in disguising wrappings; even the claw-like, groping hands were held under blankets when curious eyes were near. Isa had won Joyce's everlasting gratitude by holding her tongue regarding the child's bodily deformity; and the Hillcrest doctor, who had been summoned when the fever grew, did not consider the

Harriet T. Comstock

circumstance important enough to weigh on his memory when once the payment for his services was, to his surprise, forthcoming.

But the sad, little old face with its fringe of straight black hair! That must be public property, and its piteous appeal had no power beyond the mother, to stay the cruel jest and jibe.

"Say, Jude," Peter Falstar had said in offering his maudlin congratulations, "what's that you got up to your place—a baby or a Chinese idol? That comes of having a handsome wife, what has notions beyond what women can digest."

Jude did not take this pleasantry as one might suppose he would. His own primitive aversion to the strange, deformed child made him weakly sensitive. He recoiled from Falstar's gibe with a sneaking shame he dared not defend by a physical outburst.

"He ain't a very handsome chap," he returned foolishly, "don't favour either father or mother—hey?"

Gaston overheard this and other similar witticisms, and his blood rose hot within him.

The cruelty and indelicacy of it all made him hate, where, heretofore, he had but felt contempt.

He realized most keenly that in his lonely life among the pines the few interests and friendships that he had permitted himself were deeper than he had believed.

Jock Filmer, during the closer contact of daily labour, had become to him a rude prototype of a Jonathan. They had found each other out, and behind the screen that divided them from others, they held communion sacred to themselves. They read together in Gaston's shack. They had, at times, skimmed dangerously near the Pasts that both, for reasons of their own, kept shrouded. After one of these close calls of confidence, they would drift apart for a time—afraid of each other—but the growing attraction they felt was strengthening after the three or four years wherein an unconscious foundation had been laid.

Then Gaston, too, realized that he had banked much upon the marriage he had brought about between Jude and Joyce. In saving himself from temptation, he felt he had sacrificed the girl, unless he could bring into her life an element that would satisfy her blind gropings.

To argue that in saving himself he had saved her, was no comfort. He had not been called upon to elect himself arbiter of Joyce's future. No; to put it baldly, in his loneliness he had dabbled in affairs that did not concern him—and he must pay for his idiocy.

To that end he had, at first, put himself and his private funds at Jude's disposal. He had had hopes that by so doing he might help Jude to decent manliness. But that hope soon died. Jude, lazy with the inertness of a too sharply defined ancestry, became rapidly a well-developed parasite.

Even when he accepted the contract to build Ralph Drew's house, he had done so from two motives. By this means he could, he found, command more of Gaston's money than in any other way, and by assuming the responsibility he placed himself on a social pinnacle that satisfied his vanity. He became a man of importance. Gaston and Filmer, glad with the intelligence of men who know the value of work, took the actual burden upon themselves. Lauzoon had the empty glory; they had the blessing of toil that brought their faculties into play, and gave them relief from somberer thoughts. But Gaston was too normal a man not to consider the gravity of conditions that were developing. His hopes of Jude had long ago sunk into a contemptuous understanding of the shiftless fellow. He had, however, believed that the hold he had upon him insured a comparatively easy life for Joyce. This, too, he now saw was a false belief.

　　　　Harriet T. Comstock

He knew the girl. He knew that mere housing and assured food were little to her, if deeper things failed.

It was this essentially spiritual side of Joyce that had interested him and appealed to him from the beginning.

One by one he gave up his hopes for her happiness. He saw that Jude was impossible long before Joyce did; then he put his faith in the little child—and now that had failed! Poor girl! he thought; and in the inner chamber of his shack with the doors and shutters barred, the pistol lying at hand upon his desk, he cursed himself for a fool who had tried to enrich his own wasted life with an interest in the lives of others that had brought about as bad a state of affairs as any meddler could well conceive.

Then he grew reckless. Things couldn't be much worse, anyway, and if he might brighten that dull life in the little house, he'd brighten it and Jude be—the laugh that Gaston laughed was perhaps better than the word he might have used had he finished his sentence.

There was the regular income from the outer world; as long as that was at Gaston's command he felt he could control Lauzoon, and who else mattered, except Filmer? Well, Filmer had sense to keep his opinions to himself—although the look in his eyes when he disapproved of anything, was unpleasant and—impertinent.

A clam like Filmer had no right to personal opinions of other folks' conduct. Unless he let light in upon his own excuse for being, he should withhold condemnation.

So Gaston spent his days' ends on Jude's little piazza, or in the bay window of the sitting room when the air was too cool for the baby snuggling against the young mother's breast.

Gaston brought his fiddle along, and those were wonderful tunes he drew from the strings. Sometimes he explained what they meant, his words running along in monotone that yet kept time to the alluring strains.

Joyce smiled, and her ready tears came, but the colour was coming back into her beautiful face; the brooding eyes once again had the glint of sweet mischief in them, and the lip curled away from the pretty teeth.

She had never been so beautiful before. Living in the ideal where her baby was concerned made it perilously easy for her to live ideally in all other ways.

Jude became a blurred reality. He was, when she thought of him at all, endowed with the graces and attractiveness of Gaston. Joyce did not consider Jude as he really existed. She smiled vaguely at him—his personality now, neither annoyed her nor appealed to her. While living with him outwardly, she was to all intents and purposes, spiritually living with Gaston. For she gave to Jude the attributes that made Gaston her hero, just as she gave to her poor, twisted baby the beautiful contours and heavenly beauty of the Madonna's exquisite Child.

The summer throbbed and glowed in St. Ange.

Was it possible that things were as they always had been? Jared Birkdale kept his distance and silence; and Joyce grew to forget him.

The Black Cat flourished, and Jude made no attempt to curb his growing desire for popularity there. He was developing a talent for instructing his elders, and laying down the law. He was endeavoring to fill Birkdale's place. Jared had always been the tavern orator. Some one has to occupy that pedestal in all such places, while the others enjoy their pipes and mugs in speculative contemplation.

But nothing was as it *had* been with Joyce. She had the look of one on the threshold of big happenings. Her pale beauty had a

Harriet T. Comstock

new glow. The thinness of girlhood had given place to a slender womanhood, all grace and charm.

She was rarely seen without her baby on her bosom. Even in her work she managed to bear him on one arm.

Away from her, he wailed pitifully and almost constantly; while pressed against the warm, loving heart he sank into comfort and peace. When he was awake his elfish eyes were fixed in solemn stare upon the mother-face. Not knowingly nor indifferently, but intently, as if from the depths of past experience he was wondering and endeavouring to understand.

One evening, and such an evening it was in late July, Joyce, in her low rocker, the baby on her knees, sat on the piazza facing westward, when Gaston came around the house, fiddle in hand.

"Alone, Joyce?" It was an idle question, but it would do.

"Yes; Jude seems to have a lot to do about Mr. Drew's house, you know."

Joyce still kept up a pretty defence of Jude. Not that it was in the least necessary, or even sensible, but it had its part in her detached and dreamy life.

"The house is about finished," Gaston replied, tuning up the fiddle. "And then what?" he said, placing the instrument.

"I wonder?" Joyce looked down happily upon her child.

It did not greatly matter, for now Gaston had struck into one of those compelling airs, so intensely sweet and melodious that it all but hurt; and the red sunset trembled as the tear-dimmed eyes beheld it.

The tune changed. It danced elfishly, and trippingly—for very joy it made one laugh. The tear rolled down Joyce's face, as the smile replaced it, and dropped upon the thin cheek of the baby. He did not flinch, and the staring eyes did not falter, but something drew the mother's attention. As the final tripping notes died away, she said softly.

"Mr. Gaston, just look—at the baby."

The child had rarely drawn them together. It was to make her forget the child—and other things—that Gaston called so often.

He came now, and bent over the two.

"Does—he—look—just the same to you?" she asked.

"Why, yes!" Gaston repressed the desire to laugh. "You see babies are not much in my line. I don't think I ever saw such a little fellow before. They look about the same for a long time, don't they?"

"Oh! no. They change every day, and many times during the day. I weighed baby to-day," she faltered, "and do you know, he weighs *less* than when he was born!"

"The ungrateful little heathen!"

"I'm afraid—I'm not a good mother." The sweet face quivered. "And I want to be that more than anything else on earth. You see if I can get him through—through this awful time when I can't tell just what might be the matter—it will be easy enough. But young babies are so—so—unreal. You don't know whether you've got them to keep or not. They seem to be kind of holding on to another life, while they clutch this. A good mother knows how to unloose them from that other hold."

Gaston was touched by the yearning in the low voice, but the weazened face of the child repelled him, even while it attracted him.

"Would it be so—so terrible if he did not let go that—other hold?"

It was a stupid thing to say, and Gaston despised himself for being so brutal when he saw the look of horror on the upturned face.

"Terrible?" Joyce gasped. "Why, if—if he should leave me, I couldn't live. You don't know how it seems to have him warm and little and soft against your heart. The whole world would be empty—empty, until it would kill me with the emptiness— and I'd always think, you know, he'd found out I wasn't fit to be his mother. It's a foolish fancy, but you know, Mr. Gaston, I think they come to try us mothers—if they find us out—not fit—they don't stay. Such a lot of babies don't stay!"

"Why Joyce!" Gaston tried to turn his gaze from that awful baby-stare. "Full of whim-whams and moonshine. You must get about more. You must come up to Drew's house to-morrow. It's a palace of a place—and Filmer had a letter from Drew to-day. He's coming before the autumn cold sets in— he's going to bring an aunt and a sister—just get your idle fancy on the doings, and let Master Malcolm jog along at his own pace. If he doesn't like you for a mother, he isn't worth considering. Look at him now—he sees the joke, the brazen little cuss, he's actually laughing in our faces."

"Oh!" Joyce sat rigidly up, and her own face became transformed. The moment she had lived and waited for had come! The blank stare gave place to a broken, crinkling expression; the thin shapeless lips trembled over the toothless gums, and into the big eyes a wonder broke. A light seemed to shine forth—and the baby smiled into the adoring face looking down!

To Gaston, the sight was, in a sense, awful. The majesty of Joyce's attitude toward the change in the child, was the only thing that saved the occasion.

"Is—it hungry?" he asked with the same dense stupidity he had displayed before.

"Oh, no!" Joyce laughed gleefully. "Don't you see, he—he knows me. He—he—*does* like—me—he's going to stay, and he takes this heavenly way to show it."

"The deuce he does!" and now Gaston laughed. "He's going to be a comical imp, if I don't miss my guess. See, he's calming down now, and regulating his features."

"But—he—smiled!" And just then Jude came around the corner of the house.

Gaston saw the expression of his face, and something stifled him for a moment. He wondered if money was always going to be a check to Jude, after all.

And if it should cease to hold him in leash—then what would happen?

He went away soon after, but he sat up until toward daylight, just outside his shack. He feared something was going to occur. But nothing did; and the next thing in Joyce's life story that tugged at his heart-strings, was the sickness and sudden death of little Malcolm.

Harriet T. Comstock

CHAPTER IX

It was the evening of the day that the baby had been laid under a slim, tall young pine tree back of the little house.

Jude felt that he had borne himself heroically throughout the trying episode.

Never having cared for the child in life, he considered himself a pretty good father to hide his relief at its early taking off.

As a man of means—what mattered if they were Gaston's means?—he had had a really impressive funeral for his son.

The Methodist minister from Hillcrest had preached for full an hour over the tiny casket. Not often did the clergyman have so good an opportunity to tell the St. Angeans what he thought of them.

He dealt with them along old and approved lines. He had heard of Drew's religious views and he took this occasion to include a warning of the damning influence that was about to enter the vicinity with the young minister's return.

"I warn you now," he thundered over the dead baby, "to make the life of this infidel, this God-hater, a burden to him."

Filmer from his rear corner, winked at Gaston at this. Gaston could see nothing amusing in the service—it was all in the passing show—a pitiful and added agony.

In that the show was a little grimmer than usual he found his resentment rising. So Gaston did not return the pleasantry of Jock's wink.

After the service, Jude had insisted that there should be no unseemly haste, and had instructed his chosen representatives to form a line and walk from the house to the tavern and back twice with the tiny remains, before they were finally laid to rest. This show of respect was talked of in St. Ange for days.

Through all the bitter day Joyce had followed dumbly whatever others did. It was like walking in her sleep, and she was grateful that she felt no sorrow.

She had feared if the baby died it might kill her, and now that it was dead she did not mind at all.

Her arms ached a little at times. She thought that was queer; they had never ached when they bore the baby.

At last she and Jude were back in the awful, quiet house. It was more awful now that Jude was there. For after the burial, and before the evening meal, he had been lessening his tension with some boon companions, down at the Black Cat, and Joyce had had the place to herself.

Jude, having relaxed to the state of geniality, was willing to let bygones be bygones in the broadest sense of the word. He had big plans afoot—he had had them the night he came home and found Gaston and Joyce hanging over the baby. These plans had been set aside while the baby was taking his pitiful leave of life after his one smile, but Jude must hurry his case now. Nothing stood in the way—and, although many a woman might get what she deserved, Jude was going to forgive Joyce again and take her to his bosom in a new life, and they'd both forget what was past.

The hold of youth and beauty clutched the man's inflamed senses. The evening meal, which Joyce had mechanically prepared, had been partaken of—by Jude—until little but fragments was left.

A black shower, which had passed over St. Ange in the late afternoon, had changed the sultry heat to ominous chill. The wind among the pines sobbed dismally as if it were a human thing and could understand.

Jude got up and shut the door. It was quite dark outside, and the lamp flickered in the breeze.

At his action Joyce sprang from the chair, and the dull calm that had possessed her for the past day or so was shattered. Her eyes blazed, and the colour came and went in the stern, white face.

"Don't—do—that!" she panted, springing to the door and flinging it back.

"What in thunder is the matter with you?" Jude stepped aside. Something in this change and fury startled him.

"Don't shut—the—door, Jude. We—we—can't leave him out there alone in the cold. He's so little—our—baby!"

Jude had a moment of doubt as to how he should deal with this foolery. If he were quite sure it was just Joyce's nonsense— but perhaps she had gone crazy. The thought stayed him.

Then he considered that in either case he must get the upper hand, and at once. All depended upon that.

"Go and set down," he commanded, eyeing the girl as she stood in the open doorway. "You don't 'spose we're going to live with open doors, do you?"

There was mastery in the tone, and, to gain her end, the woman resorted to her only course.

"Just—for to-night, Jude—just a little way open. I'd choke if I—shut him away so soon—and he so little and—and—all."

Fear of what he did not understand roused in Jude a brutish desire to overcome this something that threatened. For a moment he decided to rush from the house and leave the thing to work out its own way; but second thought brought with it his plans, which must be set in motion at once.

This attitude of Joyce's was a new obstacle, but if he conquered her, he might overcome it. So by sheer force of weak will he strode over to the woman who defied him, even while she pleaded, and grasped her roughly by the shoulder.

In that touch Joyce recognized what all suppressed and deprived womanhood has always felt, and she recoiled to reconnoitre.

"You do as I tell you, Joyce, and go and set down. The door is going to be shut and you take that in, plain and quick." He drew her away, and slammed the door with a crash.

Joyce went quietly to her chair, but a new and terrible look came into her eyes.

Jude sat on the edge of the table, disregarding the spotless cover and soiled dishes. He wanted to be near Joyce in case of an outbreak, and he had much to say.

"Are you listening to me?" he asked slowly, as if he were speaking to a child.

"Oh! yes," Joyce replied, and her tone reassured him; "I'm listening."

"Do you think you've ever taken me in any?"

The man's sullen black eyes held the clear, bluish-gray ones.

"Oh, never, Jude! You're terribly smart. I've always known that—but please—" the strained eyes turned for the last time toward the door.

"Cut that out!" said Jude. "You're just acting. You can't pull me by the nose, but it will pay you to calm down and listen to what I've got to say. I've heard from your father!"

"Have you?" The white impassive face did not change expression.

"Yes; by thunder! I have; and as it concerns you as much as it does me, you better take more interest. I heard from him more'n two weeks ago. I met him, too, in the south woods, a few nights back."

"What's he hiding for?" the monotonous tone jarred Jude more than any outbreak of temper could have done. His recent restraint, and his pent-up plans had worn his nerves to the raw edge. He was in the slow, consuming stage of emotions that was likely to lead him to a desperate move if he were balked.

"Now look here," he blurted out; "you and me has got to get down to business, and that to once! I've kept mum long of the kid's taking-off." Joyce's eyes widened as she stared through the open window over which the rose-vine was being lashed by a new storm.

"I've bided my time, and it was more for you than for me, you can bet.

"This is the big time of our lives, and I ain't going to hold back any facts what can make things clear and reasonable. Me and your father want you, maybe for different reasons, maybe not. You ain't the common sort, and we know you can help us. If you was like most women, him and me wouldn't have no compunctions about cutting, and leaving you to ways what you seem to hanker after. But he's actually pining for a sight of you, and even knowing what I do about you, I can't give you up! That's the plain situation as far as you're concerned, and you can take it for what it's worth. Are you listening?"

"Oh! yes, yes, I'm listening, Jude." And so she was. She was listening to the moan in the tree-tops. It sounded like the last plaintive cry her child had made, and it hurt her cruelly.

"I've got more money in hand, Joyce, than what I ever had— I've got fifteen hundred dollars."

Somehow this had power to reach the listener as nothing before had done. Her aching eyes fell upon Jude, and a new fear contracted them.

"Where did you get it—the money—Jude?"

"That's my business. I'm only dealing with facts."

"Yes, but I must know. It—it isn't yours, Jude."

"Isn't it?" Jude laughed. "Well, then, we'll call it mine for argerment. That pa of yours is a slick one!" The sudden change of subject relaxed the brief interest Joyce had shown in the conversation.

"Leaving here in the sulks about you, what does he do but go down to what he calls civilization, and strikes a rich claim first thing. All that was lacking was ready money. Back he comes, and finds out the lay of the land here, without so much as showing his nose. He says he had several plans to get money— but this plan of mine is the easiest, so we're going to work it. All my life I've dreamed by day and night"—a sudden glow illumined Jude's dark face,—"of the road and where it leads. Always, as true as God hears me, Joyce, always, as boy and man, when I've fancied myself on the road, and beyond the forests, I've always seen you beside me. I don't care what you are, or what temptations beset you—you've always been the one girl for me. We're going to begin a new life now—with no back flings at each other. Give me a kiss on it, girl."

Jude came over to her, and she felt his hot, excited breath on her cheek and throat.

Dazed as she was by what he had said, she was frightened at his manner, and drew back, warding him off with rigid hands.

"Don't!" she cried, hoarsely. "Don't touch me. You're all wrong—I'm not going anywhere with you. I'm going to stay right here—I swear it!"

"You won't go?" Everything swayed and trembled before Jude. "But if I promise to—to—pay it back? You know there was no time set." This was the last concession Jude was to make. His horrible suspicions were choking him.

"I'm not going. I—I couldn't—I—couldn't leave—him." The white face quivered and the big eyes overflowed with tears.

Jude had only one thought—a thought lashed to the fore by his jealous rage, and defeated hopes. And poor Joyce, distraught and grief-crazed, realized not the terrible blunder he was making.

"You're—staying—just—for him?" Jude was close to her now, and his breath came short and hard.

"Yes; I know you won't ever understand. If I was away, I couldn't bear my life—this—this longing would be always tugging at me—and I could never help it. If we stay here, Jude, I'll go on just the—same; it's being—near—that counts!"

"You—tell me this to my face—you fool!"

For an instant Joyce's dull agony wavered, and an inkling of what Jude meant rushed upon her.

"Oh!" she gasped, and put her hands out to him. But it was too late. The hot blood was surging in the weak brain. With a violence he had never shown before, the man flung the outstretched hands from him, then he struck viciously the white terrified face twice, leaving dull, red marks to bear witness.

His rage fed upon the brutality. Now that he had let himself loose, he gave full rein to his hate and revenge.

He gripped the slim, childish arm, and pushed the shrinking form before him.

"Go—you!" With one hand he drew the door back, and hurled the girl out into the black storm. "Go to *him*!"

Joyce kept her feet, but she staggered on until a tree stopped her course. The contact was another hurt, but she gave small heed to it.

Like a burning flash she seemed to see two things: Jude's true understanding of her blundering words; and her possible future, after she had made him understand. For, of course, she must go back and *make* him understand, and then—well, after such a scene, a woman's life was never safe in St. Ange. It was like a taste of blood to a wild animal. Still she must go back. In all the world there was nothing else for her to do.

Her face stung and throbbed, her arm ached where Jude had crushed the tender flesh. She leaned against the tree that had added to her pain, and wept miserably for very self-pity. She was downed and beaten. After all she was to be like the rest of St. Ange women.

Sounds roused her. Strange, terrific sounds.

What was Jude doing?

Trembling in every limb, she went forward and peered through the rose-vine into the room.

The rain was cooling her face and the wind was clearing the

agonized brain.

Inside, the scene struck terror to the watcher's heart.

Jude was crashing the furniture to pieces in a frenzy of revenge.

The chairs were dashed against the chimney; the books hurled near and far. One almost hit the white face among the vines, as it went crashing outward.

Then Jude attacked the pictures—her beautiful pictures!

The mountain peak was shattered by a blow from the remnant of the little rocker, then the ocean picture fell with the sound of splintered glass. Last the Madonna! Joyce clutched her heart as the heavenly face was obliterated by the savage blow. Then, maddened still further by his own excesses, Jude laughed and struck with mighty force, the lamp from the table—and the world was in blackness!

How long Joyce stood clinging to the vine in abject terror, she was never to know.

Consciousness of the live, vivid sort, was mercifully spared her for a space. She knew, but did not comprehend, the true horror of her situation.

No thought of explaining now to Jude occurred to her as she stood cringing and trembling against the house in the darkness. Only one thought possessed her vitally—Jude must never see her again. If he did, he would kill her. Kill her as Pierre was said to have killed poor little Lola, long, long ago.

Joyce's teeth chattered and she gripped her shaking hands over them. When her heart *did* beat—and minutes seemed to pass when it made no motion—it hurt her cruelly.

What was he doing in there? The storm was gaining power, and no other sound rose in the blackness. Then suddenly Jude rushed from the house. He passed so close to Joyce that his coat touched her. By some power entirely outside of ordinary hearing or seeing, Joyce knew that he was making for the Black Cat with the tale of his wrongs. They all did that. It was the finishing stroke for the woman.

Alone, in the blackness and storm, reason reasserted itself in Joyce's mind. It brought no comfort with its restored poise; rather, it brought a realization of her true position. Her life was as utterly shattered and devastated as was the little home. Everything was gone. The future, with pitiful choice, was as densely black as the night that shut her in with her dull misery. With Jude, there could be no possible understanding. To confront him, even with the powers of the Black Cat at call, would be the wildest folly. There was nothing to say— nothing.

Still, Jude had money. It was quite plain to the keen mind now—it was Gaston's money! Ralph Drew had probably sent the money in payment and instead of passing the amount on to Gaston, who had advanced the different sums, Jude was making off with it. She must stop that. For herself, what did it matter? But still, if Gaston, who had such power, could hold Jude and claim the money, he might find a way out of this awful trouble. She must go to Gaston, and at once.

Aching in every limb, and soaked to the skin, Joyce turned toward the North Woods. The howling wind was with her, and it was the only help she had. So she came at last to the lonely little shack among the pines.

Gaston had built a roaring piney fire upon the hearth of his outer room. He was luxuriating before this with a long-stemmed pipe between his lips.

The day had perplexed and touched him deeply. Never before in all his St. Ange life had he seemed to get so close to the heart, the human heart, of things. Joyce's white, still anguish over the death of her baby had tugged at his feelings.

So *that* was what mother-love meant the world over?

A sharp, quick knock startled him. Gaston rose at once. He knew upon the instant who it was. He knew that from some dire necessity Joyce was calling for his aid.

There was no time nor inclination for him to fall back upon that inner sense of his and seek to peer beyond the present and its need. He strode to the door, flung it open, and Joyce and the terrific storm burst into the room together!

"He—he's driven me from the house." The girl's wild face made unnecessary the idle question that Gaston spoke.

"Who?"

"Jude." Then Gaston shut and barred the heavy door. He could at least exclude the rain and wind.

"Look here! and here!" the girl pointed to her bruised face upon which the storm's moisture rested, and the slender arm with its brutal mark.

"Good God!" ejaculated Gaston, as he gazed in horror, "and on this day!"

Rage against Jude, tenderness for Jude's victim, struggled hotly in Gaston's mind; but presently a divine pity for the girl alone consumed him.

Her misery was appalling. Now that she was comparatively safe, bodily weakness overpowered her. She swayed, and put her hands out childishly for support—any support that might steady her as her world went black.

Gaston caught her and placed her gently in his deep, low chair.

"Poor girl!" he murmured, "Poor Joyce! You're as wet as a leaf. Here!" He quickly brought one of the red blankets from the inner room. "Here, let me at least wrap you in something dry. And now drink this, it will do you good."

He poured some wine into a glass and held it to her blue, cold lips.

"Come, Joyce! We'll straighten things out. Trust me."

She gulped the warming wine, and shivered in the blanket's muffling comfort.

"And now," Gaston was flinging logs on the blazing embers, "you're coming around. Whatever it is, Joyce, it isn't worth all this agony of yours."

"I'm—I'm afraid they'll come and kill us." Joyce's eyes widened and the old fear seized her again. The momentary comfort and thought of safety lost their hold.

"In God's name, Joyce, hush! You're safe and I'm not afraid. Come, don't you see if you want me to help you, you must pull yourself together?"

"Yes; yes; and we—I must hurry."

Now that he had time to think, Gaston knew pretty well what had occurred. The vulgar details did not matter. The one important and hideous fact was, that for some reason, Jude, with the crazy brutality that had long been gathering, had flung his young wife from his protection on to Gaston's.

Well, he would accept the responsibility. He was quite calm, and his blood was up. A pleasurable excitement possessed him, and he laughed to calm the fear he saw in Joyce's eyes.

The clock struck nine. All that was respectable and innocent in St. Ange was in bed at that hour.

Gaston wondered what he was going to do with the girl. The

Harriet T. Comstock

thought did not disturb him; but, of course, he must make arrangements.

Long ago he had so shut out his own world that he could not, now, call upon it for Joyce's protection. St. Ange was impossible as a working basis—his thoughts flew to Filmer. Yes; as soon as Joyce could explain, he would go for Filmer and together they would solve this riddle for the poor, battered soul, shrinking before him.

He must hurry her a little. St. Ange and nine o'clock must be considered.

The wine had brought life and colour into the white face. The glorious hair, now rapidly drying in the warm room, was curling in childish fashion above the wide eyes.

She was certainly too young and pretty to run the risk that the night might bring.

A complication arose. Divine pity made way for a sense of the girl's beauty and helplessness. The bruise upon the soft cheek cried out for tenderness and protection. Gaston strove to detach himself from the personal element. He strove to feel old and fatherly but he was still young; Fate was tempting him in the subtlest manner. The best and the worst of the man came to the fore.

The wind howled outside; the warmth and comfort held them close—together, and alone.

What did anything matter? They had both done their parts. They had tried to be what the world called good—and here they were tossed back upon each other, and not a hope beyond.

Then Gaston found himself speaking quite outside of the consciousness that was almost stifling him with its allurement.

"Joyce, I must take you home as soon as you can walk. I can straighten this out. It shall not happen again. You forget I have a certain hold over Jude."

"There is no home." The words fell dully from the girl. "He—he broke and destroyed everything before—he went to the Black Cat."

Gaston started.

"But he—did not know you came here? You see it will be in your favour, if they find you there among the ruins. I'll see to it—that they go and find you there. Can you walk now?"

"Yes, but—but you do not understand. The money—it was that I came to tell you about—Jude has a great deal of money—I think Mr. Drew has just sent it. He's going to—get away—with my—father."

Gaston now saw that no time must be wasted. If necessary he must carry Joyce, and set her down near her fallen shrine—then he must stop Jude. The money did not matter; but a frenzy of self-preservation, mingled with his desire to save Joyce, rose within him. The money was his hold on Jude; it was the only salvation for this critical moment.

Now that he faced the grim possibility, he found that he was as eager to preserve a clean future for himself as for her.

He must get her back. He must find Filmer, and he must lay hold of Jude.

"Come, Joyce, trust me, I swear to you that it will be all right."

He took her hand and led her toward the door. Then a confused noise outside stayed them.

There was a crushing of underbrush as if a light wagon was being driven over the narrow path; a mingling of voices rose excitedly.

"You damned scoundrel!" It was Filmer's voice. "Don't you utter that lie again until he's had a chance to fling it back in your teeth. Whatever your cursed row has been, he's got nothing to do with it. Shut up!"

"Hold on there, Filmer." It was Tate speaking. "This here wagon's got wedged in the trees. I want to see this thing settled square. If she's—" a bristling string of epithets followed, then Tate apparently freed the vehicle he was in, for he jumped to the ground and joined the knockers at the door.

So the morality of St. Ange was at stake! Gaston showed his teeth in a hard smile. There was but one conclusion for them all to come to, of course.

"Say, Gaston, old man!" Filmer shouted; "open up. I thought maybe you'd like to bid Jude an affectionate farewell before he skipped. If he owes you—*anything*, here's your chance!" Another knock shook the door.

The two inside looked at each other—man and woman! They both knew with what they had to deal. A dare-devil expression rose to Gaston's face. He tossed precaution to the winds.

Abject terror possessed Joyce and she reeled as she stood, clutching the blanket closer. Gaston put an arm about her, strode to the door, unbarred it, and flung it back.

"Well," he said to the men on the threshold, "what are you going to do about it?"

Filmer staggered as if Gaston had struck him, and the look in his eyes went scathingly to Gaston's heart. But while it hurt, it aroused resentment. What right had Filmer to judge—Who knew *his* past? But Gaston knew Filmer was *not* judging. He knew he was only bidding farewell to his one friend of the Solitudes. The friend he had trusted and revered.

The effect upon Jude was quite different. No doubt swayed him—he was merely debating in his mind whether he could now get away with the money and the wagon he had hired.

"Since you've got her—" he stammered, "how about—the—the money?"

The question nerved Gaston.

"Money?" he cried; "get out with it, you thief and would-be murderer. Use it to get as far from here as you can, for as true as there is a heaven above us, if you ever interfere with me or—mine—again, I'll shoot you at sight. Get out—all of you!"

He slammed the door violently shut, and with clenched hands and blazing eyes, he faced his companion.

He and she were the only ones in the new world. Stung by the memory of the look of lost faith in the eyes of the one friend to whom he had planned to turn in this emergency; recalling Jude's glance of triumph as he turned away, Gaston's moral sense reeled, and the elemental passions rose.

Joyce stood shrinking before him. Beaten, bruised and trapped, she awaited her doom.

Her primitive love for this man held no part in her present condition. Whatever he consigned her to, that must she accept. St. Ange standards were well known to her. The people would be quick enough to spurn personal responsibility for her, but if she were independent of them—well, they were not the ones to hold resentment!

No moral training had ever had part in this girl's life; nothing held her now but a fear, born of her past experience with man's authority, as to her future fate.

She was abandoned and disowned. Her recent loss and grief had bereft her of any personal pride and hope—like a slave

Harriet T. Comstock

before its master, she faced Gaston—and mutely waited.

The unexpected happened. Gaston laughed. Laughed in the old, unconcerned way; but presently the rising awe and question in the lovely eyes looking into his own, sobered him. He began to understand and to get her point of view. He stood straighter, and a new expression passed over his face.

"Sit down, Joyce," he said, urging her gently toward the chair, "I must mend the fire. Things look as if they had fallen to pieces, but they have not. Believe me—they have not. For heaven's sake stop trembling; every shudder you give is an insult to me. There, there, you don't understand, but, it's coming out all right. It was only when others were meddling that we got on the rocks. I've got the rudder in my hand now, and by God's help," he was fiercely flinging on the logs, "we'll sail out into the open with colours flying. When did you eat last?"

She was watching him with alert, feverish eyes. Like an ensnared animal she felt a frenzied eagerness to be ready for the snarer's next move.

"Eat?" she faltered, "why, why, I have forgotten. Yesterday—to-day—oh! does it matter? I'm not hungry."

"Well, I am. I always wanted a snatch after the play."

"The—the play?" Joyce leaned forward.

"After an infernal row, if you like that better. They both play the dickens with your digestion."

Bringing out the food, and making coffee eased the tension of the situation and after they had eaten, for Joyce struggled to follow his example, the atmosphere was less electrical.

The hands of the clock got around to ten-thirty; it was of no consequence, however, and then Gaston cleared the table, kicked a rebellious log back to its duty, and drew a chair beside Joyce.

The little bruised arm lay stretched pitifully along the arm of the chair. Gaston winced as he saw it, and he laid his strong, warm hand over the cold fingers that did not draw away.

"Joyce." His voice was almost solemn in its intensity. "I don't believe there is anything I can say that you would understand now. God knows, I pity you from the bottom of my soul and, God helping me, I'm going to help you in the best way I can. You need rest more than any other little woman in the world to-night, I reckon, go in there," he nodded toward his own chamber, "and try your best to sleep. I want to smoke and think it all out here by the fire. Remember, you are safe."

She rose stiffly and stood before him. Fear was gone from her; weakness remained; a horrible, sickening weakness, but no fear. Vaguely, gropingly, she tried to understand what lay behind his slow, solemn words, but the effort was too great. She sighed and looked down upon him as if he had suddenly become a stranger to her, then, stepping backward, with uncertain faltering movement, she gained the door of that room where no foot but Gaston's had ever before stepped.

Harriet T. Comstock

CHAPTER X

It was mid-October when Ralph Drew, his pretty sister Constance and his devoted maiden aunt—Miss Sally Drew—arrived in St. Ange and took up their new life in the bungalow which, under Jude Lauzoon's contractorship, had been made ready.

During his first short stay in St. Ange young Drew had regained not only his lost strength, but he had gained an insight into the needs of the men and women of the small place. He had always intended doing something for the village and its inhabitants after his return to town for they had appealed strongly to his emotional and sympathetic nature. But what St. Ange had vouchsafed in the way of restored health, she had begrudgingly bestowed. To have and to hold what she had given, the recipient must, in return, vow allegiance to her, and, forsaking all others, cling to her pines and silent places. He must forswear old habits and environment—he must give up all else and fling himself upon her mercy.

It had been hard. Back there in the town, where the pulse of things beat high, he had fought the knowledge inch by inch.

"Would a year be enough?" It would be useless. "If winters were spent there—several winters?" The big specialist shook his head.

High, dry mountains, somewhere, were the only hope. St.

Ange was comparatively near, she had given a hint as to what she could do—better trust her.

One after another the outposts of lingering hope were taken by the grim, white Spectre. He must abdicate, and accept what terms the enemy offered.

Wan, and defeated, but still with the high courage that was his only possession, Drew tried to get the new outlook.

If there were to be—life, then there must be work, God's work; he was no coward, he would do his part.

Mingled with the many, dear, familiar things of the life that no longer was to be his, was a slim, pretty, little girl whom he had enshrined in his college days, and before whom he had laid his heart's sacredest offerings since. She, and his splendid courage would make even St. Ange a Paradise.

Raising his eyes to her face, as she sat beside his bed the day the specialist had given his final command, Drew whispered his hope to her.

The soft, saintly eyes fell before the trusting, pitiful ones.

"Dear," he said, a new doubt faced him—one he had never believed possible; "they say I will be well—quite well, there if I stay. And you and I—" but that drooping face drove him back among the shadows.

"We—must—think of others." It was the voice of a self-sacrificing saint, but the heart-touch was lacking, and Drew received his sentence then and there.

For a few, weak days he decided to remain and finish it all and forever.

Then his manly faith bade him sternly to gather the poor remnant of his strength together; grasp the broken blade that was his only weapon, and finish the fight how and where he could.

"We'll go with you, laddie," Aunt Sally whispered, hanging over this boy whom she loved as her own.

"And, dear," Constance sobbed on his pillow, "she wasn't worth your love. I just knew it from the start. She's a selfish— egotistical—" a thin, feverish hand stayed the girlish outburst.

"Never mind, Connie, we'll fly to the woods, and try to forget all about it." And taking advantage of the golden October calm, they came to St. Ange.

Lying upon his bed in the bungalow chamber, looking out over the hills and meadows, gorgeous in autumn tints, Drew began slowly, interruptedly to be sure, but perceptibly, to gain strength.

Having relinquished finally the old ideal of life, it was wonderful, even to Drew himself, to find how much seemed unimportant and trivial. It was rather shocking, in a mild way, for him to realize that a certain girl's face was growing less and less vivid. At first he attributed this to bodily weakness; then to weakness of character; finally, thank God! to common sense. With that conclusion reached, the present began feebly to be vital and full of meaning.

Had perfect health been his, a call to serve the cause to which he had dedicated himself might have taken him farther than St. Ange from his old life. It was the finality of the decree that had put him in that panic. Well, he would not permit finality to hold part in his plans. He would live as if all things *might* come to him, as to other men. It should be, day by day, and he would accept these people—if they would accept him—not as minister and parishioners, but in the larger, deeper sense—as brothers. With this outlook determined upon, a change for the better began. Before it, while the old weakness possessed him, Jock Filmer, sitting daily by his bed, was merely some one who was helping nurse the fever-racked body; afterward, Jock materialized into the most important and satisfying personality to be imagined. He was untiring in his devotion and gentleness. Caught on the rebound from the shock Gaston had caused him, Filmer went over to the new call to his friendship with an abandon that proved his own sore need of sympathy.

The family, grateful for the signs of returning health in the sick man, thankful for Jock's assistance and enlivening humour, disregarded conventions, and admitted the new friend to the holy of holies in their bungalow life.

Jock had not been so supremely happy in years. The companionship healed the wound Gaston had given his faith, and he found himself shielding and defending both Gaston and Joyce against his own crude judgments.

Before coming to St. Ange, Drew had been kept in touch with all that the men who were working for him considered his legitimate business. Anything pertaining to his house was fully explained; village scandal, however, had been ignored, and when Drew was able to be moved in a steamer-chair to his broad porch facing the west, he had many astounding things to learn.

One morning, lying luxuriously back among his cushions and inhaling the pine-filled air with relish, Drew electrified Filmer, who sat near him on the porch railing, by observing calmly:

"Filmer, I've a load of questions I want to ask."

"Heave 'em out." Jock sighed resignedly. Of course, he had anticipated this hour, and he knew that he must be the high priest. "Heave 'em out, and then settle down 'mong facts."

"Where is Jude Lauzoon?" This was hitting the bull's eye with a vengeance.

"Gone off for change of air and scene—somewhere." Jock

presented a stolid, blank face to his inquisitor.

"Gone where?"

"Now how in—how do you expect I know? Just gone."

"Taken that pretty little wife of his to new scenes, eh? Well, she never seemed to me to belong here rightfully. I hope they'll do well."

Jock hitched uncomfortably.

"Well," he broke in, feeling it was inevitable, "Joyce didn't, as you might say, go with Jude. She's stopping on here."

"With the baby? There was a baby, I recall. My sister talked of it a good deal. She was interested in Joyce Lauzoon from what I told her."

"Well," Filmer felt his way, "there was, as you say, a—a baby, at least a kind of—a—baby. It was about as near a failure as *I* ever saw; but Joyce was plain crazy about it."

"Was? Is—the child dead?" Drew's big eyes were full of sympathy.

"Well, I should say so! And women is queer creatures, Drew. Now any one with an open mind would have been blamed glad when that poor little cuss cut loose. It never would have had a show in life; it was a big mistake from the beginning, but after it went, and was comfortably planted behind the shack, what do you think? Why, she came back one night and dug him up and put him—" In his endeavour to keep Drew from more unsafe topics, Filmer had plunged straight into an abyss.

"Put him where?" Drew felt the gripping of life. It hurt, but it stimulated him. He was suffering with his people—his people! Joyce's lovely face, as he remembered it, pleaded with him for sympathy. It was her face that had first given him assurance.

She should not call in vain.

"Oh! back of where she is stopping now. They've made the spot quite a little garden plot, and—"

"Filmer, see here, tell me all about it!"

"Well, by thunder, then, here is the yarn. You see in the first place, you didn't marry Jude and Joyce as tight as an older and more experienced hand would have done. I ain't blaming you, but I've used the thought to help me to be more Christian in my views about what happened. The knot you tied was a slipknot all right."

A shadow passed over the sick man's face.

"You mean—" he began.

"I certainly do. There was a hell of a—excuse me—there was a rumpus of some sort the night the kid was buried. It ended up with a general smash-a-reen of furniture, pictures and such— and I guess Joyce came in for a share of bruises, from what has leaked out since. But the outcome was, she walked up to Gaston's shack that same evening, and what happened there hasn't got into the society news yet; but when Jude and me and Tate went up to straighten out what *I* thought was a drunken lie of Lauzoon's, there she was all right, wrapped up in Gaston's red blanket, his arm around her, and him asking what we was going to do about it?"

"What have you—done?" the even words came slowly.

"Nothing. Jude evaporated. I got a bit of a jog about Gaston; I ain't over virtuous, but Gaston was a sort of pattern to me, and I'd got him into my system while we was working on your house. He made me—believe in something clean and big— and I didn't enjoy seeing him spattered with mud of his own kicking up. But Lord! It ain't any of my business."

"And the others here? Do they make her and him—feel it?"

Filmer laughed.

"You forget," he replied; "Gaston's got about all the floating capital there is around here. Where he gets it, is his own affair, and him and Joyce don't ask no favours. The whole thing has settled into shape. You needn't get excited over it. Of course, the women folks have warned your aunt and sister off. I believe they call Joyce the worst woman in the place—when they're whispering—but they don't take any chances of giving offence by speaking out loud."

"Poor little girl!" Drew's eyes were misty. He shivered slightly and pulled his fur coat closer about his chin. "How does she look, Filmer?"

"As handsome as—well, a queen would give her back teeth to look like Joyce. I never seen the like. Head up, back as straight as a pine sapling, eyes shining and hair like—like mist with sunlight in it. Gaston has taught her to speak like he does. You know he always kept his language up-to-date and stylish? Well, she's caught the trick now. You'd think she'd travelled the way she hugs her g's and d's. She trips over the grammar rules occasionally—but I always said they had to be born in your blood to make you sure, and even then—you have to exercise them daily."

"Poor little Joyce! I always felt she was only half awake, as she stood that day before me. If I had it to do now—I would wake her up, before I made the tie fast."

"Lord help us!" Jock felt the relief of an unburdened mind; "is it in your religion to tie anything fast?"

"Yes; yes." Drew was looking over the sunlighted hills and thinking of that lovely, dreaming face of a year ago.

"And now," Filmer was drawling on, "while you and me are on

this sort of house-cleaning spell, let me drop another item of interest into your think-tank. We-all up here ain't going to stand for any preaching business. I say this outspoken and friendly, meaning no ill feeling; just plain, what's what. You see them ideas of yours what you handed out last year set folks thinking. They sounded so blasted innercent and easy that we all chewed on 'em for a time, and some of us got stung. Now them as is native here can't think without suffering; and them as came here, came to get rid of thinking, and so you see none of us want to be riled along that *line*. See?"

"I see." Drew smiled, and stretched his thin white hand out to Filmer. "Thanks. But if they'll let me live—that's all I want. It's my only way of preaching, anyhow—and Filmer, I *am* going to live. I feel the blood running to my heart and brain. I feel it bringing back hope and interest—a man can make a place for himself anywhere if there are men and women about. *I* thought first—back there—when I dropped everything, that there never could be anything else worth while, but I tell you old man, if you take even a remnant of life and love to Death's portal you're always mighty glad to get the chance to come back and see the game out. It's when you go empty-handed, that you long to slip in and have done with it. Filmer, there's something yet left for me to do."

Jock was holding the boyish hand in a grim grip. He tried to speak, but could not. He stared silently at the muffled figure in the long chair, then with an impatient grunt, dropped his hold and actually fled in order to hide the feelings that surged in his heart.

Left alone, Drew sank wearily back and closed his eyes. The lately-acquired strength proved often a deserter when it was tested, and for the moment the sick man felt all the depression and inertia of the past. He *felt*, and that was his only gain. Before, he had been too indifferent to feel or care.

"Poor, little, pretty thing!" he thought, with Joyce's face before him against the closed eyelids. "She couldn't stand it. She

Harriet T. Comstock

didn't look as if she could. I'm sorry she had to find her way out by such a commonplace path. What was Gaston thinking of to let her? He knew—he should have kept his hands off and not blasted what little hope might have been hers."

Half dreamily he recalled what Filmer had just told him. His weakened body held no firm clutch on his imagination at that time of his life—it ran riot, often giving him abnormal pleasure by its vivid touches; occasionally causing him excruciating pain as he suffered, in an exaggerated way, with suffering.

He saw Joyce, bruised and shuddering as a result of Jude's cruelty; he saw her poor little idols dashed to pieces before her eyes; he felt her grief for the dead baby, and when he remembered Jock's account of her taking the small casket to the only spot where she herself was safe, the weak tears rolled down his cold, thin face. He was too exhausted and full of pain to wipe them away.

He heard his aunt and sister come out of the house.

"Asleep!" whispered the older woman in a glad tone.

"I'll go for a walk," Constance added, tip-toeing away. "Have the milk and egg ready when he wakes, auntie. Did you ever see such a day? I feel as if I had just been made, and placed in a world that hadn't been used up by millions of people."

They were gone, and Drew sighed relievedly.

Presently he opened his eyes, if he had slept he was not conscious of it, and there sat the girl of his dreams near him.

"Mrs.—" he faltered, "Mrs. Lauzoon, how good of you to come and see me. I hope you know I would have come to you as soon as I was able?"

Joyce had been studying his face—nothing had escaped her: its wanness, the sharp outline, and the tears congealed in the hollows of his cheeks. She pulled her chair nearer, and took his extended hand.

"I'm sorry you've been sick," she said simply.

Then they smiled at each other.

It was hard for Drew to readjust his ideas and fit this beautiful woman into the guise of the Magdalene of his late thoughts.

Vaguely he saw that whatever she had undergone, she had brought from her experiences new beauty; a new force, and a power to guard her possessions with marvellous calm. She was being made as she went along in life. Her spiritual and mental architecture, so to speak, could not be properly estimated until all was finished. This conclusion chilled Drew's enthusiasm. He would have felt kinder had she been less sure of herself.

"You are looking—well, Mrs. Lauzoon." Drew felt the awkwardness of the situation growing.

"Please, Mr. Drew, I'm just Joyce again. Perhaps you have not heard?" Her great eyes were still smiling that contented, peaceful smile.

"I've heard. Need we talk of it, Joyce?"

"Unless you're too weak, we must; now or at some other time. You see I have been waiting to talk to you. I've been saying over and over, 'He'll understand. He'll make me sure that I've done right.'"

Drew, for the life of him, could not repress a feeling of repulsion. Joyce noticed this, and leaned back, folding her hands in her lap.

Drew saw that her hands were white and smooth. Then she gathered her heavy, red cloak around her, and hid those silent marks of her new refinement.

"They call me"—the old, half-childish smile came to the face looking full at Drew—"the worst woman in town. At least, they call me that when they think I won't hear. You know they were always afraid of Mr. Gaston a little. But I hear and it makes me laugh."

The listener closed his eyes for a moment. He could better steady his moral sense when that sweet beauty did not interfere with his judgment.

"You see, if I had stayed on—with Jude, and lived—that—awful life": a sudden awe stole into her voice—"then, if they had thought of me at all, they would have thought of me as—good. It would have been—good for me to have—poor, sad little children—like—like my—my baby—You've heard?" Her lips were quivering. The play of expression on her face, the varying tones of her voice unnerved Drew. He nodded to her question.

"It was such a—dreadful, little, crooked form, Mr. Drew—such—a hideous thing to hold a—a—soul. Just once, the *soul* smiled at me through the big, dark eyes—it wanted me to know it *was* a soul—then it went away."

Even while the smile trembled on the girl's lips the tears stood in her eyes.

"You see," she went on, "no one would have blamed me if I had gone on like that—the misshapen children, and soon they would have stopped having souls—and Jude's cruelty,"—again that fearsome catch in the voice—"they would have called me good—if I had stayed on—but you will understand?" She bent toward him with pleading and yearning in her face. "Oh! how I have just hungered to talk it over with you—and to feel sure! There isn't any one else in all the world, you know, to whom I could say this."

"How about Gaston?" Drew heard his own words, and they sounded brutal, but they were forced from him.

Joyce stared surprisedly.

"Why—we never talk of—of that. How could we? But I read—and Mr. Gaston has taught me to think—straight—and don't you notice how much better I talk?"

"Yes—and dress." All that was hard in Drew rose in arms. This girl was like the rest of her kind for all her wood-setting and strange beauty. The only puzzling thing in the matter was her desire to talk it out with him.

"I have lots of pretty things to wear." Joyce smoothed her heavy cloak. "He's the kindest man I ever knew. That's another reason I had for wanting to come to you. I want you to show him just *how* you understand. I begin to see how lonely he is—how lonely he has always been up here—there is no one quite like him—but you. But Mr. Drew, do you remember what you preached that day you—married us—Jude and me, I mean?"

"I'm afraid not—so many things have happened since." Drew tried to keep his feelings in check.

"Well, I remember every word." The glowing face again bent toward Drew. "Can't you think back? It was about what we've brought into the world, what we get here and shape into *our* lives, and then what we leave when we go—away. The blazed trail, you know, and clearing the way for others. Oh, it was the sort of thing that when you thought about it you didn't *dare* go on being careless."

"I do—recall." Her intensity was gripping Drew in spite of himself. "It was an old fancy. But it has helped me to live."

"It has *made* me live. I tried it fair and honest with Jude, Mr. Drew, but no one could do it with him. The trail got choked with—awful things—and I only had strength enough to run away, after one year. If I had stayed—I—I would have rotted as I stood." She breathed thick and fast. Her old life, even in memory, smothered her. Drew caught a slight impression of what it must have been for this strange-natured woman. He began to think she was not yet awake, and the thought made him kinder in his estimate of her.

"But," he said gently, "was there no other way out of your difficulty?"

She looked pityingly at him.

"I didn't go to Mr. Gaston to—to stay," she whispered: "there was a reason for my going—a reason about Jude—then things happened that I guess were meant to happen. There was no other way out for me—but I had not thought that far. I guess if God ever took care of any one, he took care of me that night."

This utterly pagan outlook on the proprieties positively stirred Drew to unholy mirth. But it did something else—it made him realize that the girl before him was quite outside the reach of any of his preconceived ideas. He could afford to sit down upon her plane and feel no moral indignation. Perhaps, after all, she had brought his work to him when she came herself.

"You see, after Jude and Mr. Tate and Jock Filmer found me there late at night—there was nothing else for me to do. Jude would have killed me—if I had gone away alone—he was—awful. Besides, where could I have gone?"

"Gaston should have acted for you. He knew what he was doing to you."

The righteous indignation confused the girl.

"Why, he did act for me." The fire sprang to the wondering eyes. "He is the best man on earth. There are more ways of being good than one. The people here can't see that—but surely you can. Mr. Gaston made my life safe and clean. I could grow better every day. Why, look at me." She flung her arms wide as if by the gesture she laid bare her new life.

"He has taught me until I can see and think, wide and sure. He is always gentle—and he never lets me work until—until I'm too tired to want to live.

"Isn't it being good when you are growing into the thing God meant you to be? Ought you not to take any way God offers to reach that kind of life?" Joyce flung the questions out fiercely. She was perplexed by Drew's attitude. If he were as much like Gaston as she had believed, why did he look and act as he was doing?

"If—if you have, and if you are, all that you say, why do you question me so?" Drew asked. He was feeling his way blindly through this new moral, or unmoral, thicket.

"Because sometimes a queer thought comes to me. I know it is because these people can not understand; but *you* can, and when you have told me it is all right—I shall never have the thought again."

"What *is* the thought, Joyce?"

"You see," she almost touched him now in her intensity, "I do not know anything about Mr. Gaston—really. About what he was, what his life was before he came here. I would not hurt him for anything God could give to me—and sometimes I have wondered if—if in that life that was; the life that *might* come again to him, you know,—for for he is *so* different from any one here—I wonder if what he has done for me, could hurt him? Could anything that is so heavenly good for me— hurt him?—tell me, tell me!"

And now Drew dropped his eyes and sent a swift prayer to God for forgiveness.

He had thought her without conscience, without soul. He felt himself in a dim valley, and he hardly dared to raise his eyes to her.

"I am perfectly happy." The words quivered to him, and belied themselves. "And he says he—is—but would he be if he were back there—where he came from? In my getting of *my* life, am I taking from *his*?"

"Good God!"

"You—you do not understand, either?"

"Yes; I do, Joyce—I understand. I understand."

"Am I hurting him?"

"He must answer that, Joyce, no one else can. He must face that some day, and also whether he is hurting you or not. We cannot any of us choose a little sunny spot in life for ourselves and shut out the past and future by a high wall. The present faces both ways, Joyce, and light is let in from all sides. Light and blackest gloom, God help us!

"What Gaston's other life was—he alone knows—he ought to tell you if he hopes to help you really. If he's the good man he seems to you, Joyce, he *will* tell you, and give you a chance to play the game." Suddenly an inspiration came to Drew. "Tell him," he said slowly, "that I have friends coming here—friends who will probably build summer homes and introduce a new life. It's none of my business, perhaps, but you've come to me for help—and as God shows me, I must help you. Gaston has no right to injure your future by playing a game with you that you in no wise understand. It isn't fair—and he knows it, if he stops to think. Perhaps there was no way for him to help you that night, but the way he took. Perhaps he nobly did the only thing he could—I hope to God this is true; but there are other ways now, Joyce—he must know and give you a choice."

"I—I—do not see—what you mean?" A frightened look spread over Joyce's face, and she shivered even in the full glow of the autumn sunlight. "I feel—you make me feel—as if I had been—as if I am—shut in a little room, with the doors and windows about to be opened. What is coming in, Mr. Drew? What am I going to see? You—you frighten me. I cannot—I will not believe—anything dreadful could happen to him or me—when I am so happy and safe."

The excitement was wearing upon Drew frightfully. His ghastly face appealed suddenly to Joyce as she looked at him through her own growing doubt.

"I'm going," she said, starting up; "I've made you worse. What can I do?"

Drew smiled wanly and held out a trembling hand.

"Come again," he whispered. "It's all right, I'm much better—than when you came."

And so he was, spiritually, for he had retained his belief in God's goodness, somehow. Just why, he could not have told, but had the girl been what he had, for a moment, believed, it would all have seemed so uselessly hopeless and crude.

From the strange confession he had obtained but a blurred impression, but that impression saved his faith in Joyce, at least. She was not a bad, ignoble woman. Whatever she had done, had been done from the best that was in her, and if Gaston had accepted her sacrifice he had, in some way, managed to keep himself noble in her sight.

It was a baffling thing all around. A thing that he must approach from a new standpoint; the one, the only comfort was, the girl's own evolution. It was not possible Drew thought, that all was evil which had produced what he had just seen.

CHAPTER XI

Gaston often took a trip to Hillcrest, remaining several days, at times, and Joyce never questioned. Gradually she had accepted the place in Gaston's life that he had allotted her without expectation or regret. To live in the light and joy of his presence had become enough—almost enough. She studied, and sought to be what he desired. She was, after the very first, genuinely happy and full of quaint sweetness. As the black interval of her life faded, she turned with grateful appreciation to the present and played the part expected of her in an amazing manner.

Sometimes that disturbing doubt, hardly strong enough to be classified, made her pause, wide-eyed and still, but it fled before Gaston's laugh and jest.

With Drew's coming she grasped the subtle restlessness and comforted herself with the thought that he who understood so much, he, who was, in kind, like Gaston, he would clear away the elusive doubt forever.

She had never forgotten that it was Drew who had first set her feet on the upward path; he, above all others, would be glad of her better life, and sympathize with her happiness.

When she pondered upon Gaston's possible past, she felt guilty. What he did not entrust to her, she had no right to consider—so she tried to push the thought away. She was glad of so good an excuse for putting a fretting thing aside. But it would not remain hidden. During Gaston's absences it reared its hated head—with his return it slunk into shadow.

Taking advantage of one of Gaston's brief visits from home, Joyce had gone to Drew, timing her call when she knew his womenkind were away. She had an instinctive aversion to her own sex. She had thought it was contempt for St. Ange womanhood; she did not speculate about these others.

Her talk with the young minister, instead of clearing her sky of the tiny cloud, had resulted in a general atmosphere of doubts and shapeless fears that doomed her days to unhappiness, and her lonely nights to actual misery.

Things were *not* right. That was the overpowering conviction that grew apace. If she knew all—all what? Well, if she insisted upon knowing all—what would happen?

She caught her breath sharply, and frantically turned to bodily toil in order to down the spectre which now confronted her with brazen insistence. Things must go on as before. Ralph Drew was nothing but a boy—what were his opinions compared to Gaston's? Gaston could do no wrong. She was content to abide by his decree.

She sang, and turned from one task to another with determined haste. At one moment she vowed the subject should never be thought of again; the next, she promised herself that she would put the whole matter before Gaston as soon as he returned, and, by so doing, prove the unimportance of the thing. But whichever way she looked at it, she hourly grew to dread Gaston's return. Life was never going to be the same. Something was going to happen!

Oh, she had often had these premonitions before. Gaston laughed at them, and called her funny names when she voiced them to him.

Three days and nights dragged on, after that visit to Drew,

before Gaston came back.

The house had been cleaned and recleaned until it shone. The fire was kept brilliant, and Joyce donned, in turn, every pretty bit of adornment that she owned. She decked the pictures with ground-pine, and, in the act of preparing the dishes for supper that Gaston liked best, he found her.

"Hello, little girl," he called cheerily; "it look like Christmas. It's lucky I have some presents in my pack. I believe you fixed up to catch me, and make me feel like a tight-wad. But I'm one to the good. Don't peek. After supper we'll have a lark. Have you a kiss by way of welcome?"

Joyce turned from the lamp she was lighting, and put both her hands on his shoulders.

"Oh, but it's good to have you back!" she said, and raised her lips to his.

This fond response to him was the greatest recompense the change in their lives had brought to Gaston. It warmed the lonely places of his heart.

It was a jovial meal that followed. Gaston was hungry, the food was excellent, and Joyce glowed and beamed in the atmosphere of regained trust.

It was, though, a fleeting peace. When the dishes were removed, Gaston noticed how tired she looked.

"Happy?" he asked, with a laugh.

"Perfectly." Joyce was filling his pipe.

"Perfectly *nothing!*" he exclaimed, drawing her down to the arm of his chair. "Now own up, my lady, what have you been doing?"

Gaston expected a rehearsal of daily tasks, more energetically performed, perhaps, than was necessary.

"I went to see Mr. Drew." The smile fled from Gaston's face. So it was not housework!

"How is the young D. D.?"

"He looks very ill, but they say he is getting better."

"Did you have a pleasant call?"

Gaston was unreasonably annoyed, but he was curious also.

Joyce dropped her eyes. In a subtle way Gaston felt a change in her. She was never anything but direct and truthful with him, her attitude was now, therefore, more significant. He had beaten his life, his personal life, into a monotonous round outlined on that first night when Joyce had been thrust into his care. He had grown to think that emotions were dead and done with; this sudden realization that the first touch from the outer world could disturb his calm, irritated him beyond measure.

"Mr. Drew was very—kind," Joyce's voice fell dully upon Gaston's impatience; "he's coming—to see us!"

"The devil he is!" The outburst seemed so childish that Gaston laughed, and his gloom passed.

By persistent practice he had felled every circumstance to a dead level—he would raze this new element, too, to the ground, and things would assume the old placidity.

"We'll welcome him when he comes, Joyce. I'm a selfish brute and don't want to be disturbed; but of course any one who cares to come will be welcome."

She shot a swift glance at him, then her eyes fell.

Gaston stared at her, and his face flushed. It had not been easy during the past year to keep the man in him under control, but he had begun to think, lately, the victory was assured. So confident was he of himself, that he had planned a final test in order to make sure the future held no danger for him—and her!

He sometimes wondered, if she were placed in different environment, surrounded by luxuries and admiration, how she would appear; and how she would affect him. In a way he had educated her and refined her. He had grown used to her and taken her for granted, but there were moments when she perplexed him.

His visit to Hillcrest was connected with his little plan to test, in a fashion, this woman he had helped to form.

Her announcement about Drew had diverted his thought, but he returned now to his own interests. Again he wondered if, after all he had done for her, she could rise above Jude and St. Ange to a degree that might touch him—that part of him that he hoped he had conquered forever.

If she could—then—but he would not anticipate. Drew's advent had focussed his desire to put himself, and her, to the test. Joyce had precipitated matters, that was all.

"Joyce!"

She was bending to place a log upon the fire.

"None of that! When I'm at home, the big logs are for me."

She laughed brightly. To be so guarded and cared for never ceased to be exciting.

"And now for my surprise! It's a corker this time, Joyce."

Gaston walked to the lean-to room and brought out

two boxes.

"Take them to your room, and put them on," he said.

There were always surprises when Gaston returned from Hillcrest. From out the Somewhere, somehow there drifted marvellous things—books, pictures, dresses, dainty slippers and home furnishings. Things that St. Ange gaped silently upon. Joyce never asked questions. Like a child she shielded this fairy-like mystery from her own curiosity. She was happier not to know.

But to-night the boxes seemed heavy. Not from what they held, but from the weight of her unrest, which was returning with added force.

She obeyed, however, with that quivering smile still upon her lips. Almost staggering under the load, she turned and entered the chamber that had once been Gaston's. It was a woman's room now in every sense. Gone were the rough furniture, the pipes and books. In their places were the white bed, the low rocker, the many trifles that go to meet the endless whims of a woman's fancy and taste. It was an odd room for the shack of a backwoodsman. It had taken Joyce long to settle into it comfortably. Her brief apprenticeship in the home that Gaston had helped Jude make for her was the only preparation she had had for ease among these refinements.

Once within the shelter now, Joyce almost flung the boxes from her. It was dark and cold in the room, and the stillness soothed her. She groped her way to the window and looked out at the little mound near the pines, where all that was really her own—her very own—lay. It had always been a comfort to have the little body so near her place of safety. She had ceased to grieve when once the baby was brought away from the ruin of the former home; but to-night the small oval, under its crust of glittering snow, made her shudder. It was her own—but oh! it was cold and dead like all the rest of her hope and joy. She knew it now. Not even Gaston's coming had cleared

Harriet T. Comstock

the doubt.

She had believed herself so good and happy—and here it was made plain, horribly plain. Everything was wrong. It had always been wrong.

But she dared not shrink into her pain. She must obey, and play her part. Awkwardly she lighted her lamp; tremblingly she untied the boxes—they bore the same mystic signs and the oft-repeated words, "New York." It did not matter. New York or the New Jerusalem, one was as unreal as the other to the backwoods girl.

Oh, but here was surprise indeed!

Joyce had not, as yet, sunk so far in doubt and apprehension, but that the contents of the boxes moved her to interest and delight.

A gown of golden silk, clinging and long. The daintiest of gloves, silken hose, and satin slippers. Filmy skirts, and bewildering ruffles of cobwebby lace. What wild imagination ever conceived of such witcheries; and what power could command their materialization in the North Woods?

Joyce sank beside the boxes, gasping with delight. Then suddenly, as the shock of pleasurable surprise passed, the mockery of the gift struck her. Down went the humbled head, and the girl wept as if her heart would break.

Gaston was playing with her. She had not been keen enough to understand, but all along he had amused himself at her expense. Having had her thrust upon him by circumstances, he had accepted the situation in his good-natured way, but underneath it was as cruel as—all else in her life.

She had been an ignorant, blind fool. Never had Gaston been so daring with her. Other pretty gifts had found a place, and supplied a want, in their common life; but this—this—oh! the incongruity was cruel and—insulting.

Joyce could not analyze all this—she merely felt it. But when it had sunk to the depths of her aroused instinct, the reaction took place. Had the girl been ugly physically, or had Gaston debased her, her doom would have been fixed; but there was a—chance!

In the death throes of her false position, she retraced the steps of her life with Gaston. With a sickening shudder she recalled her mad fear that first awful night when he had shut the door upon Jude and the others. How he had made her feel, and at once, that from the high place that was his, he could afford to help her, and only the low and vile would misunderstand. It was because she was low and vile as Jude had made her that she had feared—what?

How the knowledge had stung, then stunned her! She might have known, had she remembered, from the first Gaston had always driven her back upon herself when her foolish passion for him reared its head.

No one of his own kind would ever have been led into a misunderstanding of his motives and goodness.

Then in the days that followed that first terrible night, she had abased herself and striven to fill the role Gaston prepared for her!

Later she studied and silently prayed that, in a small way, she might repay him for his divine kindness!

But with the patient effort and the marvellous results of quickened mentality, a clear space was left in the new woman for harrowing doubt. She never again sank to the thought that Gaston could love her; but she could not utterly blind herself to the fear that he might be hurting himself through others *not* realizing the difference between him and her. Naturally she could not go to Gaston with this doubt—it would seem an

Harriet T. Comstock

insult to him, and a shameless suggestion.

Therefore she hailed Drew's advent with mingled apprehension and relief. Had he taken for granted that all was well; had he seemed glad that Gaston had saved her from her evil fate; then she would have known that such people as Gaston and Drew would understand and think no evil. But the effect of Gaston's training and influence had sunk deep. Joyce had risen above the vile thing Jude and St. Ange had tried to make her. She was, for all the wide difference between her and Gaston, a woman! A woman beautiful and alive to the highest degree. She dared not any longer ignore that. For Gaston's sake she must face the blinding truth.

Crouching beside the boxes of finery that he had thought she could not understand, Joyce clenched her hands in an agony of consecration and renunciation. Then despair seized her, and for a wild moment she was tempted to use Gaston's own weapon against him.

Heretofore she had accepted his gifts with a child's delight—what a fool she had been! Suppose now she should—well, take what she could get from life in spite—yes, in spite of Gaston himself?

Dare she? Could she? Would she be able to do anything when she faced him, but fall at his feet, beg for mercy, and implore him to tell her what her awakened conscience demanded?

She would try.

The colour rose and fell in the lovely face. She was beautiful, and she loved him. She had never let him see how much; or how. He should see now! She would try her meanest and basest weapon—and if—if—it conquered, she would make—terms. She, poor, dependent Joyce of the backwoods. Old Jared's girl. Jude Lauzoon's discarded wife. If she won a victory, *what* a victory it would be!

It would prove to Drew—she rose defiantly, and snatched the finery from the boxes. Her eyes were blazing and her blood ran hotly. Before her little mirror she let the garments of her past life fall from her. She unpinned her glorious hair, and thrilled as its convincing beauty gave added power to her plans.

Slowly, carefully, with a pictured ideal in her memory, she fashioned the wonderful tresses into form. High upon her head the glistening mass was fastened, then cunningly the little curls were pulled loose, and were permitted to go free about the smooth brow and white neck.

Then with an instinct that did not play her false, she donned the marvellous garments.

She was finished at last. The new, palpitating woman. All that belonged to the old Joyce seemed to have fallen, with the discarded garments, to the floor.

She did not doubt her power now. She was not afraid. Something was going to happen—again she experienced the sensation. It had come first in this very shack, when her childhood had departed, and the woman in her had been born. A poor, dull woman, to be sure; still, a woman.

She had felt it, too, the Sunday of her marriage, when Drew had called to her conscience and spirituality, and set the chords of suffering and hope vibrating. From that hour to this she had been climbing painfully to what was about to occur.

Well, she was ready. The bewitching smile played over her face. Tiptoeing across the bedroom floor, she noiselessly unfastened the door, and silently reached Gaston's side.

He had quite forgotten her. Weary from the day's work, perplexed by later developments, with closed eyes, and hands clasped behind his head, he was lost in thought.

Joyce touched him lightly, and he looked up.

She had taken him off guard. Her bewildering beauty attacked his senses while his shield of Purpose was down.

"Good God!" he exclaimed staring at her. "You—you glorious creature!"

She laughed, and the sound thrilled the man as her beauty did. It was new, and wonderful. He staggered to his feet and reached out to her like a man blinded by a sudden glare.

She evaded his touch, and gave that wild little laugh again.

"You like it?" she asked, from across the table.

"Like it? You—are—divine!"

"Why—did—you—do it?"

"I had a mad fancy to see just how great your—beauty was."

"And—you see?"

"Heavens! I do see."

"And you think?"

"What any man would think," Gaston's excitement was rising, "who had been starved for—years—and then finds all he's hungered for—alone in the North Woods. Think?"

The breaking of a flaming log startled them, and it steadied Gaston for a moment. Joyce had herself well in hand. The victory was hers if only she could command this new power long enough.

"Please," she pleaded, "please sit down. I have something to say to you."

CHAPTER XII

Gaston sank back in his chair, and Joyce sat down opposite. The table was between them, and the light of the fire and lamp flooded over the girl.

She was wonderful in that gown, and with her splendid, pale hair framing her face with its fair glory.

The shock of surprise was passing, but Gaston still looked at the girl as if he had never seen her before.

"What is it, Joyce?" he asked presently; "what has changed you so?" Then he smiled, for the question seemed crude and ill-advised.

"The dress—isn't that what you wanted?"

"I do not mean the dress—there is something else."

"So there is—but it came with the dress. Perhaps you—did not order that—well, then, it must be *your* part of the surprise. Don't you remember that story you read to me once—about the mantle of Elijah? You know it made the humble wearer—great. Well, these pretty things,"—she touched them lightly—"they make me—a woman. The sort of woman who must—ask questions—and get answers—true answers."

"Why, don't you trust—me?"

Harriet T. Comstock

The pained question was wrung from Gaston's lips. The steady look from the big eyes went strangely to his heart.

"I—do—not know—you—as you—are now," she said firmly.

"It is not I who am changed, Joyce, it is you. Everything is just the same except that I see you are more—wonderful than I dreamed."

"Nothing is going to be the same again. I knew it while Mr. Drew was talking the other day—I have thought it all out since."

"Curse him!" Gaston broke in; "what did he say? Why did you go to him Joyce? How could you?"

There was pain in the words—pain and a dumb fear.

"It only happened to be Mr. Drew. Some one would have made me know in time."

"Joyce;" he was actually pleading with her! The knowledge burnt into the quickening soul. "Joyce, what did you trust in me, before you went to Drew?"

"Your goodness—your—unselfishness. I knew the goodness— I have only begun to see the—unselfishness."

"My unselfishness? Good heavens!" In spite of the strangeness of it all, Gaston laughed. Then an impatience stifled him. A brute instinct drove him on. Her beauty had captured his senses, and he meant to tear down the pitiful wall he had upbuilded between her and him, and force her to see the inevitable.

He had wondered if she could stir him—well he knew now. What idiots they had both been!

He was through with the Past forever. The Past that had held him to a false ideal. There should be no more imbecile philosophy in the North Woods as far as he and she were concerned.

"See here," he began, and his voice was almost hard; "don't you know when I shut you away from what you knew as danger—Jude and all the rest of the hell that went with him—I shut you away from what people—people like Drew and his set—know as mercy?"

Joyce's eyes widened, but she did not speak. Gaston rushed on—he wanted the scene over. She was too heavenly beautiful sitting there, he must bring her closer.

"They would call you—well, they wouldn't call you a good woman. They are very particular about their women. In a way, you must have known this, Joyce. You've played the game like a thoroughbred, and when one considers *how* you've played it, the wonder grows—but they'd never believe that—even if we told them. Great heavens! how could they, if they saw you?

"That there was no other way for me to help you then, that you had no other shelter in God's world would not alter the case at all. And I've been a fool, Joyce, a maudlin fool—all along!"

The woman opposite was looking at him through tears, but the sweet mouth was quivering pitifully.

"Joyce"; the tone caused the tear-dimmed eyes to close; "let us face the music—and—dance along to the tune."

Gaston leaned toward her and when she dared to look at him she saw that the future was in her hands!

"You—you thought I knew this all along?"

"In a way—yes!"

Joyce's eyes dropped and a flush rose to her pale, still face.

"Then those—those people—the good people, what would they have thought about you?"

"Oh! some would have thought me a—damned scoundrel; and they would have been right had I ever intended to leave you to their mercy. Others—well, others—"

"Please tell me, you see I want to understand everything and that world is not mine—you know."

"The others,"—and now Gaston dropped his own eyes—"the others would have forgotten all about it—had I chosen to go back!"

"But they—would not have forgotten about me?"

"No. That is their imbecile code."

"And—and men know that and yet—" Her eyes widened in a dumb terror—"why, they are worse than—the people of St. Ange!"

Suddenly Gaston flung his head back and looked full at the beautiful face. It was radiant, but the eyes were overflowing. It seemed to him as if she, coming out from her shadows, were bringing all wronged womanhood with her.

"You know Joyce, you must have known no matter what else you thought, and you must know now, I never meant to leave you to their—mercy?"

He knew that he was speaking truth to her and it gave him courage.

"Yes; yes!" she cried. "I know that above all and everything."

Joyce saw that she was gaining power. She knew that,

marvellous as it seemed, she was to shape their future lives. But she must have the sky clear. Gaston, she felt, recognized this as well as she. He expected but one outcome; he saw her love, and was willing to show his own, now that the barriers were down.

"We need ask nothing!" he said softly; "and there are deeper woods to the north, dear."

"Can you—will you—tell me about yourself before—you came here?"

The question was asked simply and it was proof, if any were needed, that the past false position was utterly annihilated.

Gaston accepted the changed conditions with no sense of surprise. He acknowledged her right to all that she desired.

"When I said, a time back"; he began slowly; "that they—those good people we were talking about—would let me into their world if I—left you"; his fingers closed firmer over her hands; "I did not tell you that there is another reason why they would *not* let me in. They could overlook some things—but not others. Suppose I should tell you that I had done a wrong that was worse, in their eyes, than almost anything else?"

"I would not believe it!"

"But that is God's truth."

She grew a little paler, but she did not withdraw her hands.

With smarting recollection Gaston remembered how, back there in the old life, two small hands had slipped from his at a like confession.

"I've been a weak fellow from the start, Joyce. I haven't even had the courage to do a big, bad thing for myself. I've let them I loved, use me. I've lost my idea of right in my depraved craving for appreciation. That sort of sin is the worst kind. It damns one's self and makes the one you've tried to serve, hate you."

He saw that she was trying to follow him, but could not clearly, so he dropped all but brutal facts.

"When I stepped off the train at St. Ange, a few years back, I took the name of Gaston, because I dared not speak my own name, and I didn't like to go by the number that I had been known by for—five years."

"Number?" she whispered, and her frightened eyes glanced about. She was not afraid of him, but *for* him. Gaston saw that.

"Never fear," he reassured her; "it was all worked out. I paid that debt, but I wanted to forget the transaction. I thought I could, up here—but I reckoned without you!"

"Go on," she said hoarsely. The clock struck eleven, the logs fell apart—she was in a hurry.

"You know there is an odd little couplet that used to please me when I was—paying up. It goes like this:

Two men looked out of the prison bars,
The one saw mud, the other, the stars.

"There were a lot of us who saw stars, for all the belief to the contrary; and even the mud-seers had their moments of star-vision—behind the prison bars.

"Birthdays and Christmases played the deuce with them." Gaston was off the trail now that he dared voice the memories of the past. They had so long haunted him. They might pass if he could tell them to another.

"Go on," Joyce said, impatiently glancing at the clock as if her time were short. "Please go on. It doesn't matter about that. What was before, and—and what must come, now?"

"It does matter," Gaston came back. "It was that determination of mine not to be finished by that phase of my life, that left strength in me to be halfway decent since. I only meant to regain my health up here. I meant to go back to the life I had deserted and make good before them all—but something happened."

"Yes." Gaston's face had clouded, and Joyce had to recall him.

"You see it was this way. There were a lot of people—but only four mattered. My mother, my brother, the girl and her father."

The hands under Gaston's slipped away, but he did not notice.

"My mother had a heart trouble, she could not bear much—and she always loved my brother best. He had the look and way with him that made it easy for her to prefer him. I believed the—girl cared most for me—that was what kept things going all right for a time—her father liked me best, I knew.

"I had a position of trust, the control of much money, and my head got turned, I suppose—for I felt sure of everything; myself included. Then things happened all of a sudden.

"My brother found that the girl cared for me, not him; it broke him up, and that brought on an attack of sickness for my mother. She never could bear to see him suffer. My own happiness was twisted out of shape by what I saw was to be the result of my gain over his loss.

"One night he came to me and told me that his investments had gone wrong; our mother's fortune along with the rest. A certain sum of money, right then, would tide over the critical situation.

Harriet T. Comstock

"There was no chance but that all would come out right. He had private information that a few days would change the current. He would come out to the good—if only—"

"And you?" Joyce held him with her wide, terrified stare.

"Oh, yes! I didn't think there was any danger, and it seemed a chance to help when everything was about to come clattering around our ears. I helped. Good God, I helped!"

Gaston dropped his head on his folded arms.

"What happened when they all knew? When you explained—couldn't they help you?" Gaston flung his head back and looked at her.

"But they didn't find out. At least, they found out that I took the money—there wasn't anything else to tell. That damnable fact was enough, wasn't it? No amount of whimpering as to why I'd done it would have helped."

"But your brother?"

"He tried to get me to go away. He said in a few days all would be right. He could then save everything. I could return and repay—and—well! I wasn't made that way. I stayed."

"And—the girl?"

"She asked me if I had done it—she would believe no one else. I said yes; and that ended it. Her father tried to get me to explain—he was the Judge who was to have tried me—I refused and he begged to be released from sentencing me—that's all he could do for either of us."

"And—your—mother?" A sob rose in Joyce's throat.

"I think, even in her misery, she thanked God, since it had to be, that it was not my brother."

The room was growing cold. Joyce shivered.

"And then?" she faltered.

"Oh! then—" Gaston's face twitched, and his voice was bitter, "then came the star-gazing through the bars—and all the rest, until I came up here. Only one stuck to me through thick and thin."

"Your brother?" Joyce interrupted.

"My brother? No! Just a plain friend. I told him I did not want to hear a thing while I was shut away. I knew it would hold me back from getting what I could out of the experience. It's like hell to have the outside troubles and joys brought to you while you are bound hand and foot. I saw enough of that—it did more to keep men in the mud than anything else. I just kept that space of my life clear for expiation. When the gates opened for me one day—my friend was there with all the news in a budget.

"You see the lash that had cut deepest when I went away was something my mother said; 'You've broken the hearts of them who loved and trusted you.'"

"Nothing had mattered so much as those words—and out of the disgrace, the loneliness, the misery and deadly labour, I had worked out a plan to make up to them for the wrong I had done. It was going to be about the biggest job a fellow ever undertook; but, do you know, I had hoped that I could do it?

"Well, my friend's words drove me back upon myself. There was nothing for me to do."

"Why?"

"The hearts were all mended—after a fashion, without my aid."

Harriet T. Comstock

"Your mother?"

"She had died soon after I went away."

"And your—brother—he surely—"

"Oh! he had gone booming ahead like a rocket. The tide turned a bit too late for me—but it carried him to a safe harbour. In a generous and highly moral way he stood ready to repay me—but conditions had changed; I must accept certain terms."

"The—the—girl?"

"She'd married my brother. She it was who changed the conditions, you see. It had been a noble sacrifice for her to marry into *such* a family—so, of course, due consideration must be shown her. Would I live abroad on an ample allowance?"

Joyce flinched before the tone. Gaston stood up and flung his arms out. "No! by God, I would not live abroad. I chose my own place of hiding. He paid, though—I saw to that—he named no allowance, it was I; but he paid and paid and paid all that *I* thought he should. He bought me off at my price—not his. I left all in the hands of the only friend I had on earth—I never wanted to hear of the others again until I was ready to go back—and I haven't. I wanted time to think out my way. I wanted strength to go back, take my name and fortune, ask nothing of the world—but a chance to defy it. I got as far as that—" He dropped back into the chair and bowed his head.

The hands of the clock were past midnight, the fire was nothing but glowing embers; a chill was creeping through the room. Presently Gaston was aware of a nearness—not merely bodily, but spiritually. He looked up. He had forgotten Joyce and his thought of comfort in knowing that she would stand by him. To see her close now, to gaze up into her glorious face was like an awakening from a hideous dream to a safe reality.

"You got as far as that," she said in the saddest, softest tone that a woman's voice ever held; "and then I came into your life. Oh! how hard you tried to set me aside with Jude—but again and again I returned to—hold you back."

"Why, Joyce, what is the matter?"

A paralyzing fear drove anguish before it. Gaston strove to recall passion, but that, too, had deserted. He and Joyce were standing in a barren place alone—nothing behind, nothing before!

"Can't you see what is the matter?"

The coquetry had left the girl, she stood fair, cold and passive like some wonderful goddess.

"Don't you think I see it all now?

"When I came out of that room I was a—bad woman! You were mistaken, I never understood before—about us!

"You see when—when I came to you that night—after Jude—" she struggled with her trembling—"I did not know such men as you—lived. I was what Jude and St. Ange had made me. I was afraid of you—but," she bent over him in divine pity pressing her wet cheek to his bowed head; "but I grew to know! You were far, far above me, I soon saw how far. You never thought about it, but it made it safe for you to help me. I can see it all so plain now.

"Then the evil that was in me, the evil that some might have made so vile, slipped away. I tried hard to be what you wanted me to be for my own sake. You did not think of the past and I tried to forget it, too; and so we came along to this night.

Harriet T. Comstock

"In that room"—she looked quiveringly at the closed door—
"for a moment, I misunderstood again. I thought you were
trifling with me. I think I felt for the first time that perhaps I
was *not* what I had been—when I came out of the old life! I
wanted to make sure, and I stooped to the meanest way."

Gaston drew her close. Vaguely he feared that she was slipping
farther and farther from him for all her sweetness and nearness.

"Joyce!" he cried wildly. "*You* are not going to desert me—
now?"

She dropped beside him and clasped her hands over his knee.
There was no need of reserve, she knew that better than he.

"Can you not see what sort of man you are?" she asked fiercely;
while the tears fell thick and fast.

"Oh! I love you many, many ways. I can tell you this now and
you must not stop me. I love you for them who left you alone
to suffer. I love you just for myself, and I love you as I would
have loved my poor baby had God let me keep him. And that
is the best way of all, for it holds all other loves.

"Oh, you must see! You shall see! The men out in your
world—could any of them have done what you have done—
for me? Even Mr. Drew could not understand. Even *he*
thought you must have harmed me—he felt sorry for *me*! And
knowing what *I* know, do you, could any of those others,
think I would let you harm—yourself?

"You have made me a stronger woman than even you tried to
make me, and I thank God for that—for you need me so very,
very much!"

The deep sobs choked her, and she buried her head against his
arm. Out of a desolation her words were creating, Gaston
spoke desperately.

"I do need you, and by heaven, I mean to have you!"

"You're right. I did not know what you meant to me; I know now, and since Fate has played us false, we'll—we'll turn our backs on her."

"Joyce, are you willing to—trust me?"

Almost roughly he raised her face and forced her to look at him.

"I—trust you! You could never be anything but good and noble. I know that. You never have been—but, there are going to be other days and nights—just plain days and long black nights—and—I think we have almost forgotten—but there is always—Jude!"

Then like a bewildering flash the words lightened the dark place of Gaston's character.

This woman whom—he saw the fearful truth—this woman whom he had helped to form, had outgrown him and left him far behind!

Now that she understood; now that her womanhood could stand alone, she rose pure and strong above his passion and the thing he called love. She only thought he had forgotten, when God knew he did not even care for the rough fellow who had all but strangled the life out of her.

"Besides"—he heard her as from a distance—"besides, you must go back!"

"Go back—good God! to what?"

"To all that you had to go back to—when you turned to help me!"

Then Gaston bent and raised the shrinking woman beside

Harriet T. Comstock

him. Face to face they stood in the cold, still room. "Joyce," he said thickly, "what I am going to say—you may never be able to forgive—but I must say it.

"It is quite true, I gave no thought to what I was doing when I shielded you from Jude. St. Ange did not matter; there seemed no other way—and I never considered others coming to complicate things.

"I was miserable and lonely; but I felt sure of myself and in helping you I found an interest in life. Lately, almost unconsciously, I've felt the change in you—the new meaning. I wanted to make sure and then be guided, since others had entered this—this fool's paradise of mine. You are very beautiful—the most beautiful woman, I think, that I have ever seen—and I know now that you are—the best!

"Joyce—your beauty crazed me, and I had not forgotten Jude; I did not care!"

"Stop!" The little cold hand was pressed against his lips, "you shall not! It was I who tempted you—you would have remembered—everything. It is you who must forgive me—I am going—now!"

The slow, pitiful words fell lingeringly.

"Going—where can you go?" Gaston stared dumbly at her.

"I think Mr. Drew will help me. I am going to tell him everything—and he will—find a way."

"You shall not!" Gaston drew her to his breast. The primitive rose within him.

"There is another way. The only way. Drew shall not meddle in my affairs—nor yours. You will stay right here in your home until I return. I'm going to Filmer; he's the only one we need, he'll act for us both."

"But—what then?" Joyce felt her heart stand still.

"Then? why I'm going to find Jude. I'm going to buy him off—if necessary. He shall free you—and then—then!"

Gaston held the pale face off from him and searched the wide, startled eyes.

"And then?" The words fell into a question.

"But how"—Joyce panted; "how could I feel sure this great thing you plan is not another—unselfish act? Suppose, oh! suppose—*she*, that—that other girl—should come back—what then?"

"Hear me, Joyce. There is never going to be any one else. We are going back together—into that other life. Why, the possibility almost blinds me.

"They shall see what I've brought out of my experience. We'll make a place for ourselves and redeem the past. They shall seek us, my darling, and they shall see at last that I am master of my life!"

His enthusiasm and exaltation carried Joyce along with him.

"Dare I trust—not you—but myself?" she whispered. "After everything is said—I am—what I am!"

"Yes—you are what you are!" Gaston pressed his lips against her trembling mouth. "And now, good-bye!" he released her, and led her toward her door. "I must make a few preparations—then get to Filmer. It's all very wonderful, but it is more true than wonderful. Until I come, then—and it may take time, dear—you will remember?"

"Always—until you come—and after!"

Gaston bent again, but this time he only pressed his lips to the soft, pale hair.

When the door closed behind her; he stood for a moment dazed and bewildered. Mechanically he turned to the first task that lay at hand. He rebuilt the dead fire. It seemed symbolic, somehow, and he smiled. Then holding to the fancy that touched him, he piled on log after log.

There should be no lack of warmth and glow in the new reincarnation.

An hour later he left the house, with the needful things for his possible, long absence packed in a grip and flung across his shoulder.

He had attended to so many small comforts for Joyce—the fire, the writing out of directions, where to find money, etc.— that he had been hurried in the details of his own affairs; he had forgotten to take the key from the lock of the chest!

CHAPTER XIII

Jock Filmer was coming to the belief that there was a Destiny shaping *his* ends *roughly*, smooth-hew them as he had ever tried to do. Jock was pursued, there was no doubt of that. For reasons of his own he had drifted into St. Ange when very young. Most conveniently and soothingly memory and old habits dropped from him—they had clung tenaciously to Gaston. Jock adapted himself to circumstances and new environment with flattering promptness.

The Black Cat felt no resentment toward him after the first few months. His English became blurred with regard to grammar; the local speech was good enough for him. When Jock's Past became troublesome, as it had done from the very first, the Black Cat had consolation for its latest recruit; and, while he did not sink quite so far as some of the natives, the shortcoming was attributed more to youth than to the putting on of airifications, as Tate said.

In a boyish, off-hand way, Filmer had always regarded Gaston as a sign-board in an unexplored country. If things ever pressed too close, Filmer believed Gaston would point him to safety.

A mystic something held them together. A common interest, consciously cast into oblivion, but perfectly tangible and not to be denied, was the unspoken passport in their intercourse.

Later, during the building of Drew's bungalow and their joint sympathy for, and with, Joyce, Filmer had acknowledged

Gaston, as a superior and, spiritually, regarded him as a leader in an interesting adventure.

Gaston, the night when he faced Jude and him with the pointed question, "What you going to do about it?" had fallen from Jock's high opinion, and the crash had affected him to a painful extent.

"Oh! what's the good?" he had finally concluded.

Another friendship that had been formed in the lonely woods yet remained to him, and he made the most of that. Drew's personality had stirred Jock's emotions from the start. To look forward to a renewal of the companionship was a distinct pleasure in the time when the dust of Gaston's fallen image was blinding his eyes and smarting his heart.

Drew came, sick but unconquered. All the chivalry in Filmer rose to the call. He gave his time to the young minister. Using up the little money he had earned as builder, resigning his chance to go into camp, he devoted himself to Drew day and night. He became one of the family at the bungalow and a jocose familiarity was as much a part of Jock's liking for a person, as were his tireless patience and capacity for single-minded service.

Drew's maiden aunt, prim, proper and worldly-wise, was as much Aunt Sally to Filmer as she was to her niece and nephew. Jock jollied the aristocratic lady as freely as he did Drew, toward whom he held the tolerant admiration that he had given him from the beginning. But poor Jock was not to have his own easy planning of the new situation in all directions. Constance Drew took a hand in the game, and Jock, with trailing plume, plodded on behind her.

If *he* could gibe and tease, she could bring him about with her cool audacity and comical dignity.

The girl's splendid physique, her athletic tendencies, her

endurance and pluck, compelled Jock's masculine admiration. Her love for her brother, her tenderness and cheerfulness toward him, won his heart; but her mental make-up, her strange seriousness where her own private interests were concerned, caused the young fellow no end of amusement and delight. He had never seen any one in the least like her, and the new sensation held him captive.

Poor Jock! He was never again to walk through life without a chain and ball; but little he heeded that while he had strength and spirit to drag them.

With Drew's partial recovery the bungalow household lost its head a little. Aunt Sally's gratitude overflowed into every house in St. Ange. She felt as if the natives, not the pine-laded air, had been instrumental in this regained health and joyousness.

"I can never thank you enough," was her constant greeting; and so sincere was her gratitude that eventually the back doors of the squalid houses opened to her unconsciously—and of true friendship there is no greater proof in a primitive village. Sitting in their kitchens, it was easy for her to reach down into their hearts, and many a St. Ange woman poured her troubles into Aunt Sally's ears, and went forever after with uplifted head.

"Why, my dear," the old lady said to Ralph, after Peggy Falstar had taken her into her confidence, "these people are much like others, only they have the rough bark on. They are a great deal more vital—the bark has, somehow, kept the sap richer."

Drew laughed heartily.

"The polishing takes something away, Auntie," he replied. "The bark is hard to get through; it's tough and prickly and not always lovely, but it's the sap that counts in every case, and that's what I used to tell you and Connie. Every time I tapped these people up here, I saw and felt the rich possibilities."

"Now, you go straight to sleep," his aunt always commanded at that juncture.

She was not yet able to face the probability of a final settlement in these backwoods, but she saw with alarm that her nephew was planting his hopes deep and accepting the inevitable.

"It's all such a horrible sacrifice of his young life," she confided to Constance.

"His young life!" the girl had returned with a straight, clear look. "Why, I begin to think the only life he has, Auntie, is what St. Ange offers—he must take that or nothing. Oh! if only that little beast down there in New York had had the courage of a mouse, and the imagination of a mole, she might have made Ralph's life—this life—a thing to go thundering down into history! It's splendid up here! It's the sort of thing that makes your soul feel like something tangible. My!" And with that, on a certain mid-winter day, the young woman strode forth.

A long fur-lined coat protected her from the deceiving cold. The dryness of the air was misleading to a coast-bred girl. A dark red hood covered the ruddy, curly hair, and skin gloves gave warm shelter to the slim, white hands.

Down the snow-covered road Constance walked. She was tingling with the joy of her life—her life and the dear, new life given to her brother.

The pines pointed darkly to a sky so faultlessly blue that it seemed a June heirloom to a white winter.

The snow was crisp and smooth; a durable snow that must last until spring. It knew its business and what was expected of it, so it was not to be impressed by mere footsteps, or the touch of prowling beast.

Constance slid and tripped along. She sang snatches of old, remembered songs, and talked aloud for very fulness of heart and the sense of her Mission rising strong within her.

Since coming to St. Ange she had not, until now, had time to think of her Mission—her last Mission;—for Constance Drew was a connoisseur in Missions. But now she must waste no more time.

She patted her long pocket on the right-hand side—yes, the book and an assorted lot of pencils were there. She preferred pencils to fountain pens. The points were nicer to bite on, and she wasn't sure, in this climate, but that ink might freeze just when a soul-flight was about to land genius on a mountain-top.

There was a beautiful log halfway between the bungalow and Gaston's shack. It was a sheltered log, with a delectable hump on it where one could rest the base of one's spinal column when victory, in the form of inspiration, was about to perch.

Constance sought this log when long, ambitious thoughts possessed her. The snow had been removed, and a cushion of moss, also bare of snow, made a resting place for two small feet, warmly incased in woollen-lined "arctics."

Constance sat down and drew the red-covered book from her pocket, and placed the seven sharply-pointed pencils, side by side and near at hand.

A sound startled the girl. Her brow puckered. Even in the deep woods inspiration was not safe from intrusion.

Well, since some bothering person must take this time for appearing, Constance hoped it would be Joyce, for she wanted to see her and talk with her. Joyce did not invite intimacy. Up there alone in her shack, waiting for Gaston's return, she was grappling with matters too sacred and agonizing to permit of curious interruption. That Drew's family should overlook any

Harriet T. Comstock

little social shortcoming in her and seek to meet her on an equal footing, did not interest her in the least—she wanted to be alone, and for the most part she was.

But it was not Joyce who appeared on the road. It was Jock Filmer and he came, without invitation, to the log and put his foot on the end nearest the girl.

"Pleasant summer weather, hey?"

Constance raised her eyes from the little book in which she had been writing, and gave Jock the benefit of her honest inspection.

"If you had ever lived where winter was meted out to you in the form of frozen moisture," she said, "you'd know how to appreciate this nice, clean, undisguised cold."

"I know the other kind." Jock nodded reminiscently. "It is like being slapped in the face with a sheet wet with ice water, isn't it?"

"Ha! ha! so you haven't always lived here? I thought as much. Indeed I have a note to that effect—here." The girl tapped the red-covered book.

"No; I've travelled some," Jock confessed, "I've been to Hillcrest several times."

"I believe you are masquerading." Constance viewed him keenly. "I've written to my married sister about you all up here; I call you and that—that Mr. Gaston, the Masqueraders."

"So!" Jock smoothed his chin with his heavily gloved hand. "That sister of yours, doubtlessly, could spot us all on sight just by your description. It ain't safe. How's your aunt and the Reverend Kid?" Jock grinned amiably. The past weeks had given him time and opportunity for broadening his views of life and enjoyment.

"Ralph is fine"; the clear, gray eyes shone with the joy of the fact; "and Auntie is having the time of her life. You know she never had her lighter vein developed. Our city connection is awfully proper and cultivated. I always knew auntie was a Bohemian, and up here—she's plunging!"

"Umph! And you?"

"Oh! I'm getting—material."

"Excuse me." Jock passed his hand over his mouth. "There are times when I think you're a comicaller little cuss than your brother!"

"Mr. Filmer!"

"Oh, come down! Mr. Filmer don't go in the woods in the middle of winter. What do you want for your Christmas?"

"When you make fun of me"—the girl was trying hard not to laugh—"you anger me beyond—expression."

A guffaw greeted this. Then:

"What was you making in your little book when I came up?"

"Character sketches."

"Sho! Let's have a look. I like pictures."

"They're pen-pictures."

"All the same to me. Pencil, pen, or paint-brush."

"But you do not understand. They are *word* pictures. Descriptions, you know."

"Well, now you have got me! Show up, anyhow."

Constance opened the little book, and spread it out on her knee.

"I am getting material for a novel," she said impressively. "The great American novel has yet to be written. I do not want you to think me conceited, Jock, but I have had exceptional advantages—I may be the chosen one to write this—this great novel."

"Who knows?" Jock's serious gaze was a perfect disguise for his true inward state.

"Yes; who knows? You see I can speak freely to you."

"Sure thing," assented Jock. "Dumb animals can't blab, and once you turn your back on St. Ange I'll be a dumb beast all right!"

"My back will never be turned permanently on St. Ange, I think!" the girl spoke slowly. "I agree with Ralph that for the future his home will probably be here; and where Ralph is—"

"The lamb will surely come. Go on, child, and hang up your pictures." They both laughed now.

"First," Constance folded her hands over the open pages of her book, "I wonder, Jock, if you would like to hear—something of my life? It would explain this—this—great ambition of mine."

"Well," Jock drawled, "if you don't think me too young and innocent for such excitement, fire away. Histories have always had a hold on me. Most of 'em ain't true, but they tickle your imagination."

"Jock! But I'm in earnest. I have felt that I must have a confidant. Some one who will—sympathize. I'm going to have a woman friend in a day or so—but a man—one who is disinterested, so to speak, is always such a comfort to a girl when she faces a great epoch in her life."

Jock swallowed his rising mirth and his face became a blank so far as expression was concerned.

"I have had wonderful advantages," Constance began, "that is what makes me dare to hope. Advantages of wealth, society and—and a deep insight into people's innermost souls."

"Gosh!" Jock exploded; "excuse me; I always burst out that way when I'm—moved." He sat down on the end of the log, and clutched his knees in his strong arms. "Somehow you don't look like such a desperate character," he added blandly, "known sin and conquered it, and all the rest?"

Constance sniffed, but a little jocularity was not going to deter her from the luxury of confession.

"Money should only be regarded," she went on, "as a sacred trust, and a means of enriching one's life. And as for Society— that is a bore! Dances, theatres, dinners and luncheons. Chaperons tagging around after you, suggesting by their mere presence that, unless you're watched, you'll do something desperate in the wild desire to break the monotony. Well, I drank deep of *that* life," Constance looked dreamily over the stretch of meadow and pine-edged woods, all dazzling with a shimmer of icy snow, "before I took to—"

"Crime?" Jock suggested. "It would seem that that was the natural sequence to such a career."

"Jock Filmer—I took to philanthropy."

"As bad as that?" Jock roared with laughter.

"I only tell you this to explain my present position." Constance drew her fur-clad shoulders up. "I became a Settlement

Harriet T. Comstock

worker; but," confidently, "that was worse than Society. It *was* Society with another setting. 'Thanks be!' as Auntie says, I have a sense of humour and a remnant of Scotch canniness. It made me laugh—when it didn't make me ashamed—to put on a sort of livery—plain frock, you know, and go down to the Settlement in the most businesslike way to 'do' for those poor people. It cost an awful lot to run our Settlement, about two-thirds of all the money. One-third went to the poor. We had plenty of fun down there. All slummy outside and lovely things inside, you know. It was like making believe. You see," she paused impressively, "when you have a Mission like Settlement work, you don't have to have a chaperon."

"Ten to one, they're needed, though." Jock was keenly interested. "Cutting loose from familiar ties and acting up sort of detached that way, must have a queer effect upon some."

"Well, I just got enough of it. Why, one Christmas, we at the Settlement House had a tree and gifts that cost hundreds of dollars. We had a big dance. Evening dress and all the rest. Young men and women who, had they been in their own homes, would have been under some one's watchful eye, were having a jolly, good fling down there that Christmas Eve, I can tell you.

"Right in the middle of the evening, a call came from a family in a tenement around the corner. I knew all about them—or I thought I did—so I went. I just flung a cloak about me and ran off alone. Somehow I did not want any one with me."

Constance's eyes grew dim, and her under lip quivered.

"It was awful." Her voice sank low. "You see, with all the preparations going on at the Settlement House, we had sort of forgotten this—this family. They were not the noisy, begging kind, but there was a pitiful, little sick girl whom I had taken a liking to and to *think* that I should have forgotten her—and at that time, too! There was no tree in that home, Jock, there was nothing much, but the little dying girl and her mother.

"They didn't even blame me—oh, if they only had!" The honest tears ran down Constance's cheeks. "But they didn't. The mother said—and she apologized for troubling me, think of that!—that the baby wanted me to tell her a Christmas story. She just wouldn't go to sleep until I did, and she had been ailing all day. I—I forgot my dress, and tore off my cloak in that cold, empty room and I took that poor baby in my arms. Then—then the hardest part came—she—she didn't know me. She got the queerest little notion in her baby head—she—she thought I was an—angel. Oh! oh! and I wanted her to know me."

Down went the girlish head in the open pages of the character sketches.

"Well of all gol-durned nonsense!" Jock blurted out. "The whole blamed show oughter been exposed. I reckon the best job the company ever had to its credit was that happening of yours—the dress and the—the—rest of the picter. Lord!" Jock's feelings were running over as he looked upon the bowed head. The story had got hold of his tender heart. "Lord above! Just think of that sort of rum suffering going on back there. It's worse than what happens here. We've got wood to keep the kids warm in winter, and there's clean air and coolness in summer. I'm durned glad I cut it when"—he stopped short. Constance was looking at him with wide, questioning eyes.

"When I did," Jock added helplessly. "And now go on with that poor little child what you took to your bosom."

"That's all." Constance choked painfully. "The baby—died while I was telling her about the wonderful tree, and Santa Claus and the other joys she should have had, and never did have. I can see that hideous empty room, and—and that poor baby every time I shut my eyes."

"Here, look up now," Jock commanded, his feelings getting the best of him. "When life's so empty that you can't find

Harriet T. Comstock

things to do by opening your eyes, you better keep your eyes shut to all eternity. Calling up the past is the rottenest kind of folly in a world where things is happening."

Constance rallied to the stern call.

"And now," she said briskly, "I've given myself, heart and soul to—literature. I'll *write* of what I have seen, and lived!

"Listen, I'll read you a sketch or so. But first I'll explain. The local colour of my novel is drawn from—here."

Jock pulled himself together.

"Well, I'll be blowed!" he sympathetically ejaculated, "Here where there ain't, what you might say, enough local color to more than touch up the noses of the Black Catters."

"Jock! Now, see if you'd know it." She read a scrappy description of the village. "Would you recognize it?"

"With a footnote, it would go." Jock was all attention. "But I have my doubts as to whether Pete Falstar will take kindly to his place of residence being classified as a human pig-sty. That's laying the local colour on, with a whitewash brush, don't you think? A little dirt and disorder don't seem to call for such language."

"That is artistic license." Constance explained.

"Well, you ought to pay high for that kind of license—but maybe you do. Go on."

"I handle my subject without gloves," Constance began again.

"By gosh! I'd keep 'em on when I was tackling pig-stys and such; but don't mind me."

"And here; see if you can guess who this is?

"'The sleek, fat proprietor looked oily within and oily without. He oozed oil on the community that he was demoralizing with his poisonous whiskey and doctored beer.'"

"God bless and save us!" Jock rolled from side to side. "If you don't beat all for gol-durned sass. Why, Tate will sue you for damages if that great American novel ever strikes his vision. Oil! Thunderation; and poisonous whiskey, and doctored beer. Was it Society or Settlement what let light in on you, about such terms?"

"Neither. It's—inspiration."

"It's just plain imperdence, and it'll get you in trouble. Are you going to use names in that novel of yours?"

"Certainly not. Do you think I do not know my art? But you recognize Tate? Then he lives!"

"Good Lord! Know him? How under the everlasting firmament could I help knowing him? What other proprietor is there in St. Ange, you comical little bag of words? specially one as demoralizes the community with poisoned whiskey and doctored beer? Balls of fire! but this beats the band. Go on; go on."

When a man of thirty steps out of a starved exile and comes in contact with a girl like Constance Drew, it may be dangerous to "go on," but the exile will certainly *want* to.

Nothing loath; all sparkling and radiant, Constance swept along.

"And I've got—you, but maybe you will never forgive me. I took you at your—your worst—for don't you see when I use you—later—I'm going to redeem you and have you come out truly splendid."

Jock's jaw dropped, and the laugh fled from his overflowing eyes.

"Me?" he gasped. Constance nodded, and waved a pointed pencil toward him.

"Wait!" she ran her eye down the page. "'Beautiful woman— with a—Past'—that's the girl up in the other Masquerader's shack, that girl Joyce, you know, and Gaston—and here's Peggy Falstar—'woman sunk to man's level and reproducing her kind'—brief note of Billy Falstar as 'impish child'—oh! here you are!

"'Village Bacchus. Tall, handsome, but lost, apparently, to shame. Swaggering criss-cross down the road, laughing sensc-lessly and shouting songs. Slave to appetite. Controlled by his brutal passions. When spoken to in this state, assumes manner of gentleman. Subconscious self—study in heredity.—Let a strong influence enter his life—handsome noble girl—redemp-tion at end—splendid character.'"

"Good God!"

Constance dropped the book. The eyes that met her own had a look in them that drove the cold, which she had not felt before, to her very heart.

"What—what—is the matter?" she gasped.

"Did you—ever see me—like that?" The words came hoarsely.

"Yes. One day a few weeks ago. Ralph wanted you. I went to find you—and"—the girl's eyes dropped. She felt a sudden humiliation as if he had detected her reading his private letters.

"And I talked—rot and all the rest?"

"Yes. I never told Ralph; I knew it would hurt him—I had— no right to tell you this—it is only—copy for me."

"Copy?"

"Yes; stuff to work into the—novel."

"The novel? Ah, I remember. I'm going to be stuffed in with Tate and—and the others?"

"Yes; but don't you recall, *you* are to be redeemed—you are to be my—my hero—in the end you are to be—splendid."

A deep groan was the only reply to this; the groan and the look of growing misery on the man's face.

"You're to go back—you see I feel you once belonged some-where else—and take up your life-work with—"

"With?" Jock repeated the word hopelessly.

"With her—the girl."

"What girl?"

"Why the girl I'm going to create. First I thought I'd have her—Joyce; but that doesn't stand clear in my thought—I cannot quite see just the sort of girl—that could rouse you to—to great things."

Filmer was staring at the speaker with dazed and pitiful eyes. Then Constance beheld a miracle. The stony misery melted as an infinite sadness and pity overflowed.

Jock stood up, plunged his hands in his pockets and looked down at the dissecter who had bared every sensitive nerve in his heart and soul.

"When—you write that book," the words drawled out the bitter thought, "just omit—me—please—if you have any mercy."

"Jock!" Constance sprang to her feet. "Jock—how could I know that you would care?"

"You—couldn't, of course."

"Is it because I saw you so?"

"No."

"You know of course—that I'd never speak of that to any one—I only used it for my book."

"If that will help your book—take it; but leave out—"

"What?"

"The girl—the redemption—and—"

"Why?"

"Can't you—guess?"

"No." But as the word passed her lips, she did guess—and what she surmised sent the blood rushing through her body.

"Don't be frightened, Miss Drew," Filmer was getting command of himself; "there isn't going to be any redemption; nor any girl—that's all; don't you see? There never is in such cases, and you want to be true to life in that first, great American novel. You got your brush in the wrong pot of local colour when you daubed me. No offence intended, or taken, I hope. God bless you! strike your pencil through all that came after the spree part. You're welcome to that, but I decline to let you ruin your reputation by offering up the rest to the public."

He was laughing again, and the agony had passed from his careless face.

"And now?" he asked, "which way?"

"I'm going—home."

"Well, well, come along. I'm bound for the Reverend Kid myself. I've got his mail in my pockets—and yours, too by thunder! You're too diverting, Miss Drew, you took my thoughts off business. Come on."

CHAPTER XIV

Joyce, waiting in the solitude of the shack under the pines, heard and saw little of what was going on in St. Ange. She was living at high pressure, and she had not even the relief of companionship to divert her from her lonely vigils.

Naturally the exhilaration of the night that Gaston left her, passed and the dull monotony of the daily tasks performed perfunctorily with no charm of another's approbation and sharing, lost the power of holding her thoughts.

She ate, and made tidy the little house in quite the old way, but the large dreaming eyes looked beyond the narrow confines, and grew pathetic as they searched the white fields and hidden trails off toward the Northern and Southern Solitudes.

Which way had he gone? From which direction would he return? Everything was ready for him—it always had been since the night he left—and she, herself, once the daily routine was over, donned her prettiest garments, not the golden gown! and waited either by the glowing fire or by the little windows.

Early in the day following Gaston's departure, she had discovered the key in the lock of the chest! The sight for a moment, made her tremble.

Had he left it by mistake? Had he left it designedly, now that he had taken her completely into his confidence?

But had he? Joyce flushed and paled at the thought. After all, what had he really told her? She did not know, even, his true name nor the place from which he had come.

No; she knew very little. Shaken from his indifference by her beauty and charm into a realizing sense of the woman he had helped to form, Gaston had indeed broken his silence and voiced the one great tragedy of his life to her—and she had superbly stood the test; but that was all!

In the chest lay, perhaps the rest! His name; the name of those who had taken part in all that had gone before the terrible time of his trouble. For a moment a paralyzing temptation came to Joyce to solve for herself, by the means at hand, the mystery which still surrounded the man she loved with a completeness and abandon that controlled every thought and act of her life. But it was only a momentary weakness. Her love shielded her from any shortcoming that could possibly lower her.

Bravely she walked up to the chest, and proved herself by trying the lid to see if the chest were unlocked. It was. Gaston had not even taken that precaution.

Joyce smiled—all was now safe with her. She would never feel tempted again. It became a comfort to sit near the chest. She deserted the living room and made a huge fire upon Gaston's hearth. Evenings she took her book or sewing there, and the chest with its secrets seemed like a friend who, from very nearness of comradeship, had no need to speak its hidden thoughts.

In the desolation of the mid-winter loneliness, the pale woman grew to feel, when in Gaston's room, a high courage and strength. Everything would come out right. Details were not to be considered. Gaston had always been all-powerful; he would conquer now. What did the waiting count? He, meanwhile, was tracing Jude. Soon he would return, having freed her from every evil thing of the past. He would find her as he had left her—a woman fitted by a great love to follow whither he led.

　　　　　Harriet T. Comstock

And then—as the long evenings pressed silently cold and dark around the shack, her fancy ran riot. All that she had yearned for; all, all that the books had suggested, she was to see. Mountain peaks and roaring ocean; strange people like, yet so unlike, Gaston. To think that all this was going to happen to her—old Jared's little Joyce.

A few days after Gaston's departure Jock Filmer walked into the shack quite as easily as if months had not passed without a sight of him; he came almost daily afterward. It was like Jock to assume the new relation in this easy, companionable way.

Joyce was grateful. This was but another proof of Gaston's greatness.

"Everything going straight, Joyce?" The question came one day while the keen eyes were taking in the store of wood, water and other necessaries.

"Everything, Jock; and the store-room is stocked. Sit down— and tell me the news."

Joyce was not particularly interested, but it would put Jock at ease.

Jock gracefully flung himself into Gaston's chair. The two were, of course, in the living room.

"There's company up to the bungalow," he spoke from the fullness of his heart; "a widder girl."

"A—a widow?" Joyce was for a moment perplexed.

"Yes. She don't look a day older than Drew's sister, and she's powerful cheerful for an afflicted person. But maybe she ain't afflicted. They ain't, always. She looks as if she was dressing up in them togs for fun, and at first glimpse it strikes one as sacrilegious. Something like a kid using holy words in its play."

Joyce smiled. After all it was good to have the dear human touch, even if the vital spark were lacking.

"Is—the widow-girl pretty, Jock?" she asked in order to detain Filmer.

"Well," a line came between Jock's eyes, "that's the puzzler. Now Drew's sister—" Jock spoke in this detached way of Constance Drew for self-defense—"Drew's sister stands for what she is; a good, honest, handsome girl. You own up to that and that's the end of it. This one sets you thinking. Is she, or ain't she pretty? you keep putting to yourself. Do you like her, or don't you? Is she thinking about what you're saying, or ain't she? That's the way your mind works when you are with her, till it seems a plain waste of time, and riles you way down to the ground. I like a woman what, having passed up her personality, lets you alone as to further guessing 'less you have a mind to guess. Joyce!"

"Yes, Jock."

"They want you up to the bungalow to help along with the Christmas doings. I never saw such happenings in all my life. All St. Ange is going to see what's what for once. Presents for everybody; big party at the bungalow Christmas night; the overflow is going even to reach up to the camps. Boxes and barrels arriving every day from down the State. Lord, but you should see Tom Smith's curiosity! There are big doings. They call it a kind of thanksgiving for the Reverend Kid's recovery; and they want you."

Joyce started back. She was interested, but only as it was apart from herself.

"Oh, Jock!" she cried. "I couldn't. I just couldn't."

"I thought you couldn't," Jock returned calmly; "and you shan't if you don't want to."

Harriet T. Comstock

"Thank you. Don't let them feel hurt, but I could not go."

Jock cast a sympathetic glance toward her; and changed the subject.

"It's wonderful the grip that weak little Reverend has already got on this town," he went on. "He's a sly one. Preaching ain't in it with the undercurrent he's let loose here. It's just sapping the foundations of society. It's setting free a lot of good stuff, but it's striking Tate an all-fired blow."

"Tell me about it, Jock. It seems as if I had been asleep a— long while."

"Well there are sermons *and* sermons." Jock was flattered by the look in Joyce's large eyes. "If the Reverend Kid had opened shop in the regular way, Tate and his pals would have downed him in no time; but what you going to do about sermons that are slipped in with talks to women over their wash-tubs, and what not?

"Him and me was going by Falstar's the other day, and Peggy was washing uncommon hard. Drew, he steps close to the tubs and says he, 'I tell you, Mrs. Falstar, I don't know no better religion than getting the spots out instead of slighting them. It's like the little Scotch girl who said she knew when she got religion, for she had to sweep under the mats.' Peggy was all a-grin, and Lord! how she went at it. Later, she attacked the mats. It had set her thinking. I saw 'em hanging out, and she beating them as she must often feel like beating Pete." A real laugh greeted this, and Jock glowed with approval.

"And then what does that young lunger do, but gather in all the floating population in the kid line, and play games with 'em, and read thrillers to 'em up at the bungalow every evening. He's teaching them as wants to learn, too. He's got Tate flamgasted. You see, the old man depended, for the future, on them youngsters that haunted the tavern and got the drippings that fell from within. The Black Cat Tavern

Kindergarten is busted, and the Bungalow stock is going up."

"Kindergarten? What's that, Jock?"

"Oh, it's a new-fangled idea in the way of schools. Sort of breaking up the ground for later planting."

"Who told you about it?"

"Why—Drew's sister." Jock's face looked stern and he gazed into space.

"It's a splendid idea, Jock." Joyce's interest was keen enough now. "Some one, even St. Ange's folks, should have seen how fine it is to keep the children away from the tavern. How we have let everything drift! Why Jock, if the boys and girls learn to hate the Black Cat; if they are given something good, why of course St. Ange is going to be another kind of place. Does Miss Drew help in teaching?"

"Does she?" Poor Jock smiled pitifully in his effort to appear unconcerned. "They sit at her feet lost to everything but what she tells 'em. Billy Falstar, before he left to be a camp fiddler, was a reformed brat. She had smote him hip and thigh, and finished him, as far as a career of crime is concerned. Do you know, he went up to see her with his red hair plastered down with lard until it was a dull maroon colour; his square cotton handkercher was perfumed with kerosene, and I tell you he was a sight and a smell to remember; but Drew's sister stood it without a word. She told me afterward that it was a proof conclusive—them's her words—of Billy's redemption.

"I saw the brat the day he started for camp. I tell you the ginger was all out of Billy. When he was obliged to swear he did it in whispers."

"Poor Billy! He's pretty young to begin camp life. There's good in Billy. I wish Mr. Drew would make Peter send him to school."

"That's what he's planning to do."

Soon after this, when Jock started to go, he said: "So every-thing's fit for a spell?"

"Everything Jock, until—"

They looked at each other mutely. Then Jock put his hand out awkwardly and took Joyce's.

"Good-bye," he said quietly. His manner puzzled the girl.

"Life's a queer jamboree," he laughed lightly. "It's a heap easier to stand it if you give yourself the hope of cutting it if you find the pace too fast. So 'good-bye' is always in order even if you're going to drop in to-morrow. Good-bye."

Joyce walked with him to the door. "Good-bye," she said with a growing doubt in her heart; "good-bye, Jock—and I can never tell you how I thank you."

It was many a long day before Joyce was to see Filmer again, and she always felt that she knew it as she saw him pass beyond the pines after that "good-bye."

*   *   *   *   *

Perhaps it was the boyish longing for Christmas cheer that struck such a deadly blow at the heart of Billy, the fiddler, in Camp 7. Perhaps it was the arrow that smites all, sooner or later. Be that as it may, as Christmas drew near the mournful tunes Billy managed to saw from his fiddle got on to the nerves of the men.

From remarks aimed at his efforts, pieces of wood and articles of clothing were aimed at him, and Billy's life became a burden in the dull, deep woods.

"I can't make jigs come," he whined one evening, "when I'm

chock full of hymn tunes."

"You'll be chock full of cold lead if you fill this hull camp with them death dirges," warned one man who was bearing about all he could anyway.

"I wish to—I just wish I was plugged full of lead—and done for," was Billy's unlooked-for reply; and then, to the surprise of all, he bent his red curls over the fiddle and wept as only a homesick youngster can weep when the barriers of his fourteen years are down, and the flood has its way.

That night, Billy in his bunk, sleepless and consumed with longing for home and the excitement of the bungalow element, planned desertion. At midnight he crept to the larder and packed enough food to last for a couple of days, at four o'clock he stole from the sleeping-shed, and, cheered by the unanimous snores that rang in his ears, he turned his freckled, determined face toward St. Ange and the one absorbing passion of his life.

The outlook of the Solitude at four in the morning was not an altogether cheerful one even to ambitious youth. Indeed there was little, if any, outlook.

Blackness around; cold starlight overhead. Snow and ice everywhere except on the trail that a "V" plow had made through the forest.

It was cruelly still and lonely. "Gawd," said Billy raising his eyes to the emptiness above him, "you see me to the end of this, and, by gosh! I'll swear to go to Hillcrest to school."

From irreligious depravity, Billy had risen to reverent heights, and Hillcrest restraint was beautiful in his thought, as a method of preparing him for—Her.

A fear he had never known had birth in Billy's heart then as he slipped and slid down the icy trail that had been flooded and frozen for the passage of the logs. Even his unprotected boyhood had been shielded from four-o'clock journeys in the wintry woods heretofore.

The only help Billy could draw from the situation was, that so far he could refrain from whistling. When in this tense state a boy is reduced to whistling all hope for strength is gone.

A distant groan; swish! ah! ah! and crash! rent the stillness. The boy drew his breath in sharp.

"D—blast that tree!" gurgled he, "what did it have to fall for now?"

Suddenly a deer darted across the trail and turned its wondering eyes on the small brother of the woods. Billy's spirits rose. The wild things were friends. The boy's depravity had always been redeemed by a lack of cruelty.

A little farther on the way, Billy seated himself on a fallen log, and cheered his inner man by a "bite of breakfast." Presently a shy, wild creature drew near; took note and courage and scurried to Billy's feet. With generous hand the boy shared his early meal, and made a familiar noise that further won the little animal's confidence.

Billy had his plans well laid. There was a lumberman's hut a day's walk from the camp; he must make that by night. There would be a rough bed and chopped wood; he could sleep and rest and then, if all went well, he ought to make St. Ange by the end of the following day, particularly if he got a "lift," which was not impossible.

Just then, for the morning was beginning to show through the gaunt trees, a bird-note sounded. Billy rose quickly—there was no time to waste. Sometimes a bird sounded that warning when a storm was near. It would never do for him to face a storm so far from shelter.

All that day Billy trudged on. Fortunately it was a constant, though gradual, decline and the journey was made easier. He ate occasionally, and gained courage and strength, but it was nearly nine o'clock—though Billy was not aware of it—before the landmarks proved his hope true—the woodman's hut was near at hand.

The boy had all the keenness of his age and environment. He knew that others besides himself might avail themselves of the shelter, and he had reason for choosing his company; so, before he reached the house, he took to tip-toeing, and keeping clear of the underbrush.

The hut had one small window, before which hung a dilapidated shutter by a rusty hinge. The door opened, Billy knew, into a little passage from which the room door opened, and from which a rickety ladder led up to a loft, unused and apparently useless.

As the boy neared the house his trained senses detected the smell of fire and the sound of muffled voices. He crept to the window, and through the broken shutter saw two figures crouching by the blazing logs, but the faces were turned away, and the gloom of the room made it impossible for Billy to decide whether the men were familiars or strangers.

Meanwhile the wind was rising with a storm in its keeping; there was nothing to do but seek refuge, for, until he could determine his further course, Billy decided to take to the loft in order to reconnoitre.

Cautiously he made his way to the door, lifted the latch and gained the entry. There he paused, for the voices had ceased speaking and the boy feared that he had been heard. After a moment he concluded it was safer to be in the loft in case the men were suspicious, so he hurriedly mounted the ladder and crawled along the dusty floor of the space overhead.

Gratefully, to his half-frozen form, the heat from below rose,

Harriet T. Comstock

and with it came the odour of frying bacon, and the sound of sizzling fat.

Fortune was still further with Billy. There was a pile of discarded bedding and clothing on the floor. If worst came he could stay where he was and be partially comfortable.

As he reached this conclusion a voice from below caused his heart to stand still.

"I thought I'd seen the last of yer. You got all I had—what more do you want with me?"

It was Jude Lauzoon who spoke.

"See here, son"; and the smooth tones filled Billy with an old fear; "that was all a big mistake. My hand was out of the game. St. Ange had taken the nerve out of me. I've got my steam up now." It was Jared Birkdale! and Billy had hoped he was never to see the man again. From his babyhood up, a look from Jared had had power to quell him when a blow from another might fail.

"Well, I ain't got nothing more to give you." Jude sounded sullen and ugly.

Through a crack in the floor Billy could see that it was Jude who was preparing the evening meal, while Jared, as usual, was taking his ease, and discoursing at his leisure.

"You've got more to give than what you know Jude, my boy. What you doing here, anyway?"

"You see what I'm doing. Here, take this hunk of bread, and come nearer so I can flip the bacon on."

The sight and smell made Billy's mouth water, even while something in him foretold danger.

"Now, see here, Jude." Jared spoke through a full mouth. "You and me can't afford to work at cross purposes. Where we failed once, we are going to succeed next time."

"You darsn't show your face down there beyond the woods again, and you know it." Jude spoke doggedly. "They was after us both. Besides I can't stand transplanting. It would be the death of me. It nearly was."

"Don't be white-livered, Jude. You see the laws have changed more than any one could have thought, while I was browsing away in St. Ange. That's where I made my mistake. I ought to have taken time and got the lay of the land 'fore I beckoned to you; but it looked safe enough, and I had to take, or leave the Joint, sudden. How could any man know it was spotted, and so had to be got rid of? It was one on us and no mistake.

"Fill up my cup, Jude, you're a tasty one with cooking."

Jude obeyed and muttered as he did so: "Luck or no luck, I ain't got nothing, nor ever will have again, so that's an end of it."

"Jude, where you going to?"

"Where be you?"

Up aloft Billy waited.

"I'm going to St. Ange." There was defiance in Jude's tone—defiance and a sort of shame; Jude had again lost his grip.

"I've just come from there," said Jared.

And now Billy could see through his peephole that Jude started into life.

"You been there?"

Jared gurgled assent.

"How is—she?"

"That's it, Jude. Now let's get down to business. Having to hide somewhere after that little unpleasantness down State, I ran up to St. Ange. Knowing the way about, it was a better place than some others, and I could keep from sight and find things out. I stopped at Laval's haunted shack." Billy shivered. "I kept clear of my place."

"Guess you wasn't disturbed none at Laval's," sneered Jude and he gave an unpleasant laugh.

"'Twas blasted cold, and I had the devil's time getting enough at night to keep me going by day; but I learned a heap, and I struck your gold mine all right, sonny."

"What you mean? Spit it out."

Billy crouched closer, and his breath came thick and fast.

"He's—left her!"

"Gaston?" An ugly oath escaped Jude.

"Gaston. But not for what you think. Jude, he's after you." Jared paused for effect.

"After me?" The ugliness gave place to a dull fear.

"You, my son. He wants you to free Joyce." Evidently this announcement failed to reach Jude's intelligence.

"Free her? Me? What's got you, old man? Didn't she cut, herself?"

"You don't catch on, Jude. He wants to do the big, white thing by the girl—marry her out of hand clean and particular, and he wants to get your word that you won't make any trouble."

A silence followed this. Jude was struggling to digest it; but the result was simple.

"Well, by thunder! Won't he have to pay high for it?"

There was excitement and feverish energy in Jude's voice now.

"Maybe he'll fling a bone to you—but don't you see, son, you can hold off and make him pay, and pay and pay?

"Now tell me, so true as you live, what was *you* going down to St. Ange for?"

"I was going down to"—Jude hesitated. "Well, I was tired of being hounded, and having to hide and starve. I was going down to get—what—I could—and no questions asked." A foolish laugh followed. Beside Jared's subtlety, Jude seemed a babbling infant with feeble aims.

Jared was contemptuous.

"Gosh darn it, Jude! It's good I fell across your path again. You might have thrown away the one, great, shining opportunity of your life. Listen to *my* plans. You better stay where you are, and let me run this here show. I got the tracks all laid out. I'm sort o' inspired where it comes to plotting for them I love. I'm going to write a touching letter to her. It's going to state that Gaston is laid up from an accident in a hut, further up to the north. A lumberman is going to write the letter—catch on? and she's wanted up to Gaston's dying bedside. The lumberman is going to meet her at Laval's. When she's caught safe and sure, Jock Filmer—he's the go-between in all this—will get that information, or the part about her going away, to Gaston; then the game's in our hands. If Gaston means business, he'll pay what *we* say. If he ain't sharp set as to a big figger, we've got Joyce; and by thunder! who's got a better right? Then we'll make tracks, after the spring freshet, to another place I know of where laws is stationary and folks ain't over keen, and where a handsome woman like Joyce will help. I've got money enough left from the wreck to tide us over, my son—unless Gaston planks down."

All this completed Billy's demoralization. His teeth chattered louder, and for the life of him he could not control an audible sound, half sob, half sigh. But Jude was evidently as much overpowered as Billy, for the boy suddenly heard him emit an oath, and then a volley of questions designed to clear the air after Jared's storm of eloquence.

"She'll come, all right." Jared had his answers ready. "It's an all-fired queer state of things down there to St. Ange. You and me ain't never struck Gaston's kind before. Joyce'll go when he calls, and don't you forget it—all I've got to do is to make the lumberman's letter real convincing.

"Sure! I'm the lumberman, all right. Camp up north? Nothing. I'll land her here where her rightful and loving husband will be waiting for her till further developments. How did I find out the lay of the land? Gosh! that was a tight squeeze. I found out he was over to Hillcrest, Gaston you know; and I run up, after dark to his shack, planning to get a haul from Joyce. I got into the back kitchen while she was outside, and before I could get away—in walks Gaston. What I saw and heard that evening, Jude, ain't necessary here, but it blazed our trail, boy, and I cut later—taking more than I planned for." Birkdale breathed hard. "You leave Gaston to me, curse 'im!

"Make trouble for us? How in thunder is a man to make trouble for a husband who is taking his own wife to his dishonoured bosom? Lord! Jude, you've got about as much backbone as an angle worm.

"What?" Some muttered words followed that Billy could not catch. Then—

"Trust me! Does any one know to this day, you blamed fool,

who shot that government detective that was snooping into that clearing you and me made—five years back? Gaston'll pay or you'll take one of them never-failing shots of yours, and—"

It had been a hard day for Billy, and he was only fourteen.

The low, smoke-filled loft seemed to draw close about him, and it smothered the life out of him. He thought he screamed, but instead, an unseen power laid a kindly hand upon his trembling mouth, and a pause came in his troubled life. It was not sleep, nor was it faintness that struck like death the frightened boy—but an oblivion, from which he issued clear-headed and strengthened.

When he again realized his surroundings he was cramped and cold, and hungry as a wolf. From below two deep, unmusical snores rose comfortingly. There was but one thing to do—and Billy must prepare for it.

He ate every crumb of food that remained in his bag; then he rubbed himself until his numbness lessened. At last he was ready to set forth for St. Ange, and, be it forever to his glory, Billy the Redeemed, had only Joyce in mind when his grim little freckled face once more turned toward home!

Christmas, the joys of the bungalow, all, all were forgotten. It was a big and an awful thing he had on hand, but he must carry it out to the end. Floating gossip gained strength in Billy's memory as he trudged through the black morning of that second hard day.

Childhood was not much considered in St. Ange, but childhood protects itself to a certain degree, and Billy had never fully understood what the gossip about Joyce had meant. All at once he seemed to have become a man; and, oh! thank God, a man with a warm heart. A kinship of suffering and hope with Joyce made him wondrous tender. He'd stand by her. They should all see what he could do. And that hated Jared Birkdale should be driven forever from St. Ange.

Harriet T. Comstock

It was a long, dreary journey which Billy took that day. The plentiful morning meal had beggared the future, but it had given the boy power to start well.

With daylight and home in view, although at a dim distance, Billy felt that he controlled Fate.

It would be some days before Jared could possibly get the letter to Joyce. Long before it came he, Billy, would be on the spot, and nothing could pass unnoticed before his eyes.

At eight o'clock of that second day, the boy, worn to the verge of exhaustion, staggered into his mother's kitchen, and almost frightened Peggy to death by simply announcing:

"I've cut, and I'll be eternally busted if I ever go back, so there! And I'm starved."

With the latter information Peggy could deal; the former was beyond her. She prepared a satisfying repast for her son; noting, as she hovered over him, the change that had come. He was no longer a child, therefore he was to be respected. An awe possessed Peggy. The awe of Man as she had ever known him. Her Billy was a man! Then she noticed how thin he was, and how his mouth drooped, and how black the circles were under his big eyes.

Had they been cruel to him in camp? They could be so cruel; but then, Billy was a favourite.

What had happened?

It was proof of Billy's spiritual and physical change that Peggy did not cuff him and demand an explanation.

CHAPTER XV

Billy ate long and uninterruptedly. Peggy supplied his demands before they were voiced, and Maggie, the small and unimpressed sister, eyed him from across the table with keen, unsympathetic stare. Occasionally she made known her opinions with a calm, sisterly detachment that roused no resentment in the new being who had hurled himself upon them.

"You eat like a real pig," Maggie remarked with a sniff. She was being trained for the bungalow fete, and she had suffered in the process.

Billy eyed her indifferently.

"Push them 'taters nearer," was all he replied.

"Your father'll kill you," Peggy ventured timidly, as she filled Billy's cup for the fourth time with a concoction which passed in St. Ange for coffee, because Leon Tate so declared it.

"No, he won't, neither," Billy said; "nobody ain't ever going to kill me, never!"

He turned a tense, defiant face to his mother, but there was something in his eyes that drew tears to Peggy's. She came behind his chair and, half afraid, let her hand rest upon his thin shoulder.

Wonder of wonders! Billy did not shake off the unfamiliar

caress. On the contrary he smiled into the work-worn face above him.

"Ain't Billy terrible speckled when the tan's off?" Maggie broke in, "and his hair's as red as my flannel petticoat."

Peggy cast a threatening glance at her daughter.

"Clear off the table!" she commanded, for Billy was at last finished.

Maggie set about the task with relief. Something was afoot that she could not understand. Maggie was not spiritually constructed, but she was going to be a woman some day!

"Mother!" Generally Billy addressed her as "say!" "Mother, I'm going over to Hillcrest to school. I'm going to work when I can, and—make somewhat of myself."

Maggie dropped a cup, and, because she happened to be near her mother, Peggy relieved her own feelings by boxing the girl's ears. Then she turned again to her man-child and stared stupidly.

Poor downtrodden Peggy! She was at a crisis of motherhood that is common to high and low. Since Mary of Galilee found her son in the Temple questioning Wisdom, and with awe beheld that he was no longer her little child, the paralyzing question, "What have I to do with thee?" has set maternity back upon itself over and over again, in order that the suddenly arrived Man might be upon "his Father's business."

"Going to—make—something of yourself?"

Peggy's trembling hands groped feebly, and then, thank heaven! Billy drew near and glorified this new, but lonely place of his own creation.

"You've done your best, mother; I see it now, but I was—I

ain't going to say what I was—but I'm going to be something different; and you're going to help me now, like you always have."

A pain gripped Peggy's throat, and the room whirled about. Then the mist cleared from the dim eyes and Hope lighted them.

"Son," she said solemnly, "I am. I don't quite see how, but the way will be opened. Go in, now, and rest; you look clean done for."

It was humiliating, but Billy had to feel his way to the door of the bedchamber beyond.

Alone with her daughter, Peggy's Vision on the Mount faded.

"Billy's aged terrible," she said to Maggie, who was still sulking because of the boxed ear.

"I know what's the matter with him." Maggie's lynx-eyes glittered. "I found some po'try he writ on the back of the wood-shed door. He thought nobody but him ever went there. It's grand po'try."

Maggie struck an attitude, and drawled:

My heart feels like a chunk of rock
When I am far from you,
But when you trip acrost my vision
My heart melts same as du.

"I learned that in one morning!" Maggie proudly declared. "I don't care if he is my brother, that's grand."

Peggy dropped helplessly in her chair. She had never looked for glory in her modest dream. That Billy should escape the degradation of the Black Cat, and that Maggie might have a lighter cross than her own to carry, had been the most she had plead for when she had had time to pray; and now—why God had crowned her lot by children who were undoubtedly geniuses! Maggie, too, had a circle of light about her head. And it had all dawned upon Peggy in a flash of an eye.

"You ain't sick to your stomach, are you, mother?"

Peggy repudiated this with scorn.

"Maggie," she said softly, "I want that you should write that out real plain for me, in print. I'm going to take it up to the bungalow."

"Billy'll cuss us." Maggie turned coward.

"Oh! I ain't going to let Mr. Drew think Billy done it." Peggy was waxing bold. "I'm going to tell him it was writ by a noted po'try-maker, and I want to find out what his views is as to its fineness."

Maggie looked dubious.

"He might guess," she said.

"How *could* he?" Peggy raised her face ecstatically. Then Maggie came close to her mother.

"Ma," she whispered, "don't you know why Billy writ that, and why he wants to get learning, and what not?"

"No," gasped Peggy, and she felt that the heavens were about to open.

"He wants to be different so he can spark—her!"

"Spark?" Peggy panted inanely as if the word were of foreign tongue.

"Yep, spark."

"Her?"

"Yep. Her. Miss Drew."

Peggy's jaw dropped.

Since the sudden opening of the door, and Billy's unlooked-for entrance, events had crowded upon Peggy Falstar's horizon.

Her children had been translated. She felt desolate and stricken, although her heart glowed with pride as she viewed them from afar. In a last attempt to cling to her familiar attitude toward Maggie at least, Peggy vaguely remarked:

"I wonder if your being a girl makes you such a plain fool?"

"I 'spose it might," Maggie returned indifferently.

"Well," her mother continued, "don't you go upsetting Billy with any of your fool ideas."

"I ain't going to hurt 'im." Maggie tossed her head.

"Hurt him!" Peggy sniffed. "You lay this up for future hatching, Maggie Falstar. You, me, nor nobody ain't ever going to hurt him again and *know* it. What hurts he gets, from now on, he ain't going to howl about."

Just then the supposedly slumbering Billy came out of the inner room. Mother and sister eyed him critically. He was magnificently attired in all the meagre finery he could call into service. What he lacked in attire he made up in the grooming. Billy shone. Billy was plastered. Billy smelled to high heaven of soap and kerosene. But there was that about Billy which checked Maggie's ribald jeers, and the mother's question as to where he was going.

However, Billy was magnanimous in his power. He turned at the outer door and satisfied his mother's curiosity.

Harriet T. Comstock

"Anything you want sent up to Joyce's?"

"Joyce's?" gasped Maggie. "Joyce's?"

Billy held her with a glance.

"Joyce's," he repeated. Then receiving no reply, he went out into the still, cold night.

Billy felt like a man who held the fortune of many in the hollow of his hand.

Knowing the ways of St. Ange men he felt sure the letter from "the backwoodsman" to Joyce would be several days, or a week, in materializing, perhaps much longer. It was for him to be ready and watchful; but there was no immediate call for action. His sympathies were so largely aroused for Joyce, that he meant to overcome his yearning to be with the object of his passion, and on that first night he intended going to Gaston's shack and setting Joyce right about the future and his own part in the drama.

Billy realized that he must shield himself. Birkdale and Lauzoon must never know of his presence in the hut. Joyce, Billy felt sure, would cooeperate with him. If he and she could find Gaston, all might be safe and well; but while Gaston was absent, danger lurked. However, Joyce must refuse to meet "the backwoodsman"; after that they two, Billy and Joyce, must find a path that connected Gaston with them, and make him secure from the plots of the evil Birkdale and the weak, foolish Jude of the unerring shot.

All this Billy thought upon as he strode forward whistling comfortably, and his chest swelling proudly.

It was one thing to whistle on the highway of St. Ange, and quite another to whistle in the wilds of the North Solitude.

Billy was full of creature comfort, and the scattered lights of the houses gave cheer and a feeling of security to the boy.

The Black Cat's twinkling eyes had no charm for Billy. They were never to have a charm for him; but as he neared the bungalow his whistle grew intermittent and his legs had an inclination in one direction while his heart sternly bade him follow another. Then, without really being aware of his weakness, Billy found himself knocking on the bungalow door, and his heart thumped wildly beneath the old vest of his father's which he wore closely buttoned under the coat he had painfully outgrown.

In response to his knock, the wide, hospitable door was flung open, and Billy faced a stranger who quite unnerved him, by the direct and pointed question:

"Why, good evening, little boy; what do *you* want?"

The glow from within set Billy's senses in a mad whirl, but the "little boy" was like a dash of cold water to his pride and egotism.

"I—I—want—her!" Poor Billy was in a lost state.

"It is—I do believe it is my delectable Billy."

It was *her* voice, and it floated down to the boy at the gate of Paradise, from the top of a step-ladder. Halfway up the ladder Jock Filmer stood with his hands full of greens and his eyes full of laughter.

"Billy, come up and be welcomed. Get down Jock, you've had your turn."

His turn! A fierce hate rose in Billy's heart; but the stranger closed the door behind him; Aunt Sally and the minister were saying kind things to him, and informing him that the angel who had admitted him was Mrs. Dale, the Fairy of Christmas, and a great admirer of little boys.

Little boys! Were they bent on insulting him?

Jock descended with that laugh of his that always disturbed Billy's preconceived ideas. Then Billy was facing *Her* as she bent to meet him halfway.

The glad smile passed slowly from Constance Drew's face. The others, below, were talking and forgetting the two upon the ladder.

"Why—Billy—have you—been sick?"

"No, ma'am."

"Did they let you come home for Christmas?"

"No, ma'am. I jest cum."

Constance looked long at him, and at last the laugh was gone even from her dear eyes.

"Billy," she said softly, laying her hands on his shoulders, "you've been keeping your word to me, about swearing, and—and all the rest?"

"Yes'm."

"It's been hard, too, dear, I know; but it has made you into something—better." And then with a shining look on her face she bent and kissed him.

The heat rushed all over Billy's body, following a cold perspiration. His mouth twitched, and a maddening feeling of tears rose to his smarting eyes.

"I'm—going—over—to—Hillcrest school!" He whispered feebly, "I'm going—to get—learnin', an' things."

"Oh! Billy!"

"Yes'm."

"Oh! my dear Billy."

But such moments in life are brief. They are only permitted as propellers for all the other plain moments which are the common lot. Billy and Constance came down from the heights morally, spiritually and physically and joined the commonplace things below.

There was corn to pop, and candy to make. There were boxes to unpack, and goodies to eat; so was it any wonder that Joyce and her poor affairs should be relegated to a place outside this Eden?

Then, too, Jock complicated matters. He was shameless in his mirth and jokes. Even the stranger-lady with her wonderful aloofness could not daunt him, but Billy fiercely resented his attentions to the girl for whom he, Billy, had forsaken all else.

To leave the field to Jock was beyond the strength of mere man, so they stayed it out together, and left the bungalow in company just as the clock struck twelve.

It was then that the events of the past forty-eight hours began most to tell upon Billy. His exhausted nerves played him false, and cried out their desperate state.

As he and Jock left the warm, scented room behind them, and faced the white, still cold of an apparently dead St. Ange, the boy turned a drawn face upon Jock, and cried tremblingly, "Say, you better—keep—yer—hands—off!" Jock stood still, and returned Billy's agonized stare with one equally grim.

"I've just reached that conclusion myself, Billy," he said, with every trace of his past mirth gone.

Billy was hoisted on his own petard.

Hatred fled before the sympathy he felt flowing from Jock to him. He wanted to cry; wanted to fling himself upon his companion and "own up," but Jock anticipated all his emotions.

"See here, kid," he said in a voice new to St. Ange's knowledge of Jock; "you're not the fellow to grudge a poor devil an hour or so of heaven. There's the hope of an eternity of it for you; but for me there's going to be only—the memory of this hour. Shake hands, old man, and take this from me, straight. Keep yourself *fit* to touch. Lay hold of that and never let go. The more you care, the more you'll curse yourself, if you don't. It's the only decent offering a man can take to a woman. Everything else he can hope to gain afterward. A place for her, money, and all the rest; but if he goes to her with dirty hands and a heart full of shame, nothing can make up for it—nothing!

"Billy—I'd give you all I ever hoped to have here or hereafter if I could begin to-night where you are—and with the power to *want* to keep straight."

Billy shivered and looked dumbly, pathetically into the sad face above him. He had nothing to say. When Jock next spoke he was more like himself.

"Billy, will you see to a little business for me, and keep mum?"

This was quite in the line of the over-burdened Billy, and he accepted off-hand.

"I may—go—into camp before Christmas."

"Don't yer!" advised the boy magnanimously. "I ain't ever going to care again. You can stay here." Jock forbore to smile, but he laid his hand on Billy's shoulder.

"There's two big stacks of young pine trees up to my shack done round in bagging and ticketed to a place down the State.

They're Christmas trees for poor kids, and I want you to see to getting them off for me to-morrow or next day, and if Tom Smith airs any remarks, you let on as how they hailed from the bungalow; for that's God's truth, when all's told."

"They'll go, Jock, you bet!" Billy gulped.

Curiosity was dead within him. Human suffering gave him an insight that soared above idle questioning.

"And Billy, there's another thing. I want you to go to Gaston's shack; tote water and wood for Joyce—and keep your mouth shut. And lay this by in your constitution. Gaston is a man so far above anything God ever created round here, that you can't understand him, but you *can* try to chase off the dirty insects that want to sting him. Catch on?"

"Yes"; murmured Billy, while unfulfilled duty clutched his vitals with remorse.

"I'm—I'm going up to Gaston's to-morrow," he said.

"And now, you old rip," Filmer shook off his strange mood, "walk up to a fellow's bunk with him. It's good to keep clean company when you can—and for as long as you can."

"Shall—shall I stay all night with you?"

Billy asked this doubtfully from the new instinct that was stirring within him. For an instant a gleam of pleasure lighted Filmer's face. It almost seemed like a yearning, then he said roughly:

"No, get home! You're afraid? If you are I'll turn back."

"What you take me for?" Billy sniffed scornfully, and then they parted company.

* * * * *

Harriet T. Comstock

It was just when the hands of the clock in Drew's study pointed to half-past twelve, that the young master, sitting before the glowing logs, bestirred himself preparatory to turning in for the night.

A satisfied feeling had kept him up after the others had bade good night. He always enjoyed the anticlimax of pleasure, and the day had been a happy one.

He felt well. The companionship of the widowed wife of his closest friend, added interest to the new life in the woods. She had brought news and had awakened memories, but she had timed the Past and the Present to perfect measure. At last he could hope that the old wound was healed and that he could live among his people—his people! the thought thrilled him—with purpose and content. The rough men and women about him were drawing closer. He knew it in the innermost places of his heart. He was brightening their lives. He was holding their children for them, and opening a way for them to seek higher paths. It would all come out as he desired. It was a splendid field of work that had been given him—and he had rebelled so in his ignorance!

How he wished that Philip Dale could have lived to see and know. Of all the men whom he had known, Dale was the one man who could have comprehended this opening for service. What a noble fellow he had been! How his personality and charm struck one at the first glance. He had been one of those men who claimed friends as they came his way, without pledge of time or intimacy. He knew what was his own in life, and gripped it without question or explanation. He had been the first to understand Drew's ambition, so different from the ones of the social set in which they both moved.

"You'll always find me at your elbow, Drew," he had said, "in any scheme you start." But when the time came—Dale had slipped out of life as bravely and cheerfully as he had always lived. "And he had his own deep trouble," Drew mused as he prepared to bank the fire; "he never talked about it; but it made him what he was. One must go through some sort of fire to be of real service."

A light tap on the door startled him. He had been, in thought, far, far from St. Ange.

"Come!"

The door opened slowly and Ruth Dale entered.

She was all in white—a soft, long, trailing gown. Her hair had been loosened from the coronet, and fell in two shining braids over her shoulders. She looked very girlish as she came to the fire and dropped into a deep chair.

"Please put on more logs," she said softly. "Father Confessor, I've come to confess." There was something under the playfulness that touched Drew. "I told Connie that I wanted to talk to you about a plan of mine; well, so it is, but I want you to put the stamp of your sage approval upon it."

Drew shook his head.

"Hardly that," he said with a laugh, "but I'm willing to plot with you."

"I always think of you now," Ruth Dale continued, leaning toward the crackling logs, and holding her little benumbed hands open to the heat, "as 'the man who lives in his house by the side of the road, and is a friend to man'. Ralph, I need a friend! I must have one or I shall fail in that which I have set myself to do."

There was no lightness in the woman's manner now. She looked tragic; almost desperate.

Ralph Drew waited for her to go on. He was prepared to follow, but he could not lead.

Her youthfulness of appearance struck him now as it often had before; but the worn look in the eyes emphasized it to-night.

"You look tired, Ruth," he said kindly; "won't to-morrow— or"—for he saw it was well on toward one o'clock—"later in the day do?"

"Unless you are too weary to bide with me one little hour?" she replied wistfully; "it had better be now."

"You know what an owl I am, Ruth. With returning health my old habits seem to gain strength. I sleep more satisfactorily if I do it after midnight." He settled back comfortably in his chair, and the fire, encouraged by several small logs, rose to the occasion.

"I've been thinking about—Philip to-night."

"Poor girl. It was a year ago! To remember Phil best, we should be cheerful, but the subconscious sadness ran through all the evening's fun for you—and me, Ruth."

"Yes. Ralph, you only knew Phil a few years—never before he was married?"

"No, but he was one of those men who do not belong to time limit nor letters of introduction. His own knew him at a glance. There was no time to be lost with Phil. I've often noticed that faculty for deep and ready friendship among people who are here for only a short life. Others can afford to weigh and consider; they must garner quickly, and the Master seems to have equipped them."

"Ralph, was Phil a man that you felt you knew, really knew, I mean?"

"Yes; as to essentials. I never saw any one so positive as to the high lights. Honesty, truth, good faith, and a broad humanity. I always knew he had trouble that he did not talk about; he hinted that much to me once or twice, but the silence regarding it only intensified his own personality, of which he gave lavishly."

The woman bending toward the fire, shivered, and as her head sank lower, one shining braid of hair dropped forward, shielding her face.

"Ralph—I sometimes think the thing I have to do is the—hardest that ever woman had to do." The words were uttered with a moan that drove Drew into a silence more eloquent than any question he could have put. He realized that the woman beside him must tread the rough path of confession alone, and as she could. In his heart he prayed for strength to be beside her when all was done.

"If ever a sin saved, Philip's sin saved him, and yet he counted it as nothing at the last. He bade me do for him what he could not do for himself—I have never been able to begin until—to-night. He said—he had no right to friends nor the trust and favour of love. But he never was able to renounce them; I must strike them down one by one—now he is gone.

"I must do as he would have me do—I see the justice, if the end is to be obtained, but thank God, I, who loved him—can still love him—and he has been dead a year!"

The pain-racked eyes looked straight into Drew's with a sort of challenge. But Drew was too sincere a man to give, even to friendship, a blind comfort and assurance. He merely smiled at the troubled glance, and said quietly:

"I am sure where you loved, there was much to love."

"Yes; yes; that is true; and I begin to think the nobility of it all lay in his unconsciousness of the splendid character he builded so patiently and laboriously out of all the wreck.

"Philip had a brother, Ralph! His name was never spoken. He

Harriet T. Comstock

was two years older than Philip, and as different as it was possible for a brother to be.

"John was all strength and concentration; Philip all brightness and charm—in the beginning! Their mother adored Philip; she never understood John, and yet he was a good son, brave and faithful. But he could not show his nature—it lay so far below the surface. It was always easy for Philip. His charm attracted nearly everyone. My father always liked John better. He said there was splendid power in him, and—I must keep nothing from you, Ralph—I loved John—loved him, oh! how I loved him. I pitied him because he could not win what should have been his—I loved him for myself, and for all the others who were too dull to realize his worth. It was like mother love and all the rest, in one."

"Yes; the most God-like love of all. Only women know it, I fancy," Drew murmured.

"And then"; the agonized eyes seemed to plead even while they confessed, "then the awful thing happened. John took—he stole many thousands of dollars from men who trusted and honoured him."

"Ruth!"

"I could never have believed it, but he told me so himself. To the day of his death my father believed the half had never been told, but how could I think that, when John told me himself that he was guilty? Father was a judge—he was to have been the judge before whom John Dale was tried, but they relieved him of that horrible duty. John Dale was sentenced to five years—in prison! They said it was a light sentence."

"My God! Poor Phil! How terrible for you all!"

"Don't! don't!" Ruth Dale put out her hands as if warding off a blow. "Haven't you guessed? Can you not think?"

Drew shook his head slowly. He did not seem to be able to think at all.

"Mrs. Dale died soon after. She had a weak heart—it killed her. Philip was everything to her—he was heavenly good in his attention and devotion. Somehow, I wonder what you will think of me, but suddenly I became possessed with a passion for making happier them whom John had blighted. I grappled with my own love—I knew it would kill me if I let it gain power over me. I knew I never could be anything to John—I was not the sort of woman, Ralph, who could love the sinner—forgetting the sin. I could forgive—I thought I could—but I remembered all the more sharply.

"Philip had always loved me. I saw my way. I would ignore the stigma on the family, I would marry Philip and carry what joy I could to him and his mother. My father tried to restrain me. He called me martyr, sacrifice, and all the rest, but I married— and I know I took comfort into poor Mrs. Dale's life, and—I never doubted what I did for Philip. But—" Ruth whispered the horrible secret—"John Dale *took* the money for—Philip! He never wanted it for himself. He never used one dollar of it. It was Philip who ran the family honour, and his own, into danger—he made it seem to John that to tide him over the critical hour would be to save them all and bring no harm. But he was wrong. The crash came. John never cringed under the blow. To his simple nature the mere act was enough. He did not try to shield himself by one word of explanation—he went away!"

Drew's throat and eyes burned. He seemed to know all this like an oft-told tale that still had power to awe and control him.

"Then the years of agonized consecration began for Philip. I never knew until a week before his death, but the memory scorches into my soul day by day now.

"You see I thought it was love for his brother, and the shame,

Harriet T. Comstock

that had changed Philip—and *that* endeared him to me. All the lightness and carelessness of manner departed. A great, strong, tenderness took their place. But you know, it was so that he came into your life. He had a wide sympathy and charity, for all—oh! how it drew people to him. But think of his suffering—alone and through all those years!

"The money that was John's ruin was the force that brought success to Philip. You see—he could not explain—at least he thought he could not, he was too cowardly—and the knowledge spurred him on. Wealth flowed in and in. He paid, and with interest, all that had been taken. How the world praised him—and how he suffered as they applauded him! He gave great sums to charity—mostly to those charities that mitigate the misery of—the outcasts. Men and women who come under the law. Can you understand?"

"Yes! yes!" Drew's head was buried in his thin hands. His voice was full of anguish.

"They used to come to him, those sad creatures,—and he never turned them away. I have seen and heard them bless him as they knelt beside him. He helped them so wisely because—oh! because he was—one of them, and they never knew! Then the disease came—the cancer. I think he welcomed it—it was so sure to open the door for him—and I think he even loved the suffering as a kind of expiation.

"Never once did a murmur escape him of impatience or regret. It was he who cheered us. It was he who stood by my father's death-bed and comforted him, and strengthened me. Always cheerful, always helpful until—just before he went. When he knew the days were few—when the coward in him—his last enemy—died, he told me everything.

"He said—" a sob choked the words—"that I must find—John. I must lay waste the beautiful memory of him. Show the *coward* who had not been able to stand before men! I must redeem the past as best I could. I must begin with you—the friend he most loved—for you must help me find—John."

Ralph Drew rose weakly to his feet. Something had gone out of him. Something that he groped after, but could not grasp. He felt as if he and the stricken woman before him were lost upon a black and dangerous road. Their only salvation was to cling together spiritually and bodily. He caught the back of her chair for support, and bent over her.

"Is there no one, who kept in touch with—the brother? Was he utterly forsaken? God help him!"

"They said it was his desire. But there was one—I never knew who it was; that was part of the mystery—but some one claimed and claimed money for him, for John. I knew sums of money were paid regularly, I used to think it was another of Philip's charities—but I know now that there was a constant lash laid upon him. Oh! if they had only known all.

"Ralph, Philip left nearly all his fortune to his brother. There is only my portion reserved for me. So you see I must find him. I was left sole executor."

"I will help you, Ruth."

"I was sure you would. Philip spoke your name last; he said you could see the man he tried to be, even in the man he was."

"Yes! yes, a thousand times more than he ever hoped. What was the poor crumbling shell compared to the splendid soul that he builded through those horrible years? Years when he could not quite free himself from the craven thing that was his curse—the fear! fear! fear!"

The two were silent for a moment while the red glow showed them haggard and worn. Then it was the woman who spoke.

"Ralph—do you think a woman can love—really love—two men?"

He stared at her.

"Perhaps," he faltered; "perhaps, but in different ways."

"I loved them both. When—when I find John—if he wants me—if he asks me—I shall marry him." She shuddered.

"Ruth!"

"Yes; I think Philip would give him even—me. His renunciation was wide and deep. He, the great, strong soul of him, went on—alone. It had no real part with his weakness and all that was bound up in his weakness—he wanted John to have everything of which he had deprived him. You can understand, can you not? At the last, when fear had no further power, he was almost mad in his abandon of recompense.

"He did not tell me this, that awful night when he told me—the rest; but I felt it. I saw that I, with all else that had meant anything to him, was included in his shame; and the new nature that had evolved from the agony and remorse—had nothing to do with us any more!"

A deep sob shook the slim form. For a moment Ruth Dale rocked to and fro in her misery, then she let the wild confession again have its way.

"For myself—" the haunted eyes fixed themselves upon Drew's rigid face—"for myself—in a strange fashion—and oh! you shall *not* misunderstand me, I want to give to him that which I withheld from him when he needed it most. I want to bring back the gladness of life to him—if I can," she gasped; "it has all been such a hideous nightmare. If he wants me—if he wants me, he shall have me!" The words were flung out defiantly, fiercely.

Drew started to his feet, and went quickly to her. In all his life he had never seen on a woman's face such desperation and remorse.

As his friend's wife he had loved her as a sister. Her beauty had always fascinated and charmed him. To see her now, cast adrift on this troubled sea of love and fear, was a bitter, almost a terrifying sight.

He bent over her, and raised her face firmly and gently with one trembling hand. He felt that he must calm and steady her by physical control.

"Ruth," he said gently, but distinctly, "why do you look as you do? Tell me, what is in your heart?"

The woman tried to shrink from the hold he had upon her. He saw that the vital point of her confession she would keep from him unless he commanded, and, if the future were to be saved from the grip of the miserable past, he and she must thoroughly understand each other.

"Ruth, you must tell me everything."

She panted, but no longer struggled mentally or bodily.

"Because," she said, "even now, I could accept the man who was the true sinner easier than the man who was sinned against! Not because of a greater love; but because of the slime of the punishment that the one was doomed to suffer.

"That's what life has done for him—and me!" Again she shuddered. "Don't you see, even when my heart is breaking with love for him—and the old love is growing stronger as—as Philip seems to be going further from me—I shall always think of the hideous—detail that—he suffered. It was what Philip could not face—it is what I—must!"

The words came pantingly, grudgingly and full of soul-terror.

Drew sought for comfort to give to this poor, distracted woman whose white, still face rested in the hollow of his hand, like a dead thing.

Harriet T. Comstock

"Ruth, you shall not lash yourself unnecessarily. God knows you have borne the scourge of others bravely enough. It is not the detail alone that rises before you, and keeps you from what you have set up as your duty—it is the weakness of the man. That is the pitiful difference. The sin is the sin—but the man who *planned* was more the master, than he who became the slave. Do not blame yourself entirely—can you not see, it is the instinctive homage humanity pays to even an evil interpretation of the Creator!"

A blur, for an instant, shimmered over the beautiful, solemn eyes.

"No." The woman would not shield herself in this hour. "No; for you forget Philip's cowardice—and weakness. But he was not—smirched with society's remedy for wrong-doing. No; even if I found John had come out of the—the detail, strong and purified, I know, as God hears me, I should always, when most he needed me, see the *prisoner* instead of—him. Oh! Oh! Oh!"

She closed her eyes, and the great tears were pressed from under the quivering lids.

Drew for very pity released the suffering face, but his hand rested on the bent shoulder. Then out of the strain of the black hour, he asked a question that seemed to have no part in the present trouble; no meaning.

"Ruth have you ever loved just for yourself—just because *you* wanted what you loved?"

"Just for myself? Who ever does in this world, I wonder?"

She sighed deeply, and sank back in the chair.

It was over at last. There was nothing now to do but to take up her cross and follow as she could; there was no more to be said.

Drew waited for her a moment, still standing behind the chair. Then he spoke clearly and firmly:

"Ruth, in Phil's going he left our love to us; for we are permitted to remember the splendid man in spite of the weakness which crippled him. We must carry out every wish of his. I think when this is done—his brave soul will be free from every earthly stain. The good he did; the man he was, must claim recognition as well as the sin that stamped him. Both are actual and real.

"We'll find John Dale if he is to be found. We'll give him all that is his own—his own. But I pray God he is still man enough to claim no more.

"And now, go to bed. You may sleep safely, for you have made yourself ready even for—sacrifice."

"No! no! Ralph."

"Yes! yes!"

He opened the door of the study, and with bowed head she passed out. Then Drew turned and mechanically banked the fire, and left the room orderly, as was his habit.

As he followed a few moments later, the little clock struck the half-hour of one. Much had been lost and gained in an hour's time.

CHAPTER XVI

Billy arose the morning after his eventful evening, with a feeling of physical discomfort. He attributed it to his neglected duty, when in reality it was merely a disordered stomach.

The past day or two, ending in a feast of unwonted dainties, had created havoc with Billy's newly acquired, higher nature.

He was sulkily belligerent with Maggie, but Maggie viewed the lapse with considerable relief. Billy of the night before awed her in spite of herself. Billy of the morning after cast no reflections on her own inferiority.

Poor Peggy wondered, in her dull way, if she had been dreaming the astonishing things that had set her heart beating. To reassure herself she took a candle and went out to the wood-shed. No; there, in the dim shadows of the cobwebby place, was the stanza that was proof of her son's genius. Then Peggy reflected with a glad heart that it was the accepted belief of the world that geniuses were always cranky and uncomfortable, and, womanlike, Peggy gave thanks that it was permitted her to have a genius for her own.

Soon after breakfast Billy began his life work with a dull pain in the region of his heart.

He went up to Filmer's shack and found him out; he then hauled and pulled the tagged bundles of pine trees, which Jock had left standing by the door, down to the Station.

"What in the name"—Tom Smith paused to expectorate—"of all," (it is needless to enumerate the name of the gods by which Tom swore) "yer doing with them sapling pines?"

"Mind yer business," Billy returned, panting under the last load. "Put 'em on the train; that's you're lookout; and here's the money to pay for their ticket down State." Billy had found the money in an envelope tied to the trees.

"Well, I'll—be—blowed." Tom spelled out the address and took the money.

"Where does these hail from?" he asked.

"From the bungalow," Billy replied with unlooked-for promptness.

Tom had nothing more to say. The bungalow people had the right of way on the branch road. To and from the Junction the name of Drew was one to conjure with.

"I guess," Tom spat wide and far, "I guess she's aiming to decorate the hull blamed town, back there, with greens. She don't mind slashing, she don't."

"Shut up!" Billy commanded. Tom turned to look at the boy, who in the recent past had been his legitimate property, in common with others, to kick and swear at.

"Well by—" But he neither kicked nor swore at Billy. He relieved himself by expressing his feelings to inanimate objects.

Then Billy went up to the tavern. The dull pain was relaxing. The fine, cold air was clearing his muddled wits, and he felt the milk of human kindness reasserting itself in his new-born nature.

"Mr. Tate," he asked boldly, stepping behind the screen to the men's side. "Any letters here for Joyce?"

Tate, bending over a cask of beer, raised himself, and gave Billy the compliment of a long, hard stare.

"Your voice changing, Billy?" he asked blandly. "Gosh! you've growed up terrible suddint. What you doing home in the middle of the season?"

"Got—sick," Billy muttered quite truthfully. "Any letters for Joyce?"

"I don't keep letters on *this* side, son."

Tate felt compelled to cater to what he recognized in Billy. "And whoever heard of Joyce having letters? If you mean Gaston's mail she's sent for, then I reply straight and honest, and you can tell her—I know *my* business!

"When Gaston calls for his mail, he gets it. When he wants Joyce to have it—he's got to send order for same. The Government down to Washington, D.C., knowed who it was selecting when it chose Leon Tate for Postmaster.

"Billy, you've changed more in a few months than any one I ever seed. You—" he hesitated, and grinned foolishly—"you feel—like a drink o' anything?"

The subtle compliment to his manhood thrilled Billy; but oh! if Tate had only known to what that manhood was due.

"No, thank you," Billy replied, pulling his trousers up ecstatically. "I don't want nothing to drink—to-day. But won't you please look and see if there ain't a letter for Joyce—with her name to it?"

Tate walked around the screen, followed by Billy, and began fumbling in the row of slits that answered for letter-boxes.

"Bet she's expecting word from Gaston."

Tate moistened his dirty fingers, and shuffled the envelopes.

"Here's five or six for Gaston hisself—one done up with a broad streak of black round it. It's got a dreadful thick envelope! Well, if I ain't blowed. Here *is* one for Joyce, and did you ever?" Billy was beside him now. "Done in printing. Well, if that don't beat the Injuns. Mis' Joyce Lauzoon—that's good, Lauzoon! No wonder it didn't strike me first; I guess I read it Jude Lauzoon. Here, you want to tote it up the hill? Shouldn't wonder if it was *from* Jude. If he's got over his sulks, and finds no one to do for him, it's just like him to wheedle his woman into coming back and—beginning all over."

Billy had grasped the letter with trembling hands. He was breathing short and hard. Jared had evidently written the letter before talking to Jude.

"Do you know who that's from?" Tate eyed the boy suspiciously.

"How should I?" Billy impudently turned away, "*I* ain't Postmaster, am I?"

Tate glared after the fleeing figure. He did not like the sense of insecurity that pervaded St. Ange. If coming events cast their shadows before, then Tate's future looked as if it might be one encompassed by darkness.

When Billy reached Gaston's shack a silence of desolation pervaded it. Had all reputable St. Ange gone a-visiting?

Jock's absence, and now Joyce's, gave Billy a creepy feeling such as a cat must feel who has been deserted by them he trusted.

But there had been no fire in Filmer's shack; on Gaston's hearth a roaring, recently builded fire gave evidence of late companionship.

"Joyce!" called Billy. There was no reply. Then the boy opened the door leading into the lean-to. He had no reverence for retreats. If any door opened to Billy's hand, Billy's feet carried him further.

A fresh fire also blazed on the hearth of Gaston's sanctuary.

All at once Billy's childhood rose supreme over his recently gained moral viewpoint. Ever since he and the other St. Ange children had spied upon Gaston as a stranger, Gaston's possessions had filled their souls with curious wonder.

Maggie was responsible for the story about a certain chest.

"It's as big"—here Maggie had stretched truth to the snapping point—"as this! And it's all thick with iron strips, and it has a lock as big as my head. Once I saw him open it—I was in the next room—"

"What was in it?" St. Ange youth whispered.

"That's telling," Maggie had sniffed.

But after all the earthly wealth that St. Ange greed then held in the way of strings, old postage stamps, etc., had been laid at her feet, Maggie revealed what she had *not* seen.

"There's hundreds of dollars of gold. Umph! And candy and—and"—Maggie's imagination in those days had been awakened by Gaston's fairy-lore—"and a box tied up with a blood-stained cord! And a gun, and a knife, with queer spots on it, and things that made me turn sick as I looked!"

As Billy viewed the chest now—somewhat dwindled as to size—the old story moved him.

There was no low curiosity of a thieving kind in his feverish longing to test the truth of that old story of Maggie's. Money had no lure for him, candy he was surfeited with, but he'd chance much to get a glimpse of the box tied with the blood-stained cord, and the knife with the queer spots.

Joyce had apparently gone on an errand. Billy stepped back into the living room, then went to the wood-shed, and all around the house.

Perhaps she had gone to the store by a back path—she had a love for unfrequented places.

Billy returned to the shack, laid the letter on the table of the outer room, and tiptoed back to the lean-to.

The particular kind of thrill he experienced then was delicious. Quite different was it from the one that had driven him almost mad with fear as he listened to Jude and Birkdale a time back. This was a thriller that appealed to the familiar in him,—the impishness that died hard.

He went across to the chest and leaned over it. The fire crackled—and he leaped back! Then, loathing himself for his weakness, he knelt before the treasure trove and tried the key in the lock.

It turned easily, and the lid flew back; for the chest was filled to the brim. Several small articles, like letters, pictures and books, fell onto the floor; but Billy heeded them not. He was after bigger game. He tossed the contents hurriedly out. Maggie had lied foully—not a blood stain anywhere, nor knife, string, nor box! Not even a gun, nor candy nor gold dollars.

Billy's contempt for Maggie at that moment was too deep for expression.

Disappointedly he began to replace the poor trash that Gaston evidently prized—the last thing to put back was a photo-graph—and from sheer disappointment Billy was about to vent his disgust by tearing this in two, when the face riveted his attention. It was a face that once seen could never be forgotten. Pale and sweet it looked up at him. It was part of the clean, better life that he was trying to lead. It made him, all in the flash of an eye, see what a mean, low scamp he was to—

The outer door of the shack opened and shut! Hurrying feet ran across the floor of the living room, the lean-to door was flung back, and, all palpitating and wide-eyed, Joyce confronted the boy.

"You—Billy!" The glorious light died out of the big eyes, the pale, expectant face set into lines of hopeless disappointment. "I thought—" the mouth quivered pitifully, and Billy felt the added sting of discovered shame.

In a moment things steadied themselves, Joyce was mistress of the situation.

"What have you there?" she asked sharply. In the distraction she had not noticed that the chest was open.

"Her picture!"

"Her! Who?" Joyce came over to Billy, and looked at the face he held at arm's length.

Something numbed every sense but sight. That sense must convey the image of the girl-face to Joyce's brain, and implant it there so effectually that it could never be forgotten. And that very morning Joyce had seen its counterpart on the highway!

"Who—is—that?" she demanded.

"It's her up to the bungalow. They call her—Ruth. See! here it is writ on the back—'Ruth'; her other name is Mis' Dale."

The face was burned in now for all time; and the other faculties began to throb into life.

"Billy, where did you get that?"

Then both boy and woman looked at the desecrated chest—and all was told.

Even while she was wildly pushing facts from her, Joyce saw, rising before her, a completed structure of John Gaston's past.

That exquisite girl was she who had held his love before—and she had married the brother! Then Gaston's name was Dale. Oh! how vividly, hideously clear it was. It seemed as if she had always known it. Even the pictured face was as familiar now as Gaston's own. But Joyce's cold lips were forming the words:

"Billy you lie! You brought that over to show me. Tell me the truth." She had him by the shoulder, and her fierce eyes frightened him.

"I have told you the truth; so help me! There she is now; look!"

Joyce turned as Billy pointed to the window.

Outside, near the grave of *her* baby, stood Constance Drew and the girl whose picture Billy held limply in his hand.

Constance Drew was talking, but the stranger's sweet face was turned toward the house, and Joyce saw that her eyes were full of tears.

"Billy"; Joyce clutched the thin shoulder; "put that back! Now lock the chest, and listen. If you ever tell a living soul what you have done—Mr. Gaston will—kill you!"

Billy obeyed with dumb fear.

"Now, go out of the shed door. Go—don't let them see you!"

Billy was gone, forgetting even to mention the letter lying on the living-room table.

Then Joyce waited. Out in front, they two—Miss Drew and

Harriet T. Comstock

that girl—seemed rooted to the spot near the baby's grave.

Feeling had departed from Joyce—she simply waited.

Finally they, outside, turned. They walked directly to the house, and knocked. They knocked again.

"It's etiquette to go in, if the house is empty." It was Constance Drew's voice. "St. Ange and New York have different ideas. Leave things as you find them, that's the only social commandment here." A hand was on the latch.

"Connie, I cannot! It does not seem decent." *That* voice sank deep into the listening heart behind the barrier.

"Well, then, I'll write her a letter. I'm sorry I asked Jock Filmer to take a verbal invitation. She might think—"

"That's better, Connie, and while you and Ralph drive over to Hillcrest this afternoon, I'll bring it here; perhaps she will be at home then."

Joyce heard them turn. She watched them until the pine trees hid them; then her heart beat feebly.

Presently she went to the table, and there her eyes fell on the letter Billy had brought. Quietly she took it up, opened it, and read it once, twice, then the third time.

Finally it dropped to her feet, and, with hands groping before her, Joyce staggered to Gaston's deep chair and fell heavily into it.

CHAPTER XVII

Joyce did not faint, nor did she lose consciousness. A dull quiet possessed her, and, had she tried to explain her state of mind, she would have said she was thinking things out.

In reality Destiny, or whatever we choose to call that power which controls things that *must be*, had the woman completely in its grip. Whatever she was to do would be done without any actual forethought or preparation; she would realize that afterward as we all do when we have passed through a crisis and have done better, perhaps, than our poor, unassisted thought might have accomplished for us.

Joyce was on the wheel, and the wheel was going at a tremendous speed. There was no time for plotting or planning, with all the strength that was in her, the girl was clinging, clinging to some unseen, central truth, while she was being whirled through a still place crowded with more or less distinguishable facts that she dared not close her eyes to.

One cruel thing made her cringe in the deep chair. She was losing her clear, sweet vision of that blessed night when Gaston and she had stood transfigured! If only she could have held to that, all would have been so simple—but with that fading glory gone she would be alone in a barren, cheerless place to act not merely for herself, but for Gaston also.

She was no longer the beautiful woman in the golden dress; nor he the man of the illumined face and pleading arms. No;

Harriet T. Comstock

she was old Jared's wild little daughter; Jude Lauzoon's bruta-
lized and dishonoured wife. Nothing, nothing could do away
with those awful facts.

He, the man she loved—who thought in one wild hour that he
loved her—was not of her world nor of her kind. He had
given, given, given to her of his best and purest. God! how he
had given. He had cast a glamour over her crudeness by his
power and goodness, but underneath was—Jared's daughter
and Jude's wife.

If he took her courageously back to his world they, those
others like, yet unlike him, would see easily through the
disguise, and would be quick enough to make both him and
her feel it.

Without her, they would accept him. The past would be as if it
had not been; but if he brought her to them from his past, it
would be like an insult to them—an insult they would never
forgive. And then—he would have no life; no place. He would
have to go on being kind and good to her in a greater loneliness and desolation than St. Ange had ever known.

She could not escape the responsibility of her part in his life.
She might keep on taking, taking, taking. On the other hand
his old life had come back to him, not even waiting for his
choice.

The woman who had misunderstood, had failed him in that
hour of his need, had been sent by an all-powerful Force into
the heart of the Northern Solitude to reclaim him, now that he
had accomplished that which he had set himself to do.

Every barrier was removed. Even Death had been kind to that
sweet, pale girl—she was ready to perform the glorious act of
returning Gaston's own to him, if only she, Joyce, would let go
her selfish, ignoble hold.

Now, if she were as noble as Gaston had striven to make her, there was but one thing to do. Go to that woman up at the bungalow, tell her all that she did *not* know. All about the heavy penalty weakness had paid for the crime committed by another. Tell of the splendid expiation and the hard-won victory, and then—let go her hold and, in Love's supreme renunciation, prove her worthiness to what God withheld.

The little living room of Gaston's shack was the battle-ground of Joyce's soul-conflict that winter day.

Pale and rigid, she crouched in the deep chair, her head buried on the arm where so often his dear hand had lain.

No; she could not! She would not! Then after a moment—"I must! or in all the future I shall hate myself." Then she grew calmer, and instinctively she began to plan about—going. She would leave both fires ready to light—he might come now at any time.

The letter Billy had brought had not for a moment deceived her. She counted it now as but one of the links in the chain that was dragging her away from Gaston.

It was either Jude or her father who had sent the note. Well, it did not matter, it was the best possible escape that could have been conceived.

Then her plans ran on. She would pack her own pretty things—out of sight! They must not confuse, or call for pity. There would be no note. She, that woman at the bungalow would explain, and would tell him that there could be no reconsideration, for she, Joyce, had gone to her—husband!

At that point Joyce sprang up, and her eyes blazed feverishly.

No; she was going to do no such thing. She was going to wait just where she was with folded hands and eager love. When Gaston came he should decide things. She would not interfere with her future. She would hide nothing; neither would she disclose anything. Why should she strangle her own life, with the knowledge she had neither sought nor desired?

The brilliant afternoon sun crept toward the west, and it shone into the side window and through the screen of splendid fuchsias which clambered from sill to top of casement.

Gaston might come—now! Perhaps he had failed to locate Jude, and would return to consider. Well, then, she could put him on Jude's trail. Gaston, not she, should meet the "woodsman" in Lola Laval's deserted house.

In the sudden up-springing of this hope, Joyce quite forgot the face of the woman at the bungalow.

A freakish yearning to reproduce the one crowning moment of her life possessed the girl.

She would build a great fire upon the hearth, and make the room beautiful. She would don—the yellow gown, and, if he came, he should find her as he had left her.

If he still loved her—and she saw it in his eyes—then nothing, nothing should part them.

She would go with him to Lola's house and together they would finish the dreary search. She would beg him never to return to St. Ange. What did the world matter, the people of the world? Nothing mattered but him and her.

So Joyce flew to the bidding of her mad fancy. She drew the shades and flung on log after log. She swept and dusted the room. Put Gaston's slippers and house-coat close to the warmth. She lighted the lamp to keep up the delusion, then stole to her room and made ready.

Again, as the garments of the daily task fell from her, Joyce felt the sordidness and fearsomeness depart.

The lovely hair lent itself to the pretty design, and the golden gown transfigured the wearer.

She felt sure Gaston was coming. The premonition grew and grew. He would never leave her to bear the Christmas alone. He might return later to search for Jude but, remembering her in the shack, he would come to her for that one, holy day.

He would surprise her. And she?—why, she would surprise him.

How he would laugh and take her in his arms!—for it was all clear ahead of them now. She would lead him to Jude!

A knock at the outer door startled her. She was about to leave her bedchamber complete and beautiful—but the summons stayed the little satin-shod feet, and the colour left the quivering face.

Perhaps Gaston had knocked to keep up the conceit of his home-coming surprise!

Tiptoeing across the living room, Joyce took her stand by the table and called timidly, expectantly and awesomely:

"Come."

The latch lifted and some one pressed against the door, and then, in walked Ruth Dale.

She wore the heavy crimson cloak of Constance's, the fur-trimmed hood of which encircled her face.

Coming from the outer sunlight into the lamp-lighted room, Ruth Dale stood for a moment, dazzled and confused. Then her grave, kindly eyes were riveted upon the splendid, straight young form confronting her.

Never in her life had Ruth Dale been so utterly confounded

and taken aback. For a full moment the two faced each other in solemn silence. It was Joyce who spoke.

"I heard you say you were coming. I was in when you and Miss Drew called before, but I wasn't ready for company then. Won't you sit down?"

Mrs. Dale sank into the nearest chair from sheer helplessness.

"Please take off your cloak. The room is very warm."

It was stifling, and Ruth Dale unfastened and let fall the heavy fur-lined wrap.

Joyce took Gaston's chair. The contact seemed to strengthen her.

"Miss Drew—has—sent—this note." Ruth held it out helplessly.

"Thank you. I know what is in it; but I cannot come. I am going away." The proffered note fluttered to the floor.

"Going away?"

"Yes." The word was almost agonizing in its intensity. "Yes!"

"Please—Mrs. Lauzoon," Ruth Dale stammered the name; "please may I hear where you are going? My friends are so interested in you. I—I—am sorry for you. We could not bear to have you lonely and sad here—on Christmas—but if you are going away to be—happy, we will all be so glad."

"Please tell Mr. Drew," Joyce clutched the arms of the chair, and Ruth Dale continued to stare helplessly at the exquisite beauty of this mountain girl, "tell Mr. Drew—I am—going— to my husband."

"Your husband!"

"Yes; he will be so glad, Mr. Drew will. He has always been so—good. Tell him, please—and I think he will understand—that he made it possible for me—to do this—thing."

The human agony contained in these words carried all before it. Ruth Dale got up from her chair, and almost ran across the room to Joyce's side. She leaned over her and a wave of pity seemed to bear the two women along to a point where words—words from the heart—were possible.

"I—I have heard your story, dear. Ralph Drew is such a kind *gentleman*, and he—we, all of us—pity you from the bottom of our hearts. Believe me, you are doing the right thing, hard and cruel as it may seem now. When God sets you free—then alone can you really be free. I think every good woman knows this. Man can only give freedom within limitations. I know I am right. Have you heard from—your husband?"

"Yes. He has sent for me."

"Have you any message to leave? I will tell Mr. Drew anything you care to entrust to me—he will deliver the message to—any one."

"Please—sit down." Joyce motioned stiffly to a chair across the table. "I have a great deal to say to you."

Ruth obeyed with a dull foreboding in her heart. She felt constrained and awkward. The unusual and expensive gown Joyce wore acted as an irritant upon her, now that she considered it. It seemed so vulgar, so theatrical for the girl to deck herself in this fashion; and the very gown itself spoke volumes against any such lofty ideals as Ralph Drew had depicted in the woman. Evidently Joyce was expecting Gaston back; the statement as to her going to her husband was either false, or a subterfuge.

With Ruth Dale's discomfort, too, was mingled a fear that Gaston might return and find her there. From Drew's description of Gaston she knew he was a person above the ordinary St. Ange type, and might naturally, and rightly, resent her visit. But Joyce, more mistress of the situation than the other knew, was feeling her way through the densest thicket of trouble that had ever surrounded her. Here was her chance, in woman-fashion, to test that strange double code of honour about which Gaston had spoken, and Drew had hinted. Here, woman to woman, she could question and probe, and so have clearer vision.

This woman visitor was from his world. She was kind and was, perhaps, the best that existed down beyond the Southern Solitude. If she bore the test, then Joyce would relinquish her rights absolutely—but only after that woman knew why she did so.

"I—I suppose you think I have been a very bad woman?" Joyce turned sad, yet childlike eyes upon her companion.

"I think you have acted unwisely." Ruth Dale crimsoned under the steady glance. "You see, Mr. Drew has always had a deep interest in you. His sister and I heard about you long before we came up here. He says you had grave provocation. What you have done was done—in ignorance. It would only be sin— after you knew the difference."

"I see. But what—what would you think about Mr. Gaston?"

The colour died from Ruth's face, only to return more vivid.

"I think he has treated you—shamefully. He knew how such things are viewed. He took advantage of your weakness and innocence. I hate to say this to you—but I have no two opinions about such things. I think this Mr. Gaston must be a very wicked man."

A sudden resolve had sprung up in Ruth's mind. If she could rescue this poor, ignorant girl from the toils of the man who had misled her, she would befriend her. She might even save

her from the depraved husband who was now her only apparent safety. The girl was lovely beyond expression. It would be
a splendid thing to do.

With this in sight, her interference took on an appearance of
dignified philanthropy.

"Will you let me help you?" she asked wistfully; "be your
friend? I have money; I would love to do what I can. I have
deep sympathy with you and—I am very lonely and sad
myself. I have recently lost my husband—I have no one."

Joyce continued to hold her visitor with that solemn, intense
glance.

"You loved your—husband—very much?" Ruth winced. She
could hardly resent the curiosity, but she stiffened.

"Of course. But if I had not, I should have been—lonely and
sad. It is a relationship that cannot be dissolved either by death
or in any way without causing pain and a deep sense of loss."

"Oh, yes, it can." Joyce spoke rapidly. "The loss may mean—
life to you. It may take fear away and a hideous loathing. It
may let you be yourself, the self that can breathe and learn to
love goodness."

This outburst surprised and confused Ruth Dale. The expression of face, voice and language swept away the sense of
unreality and detachment. Here was a vital trouble. A tangible
human call. It might be that she, instead of Ralph Drew or
Constance, or any other person, might touch and rescue this
girl who was finding herself among the ruins of her life.

Ruth Dale was no common egotist, but her charm and magnetism had often taken her close to others' needs, and she was
eager, always, to answer any demand made upon her.

"Joyce," she said softly, "please let me call you that. You see, by

Harriet T. Comstock

that name I have always heard you called, and Constance Drew and I felt we knew you before we saw you. I believe you have suffered horribly. All women suffer in an unhappy marriage—but you suffered doubly because you have always been capable of better things, perhaps, than you have ever had. You do not mind my speaking very plainly?"

"No. I want you to."

"But you cannot find happiness—I know I am right about this—by taking from life what does not really belong to you. Do you see what I mean?"

"No, but go on; I may see soon." The quiet face opposite made Ruth Dale more and more uncomfortable. She had, for a moment, forgotten the possibility of Gaston's return; the yellow gown was losing its irritating power; she truly had a great and consuming desire to be of service to this woman who was following her words with feverish intensity, but she was ill at ease as she proceeded.

"If we have bungled our lives, made grave mistakes, it's better to abide by them courageously than defy—well, the accepted laws.

"Perhaps you ought not go back to your husband; I would not dare decide that; Ralph Drew would know, but this I know, you should not stay here. I will befriend you, Joyce, in whatever other course you choose. Please let me help you; it would help me."

She stretched her pretty, pleading hands across the table, and her eyes were full of tears. She felt old, and worldly-wise beside this mountain girl, and she was adrift on the alluring sea of personal service.

Joyce took no heed of the waiting hands, the inspired face held her.

"Don't you see, Joyce, even if this is love that controls you, you would not want it to be selfish?"

"No. Oh! No."

"What do you know of this man Gaston, really? Mr. Drew says he is quite different from the people hereabout. You do not even know the true man, his name, nor antecedents. The time may come when he will return to his former life, whatever it was; can you not see how you would—interfere with such a plan? If he left you—what would he leave you to? And if he were one of a thousand and took you with him—what then? In either case it would mean your unhappiness and his— shame."

Joyce winced, and Ruth Dale saw the hands clutch the arms of the chair. She felt that she was making an impression, and her ardour grew.

"I do not know Gaston," she went on, "but I do know the world; and for women placed as you are, Joyce, there is no alternative. Your very love should urge you to accept the situation, hard as it may seem."

"It does." For a moment the lovely head drooped and the white lids quivered over the pain-filled eyes.

"No matter how—good a man—this Mr. Gaston has been to you—he knew the price you would have to pay some day. He has been either wilfully weak—or worse. A man takes a mean advantage of a woman in all such matters. It is not a question of right or wrong altogether—it isn't fair.

"I have burned over such things ever since I was a girl—I am ready now to prove to you my desire to help you. Will you let me, Joyce?"

"You are very, very good. I can see you are better and kinder than any other woman I ever knew. I believe all that you say is true. If I did not think that, I could not do what I am going to do."

Joyce spoke very quietly, very simply. She was not even confused when she poured out the deepest secrets of her heart. She was worn and spent; loneliness, conflict and soul-torture had torn down all her defenses.

"You are right in all that you have said—but you don't know all!" The flame rose in the pallid face; "but if you did, the truth of what you have said would be all the deeper.

"My love has been a selfish one because I never thought it lay in my power to do anything for—him. I see there is something now that I can do—and I mean to do it so thoroughly that even his goodness cannot prevent. He is so very, very good; oh! if you could only know him as I know him!

"I am—going to my husband, then—that will finish it! But I must tell you something—first."

Joyce caught her breath, and she sat up straight and rigid.

"I suppose in your life you could not believe that a man like Mr. Gaston could be just good to me—and nothing else?"

Woman looked at woman. The world's woman noted the beauty and tender grace of the unworldly woman, and her eyes fell.

"It would be difficult to believe that. I have heard of such cases—I never knew one—and for that very reason of unbelief, it does not greatly matter—the outcome would be the same— for the woman and the man."

"Yes; but they would know, and God would know; might that not be enough?"

"No. Believe me—it would not be enough."

"Do you believe me when I tell you that, in this case, it is true?"

Again the two held each other in a long challenge. Then:

"Joyce, as God hears me, I *do* believe you. Now I am more eager than ever to be your friend."

"You—cannot be mine—but you must be his!"

"His?" Ruth started back.

"Yes. I do know—something of his life. He belonged—to your world. He had a great, a terrible trouble—but through it all he saw the stars, not the mud, and he came out of it—a strong, tender, brave man."

A dull sob shook the low, sweet voice.

"All the shameful sorrow served as a purpose to make him noble—and splendid; but his soul was sad and hurt. He never blamed any one, though there were others who should have suffered more than he. He just gave himself up to the chance of gaining good out of all the evil. Then he came here—to rest. But he could not help being kind and helpful. He found—me. He taught me, he gave me hope and showed me—how to live. Oh! you can never understand. You have always had life—I never had it until he took the blindness from me.

"He tried to do the best for me—he wanted me to marry Jude Lauzoon. He tried to make Jude good, too—but that was more than even *he* could accomplish. Then I'm—afraid I cannot tell you—this it might—soil your soul."

"Go on." Ruth spoke hoarsely. She was spellbound and a deathly coldness crept over her.

"Well, Jude dragged all of me down, down, down—all of me but the part that—Mr. Gaston had made. That part clung to him as if he were its God."

"I see, I see. Go on!"

"It was all low—and evil, that life with Jude, except the poor baby. That had a soul, too, but the dreadful body could not hold it. It had to go—and oh! I am so glad.

"Then, in all the world, there was nowhere for me to go but—here. I did not mean to fling myself upon him. I came to save him. There was money Jude had—oh! it doesn't matter, but anyway, things happened, and I was left—on Mr. Gaston's mercy.

"I had only one idea of men—then. You see Jude had almost made a beast of me, too." The great eyes shone until they burned into Ruth Dale's brain.

"But Mr. Gaston rose high and far above my low fear and thought. How I hated myself then for daring to judge him by—Jude. No, he made a clean, holy place for me to live in. He saw no other way to help me—perhaps he did not look far enough in the future, it did not matter—but he never came down from his high place except to make me better by his heavenly goodness.

"After a while it grew easy—after I comprehended his thought for me—and we were very happy—just as we might have been had we been brother and sister. I grew to think his own kind would know and understand how impossible it would be for him to be other than what he was; and for what the lower people thought I had no care. I was—just happy!

"But something happened. Perhaps being near such goodness made me a little better; and a great happiness and lack of fear helped—I think I got nearer to his high place. He loved to give me pretty things. He gave me this"—the fumbling fingers touched the yellow gown; "and I suppose I looked—different, and then he saw that I had—changed and—and he—loved me! I know he loved me; women can tell. I could not be wrong about that. You see I had always loved him—and had once hungered so for his love that when it came I could not be deceived. It—was—that—last—night he told me—about—the past! Then he went away to find Jude—to get Jude to set me free—and we were—going to—be—" the words trailed into a faint moan. "But I see, I see! Even if it had come out right—I'd always be, for all his goodness, old Jared Birkdale's daughter, and Jude Lauzoon's wife. That, he would have to bear and suffer for me—and his world would never forgive him—nor me!

"No; I do love him too well for that. I give him back to his place, and you."

"To me?" And Ruth Dale, haggard and trembling, came slowly around the table, clinging to it for support. When she reached Joyce, she put out cold, groping hands and clutched her by the shoulders.

"You—give him back to me—why? Who is he?"

"John Gaston is—John Dale. It has all come to me so suddenly, I cannot explain, but there is no mistake. I am going to Jude Lauzoon, so that neither you nor he can keep me—from what alone is mine; but be—good to him—or God will never forgive you! Please go now. I must hurry. Good-bye."

"Joyce!" Ruth Dale was crouching at her feet.

"I am—so tired." A long sigh broke from Joyce's lips. "Please do not make it harder. It *must* be; and I have much to do."

"But—there may be some mistake." A horrible fear shook Ruth Dale. Joyce rose and confronted the woman who knelt on the floor.

"Do you believe there is?" she flung the question madly. "Do you?" There was no faltering, only a stern command.

"No," shuddered Ruth Dale.

"Then please, go. My part is all—over! But—be—oh! be heavenly good to him."

Blinded and staggering under the blow, Ruth Dale got to her feet and went from the house. The outer cold steadied her somewhat, but when, a half-hour later, she entered Ralph Drew's study, the man by the fire gazed upon her as if she were a stranger.

"What has happened?" he asked affrightedly, springing to her side.

She let him take her icy hands in his. "I've found—John!" she gasped hoarsely.

"John—who? Sit down, Ruth. You have had a terrible fright." He put her firmly, but gently in his own arm-chair. "Tell me all about it," he urged quietly.

"John Dale. Philip's brother."

"In heaven's name, where!"

"Up at Gaston's shack. Gaston—is—John Dale."

Ralph drew back and repeated dully:

"Gaston—is John Dale? Gaston—is John Dale?" Presently the wonder became affirmation. "Yes," he almost groaned, "Gaston is—John Dale."

A lurking familiarity of feature gained power in Drew's memory of Gaston. It linked itself into other details. He had always known Gaston had a hidden cause for being in St. Ange. Yes; he *was* John Dale.

For Drew to become convinced was for him to act upon the

impulse of his warm heart.

"Ruth, dear," he whispered, "make yourself comfortable. I will go to him."

Then Ruth raised her hands to hold him back. Her voice was deep and awed.

"No!" she commanded "neither you nor I, Ralph, is fit to enter—there. A miracle has been performed up among the pines. A man and woman have been created—that we are not worthy to—touch!"

"Ruth what madness is this? What has occurred? You must explain to me clearly."

Then the story rushed out in a flood. Tears checked it at times; a hysterical laugh now and again threatened; but Drew controlled the excitement by word and touch.

"And now," Ruth was panting and exhausted; "she, that— wonderful woman, has given him back—to me. Can't you see? She loves the soul of him—the great, strong man of him—but I—why even *now*, I cannot forget the evil thing—that befell— the *body* of him while he was—in—"

"Ruth! You shall not so degrade yourself."

"Yes! Yes! it is quite true. That is what I meant. I am not fit to touch—her nor him, and yet I shall shudder all my life—when I remember."

Drew saw that reason was tottering in Ruth.

"He may—not—wish—to claim you, dear," he comforted.

"But he must; he must! Now that she is going to her own; there is nothing left for me to do—but to go to mine."

"This can go no further, Ruth." Drew rose hastily. "I am going to send Aunt Sally to you, and I must think things out. Calm yourself, dear. In all such times as these, a greater power than is in us, controls and gives strength. Let go—Ruth! Let the Power that is, take you in its keeping."

He touched her cold face with reassuring sympathy, and then went to find Miss Sally.

His next impulse was to rush to Gaston's shack; his second thought restrained him. If Gaston had returned, he would rightfully resent any outside interference with this crucial time of his life. If Joyce were decided in the course she had laid out for herself—how dared he, how could he, divert her from it without involving them all in a deeper perplexity?

So Drew resigned *himself* to the Power that is.

CHAPTER XVIII

It was Billy Falstar who broke upon Joyce's solitude after Ruth Dale had left her.

Worn beyond the point where conscious suffering held strong part, Joyce was completing her final arrangements mechanically and laboriously when Billy presented himself.

"Say, Joyce," the boy faltered, standing in the doorway and kicking his heels together, "I'm blamed sorry I done that sneak job."

"It doesn't matter much, Billy. But now that you are here, will you help me pack food and things? I'm going—away."

Then Billy recalled the letter, and fear rose sharply to the fore.

"You ain't going to go—no such thing!" he cried, coming in and slamming the door behind him. "That's a—that's a fake letter."

"Yes, I know. It doesn't make any difference. But tell me, Billy, is it father or Jude down at the Laval place?"

Billy was stricken with surprise.

"How d' yer know?" he gasped.

"Oh! it was all so foolish!" she answered smiling feebly. "If

Harriet T. Comstock

he—if Mr. Gaston had sent it, don't you see that there would have been no need of this mystery? But is it Jude or father, Billy?"

"It's old Birkdale," Billy burst out, and then between fear and relief he related what had happened in the hut in the woods.

"Then it's a longer way I must go." Joyce sighed wearily. "Do you think I could get there—walking, Billy?"

The boy eyed her as if she had gone crazy.

"'Course not. But what you want to go for, anyway?"

Joyce came close to him. He seemed the only human thing left for her to cling to, the only one to call upon in her sore need.

"Billy, I'm going to Jude because—he's mine, and I belong to him—and it never pays in this world to take what doesn't belong to you."

"But—Gaston—you belong to him—and I want—you—to have him!" Billy felt a mad inclination to cry, but struggled against it.

"No, I never belonged to him, Billy. Believe that all your life— it will make a better man of you. He was heavenly good to me because he was sorry for me—and wanted to see me happy. But happiness doesn't come—that way. Sometimes it seems as if it did—sometimes it seems as if God meant it so—perhaps He did—but the people out—in the world—the people that should have known how—the people who had time and money and learning, they've muddled things so—that we can't even see what God meant for right or wrong.

"Why, Billy, they punish the wrong people, and then when they find out—they do not know the way to set it straight; but it doesn't matter, Billy, we have to go on, on, on, the best we can!"

Joyce put her arms around the boy, and bent her head on his thin, shaking shoulder.

She no longer wore the yellow gown. She was plain, commonplace Joyce, familiar to Billy's unregenerated youth.

But Billy did not fail her. Awkwardly, but with wonderful understanding, he put his arms around her, and whispered:

"I just wisht, Joyce, I was God for a minute—and it would all be right or I'd be—"

"Billy!"

"I'd be gol-swizzled," Billy tamely ended.

He could not master details. He only knew something had happened. Joyce was going to leave Gaston and go to Jude, and he, Billy, must make the way easy, and stand by her as a gentleman should. He patted her arm reassuringly as he thought it out.

"It's 'most night," he said; "I'll hitch up old Tate's mare to the sled. He won't know! It's going to be a big night down to the Black Cat. I'll drive you over to Jude—and wait for yer, if yer say so. If yer don't, then I'll cut back—and I don't care after that."

"Billy!"

"When will you be ready?"

Joyce glanced at the clock.

"It's after six now. I'll be ready when you get back, Billy!"

A moment later Billy had set forth in the black coldness.

It was eight o'clock that evening when the revellers at the

Harriet T. Comstock

Black Cat heard a crunching of the snow as a sled rapidly passed the tavern.

Leon Tate was mixing drinks, with a practised and obliging hand, when the unaccustomed sound struck his ear; he paused, but when the unappreciative driver passed, he lost interest.

"Thought some one was coming?" Tom Smith suggested.

"No; going," Murphy, the engineer, slowly answered.

"Where to, do you suppose?" asked Smith. Any new topic of conversation early in the evening was welcome.

"Like as not," Tate came forward with his brew, "like as not it's them folks up to the bungerler. I heard Mr. Drew had a cutter an' horse over from Hillcrest; and going out nights skylarking seems part of his religion."

"Religion!" sniffed Smith; "they're a rum lot, all right!"

"I wish they was!" Tate put in gloomily, but grinned as the others laughed.

"It's a durned shame to take an animile out nights for fun," Murphy interrupted; "I'd hate to run even the injine 'less 'twas important. Gosh! Tate, you must have let your hand slip when you mixed this."

"Christmas comes but once a year." Tate beamed radiantly. It was good to see that his Black Cat still had charms to compete successfully with the bungalow.

"That piece up to the minister's," Smith glowed inwardly and outwardly, "is the nervy one, all right," he remarked.

"Which one?" asked Tate; "the fixture or the transient?"

"The steady. I was setting here musing late this afternoon,

when in she come over there," Tom indicated the woman's side of the screen; "and first thing I knowed if she wasn't standing on a cracker-box on her side, and a-looking *over* the screen."

"Well, I'll be—" Tate stood straighter.

"'Smith,' says the young woman, 'what does Mr. Tate have screens for?' Then, with her blamed, sassy little nose all crinkled up; 'my! how it does smell. I should think if Mr. Tate had *anything*, he'd have an air-tight and smell-proof partition.'"

A roar greeted this.

"Like as not." Tate was crimson, "the sentiments you're rehashing ain't got constitootion enough, Smith, to stand much more airing. Something's got to be done in this here place to set matters on a proper footing. You let a woman come nosing around where she don't belong, specially one with a loose-jointed tongue, and there's hell to pay. Our women is getting heady. You men will learn too late, maybe, that you'd better put the screw on while there's something to hold to."

"It's sapping the juice, some." Murphy was beginning to relax. "But, Lord! have you seen the duds for the kids, and the costumes for the women? Mis' Falster had me in to show off hers. Every woman's to have a new frock for the jamboree Christmas night; not to mention the trappings for the kids. The old lady up to the bungerler give 'em."

Tate scowled.

Just then the door opened and Jock Filmer entered. He looked spent and haggard; and his handsome, careless face did not wear its usual happy smile.

"Hello!" he said, slamming the door after him, and walking up to the stove. "I thought I saw your Brown Betty kiting over toward the north, Tate. I was afraid something had happened."

"No; Brown Betty's safe in the barn." Tate's gloom passed as he greeted Jock. "The Reverend's got a new horse. What'll you have, Filmer?"

"Plain soda," Jock replied and walked up to the bar.

Tate almost reeled under the blow.

"Plain—thunder!" he gasped, thinking Jock was joking. But Filmer fixed him with a mirthless stare.

"Plain soda, and no monkeying with it."

The air became electrical.

"Been away?" Murphy tried to break the spell.

"Over to Hillcrest—on business." Jock was gulping down the soda. His throat was dry and burning; and the unaccustomed beverage went against all his desire. "I'm off—to-morrow—for a spell. Won't you join me in a drink, boys?"

The invitation was accepted with alacrity, and Smith asked cordially:

"Where are you bound to, Filmer?"

"Got a job?" Tate gave each man his choice of drinks and looked dubiously at the treater.

"What'll you have now, Filmer?" he asked, "maybe plain water?"

Jock's eyes grew glassy.

"No," he muttered; "make it another soda, Tate. Yes; I've got a job. Such a thundering big one that it's going to take about all the nerve I've got lying around loose."

"Bossing—maybe?" Tate cast a keen glance upon Filmer. Jock returned the look. The gleam had departed from his eyes—he was Tate's master now.

"That's about the size of it," he answered. "Bossing, and it's going to be a go, or you'll never see me again. Here's to you!"

Something of the old dash returned as Jock held his soda aloft.

"Anything happened up to Camp 7?" Tate was uneasy.

"Lord! It's further back than 7." Filmer set his glass down. "It's a new cut—started late, but it's worth trying. So long!"

The others stared after him.

When the door had closed upon the tall, swinging figure, the company turned upon themselves.

"Things are going to—" Tate did not designate the locality. After all, it was needless for him to go into particulars.

An hour later Jock, sitting in his own shack before the warm fire, eyed with satisfaction the preparations for his journey. They consisted of certain comforts in the way of sleeping-bag, provisions, gun and a bag of necessary clothing; and a general mass of debris, in the form of smashed bottles and jugs. A vile smell of liquor filled the room, and there were little streams of fluid running down any available slope leading away from the rubbish. Jock, sitting before the fire, his long legs stretched out and his hands clasped behind his head, eyed these rivulets in a dazed, helpless way, while the foul odour made him half mad with longing. His face was terrible to see, and his form was rigid.

A knock on the outer door made no impression upon him, but a second, louder, more insistent one brought a, "Why in thunder don't you come in, and stop your infernal racket?" from his overwrought nerves.

Drew entered. His fur coat had snow flakes on it. A coming storm had sent its messengers.

For a moment Filmer looked at his visitor with unseeing eyes, then his consciousness travelled back from its far place, and a soft welcome spread over the drawn face. So glad was he to see Drew that he forgot to be patronizing. He was weakly overjoyed.

Drew, with a keen, comprehensive glance, took in the scene and something of what it meant. He smiled kindly, and pulled a chair up before the hearth.

"Been away Filmer, or going?" he asked as he sat down and flung off his coat and fur hat.

"Both," Filmer returned, and although his voice was hard and strained, Drew detected a welcome to him in the tone.

"I wanted you up at the bungalow," he said quietly; "the girls cannot get along without you. It's Christmas Eve," he added quietly, "to-morrow's the big day, you know."

"I shan't be here." The words came harshly. "See here, Drew," Jock flung himself about and leaned toward his guest, his long, thin hands clasped closely and outstretched. "I wanted you to-night more than any one, but God, could know. I couldn't come to you—but you've come to me at the right moment."

"I'm glad of that, Filmer."

"I'm not much of a hand for holding back what I want to give out," Jock rushed on, "and I ain't much of an orator. What I'm going to tell you, Drew, has been corked up for over ten years—it's ripe for opening—will you share it?"

"Can you ask that, Filmer?" The two men looked steadily at each other.

"Did you ever hear of Jasper Filmer on the Pacific Coast?" Jock asked suddenly.

"Yes; he died a week ago. The papers were full of it. We noticed the name—" Drew bent forward—"and wondered."

"I'm his son. There ain't much to tell. It's a common enough yarn. The world's full of the like. It's only when you tackle the separate ones that they seem to differ. The old man—made himself. That kind is either hard as nails or soft as mush. My governor had the iron in his. He banked everything on—me—and I wasn't up to the expectation. I was made out of the odds and ends that were left out of his constitution—and we didn't get on. My mother—" Jock pulled himself together; "she was the sort those self-made men generally hanker after, all lady, and pretty and dainty. You know the kind?"

Drew nodded. His face was ashen.

"I wish you could have seen her, Drew, I've seen a good many, but none, no, not *one*, who ever came up to her for softness, and fetching ways. Lord! how I loved her. The old man might have known that if I could have gone straight I'd have done it for—mother. She never lost faith in me. Every time I went wrong—she just stopped singing for a time." Filmer gulped. "Then when I pulled myself together, after a while she'd begin again, singing as she went about, and smiling and laughing a laugh that keeps ringing, even now.

"At last the governor got tired of the lapses. I don't blame him; just remember that. He thought if I went off and nibbled—what is it—husks? that I'd come around. He didn't understand that it was the *motive power* that was lacking in me.

"Good God, Drew! I've been hungry and cold and homesick until I've thought death was the next step; but I couldn't *stick* to anything long enough to make good. Such men as my father never know what hell-suffering men like me go through— before they fall, and fall, and fall!

"I wrote—lies, home. I wanted to keep mother singing and laughing. I was always doing fine, you know. Coming home in a year or so. I was in Chicago, then New York; but I was getting lower all the time. I put up in those haunted houses— the lodging dives, but I kept those letters going to her, always cheerful.

"Then I made another struggle. I cut for the woods. I got to Hillcrest—when word came—that she had—died!" A dumb suffering stopped the words. Drew laid his hot hand over Filmer's, which were clenched, until the finger-tips were white.

"It was the hope—of making myself fit to go home and hear her sing and laugh that had brought me to Hillcrest. Well, I wrote the old man—that I was going further north. You see, he blamed me. Said the longing for me, the disappointment and the rest, had weakened her heart. I couldn't bear the thought of ever going back—then; so I tramped over the hill and—St. Ange adopted me. It's been a tame plot since then, but it's never been as bad as it was before. I dropped into their speech and ways, and things sank to a dead level. I got word from Hillcrest the other day." Filmer looked blankly into the red embers. "The governor has left—it all to me with this saving clause: if I have any honour I am not to take the money until I can use it as my parents would desire. You see, the old man had what I never suspected—a soft place in his heart for me, and a glimmer of hope. It might not have made any difference—but I wish to God I had known it before."

Drew could not stand the misery of the convulsed face. He turned his eyes away.

"Drew!" Filmer had risen suddenly and now confronted his companion with deep, flashing eyes. "Drew, I'm not going to take the fortune unless—I'm fit to handle it. I've been a tramp long enough to know that I can keep on being a tramp, but I'm going to make one more almighty try before I succumb. I may be all wrong, but lately I've thought the—the motive power has—come to me." A strange, uplifting dignity seemed to fall upon Filmer. Drew tried to speak; to say the right thing, but he merely smiled feebly and rose unsteadily to his feet.

"I wouldn't blame you if you—cut me after this, Drew, but it's got to be said. It's—your—sister."

"My—sister? Connie?" Drew was never so surprised and astounded in his life before.

"Connie?" he gasped again. "Connie?"

"If—if—I was what I might be? If I come into my own, Drew, do you think she—could care—for me?"

"How under heaven can I tell?" Drew said slowly; "she has never—how could she? shown—" he paused.

"How indeed, could she?" Filmer laughed a hard, bitter laugh.

"It would be a poor sort of reformation, Jock—" Drew was getting command of himself—"if it were only to get—her! You've got to get yourself, old man, before you'd dare ask any woman to care for you. I often think the best of us ask a good deal—on trust; but at least a man must know himself before he has a right to expect even—faith."

"Oh! I've worked all that out, Drew, I've been to Hillcrest to talk the beginnings over with a little lawyer fellow who's had my confidence all along. I'm going back where I fell, Drew, in the start. I'm going back there where the loss of her—the mother's laugh and song—will grip the hardest and where the antidote will be the easiest to get. I'm going to take only enough of the governor's money to keep me out of the filth of the gutter until I can climb on to the curb or—go to the sewer, see? But always there is going to be your sister above me. Just remember that—and if you can help her to think of me, once in—a while—"

"Filmer, until you climb up, you must not ask me to hold even one thought of my sister's for you; except—" and here Drew looked frankly in the anxious face—"except as the good fellow of—our Solitude."

"Thank you! That's all I meant. And if I pull up—and stay up—she, not I, will know how to use the money. She's got the heart that can reach down to the suffering, and hold little dying kids on her breast. If I go under, Drew, the money is going to her—anyway."

"Filmer!"

"That's all right, Drew. I know what I'm about. She'll brighten up all the dark places—and remember me in that way if in no other."

Long the two men looked at each other; then Drew extended his hand. Jock took it in a firm grip.

"Good night, Filmer, and God be with you!"

"I'm ready to start, I'll tramp back with you as far as the bungalow."

Jock dashed the crumbling, glowing logs with his foot, and left the fire dying, but safe. Then, gathering his travelling things together, he went out with Drew, closing the door behind him.

It was a snowy night now, white and dry. In silence the two trudged on to the bungalow, then Drew said, "and you won't come in, Filmer, just for a word?"

"Thanks; no."

"Where are you going now?"

"To Hillcrest. I start from there to-morrow morning, after another talk with the little fellow I mentioned. I'm going to keep to the woods for a few days—they always brace me—then I'm going to make a break—for the coast."

"You'll—write—to—me—Jock?"

For a moment Filmer hesitated; then he said eagerly:

"Yes; as long as I'm fighting, I'll keep in touch. If I get down—you'll know by my—not writing. And Drew, I want to tell you something. That religion of yours is all right. It was the first kind that ever got into my system and—stayed there. It's got iron, red-hot iron in it, but it's got a homelike kind of friendliness about it that gives you heart to hope in this life, and let the next life take care of itself."

"Thank you, Filmer. That's going to make me—fight."

Another quick, strong handclasp—and then Drew turned toward the glowing windows of his home.

Filmer stood with uncovered head in the driving storm, and looked, with a great, hungry craving, up to the house that held the motive-power of his new life, and then, with a dull pain he grimly set his face toward—the coast.

CHAPTER XIX

Drew waited until after Christmas before he took a decided part in the affairs of Gaston and Joyce. Indeed he purposely avoided any information regarding what was going on at the shack among the pines. He was determined that St. Ange's first, true Christmas should be, as far as he could make it, a perfect one; and it was one never to be forgotten. It set a high standard; one from which the place was never again to fall far below.

The snowstorm raged furiously for hours, and then the weather cleared suddenly and gloriously.

Blue was the sky, and white the world. A stillness held all Nature, and the intense cold was so disguised that even the wisest native was misled.

Early on Christmas morning, right after the jolly family breakfast, Drew called to Constance as she passed his study door:

"Connie, we cannot have Filmer with us, after all. He's gone away."

The girl stopped suddenly. Her arms were full of gifts, and her bright face grew still.

"Where has he gone?" The question was put calmly, but with effort.

"It's quite a yarn, Con; can you come in?"

"I can hear from here, Ralph; go on."

"You know that rich old fellow on the Pacific Coast who has just died, Jasper Filmer, the mining magnate?"

"Yes."

"He's was Jock's—father."

Drew heard a package drop from his sister's arms. She stooped and picked it up. From his chair Drew saw that her face never changed expression.

"So then, Filmer did not take the trouble to change even his name?"

The voice was completely under control now.

"No. I imagine this was no case of the town-crier being sent out. When the prodigal got ready to return, under prescribed conditions—the calf was there."

"I see. And has he—has Jock accepted the—conditions?"

"He's gone to make—a big fight, Con. He will not take the fortune unless he wins. Filmer's got some of the old man in him, I bet."

"Yes. Is—is his mother living? Has he any one to go to—out there?"

"No one, Con. From what he told me, I gathered that it was to be a fight with the odds—against him."

There was a long pause. A package again dropped to the floor. The girl outside stooped to gather it up; dropped two or three more, then straightened herself with an impatient exclamation.

"He'll win out!" The words sounded like a rally call. With that the girl fled down the hall, trilling the merriest sort of a Christmas tune.

At three o'clock St. Ange turned out in force, and set its face toward the bungalow.

Leon Tate had decided that to put a cheerful front to the foe was the wiser thing to do, so he closed the Black Cat and arrayed his oily person in his best raiment, kept heretofore for the Government Inspector and Hillcrest potentates, and drove his wife himself up to Drew's fete.

"Do you know," he said, as they started, "Brown Betty looks as played out as if she had been druv instead of loafing in the stable."

"She do look beat," Isa agreed. "What's that in the bottom of the sled, Tate?" she suddenly asked.

Tate picked it up.

"Now what do you think of that?" he grunted, and held the object out at arm's length.

It was a baby's tiny sock; unworn, unsoiled. The little twisted foot that had found shelter in it for so brief a time had not been a restless foot.

"Give that to me," Isa said hoarsely, and tears stood in her grim eyes.

"What the—what does that—mean?"

"How should I know, Tate? But it set me thinking. Things often let loose ideas, you know. This being Christmas—and the stable and the manger and—and—the baby. It all fits in."

Tate looked at his wife in an almost frightened way.

"You mean"—he tried awkwardly to follow her confused words; "you mean—a baby has been borned in—our manger?"

"Lord! Tate what are you thinking of? St. Ange may be wilder than Bethlehem in some ways, but there ain't never been no baby borned in *my* manger."

"Then what in thunder do you mean?"

"Nothing, Tate"; and now the tears were actually falling from Isa's eyes.

"I guess"—she strangled over her emotions—"I guess—it's more like—a flight inter Egypt—than—than—a birthday party."

"Get up, Bet!" Tate was routed by the event. Finally he said slowly, "See here, old woman, I'm going to look inter that—baby boot, and don't you forget it. This ain't no time and place maybe, but Tate's going to have his senses onter any job that takes his possessions for granted. Give me—that flannel boot."

"Tate—I can't."

"Can't, hey?"

"Well then"—and the declaration of independence rang out—"I won't!"

"What!" Brown Betty leaped under the lash.

"It don't belong to me."

"Do you know who owns it?"

"I can—guess."

"Guess then, by thunder!"

Harriet T. Comstock

"It—belonged—to—Joyce's poor little dead young-un."

"How in"—then Tate blanched, for superstition held his dull wits. "How you 'spose it got there?"

"How can I tell, Tate? But I'll ask Joyce, to-morrer."

With that Leon had to be content.

The feast began at five. Long, long did the youth of St. Ange recall it with fulness of heart and stomach. Yearningly did St. Ange womankind hark back to it. It was the first time in their lives that they had not prepared, and were not expected themselves to serve, a meal. They forgot, in the rapture of repose, their new and splendid gowns—the comfort wrapped their every sense.

"I was borned," poor Peggy confided to her neighbour, "to be a constitootional setter, I think; but circumstances prevented. It's curious enough how naterally I take the chance to set and set and enjoy setting."

Mrs. Murphy smoothed her dark-green cashmere with reverent and caressing hand.

"There's more than you, Mis' Falster," she said, "as is borned to what they don't get, sure! Now me, fur instant, I find it easier nor what you might think, to chew without my front teeth."

This made Billy Falstar laugh. It was the first genuine laugh the poor boy had had for many an hour. Constance Drew heard it, and it did her heart good. For Billy, pale, wide-eyed and laughless, was not in the order of things as they should be. She looked at Ruth Dale and whispered, "Billy is reviving with proper nourishment."

Ruth gave her a sympathetic smile. Ruth was, herself, working under pressure, but she was successfully playing her part.

"His face was the only grim one here," she said. "Just look at Maggie, Con!" To view Maggie was to forget any unpleasant thing.

Maggie Falstar was laying up for the future as a camel does for the desert. Food and drink passed from sight under Maggie's manipulation like a slight-of-hand performance, and through the effort, and above it, the girl's expressionless face was bent over her plate.

The Christmas tree, later, was in the hall. The party staggered to it from the dining room with anticipation befogged by a too, too heavy meal. But St. Ange digestions were of sturdy fibre, and fulfilled joy brought about quick relief.

Aunt Sally looked into the grateful eyes upturned toward the glittering tree, and her own kind eyes were like stars.

It was Ruth Dale who had taught the children to sing, "There's a Wonderful Tree," and the Christmas anthem now surprised and charmed the older people.

Above the shrill, exultant voices, Ruth's clear tones rang firm and true. Drew watched her from his place beside the tree, and his heart ached for her. And yet—what strength and power she had. She so slight and girlish. She had lost faith, and had had love wrenched from her. She was bent upon a martyr's course, and yet she sang, with apparent abandon of joy, the old Christmas song.

Constance Drew was an adept at prolonging pleasure and thereby intensifying it. With the tree bowed with fruit, standing glorified before them, the rapt company listened with amaze to Maggie Falstar as she sniffled and hitched through a poem so distorted that the only semi-intelligible words were: "An—snow—they—snelt—at—the   manger,   lost   in— reverent—raw."

This part of the programme affected Leon Tate in a most

unlooked-for manner.

"Say, Smith," he remarked to the station-agent, who was gazing at Constance Drew with his lower jaw hanging, "that beats anything I ever heard in the natural artistic line. Blood's bound to colour its victims—do you remember Pete's mother?"

Tom Smith had forgotten the old lady.

"Well, as sure as I'm setting here, old Mis' Falster uster come inter the Black Cat when she'd had more than was good for her out of the tea-pot, and recite yards of poetry standing on a chair and holding to the top of the screen. There hasn't been a hint of such a thing since then till—"

But *the* moment had come. The moment when the heart leaped to meet its desire. The moment when the desire materialized, and the soul asked no more.

Workworn faces quivered with happiness. Things that vanity had yearned for, but stern necessity had denied, were held now in trembling hands: precious gifts that one *could* do without, but were all the more sacred for that reason. Jewelry and pretty bits of useless neckwear, and gauzy handkerchiefs.

Useless? No. For they were to win admiration that was all but dead, and give sodden women an incentive to live up to them.

Little hungry-hearted children hugged dolls so beautiful, yet so human, that nothing more could be asked. Boys, awkward and red, shook like leaves as they fumbled with "buzzum pins" and gorgeous ties and fancy vests.

Sleds, skates and books abounded, and St. Ange, on that sacred day, revelled in the superfluous and the long-denied.

Constance Drew came upon Billy later, while games were in wild progress in the hall and study, seated in a dark corner of the dining room weeping as if his heart would break over a be-flowered vest and a rich red tie.

"Billy!"

"Yes'm." Billy was too far gone to make pretence.

"Don't you like—what you have?"

"Gosh! Yes."

"Are you happy, dear?" The gentlest of hands touched the red head.

"Happy?" Billy blubbered; "I'm busting with it."

"Billy!" and now Constance spoke slowly, impressively, "I want to tell you—something. It's something we have all thought out. It is, perhaps, another Christmas gift for you, dear. I—am—going—away!"

"Going away?" Poor Billy accepted this Christmas offering with horrified anguish.

"Going—"

"Wait, Billy, boy. When Christmas is all over and done with, I am—going back to my other—home until next—summer. But Billy—I want a part of St. Ange with me"—her eyes shone—"I have—been—so happy here—so glad—and so different. I want something to make me remember—if I ever *could* forget. Billy, I want you to come with me. There are schools there, dear. Hard work, and a bigger life—but it will make a man of you, Billy, if the thing is in you, that I believe *is* in you. It's your chance down there, Billy, your best chance, I think, dear—and I'll be there to help you—and to have you help me. Billy, will you come?"

Then Billy dropped the red tie and the be-flowered vest.

Everything seemed to fall from him, but a radiance that grew and grew. He tried to speak, but failed. He put his hands out, but they trembled shamefully. Then all in a heap Billy sank at Constance Drew's feet and hid his throbbing head in the folds of her white silk gown.

The pale moon peeped through the wide window, and cast a strange gleam over the tousled red head snuggled under the little, caressing hand. It transformed a girlish face that was looking far, far beyond St. Ange's calm and peace. The vision the girl saw was battle. Life's battle. Not little Billy's alone, though God knew that was to be no light matter. Not even Filmer's lonely struggle, but her own. Her fight against Convention and Preconceived Ideas. Against all that Always Had Been with What Was Now To Be.

But as the far-seeing eyes gazed into the future, they softened until the tears mingled with Billy's on the already much-stained silken gown.

"Billy-boy, we're crying. I wonder—what for?"

"Because," Billy's mouth was full of that silken gown; "because you and me is so plum chuck-full of happiness we're nigh to busting."

"Oh! Billy, is that really it, really?"

Billy looked up from his shrine.

"Ain't we?" he said solemnly.

"Billy—I—believe—we—are."

Late that night, standing alone by his study window, Drew's tired eyes travelled over his parish. His people had gone. They were his people at last. God-given, as he had been God-sent. He would work with them and for them. He would live day by day, and not look to the eventide. He would—then he looked down the moonlighted road to the stretch on beyond the house, where the snow lay unbroken on the way up to Gaston's shack. A tall, strong figure was striding into the emptiness. A man's form, swinging and full of purpose. It was—John Dale himself going up to meet his fate.

There was no light of welcome in the shack among the pines. All was dark and lifeless. Drew started back. Humanity seemed to urge him to follow that lonely figure and be within call should his help be needed. Second thought killed the desire.

The man plunging ahead in the night was a strong man. A man who through sorrow, sin and shame, had hewed his way to his own place. No one could help him in this hour that awaited him. He must go up to the Mount bearing his own cross—and accept the outcome according as his preparation for the ordeal had fitted him.

It was ten o'clock of the following day, when Drew was roused from his reading beside the study fire by a sharp knock on the door.

He was beginning, lately, to regard this room of his as a kind of Confessional, and every knock interested him.

"Come!" he called.

Gaston strode in. Whatever the night had meant to him, his face bore little trace of anything but stern purpose.

"Good morning, Drew," he said quietly. "Joyce Lauzoon has left my house. Can you tell me anything about her?"

"Very little, Gaston." The onslaught, so direct and unerring, rather took Drew's breath, but he caught himself in time. "Lay off your coat," he said cordially, "and draw up to the fire. The cold seems to be increasing."

Gaston flung hat and coat from him, and pulled a chair nearer the blaze.

"It will continue to grow colder from now on until the break-up. Drew, I cannot waste time, nor have I any inclination to mince matters. I know that you have, in no small measure, influenced Joyce Lauzoon's thought. I know she has spoken of the effect of your words upon her life and, finding her gone upon my return, I naturally come to you thinking that perhaps—and from the highest motives—you may have said something to her that has led her to take this step.

"Whatever has been said, has been said by some one who could affect her as one speaking, if you can understand, from my side of the question. No one else could have any power over her."

"Gaston, I have not seen, nor have I had any communication with Joyce Lauzoon, since you left this last time. While you were away before, she came to me, and I talked with her as I felt should, under the circumstances."

"I know all about that"; a sharp line formed on Gaston's forehead; "it was indirectly on account of that conversation between you that I left so abruptly again. Pardon me, Drew, but don't you think your aunt or your sister—might have followed up your line of argument by—their own?"

Drew flushed scarlet.

"I am quite sure they did not," he said emphatically.

"I've got to find her, Drew"; Gaston breathed hard; "none of you understand the situation in the least."

"Perhaps we do, Gaston." The minister-instinct rose within the weak man, and gave him the sudden dignity that had always impressed Jock Filmer.

For the life of him Gaston could not despise the young fellow. There was courage of purpose and conviction that ennobled his frail body. It was no easy thing, Gaston felt sure, for him to place himself and his youth in this attitude toward a man older than he. It was undeniable Drew lost sight of himself every time he accepted the demands of his profession,—and the renunciation won respect.

"See here Drew, I do not often give my confidence. It does not often appear necessary, and I think nine times out of ten it complicates matters instead of solving mysteries, but I'm going to speak quite openly to you—for Joyce's sake. It would not make any difference to others—they think she deserves punishment for appearing to deserve it, but I believe you will be able to comprehend the difference and perhaps help me to help her.

"Up to the night when she told me that she had seen you, and that your conversation had emphasized some doubts of her own—she had been to me, first a poor hounded creature, then, a striving, high-minded girl endeavouring to free herself from the bondage of evil that had been her inheritance. I'm not going to speak of myself in the matter, only so far as to say that my own life, under different environment, has been such—that I understood; I undertook the—task of helping her! Whatever of temptation cropped up now and then, was strangled for her sake always,—sometimes for my own, too—it died at last, and I was enabled to serve her with single purpose.

"What that task has meant to me—I cannot expect any living soul to understand. I was very lonely. I never looked for reward nor recompense. It was—I thought it was—enough in itself. But something had been going on that was no part of my plan. Like a revelation it came to me, that last evening I spent at home—that she was a splendid woman; and I knew that I loved her!

"That was why I went away. I went to find Jude Lauzoon. I meant to free her, and marry her. Her love has always been mine. This may make no difference—perhaps you cannot believe it—but it's God's truth, and now you see why I must have her."

Drew had never shifted his gaze from the speaker's face. Conflicting emotions tore him—but there was no doubt in his heart, now, of Gaston.

"In your profession, Drew," Gaston saw that he had gained his point, "you do not want to condone sin, but you want to understand the sinner as well as possible; and, Drew, you may take my word for it—I'm not in an overwhelming minority."

For a moment Drew tried to speak and failed. Every expression of his true thought seemed inadequate and futile. Presently he stretched his hand across the little space that divided him from his companion.

"Gaston," he said, "I thank you. It does make a difference. It makes—all the difference in the world."

His thin, blue-veined hand fell upon Gaston's strong, brown one, which lay spread upon the chairarm.

Gaston did not flinch under the touch. He did not seem to notice it.

"Drew," he continued after a long pause, "it will help me—to find her, perhaps, if you tell me the little that you know. I am not going to let her slip if I have to hunt every inch of the woods for her. You must see that there is danger in every moment's delay.

"Can you tell me if any one has seen her and talked with her who might influence her from an—outside point of view?"

Drew was sorely perplexed. He realized that Ruth's wild description of her encounter with Joyce had left many unexplained points. Evidently Joyce herself had, in some way, learned more of Gaston's past than Drew had at first supposed. Then, to tell Gaston, even in his trouble, that a guest of his,

Drew's, had gone into the other's home and caused this calamity, was too cold-blooded a thing to do, without due consideration.

He knew, better than his companion did, that if Joyce had carried out her intention, there was no need of haste.

Gaston was looking keenly at him.

"You are keeping something from me, Drew," he said slowly, "and you have a reason for doing so?"

"Yes, Gaston, I am; and I have."

The further he became involved, the more hopeless the position became to Drew. Gaston was seeking to solve Joyce Lauzoon's problem and his own, without the test of Ruth Dale. Not only Ruth's confession as to Joyce, but Ruth herself must enter into Gaston's future plan of action.

"You know, Drew, who went to my house?"

"Yes; I know that Joyce had a visitor who might have influenced her to take this step; but I have reason to believe that Joyce did not act upon this other's initiative entirely. She had certain knowledge of her own that—urged the course she has taken."

"That is impossible!" Gaston's eyes flashed. Recalling that last scene with Joyce, he could not doubt her simple faithfulness— unless that faith of hers had been turned into a channel which she fondly believed was for his greater good. Nothing could change Joyce Lauzoon. Whatever had been the cause, Gaston knew, she had forgotten herself in her decision.

"I am—sure I am right, Gaston."

"And you refuse to tell me who has seen her?" A slow anger was mounting in Gaston.

Before Drew could reply, a merry call from the hall smote both men into dead silence.

"Ruthie! Ruth Dale, where are you? Come, let's go and see how things look the morning after?"

Constance Drew had given Gaston his answer. By the magic of that name she had connected the Past and the Present. The shock was tremendous, but Gaston bore it with only a tightening of the lips to show the agony he was enduring.

Presently an aimless question broke the unendurable stillness of the room.

"Who—is—that, Drew?"

"Ruth Dale—your brother's widow."

"So—he is dead?" At such vital times in life, the mind leaps over chasms of events, and takes much for granted.

"Yes; he died a year ago."

"How long—have you known, Drew—about him and me?"

"Only a few nights ago. He was my friend for a comparatively few years—but he was—a dear friend!" Drew spoke as if defence were necessary.

"I wonder—how much you *do* know, Drew?" Gaston's face quivered. He began to understand Joyce's soul-struggle.

"Everything, Dale," the name clung uncertainly upon the speaker's lips; "everything—vital. Philip confessed—the week before he died."

Both men lowered their eyes. They dared not face each other for a moment.

The fire crackled and the clock ticked. Every sense was sharpened and quickened in Dale until it was painful.

Objects in the room stood out clearly to his uncaring sight; the snap of the fire, the tick of the clock smote like separate reports upon his hearing; and while he lived he was to recall, when he smelled burning pine, this tense moment. Presently he rose unsteadily and reached out for his coat and hat like a blind man.

"Well, Drew," he said, making an effort to speak evenly, "there doesn't seem to be anything more to say. I am going. Goodbye."

"Dale—where are you going?" Drew was beside him.

"I'm going to try and find—Joyce Lauzoon."

"She—has—gone—to—her husband! He sent for her—and she went." Drew spoke with an effort; but before the look on John Dale's face, he staggered back. Hopeless rage, defeated desire blanched and fired in turn the strong features. Then without a word Dale strode from the room.

CHAPTER XX

John Dale went directly to his shack. What else was there for him to do until he could find another trail through the blank that surrounded him?

When he had entered his home the night before, God knew he had been sorely distressed. He was going back to the woman he loved with her fetters still unloosened. Worn and spent, he had permitted himself the relaxation of spending a few days with her before he started out again on the quest of Jude. He had found the shack deserted, but every pitiful evidence of Joyce's thought for his comfort was apparent. He had lighted the fire and lamp; had searched for note or other explanation, and, finding none, he had eaten hastily and gone to Filmer's house. There desolation again greeted him.

Finally he had concluded that Joyce had gone to Isa Tate. This was a poor solace, but it stayed him through the long night; an early visit to the Black Cat proved this last hope vain.

Now, with the later knowledge searching into his soul, Dale noticed the careful arrangements Joyce had made, before she slipped back into the hell from which he had once rescued her.

She had taken only her own poor belongings. The shabby gowns and trinkets that had been found among the ruins of the home Jude had laid low.

One silent token of the flight brought the stinging tears to

Dale's eyes.

At the last, there must have been haste, for near the door of Joyce's bedroom lay the mate of the baby's sock that Isa Tate was hiding at that very moment.

Poor, dead baby! He was pleading for the pretty mother who in his brief life had so tenderly pleaded for him.

Isa had wept over the tiny shoe, and now John Dale picked the mate up reverently, and put it back where he knew Joyce always had kept it.

Manlike he did not give himself blindly up to his misery. Life must go on somehow—and while he sought a way out of the blackness that enshrouded him, he must prepare himself.

He replenished the fire, and then when high noon flooded the living room with a pale glow, he set forth a meagre but nourishing meal.

In the performing of these homely tasks he found a kind of comfort. It brought Joyce back to him in a sense.

During the early afternoon hours he smoked and thought. Things became clearer, more fixed in his mind.

Of course Joyce had been driven to Jude by a mistaken idea that she was proving her deep love. Almost from the first, Dale thought of Ruth Dale detached from the shock of her mere name as it had struck his brain and heart in Drew's study. The old, vital charm of Ruth's personality; her sweet, convincing power, when she chose to exert it, now rose in his memory. Joyce would be but a baby in the hands of such a woman.

A fierce indignation swayed the man. Gone was the sweet memory of the control that that same charm had once had over him. Only as it now had touched Joyce did he consider it, and every fibre of his being rose in resentment.

The savage in him gained strength. He would follow Joyce and have her yet—in spite of all that had passed!

When Joyce saw and knew—what would he and she care for the rest? He could deal with Jude—there was still money.

The wild claimed precedence over the innate refinement in Dale, and he rose to begin his search. He glanced at the clock. It was four. He could get—somewhere before dark.

The prospect of action gave him relief and he was just turning to the inner room, when a timid tap upon the outer door stayed him.

His heart gave a great throb. Had she come? Had she returned to him? Had she found the way back to hell impossible after he—the man she had deserted—had shown her a path to heaven?

"Come!" he commanded as if defying any other hold that might have power over her.

Pale, trembling and enveloped in the fur coat and hood, Ruth Dale entered and closed the door behind her.

Her eyes were wide and fear-filled, but self-possession was not lost.

"John!" she cried pleadingly; "as soon as they told me—I came."

Her outstretched hands recalled Dale to the present.

"Ruth!" he whispered hoarsely, going to her; "this is—kind of you. Let me take your wraps. Here, sit down."

It was a relief to have her a little distance from him. He took a chair on the opposite side of the hearth, and struggled to regain his composure. For the life of him he could not fix his identity in the place where the sudden convulsion of events had cast them all.

He was an exile from the past of which this lovely woman was a part, and the present had no space for her.

In a dazed way he noted how exactly the same Ruth looked. When he had dropped her hands—way back there in time, she appeared precisely the same to him as she did now, with those same little jewelled hands lying white and soft in her lap. She had worn a bright gown then, Dale recalled, but even the gloomy raiment that now enfolded her had no power to change the woman of her.

Poor Dale could not comprehend in his new birth and life, that such women as Ruth Dale are Accomplished Achievements of heredity and ultra refinement. Generations ago Ruth's type had been perfected; she and others of her kind, were but repetitions.

Her girlhood had been a brief pause before she had entered her fore-ordained womanhood—a mere waiting for the inevitable. Thus, Dale had *last* beheld her—so his photograph of her had fixed her in his mind. He saw her now the same, outwardly, and the placidity of the oft-repeated type held her afar from his rugged place.

Dale himself had been tossed into the fire of temptation, in the rough. He had fallen to the depths but to rise—a better and stronger man with the dross burned out. The strong, primitiveness of him was as alien to anything that was in Ruth as if the two had never seen each other before.

Like a man struggling with the recollections of a pre-incarnation, Dale sought to find a semblance of the old passion and fire this woman had once roused in him. Not even a reflection of them could he summon. Had she entered his life two years before she might still have been able to fan the embers into flame among the ashes; now she was powerless! Love, a great overpowering love, a love having its roots in the life of the woods and primitive things—held the man for its own.

Looking into the deep eyes that once had pleaded with hers, Ruth Dale, sitting in the lonely shack, wondered why she could not cope with this critical situation. It grieved and perplexed her—but it did not daunt her. Sweet and retiring as she was, and *consciously* self-forgetful as she believed herself, Ruth was what ages had made her. Had her subconscious self asserted itself, it would have boldly proclaimed its absolute superiority over other women of such make as poor Joyce Lauzoon. Not merely in the other's shocking lack of moral sense—but in very essence.

John Dale had suffered—and had tried, in weak man-fashion, to solace himself. The world had helped to train Ruth Dale. While not admitting that there should be any palliation for the double code—or even the appearance of it—such women as she recognized it, and were able, under sufficiently convincing circumstances, to deal with it. There were reasons, heaven knew, why she, Ruth Dale, should be lenient with this silent man across the hearth. The white-souled innocence in her thanked God, in this brief silence, that the man was *not* as evil as many a man, under the circumstances, might have been. She believed Joyce's statement. It was wonderful, it was most weirdly romantic—and it could be overlooked!

It would have been absolutely impossible for Ruth Dale to conceive that John Dale had so far outgrown her in the great human essentials of life, that he had no further need of her. The life of which she was a part, the life of which she was, she and her detached kind, the shining centre, had not enough vitality to hold this man of nature to it. But the pause was growing painful.

"John—I have come to tell you all."

He overleaped the poor past, and in his hunger to know of her part in the present, said eagerly:

"Ruth, I am waiting to hear. I might have known you would come."

Then, to his surprise, the pretty sleek head was bent upon the arm of the chair, and Ruth Dale wept, as the man opposite had forgotten women *could* weep. The sobs shook the slender form until pity for her moved him to touch and soothe her; while the savage in him held him back. Somehow, in a rough way, it seemed retribution. He was glad she could suffer. But presently the flood ceased, Ruth looked up, tear-dimmed and quivering. The torrent had borne away much sentiment; she was able to face reality.

She told of Philip's dying confession. She delicately and graphically told of the broken life—after he, John, had passed out of it—and they, who remained, bravely wound the tangled ends into a noble whole.

Dale followed her words as if the story were of another—and of a life he had never shared.

"Philip wanted you to have all—everything—of which his weakness had deprived you!"

Dale started.

"Oh! Yes," he said vaguely; "I see. Well, I can understand that. But Ruth—not even God could accomplish that miracle. In all such cases it has to be what a man himself can get out of the wreck. It has to be *other* things. New things—or he is— damned."

It was the word more than the thought that caused the shudder in the crouching woman.

"You have never forgiven us," she whispered.

"Yes, I have, Ruth. When I got to a place, cleansed by suffering, where I could forgive myself—everything else was easy."

"Oh! John, why could you not have trusted me with your—your brave secret?"

Why, indeed? John Dale could not have told; he only knew he had never paused to consider when it came to telling Joyce Lauzoon. The thought gripped him hard.

"It had to be, Ruth, I imagine. All the ugly factors had to be taken into consideration when the plan for re-making Phil and me was designed."

A grim smile touched the corners of the stern mouth.

"He left his fortune to you!"

"I cannot take it." Dale raised one hand as if pushing aside an insulting offering.

"John—I have my share—and my father's money. Think! Philip meant that you should prove your forgiveness by—finishing his work. I never saw greater anguish than in his desire. Can you, dare you, refuse?"

A mist rose in Dale's eyes. Ruth saw it, and it gave her courage.

Strangely enough, now that she groped toward this new man she saw before her, her aversion to the man she once knew was lost sight of. A dim fear arose that her sacrifice might escape him and her. Not through any unwillingness on their parts, but through a misunderstanding. She bravely strove to down the menace.

"John—I came to this house a few days ago to help a weak, erring woman, if I could. That is all I knew. Almost at once she made me see the strange thing that had happened here through the goodness of a strong man, and the simplicity of—a weak, but loving woman.

"All unknowingly I yearned to help her—save her, but she

wanted to save herself more than I understood at first. She was so brave and direct; once she saw where her weakness had placed her and the man she loved, she was strong in her determination to right the wrong. For her, poor soul, there was but one way—she returned to her husband!

"John—*she* told me who you were. In some way she knew who I was. I was so distressed and surprised at the time that I did not question how she knew me—but she did and"—Ruth could not bring herself to say, "she gave you back to me."

"John—let the cruel, cruel past be forgotten. Come back to your own. The world will see you righted. John, say that it shall be as I—as Philip—desire."

She looked like a spirit as she bent toward him full of compassion, of entreaty, and the kinship with that which she believed was still in him, and only waiting for her to call to action.

The minutes passed—her call brought forth no rush of checked emotion and controlled passion.

Dale looked at her coldly. He was far too simple a man, intrinsically, to gather the true, inward drift of her thought. He was now seeking to understand the change that had overcome him. She, the girl of his Past who had held his love, hope and desire; she no longer moved him except in wonder and aversion. But he felt that it was due her that he should meet her as far as possible on this new way they were travelling. He shifted his position. He knew something more was expected of him than he could give; but he must give as he could.

"Ruth," he began, and, because his inclination was to move away, he purposely drew nearer; "I am sure you meant nothing but kindness in coming to Joyce Lauzoon; I can see that you mean only great good to me—but you cannot understand. You haven't even touched upon the truth. I suppose some people are born complete in the little; they only have to develop.

Harriet T. Comstock

Others are—well—thrown together, and they cannot assume form and shape until by blows and chiselling they come through the machine—moulded. You have always been good and true; what you knew of me, long ago, died and was thrown aside; what little survived, was nourished apart from, and upon a life you have no conception of. I think only lately have I realized this myself. I'm a bigger and a smaller man than you knew, Ruth; I'm stronger and weaker; better and worse," his hand clenched over the arm of her chair, and her eyes dilated. She was frightened. She felt his blood rising and she shrank back. It was horrible to be there—with him alone!

"You cannot understand, but that old life seems to me now to be—used up, colourless and flabby. The people seem small and—all alike. This life—is big, free and—in the making. There are souls here that are only touched by sins that have drifted to them—they are possible of great things. They are new and keen, and they ring true when you strike them. The woman who left this house—the other day," Dale's words came hard and quick, "is the most glorious creature that ever lived. The life back there could not produce her. Strong, tender, and love itself! Not for one instant did she pause when she knew who and what I was—she loved—that was enough! God! how she loved. You—and women like you, Ruth, might lead the men you love toward heaven; she would go her way alone to perdition to add to the happiness of the man she loved. But it would be alone, mind you.

"She's gone back to such a man as your books, even, forbear to portray. Jude is one of the creatures up here who was born without a soul. She's gone to him to save me, as she thought— but she'll live alone, alone as long as she lives at all.

"So you see what trouble comes from such civilization as yours grafted on to the primitive passions of the backwoods."

"John!"

There was no fear in Ruth Dale now, only a horrible

conviction that John Dale, the man she had come to reclaim and give back to his own, would have none of her!

"John! John!" So he had sunk so low.

"Do you know where she is?" Dale looked at his companion without noting her pallid astonishment.

"No; I do not."

"Then—and you will let me see you back to Drew's? I must go and find her. She shall have the truth, the whole truth, by God! to cool the fires of that hell she has been thrust into."

Ruth covered her face with her trembling hands. Never before had she been so near the bare, throbbing heart of things.

Oh! from what had she been saved? And yet—he was standing above her and he was superb in his strength and power. He was holding her cloak for her; helping to rid himself of her. The old half-dead, but vital call of the aboriginal woman rose in her, then ebbed away at birth in a feeble flickering jealousy.

"I do not wish you to go with me." Ruth felt timidly out for her sweet dignity; the perquisite and recompense of exquisite refinement. "I prefer going alone."

"It is quite dark."

"I shall not be afraid," Dale walked with her to the door. Just before the blackness engulfed her, she turned her little, flower-like face to him:

"John—I shall always be ready to be—your—friend if you need me."

"I shall remember. Good night."

An hour later Dale walked into the Black Cat Tavern and

made a ruinous bargain with Tate for the use of his horse and sled for an indefinite time. "I'm going up into the woods," he explained, "I may be gone a week, a month, I cannot tell; when I reach Camp 7, I'll send your rig back."

"Going to join Filmer, maybe?" Tate's little eyes rolled in their cushions of fat.

"Perhaps." And Tate took this as affirmation. Now that Joyce had rejoined her rightful lord and master—for the story had leaked out—it was quite natural that Gaston should take to the woods.

"It's one on 'im," Tate confided, as Brown Betty and the sled dashed by.

*　*　*　*　*

When Dale started out his purpose was very vague. If he reasoned at all it was to the effect that Jude, after Joyce rejoined him, would seek employment as near at hand as possible. It would be like his weak vanity to parade his victory by going to the men who had known of his defeat. Besides, if he had sent for Joyce, he must have been in the neighbourhood. The heavy storm, in any case, would hinder a long journey, and the men at Camp 7 might perhaps have news of Lauzoon either before or after Joyce had met him a day or so ago.

It had been a short time. He and Brown Betty were a better pair than Jude and a heavy-hearted woman. So Dale drove on toward Camp 7.

He tried to keep to the trail, once he struck the forests, but the snow was unbroken—the heaviest fall had occurred after Billy's return—and Brown Betty intelligently slackened her speed and felt her way gingerly through the darkness. It was still as death. Above the trees the stars pricked the sky, and the intense cold fell like a tangible thing upon the flesh exposed to it. Dale pulled his fur cap lower, and gladly let Betty have her will.

*　*　*　*　*

Now when Billy had left Joyce at the end of their flight, it was near the door of the woodman's hut.

"Billy," Joyce had said, lingeringly clinging to him as the last familiar thing in her happy span of life; "Billy, you must turn back, and God bless you, dear. You see Jude must not know anything about you—and it's all right now, Billy."

Billy made an effort to speak, but ended in a sob.

"Never mind, Billy, it's *all* right now. Just remember that. Kiss me Billy."

And Billy kissed her like the true gentleman he was on the way to being. Then Joyce, with her shabby baggage, and basket of provisions went on alone.

She was stiff and cold, and her heart was like lead within her. With surprise she noticed that the door of the hut was partly open, and the snow had drifted in. It was dark and lifeless apparently, and for a moment Joyce thought that Jude had gone away, and she turned to recall Billy before it was too late. Then she boldly entered the house. The little entry was covered with snow and the room door, too, stood as the outer one did, ajar. Joyce paused and listened—then a horrible fear took possession of her. The still house overpowered her for a moment, but she knew that death awaited her in the outer cold and loneliness, so by superhuman determination she felt her way toward the fireplace—she had been in the hut more than once and memory served her now. She forced herself to think only of lighting the fire. Even when she struck a match she would glance nowhere but at the hearth.

Her teeth were set close, and her breath hardly stirred her

bosom. There had been a fire recently—but the ashes were cold. There was, however, wood nearby, and Joyce tore the paper from one of her packages and used it to ignite the smaller wood.

There was a puff, a flare, and the wood caught.

With the growing heat and light a semblance of courage returned, still Joyce kept her eyes rigidly upon her task. She laid on more wood, and yet more. It was past midnight and the terrible stillness Was numbing her reason. Presently she cautiously turned—something compelled her. She did not expect to find—anything, but she had to look! Away from the red glare, the shadows concealed their secrets from the fear-haunted eyes, but only for a moment.

Jude was there! He was lying stretched upon the floor. A bottle was near his outspread hand. He was asleep.

Joyce did not try to get upon her feet, but she crept toward the still form. She touched, with stiff fingers, the hand of the man she had come to meet—the man who was to save her from her love.

"Jude!" she whispered hoarsely; "Jude!"

A falling log started the others to a redder glow. The face of the man upon the floor lay exposed. The eyes were open—but unseeing, and Joyce knew that Jude was frozen to death!

She made no cry. Had she been capable of sensation she would have gone mad, but she was conscious of no emotion whatever.

The room grew hotter and brighter. She drew away from that horrible shape upon the floor. She must forget it or her head would burst. In the morning, and it would soon be morning, she could go for help—but for now she must forget.

Still creeping, she regained the fireplace; there she huddled with her back to—that long black shadow. Yes; it was but a shadow. She would not think of it but as a shadow.

She braced against the chimney corner, and set her face to the warm, soothing light. Once she stirred and threw on more wood, then she returned to her corner; and kept her eyes in one direction.

An hour passed. The slight form by the fire relaxed, and sank gradually to an easy position far enough away from the fire to be safe. The pretty head fell upon a bundle that had earlier been dropped carelessly there—and a great peace rested on the worn face. Suffering, hopelessness and fear fled as the calm gently settled from brow to chin; and all that was conscious of Joyce Lauzoon drifted into the oblivion that has never been fathomed.

Behind the sealed doors—the miracle was performed. The spirit freed from its suffering body—but not claimed by Death—was strengthened and purified. Where it fared—who can tell? How near the Source of eternal things it wandered none may know, but it drank deep and lost its earth-stain long enough to carry back with it a faith that would enable it to live.

The rosy light of day was showing ruddily in the window of the hut when Joyce opened her eyes. The returning spirit came slowly back with stately serenity. There was no shock nor start of wonder; it took possession of the refreshed body that was awaiting it, and accepted its responsibilities.

Joyce was lying on her back, her hands crossed upon her bosom. The fire still glowed at heart, and the room was warm. A calmness and saneness reigned supreme. Joyce wondered what had befallen her? Then slowly, like a wise mother, Nature gave into her conscious thought the knowledge of things as they were.

She turned—yes! there was Jude. But she did not shrink nor shudder now. Young as she was, she had seen death many, many times. She had gone to the portals, alone, with others beside her poor baby. She rose now, and walked over to Jude's side. The night had wrought a change in him, seemingly; or perhaps it was Joyce's regained sanity. The man on the floor looked calm, peaceful and strangely dignified. His helpless peacefulness appealed to Joyce. She began to take away all signs of degradation that remained. The inanimate tokens of poor Jude Lauzoon's weakness and undoing.

The empty bottle was hidden from sight; the disordered clothing was straightened, and the hands that were never to work harm again, were folded over the quiet breast.

God had set Joyce free! and as she did the last, sad service for the man who had no real place in her life, the words of Ruth Dale recurred to her.

No; she had never been free before. She never could have been free while Jude and she walked the same earth. There had been an intangible link that only death could sever.

Her freedom had come too late—but no! Sitting beside Jude's body, Joyce felt the convincing truth that, come what might, she could, she would live as John Dale had shown her how.

Softly, with reverent touch, Joyce covered the grim, white face, and turned away to prepare for her home journey. She must get others to come for Jude's body. Her part was all past now forever. She must go to face her new life, whatever it might be.

As she opened the outer door, the clear, stinging cold brought a sense of freshness and sweetness with it. It was so alive, and it called to all that was awakening in her. Her slow blood tingled and her breath came quick and deep.

For very relief she took off her close hood, and flung her arms wide as if in welcome to what awaited her.

The unbroken snow spread on every side. Like the first-comer in this new, pure world she set forth with a high courage and a strange faith.

So she came upon John Dale's vision, and he started back, fearing that his weariness and heavy heart were playing havoc with his senses. Having seen smoke rising from the chimney of the hut, he had left his horse and sled a short distance away, and had come to investigate.

So absorbed was Joyce that she neither saw nor heard the approach of the man she had put from her life.

Her pale beauty, as she came quickly toward him, struck Dale as almost unearthly. She was within a few yards of him when she saw him. A rich colour flushed her face as she recognized him and her eyes widened.

"Jude—is dead!" she said simply. She thought he was still upon his quest; still ignorant of the happenings that had driven her away from the shack.

The words had the effect of paralyzing Dale. Had this woman taken a life in self-preservation? Then the sweet, innocent calm of her face reassured him. Jude was dead! Every barrier was removed—every obstacle overcome.

Dale rushed toward her with outstretched arms. The look on his face awed Joyce—but before she was swept into a bliss that might not be rightfully hers, she shrank from him. She put her hands out pleadingly as if imploring him to withhold what her soul was hungering for. Dale understood.

"Joyce—I have been home. They have told me—all!"

"All?" Joyce panted the one word. "All?"

"Yes. Everything. Now—will you come?"

To his dying day Dale was never to forget the look she cast upon him as he and she stood alone in the white trackless forest.

Love, such love as worn-out civilization knows not, took possession of Joyce Lauzoon. A love that controlled and uplifted.

Dale waited—then she came to him, glorious and strong in her power of joy-giving. She clasped her hands around his neck, and lifted her face to his; their lips met and their eyes grew wondrously tender.

"And now,"—it was Joyce who recalled him to duty—"where shall we go?"

His promise to Drew followed close on the question; and Ruth Dale's farewell to him as she slipped from his life came with a new meaning.

"Sweet," he whispered, "they are waiting for us—Drew, and my sister, Ruth Dale."

THE END

Choose from Thousands of 1stWorldLibrary Classics By

A. M. Barnard
Ada Leverson
Adolphus William Ward
Aesop
Agatha Christie
Alexander Aaronsohn
Alexander Kielland
Alexandre Dumas
Alfred Gatty
Alfred Ollivant
Alice Duer Miller
Alice Turner Curtis
Alice Dunbar
Allen Chapman
Alleyne Ireland
Ambrose Bierce
Amelia E. Barr
Amory H. Bradford
Andrew Lang
Andrew McFarland Davis
Andy Adams
Angela Brazil
Anna Alice Chapin
Anna Sewell
Annie Besant
Annie Hamilton Donnell
Annie Payson Call
Annie Roe Carr
Annonaymous
Anton Chekhov
Archibald Lee Fletcher
Arnold Bennett
Arthur C. Benson
Arthur Conan Doyle
Arthur M. Winfield
Arthur Ransome
Arthur Schnitzler
Arthur Train
Atticus
B.H. Baden-Powell
B. M. Bower
B. C. Chatterjee
Baroness Emmuska Orczy
Baroness Orczy
Basil King
Bayard Taylor
Ben Macomber
Bertha Muzzy Bower
Bjornstjerne Bjornson

Booth Tarkington
Boyd Cable
Bram Stoker
C. Collodi
C. E. Orr
C. M. Ingleby
Carolyn Wells
Catherine Parr Traill
Charles A. Eastman
Charles Amory Beach
Charles Dickens
Charles Dudley Warner
Charles Farrar Browne
Charles Ives
Charles Kingsley
Charles Klein
Charles Hanson Towne
Charles Lathrop Pack
Charles Romyn Dake
Charles Whibley
Charles Willing Beale
Charlotte M. Braeme
Charlotte M. Yonge
Charlotte Perkins Stetson
Clair W. Hayes
Clarence Day Jr.
Clarence E. Mulford
Clemence Housman
Confucius
Coningsby Dawson
Cornelis DeWitt Wilcox
Cyril Burleigh
D. H. Lawrence
Daniel Defoe
David Garnett
Dinah Craik
Don Carlos Janes
Donald Keyhoe
Dorothy Kilner
Dougan Clark
Douglas Fairbanks
E. Nesbit
E. P. Roe
E. Phillips Oppenheim
E. S. Brooks
Earl Barnes
Edgar Rice Burroughs
Edith Van Dyne
Edith Wharton

Edward Everett Hale
Edward J. O'Biren
Edward S. Ellis
Edwin L. Arnold
Eleanor Atkins
Eleanor Hallowell Abbott
Eliot Gregory
Elizabeth Gaskell
Elizabeth McCracken
Elizabeth Von Arnim
Ellem Key
Emerson Hough
Emilie F. Carlen
Emily Bronte
Emily Dickinson
Enid Bagnold
Enilor Macartney Lane
Erasmus W. Jones
Ernie Howard Pie
Ethel May Dell
Ethel Turner
Ethel Watts Mumford
Eugene Sue
Eugenie Foa
Eugene Wood
Eustace Hale Ball
Evelyn Everett-green
Everard Cotes
F. H. Cheley
F. J. Cross
F. Marion Crawford
Fannie E. Newberry
Federick Austin Ogg
Ferdinand Ossendowski
Fergus Hume
Florence A. Kilpatrick
Fremont B. Deering
Francis Bacon
Francis Darwin
Frances Hodgson Burnett
Frances Parkinson Keyes
Frank Gee Patchin
Frank Harris
Frank Jewett Mather
Frank L. Packard
Frank V. Webster
Frederic Stewart Isham
Frederick Trevor Hill
Frederick Winslow Taylor

Friedrich Kerst
Friedrich Nietzsche
Fyodor Dostoyevsky
G.A. Henty
G.K. Chesterton
Gabrielle E. Jackson
Garrett P. Serviss
Gaston Leroux
George A. Warren
George Ade
Geroge Bernard Shaw
George Cary Eggleston
George Durston
George Ebers
George Eliot
George Gissing
George MacDonald
George Meredith
George Orwell
George Sylvester Viereck
George Tucker
George W. Cable
George Wharton James
Gertrude Atherton
Gordon Casserly
Grace E. King
Grace Gallatin
Grace Greenwood
Grant Allen
Guillermo A. Sherwell
Gulielma Zollinger
Gustav Flaubert
H. A. Cody
H. B. Irving
H.C. Bailey
H. G. Wells
H. H. Munro
H. Irving Hancock
H. R. Naylor
H. Rider Haggard
H. W. C. Davis
Haldeman Julius
Hall Caine
Hamilton Wright Mabie
Hans Christian Andersen
Harold Avery
Harold McGrath
Harriet Beecher Stowe
Harry Castlemon
Harry Coghill
Harry Houidini

Hayden Carruth
Helent Hunt Jackson
Helen Nicolay
Hendrik Conscience
Hendy David Thoreau
Henri Barbusse
Henrik Ibsen
Henry Adams
Henry Ford
Henry Frost
Henry James
Henry Jones Ford
Henry Seton Merriman
Henry W Longfellow
Herbert A. Giles
Herbert Carter
Herbert N. Casson
Herman Hesse
Hildegard G. Frey
Homer
Honore De Balzac
Horace B. Day
Horace Walpole
Horatio Alger Jr.
Howard Pyle
Howard R. Garis
Hugh Lofting
Hugh Walpole
Humphry Ward
Ian Maclaren
Inez Haynes Gillmore
Irving Bacheller
Isabel Cecilia Williams
Isabel Hornibrook
Israel Abrahams
Ivan Turgenev
J.G.Austin
J. Henri Fabre
J. M. Barrie
J. M. Walsh
J. Macdonald Oxley
J. R. Miller
J. S. Fletcher
J. S. Knowles
J. Storer Clouston
J. W. Duffield
Jack London
Jacob Abbott
James Allen
James Andrews
James Baldwin

James Branch Cabell
James DeMille
James Joyce
James Lane Allen
James Lane Allen
James Oliver Curwood
James Oppenheim
James Otis
James R. Driscoll
Jane Abbott
Jane Austen
Jane L. Stewart
Janet Aldridge
Jens Peter Jacobsen
Jerome K. Jerome
Jessie Graham Flower
John Buchan
John Burroughs
John Cournos
John F. Kennedy
John Gay
John Glasworthy
John Habberton
John Joy Bell
John Kendrick Bangs
John Milton
John Philip Sousa
John Taintor Foote
Jonas Lauritz Idemil Lie
Jonathan Swift
Joseph A. Altsheler
Joseph Carey
Joseph Conrad
Joseph E. Badger Jr
Joseph Hergesheimer
Joseph Jacobs
Jules Vernes
Julian Hawthrone
Julie A Lippmann
Justin Huntly McCarthy
Kakuzo Okakura
Karle Wilson Baker
Kate Chopin
Kenneth Grahame
Kenneth McGaffey
Kate Langley Bosher
Kate Langley Bosher
Katherine Cecil Thurston
Katherine Stokes
L. A. Abbot
L. T. Meade

L. Frank Baum
Latta Griswold
Laura Dent Crane
Laura Lee Hope
Laurence Housman
Lawrence Beasley
Leo Tolstoy
Leonid Andreyev
Lewis Carroll
Lewis Sperry Chafer
Lilian Bell
Lloyd Osbourne
Louis Hughes
Louis Joseph Vance
Louis Tracy
Louisa May Alcott
Lucy Fitch Perkins
Lucy Maud Montgomery
Luther Benson
Lydia Miller Middleton
Lyndon Orr
M. Corvus
M. H. Adams
Margaret E. Sangster
Margret Howth
Margaret Vandercook
Margaret W. Hungerford
Margret Penrose
Maria Edgeworth
Maria Thompson Daviess
Mariano Azuela
Marion Polk Angellotti
Mark Overton
Mark Twain
Mary Austin
Mary Catherine Crowley
Mary Cole
Mary Hastings Bradley
Mary Roberts Rinehart
Mary Rowlandson
M. Wollstonecraft Shelley
Maud Lindsay
Max Beerbohm
Myra Kelly
Nathaniel Hawthrone
Nicolo Machiavelli
O. F. Walton
Oscar Wilde

Owen Johnson
P.G. Wodehouse
Paul and Mabel Thorne
Paul G. Tomlinson
Paul Severing
Percy Brebner
Percy Keese Fitzhugh
Peter B. Kyne
Plato
Quincy Allen
R. Derby Holmes
R. L. Stevenson
R. S. Ball
Rabindranath Tagore
Rahul Alvares
Ralph Bonehill
Ralph Henry Barbour
Ralph Victor
Ralph Waldo Emmerson
Rene Descartes
Ray Cummings
Rex Beach
Rex E. Beach
Richard Harding Davis
Richard Jefferies
Richard Le Gallienne
Robert Barr
Robert Frost
Robert Gordon Anderson
Robert L. Drake
Robert Lansing
Robert Lynd
Robert Michael Ballantyne
Robert W. Chambers
Rosa Nouchette Carey
Rudyard Kipling
Saint Augustine
Samuel B. Allison
Samuel Hopkins Adams
Sarah Bernhardt
Sarah C. Hallowell
Selma Lagerlof
Sherwood Anderson
Sigmund Freud
Standish O'Grady
Stanley Weyman
Stella Benson
Stella M. Francis

Stephen Crane
Stewart Edward White
Stijn Streuvels
Swami Abhedananda
Swami Parmananda
T. S. Ackland
T. S. Arthur
The Princess Der Ling
Thomas A. Janvier
Thomas A Kempis
Thomas Anderton
Thomas Bailey Aldrich
Thomas Bulfinch
Thomas De Quincey
Thomas Dixon
Thomas H. Huxley
Thomas Hardy
Thomas More
Thornton W. Burgess
U. S. Grant
Upton Sinclair
Valentine Williams
Various Authors
Vaughan Kester
Victor Appleton
Victor G. Durham
Victoria Cross
Virginia Woolf
Wadsworth Camp
Walter Camp
Walter Scott
Washington Irving
Wilbur Lawton
Wilkie Collins
Willa Cather
Willard F. Baker
William Dean Howells
William le Queux
W. Makepeace Thackeray
William W. Walter
William Shakespeare
Winston Churchill
Yei Theodora Ozaki
Yogi Ramacharaka
Young E. Allison
Zane Grey

www.ingramcontent.com/pod-product-compliance
Lightning Source LLC
Chambersburg PA
CBHW021306250626
47155CB00002B/402